Josie tried not to look at the stone, had in fact been successful at not looking at it for months now. But she couldn't help herself. In his hands the thing fairly glowed. It must be a trick of the setting sun.

She pushed her hand through her hair and somehow scrounged up a smile. "Well, it's been nice meeting you. Glad I could help." On very shaky legs she began backing toward the door of her car, but once again his deep voice halted her.

"If ye bear me the chain, then ye bear me yerself as well, lass."

Her mouth dropped open, then snapped shut. "I don't think so. I'm really sorry." She started backing up when the gleam in his eyes grew brighter, but he merely kept pace toward her. "I—I mean, I'm flattered and all, but . . . I—I can't . . . you know . . . *bear* you anything else."

"What I know is that you bear my stone." He closed the distance and lifted the necklace toward her. "Which means yer mine now as well."

The Charm Stone

Donna Kauffman

Bantam Books

New York   Toronto   London   Sydney   Auckland

The Charm Stone

A Bantam Book / August 2002

ISBN 0-553-58457-X

Published simultaneously in the United States and Canada

Bantam Books are published by Bantam Books, a division of Random House,
Inc. Its trademark, consisting of the words "Bantam Books" and the portrayal
of a rooster, is Registered in U.S. Patent and Trademark Office and in other
countries. Marca Registrada. Bantam Books, 1540 Broadway, New York, New
York 10036.

PRINTED IN THE UNITED STATES OF AMERICA

OPM   10   9   8   7   6   5   4   3   2   1

For my sister Terri
This Scot's for you.

To my Aunt Gail,
who has her own Big Griff,
thank you for all your support.

And to all the members of the Clud Club.
Okay, who's next?

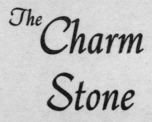

The Charm Stone

Chapter 1

*I*t wasn't every day that Josie Griffin got to rip the back end. Parker's Inlet wasn't exactly known for its monster wave action, but it was known for monster spring storms. Yesterday's had been a doozy, which was why she was here at dawn, paddling back out to take advantage of the poststorm wave surge, despite the frigid water temperatures.

Life always seemed simpler from the top of a surfboard. Waves juiced up, crested, and pounded home. If you were lucky, you squeezed the juice, and if you weren't, the juice squeezed you. Which pretty much summed up life as far as Josie was concerned. All you had to do was keep from getting your juice squeezed too often.

Pressing her belly to the board, she maneuvered her dad's newly designed shortboard as new sets built up behind her. She grinned with the sheer joy of having the whole Atlantic to herself. At least that's how it felt. Even in peak season, this part of the beach was usually deserted. It was a distance from the hotels and hard to get to through the dunes and high sea grass. But it had the best break around and today, in addition to the high surf, the wind was perfect, straight off the coast. So she'd left a message on her dad's machine and hiked in.

She probably should have waited for him, but the

siren call was too strong. He'd understand. He'd been answering that call since before she was born.

After spending weeks on graphics for some particularly fussy clients, she welcomed a day of hooky, even if she was helping her dad out at the same time. He'd be happy with her report on the new design, she thought as she caught the outside and pushed to her feet. The nose was perfect, the board mindless. One of his best yet. She was grinning fiercely as she ripped her board across the shoulder, playing it before dumping out and heading back for more.

Life doesn't get any better than this, she thought, then shivered and laughed. Well, it could be eighty degrees instead of sixty, and this could be the Pipeline in Hawaii or Australia's Gold Coast, instead of Parker's Inlet. But for South Carolina in May, this was pretty damn good.

Timing it just right, she pushed to her feet once again, then dragged her fingers through the wall of water building behind her and shot like a bullet just under the edge of the curl. She tucked again and swerved to her right, squeezing as much out of the wave as she could.

She caught another shoulder and juiced it out a little more, thinking this would only be better if her dad was out here with her. She loved watching him tackle the surf. She was still learning technique from him even after all these years.

Her mind wandered off down memory lane . . . and she never saw what struck her board and sent her flying.

She was smacking the water before she realized her board was no longer beneath her feet. The heavy undertow pulled her down, rolling her and dragging her against the bottom. The ride ended with a solid crack to the head courtesy of her surfboard, before depositing her in the surging foam near the shore.

She caught her breath and took stock. It wasn't like her to lose focus like that. Even in relatively small waves like these, losing concentration could have deadly consequences. Especially when surfing alone, but she spared herself that lecture. Instead she scraped at the seaweed and sand coating her wet suit, then tugged the hood off and brushed her hair loose. Scooping up some water, she rinsed the grit off her face, gasping again when the salt water stung her forehead. She must have taken a pretty good hit. She gingerly felt along her hairline.

"Great. Just great," she muttered as her fingers encountered a growing bump. Her face felt scraped up as well. She tried to piece together what had happened and remembered the thump just before she went flying. Her board had slammed into something. She scanned the water. "So what in the hell did I hit?" There hadn't been any floating debris when she got here. Most of it had already been deposited far up the beach during the storm surge. She ripped off the Velcro strap tethering the board to her ankle just as a trunk the size of a small suitcase tumbled onto the beach with the next breaker.

Josie rolled to her feet and jammed the nose of her board into the sand in one swift move, wincing at the throbbing pain in her forehead as she raced to catch the chest before it slid back out to sea again.

She loved walking the beach and collecting treasures. Her waterfront bungalow was a testimony to the number of mornings she'd spent doing just that. Shells, driftwood, and all manner of flotsam and jetsam cluttered her windowsills, shelves, and just about every other available surface. But this was the first time she'd ever found real treasure. Or a treasure chest anyway.

How had she missed this? She scooped up the dome-lidded box, tugged at the seaweed stuck in the hinges, then scrubbed it with the heel of her hand. It appeared to be all metal, though it was hard to tell with all the barnacles, shells, and other ocean gunk encrusted on it.

She walked back to her board, jiggling the box lightly. Something was rattling around inside. Excited now, she moved farther up the beach and set the trunk down well above the surf line, then quickly retrieved her board before sinking onto her knees in front of the box. She grabbed a heavy chunk of seashell and tried to pop off some of the barnacles stuck around the front hasp. Nothing came off easily and she really had to pry to get even small pieces of crud off the thing. She'd probably end up busting it just to get it open. What if the chest had some kind of historic significance? She could be destroying a valuable artifact from an infamous shipwreck.

"Yeah, right, and I'm Indiana Josie." *Finders, keepers* she told herself, rooting around in the sand for a sturdier piece of shell. Her head was pounding, but her curiosity was stronger. She wondered what her dad would say about her find. Probably tell her to take it to the local marine museum. With a grunt, she pried off a big hunk of barnacles and the hasp finally popped off.

Grinning, she slowly pried the lid open a crack, the hinges groaning in protest, and gasped at what she saw inside.

The seal of the box was amazingly tight as the velvet interior was totally untouched by the water. But it was what lay nestled on the deep purple fabric that grabbed her full attention.

A necklace.

She gingerly lifted out the long, heavy silver chain. "My God." Dangling from the chain was a large yellow stone set in silver. It wasn't cut like a polished gem. The stone was raw and unevenly formed, with some rough edges and some worn down. Maybe from being handled or rubbed, she thought. Other than the size of it, the stone wasn't all that remarkable. In fact, it looked like a big piece of quartz. The setting was oval with detailed scrolling around the edges.

And the chain. She ran the links through her fingers. Each one was bigger around than her thumbnail, and heavy. Really heavy. When she looked closely, she saw they weren't all exactly the same shape. "Hand forged," she murmured, suddenly wondering just how long this trunk had been floating around.

She couldn't resist slipping it over her head. It lay heavily around her neck, the chain extending down between her breasts, the stone weighty even through her wet suit.

"Och, but it's about time, if I do say so meself."

Josie let out a small squeal of surprise and twisted around on her knees. She hadn't heard anyone approaching, but she'd been pretty involved with her find.

Her train of thought evaporated like ocean mist the instant she laid eyes on her surprise intruder. She had a vague suspicion she'd whacked her head a lot harder than she'd thought. What other explanation could there be for the small man standing before her?

The *very* small man. He was barely half as tall as her shortboard. Actually, his short stature probably wouldn't have been all that startling . . . if he hadn't been outfitted in full Scots regalia. From the smartly wrapped kilt, to the sash crossing his broad little chest, the green tam on his head, to the black leather shoes that laced up over the sturdy little calves covered in red-tassled socks . . . he was a vision in plaid. All he needed was a set of bagpipes to complete the ensemble.

"I say, lass, have ye gone daft on me?"

It was quite possible, she thought. "Who are you?"

He grinned and stepped forward. "Ah yes, forgive my poor manners. Somewhat waterlogged, I suspect. I'm Bagan, Guardian of the MacNeil Stone." His brogue was heavy, but it went perfectly with his appearance, especially the bushy white eyebrows and twinkling blue eyes.

He looked like he belonged on a billboard for Glenlivet.

"Was beginning to think I'd never see the light of day again," he said somewhat wistfully, looking past her down along the shoreline. "Fish food, I thought I was." He turned back to her and clasped his small, pudgy hands. "But no longer! Ye've freed me from my briny grave."

"Excuse me?" *Briny grave? Waterlogged?* But he was perfectly dry. "I'm sorry, but I don't understand what—"

He nodded to the necklace. "Yer wearin' the MacNeil Stone, lass. 'Tis the clan charm stone. All the good for you, to be certain, but we must make haste." He looked at the dunes behind her, then up and down the shoreline again. "Might I inquire what part of the country I've landed in?"

"Parker's Inlet." *Was he drunk? Had he been wandering the dunes after a late night?*

"I'm not familiar with that area. Odd." He smiled. "But after so many years I suppose the motherland wouldn't have remained unchanged."

"The motherland?"

He looked surprised by the question. "Why, Scotland of course, lass. Oh, aye," he said with understanding. "Yer accent. New to our shores, are ye?"

He must have really tied one on. His cheeks were ruddy enough. She wasn't sure how to break it to him. "We're not in Scotland. This is America. South Carolina, to be exact."

His blue eyes widened a moment, then crinkled merrily at the corners as he laughed. "Och, don't run a man about so." Then he scanned the coast again, seeming to think a bit. "America, you say." He sighed a little. "Well, I suppose the tides can shift and move one about, can't they now? It is all as it will be, in any case. Destiny has a way of fulfilling herself and doesna always feel the need to make us privy to her reasons or methods."

Josie's head began to throb in earnest. Maybe she was hallucinating.

"So, you're to be the one, aye?" He looked her over.

"The one what?" she asked warily.

"What manner of garb would ye be wearin'?" he asked.

"A wet suit. Keeps the cold out." She'd spoken to a great variety of people in her twenty-five years of wave-trekking all over the globe with her father, but this had to rank as one of the strangest. She motioned to where her board was stuck in the sand. "For surfing."

He stared at the colorful length of fiberglass. "Surfing ye say." His bushy eyebrows furrowed. "And what manner of thing do ye hunt with a weapon such as that?"

Josie couldn't help it, she laughed. He was odd, no doubt, but he seemed harmless. "Big waves," she said. Poor guy was just old and confused.

He frowned. "I canna say I ken the need for it." He smiled then and gestured to her suit. "But I will admit to admiring yer armor. Quite flattering to the feminine form."

Josie raised her eyebrows. Great. Just what she needed, an addled dwarf hitting on her.

"Well, we've no time to contemplate the ways of the world during my absence," he said brightly. He turned and scampered up the nearest dune. He looked back when he realized she wasn't following. "Och, but me manners are truly wanting today. I've introduced myself and not asked ye about yersel. What is yer name, lass?"

She paused, unsure she wanted to play along anymore. But there was no harm in giving her first name. "Josie."

"Josie." He said her name as if he were tasting it, judging it somehow. He nodded then, as if in approval. "Would ye be a descendant then of Lady Elsinor?" He chuckled. "Aye, that would be the way of the Fates, wouldn't it? As I remember it there were several Josephines in her clan."

"I have no idea who Lady Elsinor is," she said. "And my name isn't Josephine. Just Josie."

"Not a Josephine of Clan MacLeod then?"

"No." She grinned. "I guess you could say I'm a Josie of Clan Pussycat." She laughed at his completely nonplussed reaction. "My father has a passion for corny old comics."

Now it was the dwarf who looked a bit wary. "Yes, well, however odd it might be to have the family cat as yer namesake, we've no time to ponder the curiosity. We must be off." He moved higher up the dune. "We must book passage immediately. I needs deliver ye to The MacNeil."

"Say what?" Charming and odd was one thing. Charming and seriously deranged was something else entirely.

She quickly ran down a list of possible courses of action. She could outrun him easily. But what if he were armed? Who knew what he might be hiding beneath that kilt. She surreptitiously scanned the length of the beach. The grassy dunes blocked the view of the path to the street. The rising sun hadn't burned off the ocean mist, so the taller buildings and hotels crowding the beachfront farther down were invisible. And not one early-morning treasure hunter was in sight.

She gained hope as one lone runner shuffled slowly toward them, but as she neared, Josie saw she was at least sixty. Great. Josie and a senior citizen versus the maniac midget. Even the WWF couldn't have come up with that match.

She snagged her board. "Wave hunter and dwarf whacker," she muttered beneath her breath, realizing the ridiculousness of the situation, but holding on to it nonetheless. It was the only weapon she had. She wondered if it was bulletproof.

"I, uh, I'm sorry," she began, trying to sound friendly, but firm. "I won't be able to help you out today. I'm waiting for someone." Although if her father wasn't here by now, chances are he'd fallen asleep over his drafting board again and hadn't gotten his phone messages.

Bagan was still standing near the crest of the dune. "I must insist, lass."

Josie frowned. So much for friendly but firm. "I don't know you and I'm not in the habit of wandering off with strangers."

"Hello!" a thin, high-pitched voice called out. "Do you need some help?"

Josie turned and found that the old woman jogger had stopped down by the water, about twenty yards away. What to do? She didn't want to involve anyone else in this potentially dangerous situation, but she didn't want to turn away what might be her only chance at getting help.

The old woman smiled when Josie didn't answer right away. "Don't be embarrassed about being caught talking to yourself, hon. I do it all the time.

Sorry if I bothered you." Without waiting for a reply, she waved and moved off at her slow shuffle on down the beach.

Talking to herself? Bagan might be short, but he was pretty damn hard to miss in that kilt. Josie turned back around, thinking maybe he'd disappeared the same way he'd mysteriously shown up.

But there he was, in all his plaid glory, waddling back down the hill toward her. "I should have explained," he said. "She canna see me. Only you can, lass."

Okeydokey. *This is all a head-injury-induced hallucination,* she reminded herself. But just in case it wasn't, she tightened her hold on her board and put some distance between them. "It's been real interesting talking to you, but I have to go now." She debated whether to run down the beach or go past him over the dunes.

Bagan sighed and pulled his hat off, revealing a shiny pink dome surrounded by a shock of white hair. "Lassie, I canna make it any clearer to ye. You have the stone about yer neck. Yer the one. Ye must come."

She looked down at the necklace, having forgotten all about it. "Is that what this is about? Because you're more than welcome to it. I hit the trunk with my board and—"

He shook his head, looking a tad exasperated. *Well, he wasn't the only one.* " 'Tis no' mine. I'm naught but the guardian of the thing. I must see the stone returned to the chief, as it is his to wield for the good of the clan."

"The good of the clan," she repeated hollowly. "Of course."

"The MacNeil Stone is how the laird pledges his troth. With my guidance of course," he said self-importantly. "I was heading home, en route from

Islay with the lovely Lady Elsinor MacLeod aboard, when our ship hit a spot of trouble and went down." He looked away, his bright blue eyes growing glassy. "Terrible tragedy. All was lost."

"Except for you. And the stone."

"The stone and I share a joint destiny," he explained. "I canna die." He heaved a sigh and she didn't think she'd ever heard a sound quite so sad. "So many moons have passed now." He was talking more to himself than to her. "And I've naught to show for my duties. I fear I'll be in disgrace for all eternity."

"No good luck charm can keep a ship from going down in bad weather," she said, not sure why in the world she was humoring him, much less consoling him. "Surely they can't blame you for that." Whoever the hell *they* were.

"I suppose not," he said, though he didn't sound all that relieved. "Once the stone is set upon its path, the gods take no further hand in where Fate takes it or us. But I've never failed before. The stone has always gone to the one chosen to bear—" He stopped and shook his head, then mustered a smile. "My woes are no' to be yer concern. Fate has guided me here and, like Destiny, she has her own plans for things. I am no' to judge the wisdom of who or what she chooses to put before me." The look he gave her made it clear that while he didn't judge Fate's wisdom, he did question it some. "All things will be clear when we get you home," he said confidently, then his expression faltered slightly. "Once we find the current laird, that is."

Josie wished she'd carried her cell phone. Men in white coats would be a welcome sight at the moment. Whether they'd be coming to pick up Bagan or her was a tossup at the moment. "This *is* my home," she said, as if that would make any difference to him.

"Ye wear the MacNeil charm stone, lass," he said simply, "which means yer trothed to the laird and will bear him a son. Ye canno' change what Fate has wrought. Only death can end it."

"Lucky Lady Elsinor," Josie muttered.

"I dinna think she'd agree with ye, lass," he said, obviously affronted. " 'Tis an honor to be chosen, no matter the circumstance of it. I'm certain the current laird will be happy with what Fate has brought him." He didn't quite pull this last part off convincingly.

Laughing probably wasn't the smartest thing to do in this kind of situation, but it burst right out of her. "So, let me get this straight. I'm supposed to fly off and marry some guy I've never met *and* bear his children. A guy, I might add, that you admit you don't even know. What if he's already married? What if he's a hundred years old? I don't think they even have clan chiefs anymore."

Bagan folded his arms, looking remarkably obstinate for a little person. "The MacNeil Stone has only been worn by the laird's bride. No one else. It has never failed to bring good fortune to the clan."

"I can see that." He flinched a bit and she actually felt bad for chiding him.

"I dinna know for certain why Lady Elsinor was kept from fulfilling her promise. Fate has her own mind in these things, I suppose. She'd no' put the thing on, despite my tellin' her that it was the way of things. She had her own mind and was wanting Connal to do the honors." He continued a bit uncertainly. "Perhaps it was her refusal that set Fate on a new course. In all the time it has been, the stone—when heeded—has brought good things to the clan. I canno' be held responsible for those that wouldna follow its guidance. Connal was tryin' to do the right thing, he knew it was the only way to save—"

"Just how long has this thing been sitting on the bottom of the ocean anyway?" Josie cut in, her head beginning to ache from more than the lump swelling on it. "When was the last time you dragged a bride back to Scotland?"

Bagan sniffed and looked mightily injured. "Seventeen hundred and two. And I dinna drag the lass anywhere. She was well thrilled to be the chosen one. Despite the clan's recent history, she knew it to be an honor. Why, there wasna a lass in the land who wouldn't have—"

"Well, I'm not from your land." *Or your planet*, she wanted to add. *Seventeen-oh-two?* Was he for real? "And while there might be a few places in the world where arranged marriages still happen, America isn't one of them."

"Ye canna go escaping yer destiny."

"Watch me, old chap." Josie tugged the chain over her neck and threw the necklace at him. It should have hit him square in the chest, but it didn't. In fact, it didn't hit him at all. Instead it landed in the sand where he should have been standing. But wasn't.

She whirled around, but he was nowhere to be seen. "Okay, this isn't funny!" she called out. No answer. But did she really want one? Josie swore under her breath. Maybe she should go to the hospital, have her head checked. Maybe have a CAT scan. Or three.

She looked at the necklace. She should just leave it there for some other innocent beachcomber to stumble across. But she couldn't. She stomped over, scooped it up, and tossed it into the trunk. She'd do what she should have done from the start. Deliver it to the maritime museum and let them deal with it.

By the time she hiked out to her Jeep she was exhausted and near tears. Well, who wouldn't be a bit freaked out after a morning like she'd had? She pulled her keys out from where she'd tucked them under the back fender, then put the towel-wrapped trunk under the passenger seat so she wouldn't have to look at it.

A quick check in the rearview mirror showed a good-size lump along with a healthy gouge below her hairline.

"Mother Nature: one, Josie: zero," she muttered and gunned the engine before pulling onto the road. She looked at the dunes receding from view, half-afraid she'd spy Bagan waving to her. "There's nothing there," she told herself. *There was never anything there.* If she said it enough times maybe she'd start believing it.

Ye canna go escaping yer destiny.

She shivered as Bagan's words echoed in her mind. Well, her destiny was to do graphic artwork on her father's famed boards. That, and hit the waves whenever possible.

Which didn't explain why, for the first time since her father had put her on a board at the age of two, she was in no hurry to go back to the beach.

Chapter 2

The museum was closer than the clinic, so Josie went there first. Parker's Inlet wasn't a very big place and their maritime museum was even less impressive, but at the moment she was thankful they had one at all. Until she saw the empty parking lot. Not a good sign. She swung her Jeep around to the front of the white clapboard building and squinted at the small hand-painted sign in the front window. "Closed Monday and Tuesday," she read. And it was Monday morning. "Lovely."

She was tempted to yank the trunk out and just leave it by the door. But her dad would get a kick out of seeing it—at least that's what she told herself—so she rolled back out of the lot with it still stuck under the seat.

Big Griff had spent close to twice the number of years she had globe-trotting and had seen all sorts of strange stuff. A kilt-wearing dwarf probably wouldn't even make him blink. Not that she'd decided to tell him about that part of it.

She was so busy trying to figure out just how to handle things that she was turning into her driveway before she remembered the clinic and getting her head looked at. Well, she wasn't going back now. She'd been banged up many a time and certainly knew how to handle a lumpy head and some blood.

Nothing some antiseptic and a fistful of pain relievers wouldn't cure. Toss in a hot meal and a shower and she'd be good as new.

And since she wasn't planning on going back to the beach anytime soon, the concussion she'd probably suffered wouldn't be a big setback.

She rolled down the narrow, crushed-shell driveway, wedging the Jeep between the overgrown stands of sea grass and nosed into the carport under her stilt house. As usual, she noticed the peeling paint and the jungle she whimsically called a yard and told herself for the millionth time she needed to hire someone to come over and take care of it all. Even though she knew that for the millionth time, she'd put it off. It wasn't the money, she just didn't like strangers poking about. It was why she'd chosen this place, way at the end of the strand. The water was too calm for good surfing, but she liked the seclusion, liked looking out her workroom window, watching the surf, propping her balcony door open so she could listen to the waves in bed at night.

None of that soothed her at the moment. She purposely ignored the trunk under the seat, and hauled her dad's board up the stairs. She peeled out of her wet suit and flipped it over one of the plastic beach chairs on her screened-in porch, thinking she'd rinse it off later. Right now she wanted to take a closer look at her forehead. The blinking light on her answering machine got her attention first.

"It's me, Josiecat," her dad's voice boomed from the machine. "Got a call from an interesting woman early this morning. I'll tell you all the details later. Don't do anything foolish out there today, it's rough." Then he chuckled. "Yes, I see you rolling your eyes. Just don't get hurt on me. If this thing plays out like I think it will, you'll be pretty busy shortly."

Josie smiled and hit the rewind button. "Early-morning call from a lady, huh, Dad?" Big shock there. Women loved Big Griff and the feeling was definitely mutual. He was a big man, but even at sixty-eight, he was still fit and good-looking, with charm to spare. He had a perpetual tan and the sun had weathered his face in that totally unfair way it did with men, making him even more attractive.

She was mildly curious about the new client. Her dad sounded even more excited than he usually did, and there wasn't a man alive with more boundless enthusiasm than Big Griff. But he worked hard and knew he put out a good product. He deserved the attention his work got and totally enjoyed the fame that came along with the fortune. No one seemed to mind. Josie smiled. And why would they? When Big Griff was having a good time, everyone was having a good time.

He'd instilled his pride and work ethic in his only child. Of course, he also expected her to drop everything and run off to play whenever the siren song called to him. Josie never minded. She was a chip off the old block. Too big a chip, sometimes.

"Like today," she muttered, groaning as she got a closer look at the mess on her forehead. She swore her way through cleaning it up, hoping her dad didn't drop by for, oh, at least a month. Maybe by then it wouldn't look like she'd been attacked with a two-by-four.

She grabbed some ice, although it was probably too late to do much about the swelling, and headed for her workroom. Once her head stopped pounding, she'd treat herself to a steamy shower and a big breakfast. In the meantime, work was the best antidote to getting her mind off her pain . . . and other things.

As always, shortly after she started moving her

pencil across the long sheets of paper tacked to her drafting board, the world faded away. She even managed to forget about the stupid trunk and the three-foot-tall hallucination that accompanied it, until she went outside to get her mail. She brushed along the passenger side of the Jeep on her way back in and found herself pausing by the seat where the trunk lay tucked underneath.

"Well, hell." She tossed her mail on the seat and dragged the thing out and unwrapped it, knowing she wouldn't stop thinking about it now. It looked even worse in the midday sun. She carried it up to her porch and looked it over as she finished her tuna sandwich, then continued to stare at it—without touching it—as she downed the rest of her iced tea. "Okay, now you're being silly," she told herself. It was just a harmless old trunk. She was alone for God's sake, safe in her house. Not a midget in sight.

And she really wanted to see the necklace again. She was too intrigued by it not to peek a second time. She tugged the lid up, wiped her hands off, then lifted the chain out and laid it on the corner of the towel. It was still impressive, if not aesthetically beautiful. Just how old was this thing?

Seventeen-oh-two. A little riff of unease swept along the back of her neck as she recalled what Bagan had told her about the last time the stone had been above water. And it was older than that even, if he'd been telling the truth. "Which of course he couldn't possibly be, because Bagan doesn't really exist." Saying it out loud did little to make her feel better.

She lifted the necklace and studied the stone. She moved over to the shell-framed mirror hanging on the wall next to the door and held the chain up to her chest. Her yellow T-shirt made the stone look even more off-color, but she liked the heft of it in her hands. *Put it back in the box, Josie.* She toyed with the links. It wouldn't hurt anything to see what it looked like on, right?

She wondered about the other women who had worn it as she slipped the heavy chain over her short, messy curls and beat-up face. "One thing's for certain," she told her reflection, "they had to look a lot better wearing it than you do."

"Yer garb might be a wee bit strange and yer hair hacked about the head a bit, but ye look comely enough I suppose."

Josie's heart dropped straight to her toes. *It couldn't be.* She'd locked the door. She squeezed her eyes shut, but she could feel him. Could a person have periodic hallucinations? She slowly turned around. "Oh no."

"I believe me feelings are hurt." Bagan sat on the short ledge that separated the lower half wall from the screened upper half of the porch. He was perched amidst the shells and the driftwood, his stubby legs dangling several feet off the floor.

"Okay, that does it. This is private property, you just can't come barging in here—"

Bagan merely smiled, blue eyes damnably twinkling. "I canna barge anywhere, lass. I'm rather too small for that."

"You're trespassing. I'm calling the police." She held up her hand when he went to speak. "And no more of this destiny crap. My destiny is to do the only two things I'm good at. Surf and draw. And I'm perfectly happy to do both right up until the day I die."

Die. Probably not a good word to use when the person stalking you was sitting right in front of you. So what if he'd need a booster seat at McDonald's?

"No marrying some Scottish laird," she went on adamantly. "No bearing some strange man's children. And no being stalked by—" She waved her hand at him, frustrated. "Whatever you are." *Slow down, stay calm.* She drew in a deep breath. "Now, we can avoid any unpleasantness if you'll just get down from there and see yourself out."

Completely unmoved by her edict, Bagan sniffed at the air instead. "I do believe I smell something burning."

"Don't change the sub— Oh, no." Josie smelled it then, too. Dammit, she'd forgotten all about the soup she'd put on to have with her sandwich. She pointed a finger at him. "I'm going in to turn my stove off before I burn the house down. When I get back, you'd better be gone."

She didn't wait for an answer, she was already dashing inside. The pan and its contents were scorched black and the small kitchen rapidly filling with smoke. She shoved the pan off the burner just as the smoke alarm went off. Swearing, she yanked a kitchen chair over so she could disarm the stupid thing, but when she went to stand on it, her foot went right through the wicker, leaving nice scratches along her calf. The alarm still screaming overhead, she pulled her leg free and looked around for something sturdier to stand on, finally stalking back to the porch.

Bagan had hopped off the sill and was looking at her bicycle with great consternation. "Is it possible you could make that horrible noise desist?" he asked, poking at the chain and squeezing the hand brake.

"You," she said, her voice shaking. "Leave. Now." She grabbed the plastic deck chair and dragged it through the door, but not before it caught on the screen, tearing a nice long slit in it. Swearing and not bothering to keep her voice down, she climbed on the chair and all but ripped the cover off the alarm.

She opened the window over the sink and turned the stove fan on to get the rest of the smoke out of her kitchen, then stalked back to the porch.

He was still there, sifting through some of her surf gear.

"What part of 'leave now' did you not understand?" She should have called the cops before coming back out here. A vision of police officers rushing in to save her from a dwarf swam through her mind. Maybe she'd just run out, get in the Jeep, and leave. And then what? Never come home?

Bagan sighed wearily. "Everything isna so difficult as yer makin' it, lass," he said. "And I thought being buried alive was the worst thing that could happen to me," he muttered to himself.

But she heard him. "Right now I'm thinking that wouldn't be such a bad place for you."

Undaunted, he crossed his arms. "If you tire of my company so easily, you've but to remove the necklace and I'll disappear." He raised a stubby finger as her hands went immediately to the necklace. "But no matter if I'm here or no', you canna avoid your fate."

"My fate." Now it was her turn to sigh wearily. "That would be marrying the clan chief, right?" She snorted. "Right. Bye-bye." She pulled the necklace off and where there had been a three-foot man standing indignantly before her, there was now an empty space.

She hadn't really expected it to work. Because that meant . . . she didn't even want to think about what that meant. She looked from the empty space to the stone and back again, then started to tremble. *Just put it in the trunk and take it back to the beach and toss it in the ocean.*

But the few remaining rational brain cells insisted this simply couldn't be real, no matter the alarming evidence to the contrary. So she slowly draped the necklace around her neck once again. No midget. Ha! She breathed a sigh of relief. Although why she should be relieved she had no idea. Didn't this just prove she'd actually suffered some severe head damage and was losing her mind?

"Are ye ready to heed me now, lass?"

She swung around to find Bagan leaning against the doorframe that led to her kitchen. He wiggled his fingers in a brief wave. "Shall we make our plans?"

"Jesus Christ," she breathed. She stared from the necklace to Bagan. "What the hell is happening to me?"

He waddled closer to her and took her trembling hands in his smaller, but surprisingly warm and strong ones. "Destiny, lass. Destiny."

She sank into a chair as the fight left her and dread filled her instead. Along with a healthy dose of fear. "I don't like this destiny. According to you, the last person who had my destiny drowned."

Bagan frowned. "I've given that a lot of thought and I believe it has to do with her ne'er wearin' the stone. It's never failed before, ye see." He scratched his head.

"Great, you're the guardian of the thing and even you don't know how it works."

"It's just that since I've come to be guardian of it, it's always done what it's supposed to do."

"Whatever, I don't care. I don't want it. So just vote me off the island or whatever you have to do to make this end."

Bagan's frown deepened. "It's no so simple as taking some kind of vote. Besides, I'm certain you'll love Glenmuir."

She couldn't think, she couldn't seem to get her

breath, much less put her thoughts in order. "Glen-muir?"

"Aye and it's a bonny place. Though I reckon it's changed some since I last had the pleasure of looking upon it." He sighed in remembered pleasure.

She was so far down the rabbit hole now she just gave in to it. She'd wake up from this coma eventually and have a good laugh over the whole thing. "This laird you want me to marry, I suppose he lives on this island?"

"Aye. The MacNeil has always resided there, in the clan stronghold, Winterhaven Castle."

"A castle." Right. She laughed soundlessly. Of course there was a castle. No good coma-induced fairy tale with a midget and a Scots laird would be complete without a castle.

"Winterhaven has held the MacNeils in good stead since Argus the Black had it built in 1432. Though it was called Black's Tower then. The tenth chief renamed it when he built on to it." He tapped his chin. "I think it was the tenth laird. The stone, and my guardianship, came to the clan in the seventeenth century, so I might be off a laird or two."

"Argus," she echoed. "Black's Tower. Fourteen-thirty-two." She might have whimpered a little.

Bagan patted her shoulder a bit awkwardly and peered into her face. "I see all this comes as a shock to ye, but there's no backing off. It's begun."

"You keep saying that," she said, and with enough vehemence that Bagan stumbled back a step or two. "What if I don't want to go along? In fact, I'll just tell you now, I have no plans of going with you to Scotland. It's preposterous." Her head was pounding so hard it made her eyes swim. She let her chin drop and covered her face with her hands, gently pressing her fingers over the wound on her forehead. "I want to wake up now, okay?" she said in a small voice. "I promise never to surf alone again."

But it wasn't the surfing gods that answered her.

"Och, there, there, lassie."

She felt Bagan's pudgy hand smooth her hair. His hand was very real, as was he, as was . . . all of this. She wanted to cry, but that would make her head hurt worse and wouldn't solve anything. But what would? She had no idea how to make this nightmare come to an end.

"Things seem all a jumble to ye now, but the MacNeil Stone has always brought happiness and good fortune to those who've heeded its blessings."

"Like it did the Lady Elsinor? What if a man had found the stone, huh? Would he have to marry this laird? What if I were already married?"

Bagan only smiled, his eyes crinkling in that damned wise way he had. "But a lad didn't find it, you did. And yer not married, are ye now?"

She didn't bother answering. "I should have stayed home this morning."

"It has been the experience of my many years that everything happens as it does for a reason. One event sets off another, and another, until Destiny fulfills itself."

"What about free will, huh?"

"No one made you put that necklace on, did they now?"

She felt as if her skull would crack in two. This was all simply too much to consider. "So you're saying that no matter what I choose, I can't control how things turn out?"

"Hey, Josiecat! You up there?"

A rush of tears sprang to her eyes at the sound of her dad's voice. She scrambled to her feet, pausing when the room teetered a bit. "You don't move," she commanded Bagan, gingerly holding her forehead. "That's my father. He'll deal with this. And you." She normally prided herself on her independence, and had from somewhere around the age of six, but right now she was shamelessly relieved he was here.

Bagan sighed. "I'm tellin' ye lass, only you and the laird can see me."

She ignored him and all but yanked the door off its hinges before realizing it was still latched. From the inside. She didn't even bother puzzling over that. She popped the hook free and flung herself into her dad's arms. "I'm so glad you're here."

"Whoa, baby." Big Griff stumbled back a step, before setting her back so he could look at her. "What's wrong?"

Josie took a deep breath, wondering where in the hell to start. A quick glance showed that Bagan was sitting on her porch table. He waved and swung his feet. Probably she should start with the kilt-wearing midget since her dad might have a few questions about that.

"It's been a . . . crazy day." *The key word being crazy.* She turned toward Bagan and said, "Dad, this is—"

But her father was still looking at her and didn't seem to even notice they had company. He turned her back around and took a close look at her forehead. "Board bit ya, did it?" He pulled her into his big arms again for a gentle hug. "I'm sorry, kitten. I should have been with you." He set her back again, his perpetual grin returning. "Bet that one made you see stars."

"More like dwarves," she muttered beneath her breath, not as consoled by his perpetual sunniness as she usually was. "I cleaned it up, I'll live."

"Of course you will," he said. "You've got a rock-hard noggin like your old man. Listen, why don't we go inside so you can sit down and get comfortable while I tell you all about Finola."

"Finola?" she asked, but he was already ushering her inside, right past Bagan, who winked at her as she passed. She stuck her tongue out at him, then bumped into her dad when he stopped right inside the door.

"What happened in here?"

"I left a pot on the stove too long. Listen, Dad," she said, intent on telling him what had happened this morning, then stopped. If he truly couldn't see Bagan then how could she possibly explain—

"Hey, what's this?" Griff nodded at the necklace.

"That's what I wanted to tell you about." Josie darted a look out the screen door. Bagan was still sitting there, poking through some fossils. She turned to her dad and took the necklace off, then darted a look at the porch. No Bagan. She felt her knees go a bit woozy. This was all too much to deal with.

"Whoa there, kitten." Her dad caught her, took the necklace from her, and laid it on her kitchen table before helping her to the living room and settling her on the couch. "You really took a good whack there, you're pale as a ghost." He nudged her back against the cushions, then yanked an afghan off the back and tossed it over her, pulling at it here and there. "Can I get you something to drink or anything?" he asked a bit uncertainly. "You want an ice pack for that?"

Her dad was adorable when he was flustered. He meant well and always wanted the best for her, but nurturing in the traditional ways had always been a bit awkward for him. She knew she could count on him for anything, anywhere, anytime, but, growing up, she'd probably done most of the traditional care-taking. She'd never minded, including now. As mixed up and confused as she was, having him hover about made her feel better.

"I'm okay." Which was a total lie, but she decided she didn't want to talk about the necklace, the trunk, much less the disappearing dwarf on her porch. She smiled and tried not to wince at the accompanying twinge across her forehead. "Tell me all about this Finola and I'll be even better. Sounds like something good came out of this meeting, huh?"

Her father still looked a bit worried, but was relieved enough at being let off the nursing hook to trust her judgment. He sat down across from her, apparently having forgotten all about the necklace. The excitement rolling off of him was palpable. She finally began to relax. She'd cart the necklace off to the museum Wednesday and that would be the end of that. As long as she didn't ever put it on again, she could simply pretend nothing had ever happened.

"We've done work for people all over the world, right?"

She nodded.

"Surfed everywhere."

"Right." Where was he headed with this?

"Not right. Did you know they surf in the U.K.?"

A certain dread welled up inside her. "No," she choked out. "I . . . didn't know that."

"Well, they do. Not too many of them, but the sport is growing over there. Anyway, Finola is in charge of the Scotland National Championships, which are coming up shortly. It's their twenty-fifth and she wants to commemorate the event by handing out boards designed by the world's best to the winners. And we're one of the best, aren't we, Josiecat?" He laughed and slapped his knees. "She wants us to do a special design on one of our signature longboards and come over there to award it personally."

Josie couldn't say anything. The room was closing

in on her, darkness creeping in around the corners of her vision. "We . . . we're famous enough," she heard herself say. "What do we need this for?"

Her father frowned, obviously surprised. "Because it sounds like fun," he said. "A new page in our long and colorful legacy. I thought you'd get a kick out of it." He stood and leaned over her. "You really took a knock today. We should talk about this later." He bent down and kissed her on the tip of the nose. "I'll let you get some rest. I want to hear what happened today, your report on the new board design, but you need some rest."

Josie was lucid enough to tell her father that the last thing a concussed person was supposed to do was sleep for a long period of time unmonitored, but she'd monitored her own self for years. "Okay." Though nothing was remotely okay.

"I'll check back in on you later. You call me if you need anything, okay, kitten?"

She just waved at him and forced a smile. She hated that she'd ruined his enthusiasm for this latest adventure of his, but she'd make it up to him later. Stateside.

Because though she hated disappointing her father, she wasn't going to Scotland. Not now. Not ever.

Chapter 3

*J*osie settled back in her airplane seat. It had been eight weeks since she'd found the damn trunk. Two long months spent questioning her sanity.

She'd taken the trunk and the necklace to the local maritime museum, causing a few raised eyebrows when she'd all but lunged at a visiting tourist who'd tried to put the necklace on. In the face of the woman's obvious embarrassment, Josie had let her put it on. Mercifully no dwarf had appeared. In the end, she was glad for the incident. It made it easier for her to pretend Bagan had never really existed.

Josie agreed to allow the museum director to send the trunk and necklace to a local university specializing in marine archeology. She'd left that day, hoping it would be misplaced in the bowels of scientific research, never to resurface. Weeks passed, her head healed, and she finished the board design for Finola. She'd almost convinced herself she was in control of her life again.

Then the museum had called with their report. The trunk dated to the midseventeenth century, the stone and chain were traced back to Scotland, the exact origin undocumented, but they'd classified it as likely being a clan charm stone. They couldn't find any paper trail putting it on a ship that had been documented as having sunk off the coast of South Carolina and Josie didn't bother explaining the ship might have sunk on the other side of the Atlantic. She really didn't want to know anything more about the trunk or the stone.

They'd made some suggestions as to where she could send the trunk to have it fully restored, if that were her intention. Josie had no desire to keep it, much less restore it. She'd grudgingly picked it up, telling herself to be thankful they hadn't made a media event out of her find. Back at home, she'd wrapped the trunk in a moving blanket and tucked it on a shelf of gear in the corner of her porch; out of sight, out of mind. Or so she hoped.

She'd even gotten out of the Scotland trip. Her father had been a bit confused and a little hurt by her wish to stay behind, but he'd reluctantly agreed. She'd finally allowed herself to completely relax. Episode over. Josie Griffin: one, Destiny: zero.

Then came the last-minute phone call from Hawaii. One of her father's oldest friends had passed away and he'd been asked to be a pallbearer. So he'd hopped a flight to LAX with a connecting flight to the big island . . . and she'd hopped a flight to Scotland.

Destiny. Fate.

The two words had echoed in her mind since takeoff. She leaned her forehead against the small airplane window and closed her eyes. She only wished she could shut out Bagan's voice as easily. The dwarf might have vanished from her life, but he hadn't vanished from her thoughts.

In the end, she'd decided that if Fate were indeed dragging her to Scotland, the least she could do was be prepared. So she'd done some research of her own and discovered where Glenmuir was. As it happened—and it was a coincidence, no matter what

Bagan said—Glenmuir was a Hebridean island off the western coast of Scotland . . . a three-hour ferry ride from the neighboring island of Tiree, where the championships were taking place.

So she'd decided to go to the championships, then package up the trunk and ferry it over to Glenmuir. She'd pay someone to drop it off with whoever currently resided in, or was in charge of, Winterhaven Castle . . . then she'd fly home. The trunk and stone would be with their rightful owner, her dad would be happy she'd represented the company, and maybe her peace of mind would finally be restored.

Ye can't escape yer destiny.

"Oh shut up," she muttered.

"I beg your pardon?"

She opened her eyes to find her seatmate, an older woman, frowning at her.

Josie smiled weakly. "I'm sorry, I was just talking to myself."

The older woman's frown turned to something that looked like pity. She patted her hand and said, "I know just how you feel, dear. Hard to turn off the problems in your life sometimes, isn't it?"

Josie just nodded.

"Do you want to talk about it? Sometimes that helps."

Josie just shook her head. "But thank you for offering." She could only imagine the poor woman's expression if she told her she had a magic necklace that enabled her to see an invisible dwarf.

"I understand, dear," the older woman said. "Why, when my Harold left me for that floozy that worked in the perfume department, I thought I'd never get over the shame . . ."

Josie closed her eyes and pretended not to hear, but that didn't stop the woman. In fact, for the entire flight she got to listen to every horrible thing

Harold had ever done. By the time they landed in Glasgow, Josie understood why Harold had chosen the floozy. Self-preservation. She'd rather have spent the flight talking to a Bagan. At least she could make him disappear when she wanted.

She disembarked and found Finola waiting for her. They'd spoken on the phone numerous times and Josie felt like she knew her fairly well. Finola's beaming smile and warm Scottish brogue as she welcomed her had her relaxing almost immediately. For the first time Josie let herself believe that maybe, just maybe, this wasn't such a huge mistake after all.

&

Five days later, she wasn't so sure.

"One hundred pounds," Josie offered, desperation creeping into her voice. "I'll even throw in this surfboard. It's an autographed original."

The MacBayne ferry captain sighed wearily. "Do I look like a surfer, to you?" He was in his fifties, short and quite stout, with a white beard ringing his chin. She'd seen men in worse shape attempting to shoot the tubes, but she understood his point.

"Okay, okay, name your price. I just need this package delivered. Please, it's important."

He tried a kind smile, but Josie knew she'd pushed him as far as he was going to. "Lassie, I appreciate that yer in a spot of trouble here, but this is a ferry, no' a postal service. I'll be glad to book you passage, but I canno' be responsible for deliverin' a package. I'm sorry."

"My flight leaves tomorrow," Josie said, not caring that she was whining. "If I don't take the other ferry to Oban this afternoon, I'll never make it back to Glasgow in time. I can't take the ferry to Glenmuir and get back in time for the ferry to Oban."

"That's for certain since the ferry doesn't return

this way. It goes on to Harris, then all the way to Oban itself. There won't be service from Glenmuir again for three days."

"Three days?" Josie wanted to cry. This wasn't supposed to be so difficult. She'd looked at the ferry schedule when she'd arrived and purposely made sure she got here in enough time to send the package off before heading back to the mainland. She'd have done it on her way to Tiree, but Finola had been with her and she hadn't wanted to explain. Now it looked like she was stuck.

"You could post it from the mainland," the captain suggested.

Josie had thought about that, but she really wanted to make sure it got into the right hands. Plus she had no idea to whom she was sending it. She hadn't been able to find out much about Glenmuir other than how to get to it. It was too small to make the travel guides. She'd intended to do some research on it and Winterhaven and the MacNeils after she got here, but Finola had kept her so busy that there hadn't been any time even to look at a map.

And there was no one else lined up to make the trip over that she could bribe to help her out. She looked to the captain. "You wouldn't happen to know who resides in Winterhaven Castle, would you?"

The captain laughed. "Haints maybe, no one else."

"Haints?"

"Ghosts." He chuckled. "Winterhaven hasn't been inhabited for several centuries. Not much more than a pile of rocks now, I believe, except for the tower."

"Black's Tower?"

The captain looked at her. "You know of it then? I'm surprised you didn't know it wasn't more than a ruin. Who would you be wantin' to send a package to at Winterhaven?"

"Whatever MacNeil was left in charge of it," she said, feeling more foolish by the minute.

The captain removed his hat and rubbed at his bald head before replacing it. "I'm from Stranraer, only just started on the ferry service up here, but the MacNeils have been in these islands since the beginnin', so I'm sure there's probably one or two left on Glenmuir that could help you."

"Thanks." What was she supposed to do now? Just stick the thing in a box marked "Current MacNeil Chief, Glenmuir, Scotland"?

She trudged back to her rental car at the other dock. It was easy to spot as it was the only one with a board strapped on top. Everyone else involved in the tournament was staying through the weekend and a part of her wished now she'd booked herself more time here.

She'd had a great time in Tiree, far better than she'd expected. Finola was almost fifteen years older than she was, but had the energy of an eighteen-year-old. It had been the perfect antidote to the past two months. Josie had even gotten some time in the chilly highland surf during the three-day tournament. She was honestly happy she'd come and wished her dad had been able to come along, too. He'd have liked Finola. She'd hated saying good-bye to her.

But fun and frolic notwithstanding, she was *not* going home with the damn trunk. She put the box she'd packed it in back in the car and leaned against the closed boot. She didn't see where she had a choice but to mail the thing from the mainland, but she felt responsible for its safety. Just then a delivery truck rumbled up and headed to the Glenmuir ferry. A spurt of hope shot through her. She started to take off after it on foot, but the captain unchained the gate and motioned the truck right onto the ferry. She'd never catch up.

She looked back to her dock, at the Oban ferry that wasn't scheduled to leave for hours yet, then back at the Glenmuir ferry. Damn, damn, damn. But she was already climbing into her car and pulling out of line. She wasn't going to regret this, she told herself. She knew exactly what she was doing and it had zero to do with Destiny, Fate, or anything else.

The captain waved her on with a big smile, calling out that he'd settle up with her after they'd set off on their way. *I'm doing this of my own free will,* she repeated silently as she waved back to him. She just needed to hand the trunk over to someone personally, that was all.

She'd have to reschedule her flight and it would probably cost her a mint, plus she'd have to find accommodations on Glenmuir and it was the high season for tourists. But Glenmuir wasn't exactly a hot spot so she shouldn't have too hard a time.

She parked, her heart racing as she tried to reassure herself she'd done the right thing. She knew her dad wouldn't mind her extending her stay. He'd been worried about her lately and she'd felt bad for not confiding in him. She usually shared everything with him, but not this. Because of that, she'd kept to herself more than usual, claiming the design project was giving her fits and taking more time than usual. It had, but mostly because she'd spent too much time trying to forget Bagan and his dire predictions.

So this little side trip was a good thing. It would allow her to go home rested and happy, which was good for them both. Maybe she'd even get in some more surfing, or at the very least some nice beach-combing.

"Yeah," she murmured under her breath as she

got out of the car and made her way to the rail. "It's just a few more vacation days. Totally my choice."

So why the dread built as she neared the island, she had no idea. Glenmuir first emerged as a speck on the horizon. It didn't grow much bigger as they neared. It was hilly, but the vegetation was sparse. The shoreline, on the eastern side at least, was rocky and definitely inhospitable for surfers. Right now she was more interested in finding a place to stay.

She'd studied a big map posted on board and had been pleased to find Winterhaven noted on the western shore of Glenmuir. A single road ringed the speck of an island and would take her directly to it. She'd also noted that there was only one town, Ruirisay, a short way from the ferry landing, but she held out hope that she'd find a place to stay. Surely the captain would have mentioned that being a problem before encouraging her to go.

She followed the truck off the boat, growing more uncertain as she bumped along the single-lane road into Ruirisay. They passed a few crofts on the way and numerous sheep, but no other cars and not much else. The town itself consisted of one main street with a few shops and businesses lining the only habitable side of the street. The other was railed off before falling away to the rocks far below, but provided a gorgeous view of the water.

Josie pulled to a stop behind the truck when it parked outside a small grocery that also appeared to serve as post office, bakery, butcher, and mercantile. There was only one other car parked there, but a number of bicycles were lined up against the building.

Josie went inside and looked about the place as the truck driver unloaded supplies and talked and laughed with the owner. The older woman who ran the store signed his clipboard and handed him a check before seeing him to the door. "Best ye head back to the ferry. That new one, he's like to leave you, and the poor folks on Harris won't have their bread for another fortnight."

The man waved and climbed back in his truck. Josie was tempted to follow him, but then the owner turned those warm brown eyes and pleasant smile on her. "How may I help you?"

Her brogue was as warm and delightful as Finola's, but her eyes, though brown, reminded her of Bagan. Very twinkly. Josie shut that train of thought off, put on a smile and stuck out her hand. "I'm Josie Griffin. I was over on Tiree at the surfing championships and thought I'd take a look here." She tried to look confident instead of desperate. "I sort of came on the spur of the moment and don't have a place to stay. I was hoping you could help."

The woman's smile faded to one of sincere concern. "Oh dear." She held Josie's hand a moment before letting it go. "Surfing you say? We've never had any surfers as far as I can recall. Are you certain you meant to come here?"

Josie motioned to the window where her car and board were visible. "I hoped maybe there were good waves here, with quiet, less-crowded beaches. I'm always up for an adventure," she added gamely, thinking she'd never felt less like being adventurous. She hadn't thought she could feel more foolish, but she simply wasn't up to explaining why she was really here. She'd hoped to start with surfing and work her way to the MacNeil's and Winterhaven from there.

"I'm afraid someone has misled you. No' about the beaches, we've some fine ones, if a bit remote." She smiled warmly again. "But we're no' so easy to get to, so we're not exactly a tourist stop, if you get my meaning. We've no hotel here."

"I don't need anything fancy."

The woman's expression didn't clear. "Margaery's let her spare rooms to her sister and her kids, come to stay for the summer." She smiled briefly. "Always nice to hear the ringing laughter of children. We miss that around here." Then she motioned to the door. "Come with me. We'll see what we can do."

They stepped outside, then into the pub next door. The buildings were like row houses, all attached, each painted in a cheery pastel color. It was a lively look for such a quiet little place.

"I'm Maeve, I should have said before."

Josie smiled. "I really appreciate the help."

"This is my husband Roddy's place. Maybe he has an idea."

The pub was small and dark, just big enough to accommodate a massive pool table, a few chairs, and the thick bar that ran the length of the far wall. Three men occupied stools in front of it, likely the owners of the bicycles out front, Josie thought.

All three men were of the same age as Maeve, all speaking Gaelic to one another. Maeve hailed them in kind, then switched to English when she introduced Josie.

"This is Josie Griffin, over from Tiree and fresh from the surfing tournament there." She smiled. "Josie, this is Gavin, Dougal, and the ornery one at the end there is Clud. And that's my husband, Roddy, behind the bar."

All four men grinned and raised their glasses to her. Roddy was enjoying a drink as well, she noticed.

"Can we buy you an ale, lass?" asked Dougal.

Gavin nodded. "Why, you're the prettiest thing we've seen in—" He stopped abruptly when Roddy cuffed him on the shoulder. "Since yer lovely wife there," he finished with aplomb, making all four men laugh.

"Oh, go on with you now," Maeve said, waving them

off, obviously used to their ways. "Josie is here for a few days and needs a place to stay. I know Margaery has Susan and the boys and Posey is doing some work on her place. I dinna think the Sutherlands need anyone underfoot anyhow." She turned to Josie and said, "Marital problems they have." She rolled her eyes heavenward and shook her head, then turned back to the men. "Have you any ideas?"

Roddy scratched his gray-whiskered chin and the other men seemed to take the matter under great consideration as well. Josie appreciated it, but had the sinking feeling she was going to end up sleeping in her car for a few nights. With the trunk and necklace Oh goody.

She toyed with the idea of asking if any of them were MacNeils but it didn't seem the time to impose further. She'd lasted this long, one or two more nights with the blasted thing wouldn't kill her.

"What of ol' Gregors place?" Dougal said. "He's over to Mull with his daughter what just had the babe. Sure he wouldn't mind someone doing more than just checking on the place. He'll be gone a fortnight more, I think, at least."

Josie looked to Maeve, who didn't appear all that hot on the idea. "His place is away on the western shore."

One of the other gents waved off her concern. "She can borrow my bike. I can walk back."

"She has a car," Maeve said, "but still . . ." She looked to Josie. "It's fairly remote."

It was perfect. Winterhaven was on the western shore. She could poke about a bit, then maybe come back and talk with Maeve, and maybe the men as well, about the MacNeil history here. Worst-case scenario, she could give the stupid thing to them and leave them to duke it out for possession.

"I'm pretty self-sufficient," Josie said to Maeve.

"If you're sure it's okay with him, I'd like to take you up on your very kind offer. It's only for two nights. I'll be more than glad to pay whatever rent you think appropriate."

All four men waved her off. "Och, ol' Gregor won't mind," Dougal assured her. "You might want to stock up over at Maeve's though. I doubt he has much put by."

Maeve gave in gracefully, her lined face smoothed to a smile when she turned to Josie. "Gregor definitely won't mind, dear," she said. "Come next door and we'll get you what you need. He doesna have phone service out there, but you've only to come by and ring the bell at any hour. Roddy and I live in the rooms above and will be glad to help you out." She patted her hand and her eyes crinkled at the corners as her smile widened. "Welcome to Glenmuir, Josie Griffin."

Josie was still smiling as she drove on down the road to Gregor's place. Apparently no key was needed since no one locked up their places on the island. She supposed that the population couldn't be more than a hundred or so on the entire island, and that included the sheep, so there was probably little in the way of crime. The sun was setting as she wound her way along the coastline.

She drove slowly as the road was rutted, but the scenery was so gorgeous she found she didn't mind a bit. The hills at this end were carpeted in the lovely bright green grass she'd admired since arriving in Scotland, much of it still studded with heather. It probably looked much as it had centuries ago, she thought, unable to keep herself from wondering about the original MacNeil laird, the one who'd sent the stone out to sea.

Then she rounded another curve and stomped hard on the brake. She'd reached the west shore.

The beach truly was beautiful, a long stretch of smooth sand, with decent waves that could probably entertain her for a few hours.

But that wasn't why she'd just given herself whiplash.

"Winterhaven," she whispered, awestruck. The massive pile of stones stood, proudly ruinous, on a spit of land that jutted out from the shore. The strand leading to it was so narrow that at high tide, Josie imagined you'd need to swim out to it, or take a boat. Two of the square walls had partially tumbled into the water, but still rose strong and tall into the evening sunset. A third side, facing the open water, was completely gone. But the fourth was what held her attention, as it was part of the tower of dark stone that jutted upward, seemingly untouched by the same hazards that had left the rest in ruins.

Black's Tower. She rubbed at her arms. Awed by the foreboding strength of it, she thought briefly of the men who had built it. And of her folly in coming out here alone.

She pressed on the gas before she could change her mind. *It's a ruin*, she thought *no one has lived here for hundreds of years*. But as she drew closer and the tower loomed higher and higher she couldn't keep the hairs on her arms from lifting just a bit.

She spied Gregor's spread—it was hard to miss as it was the only place around—and edged into the deeply rutted dirt lane he called a driveway. She had to stop after only several feet, unable to go any farther without getting stuck. "Doesn't anyone drive on this island?" But she'd already learned that almost everyone rode bicycles, which explained the rutted roads and lanes. Maeve explained how expensive it was to bring in petrol and most islanders preferred to hoof it or bike. The island wasn't all that big and

Josie supposed it wasn't a bad way to get around. Maeve had said there were numerous old sheep paths that most of the islanders used as shortcuts.

She spied an old dented bike leaning up against the rambling, thatched croft. Maybe she'd take a spin herself in the morning. She glanced back to the shore. But only after she'd tested out the surf, she decided.

"Okay, okay, you can't ignore it forever." She took a breath and looked back at the castle. It was truly impressive. She got out of the car and opened the boot, intent on grabbing her gear bag so she could get her wet suit out. But the box with the trunk was on top, right where she'd tucked it back on the ferry dock.

She meant to just push it aside, but something had her picking it up, flipping open the flaps. "You're home," she whispered, having no idea why she did and feeling immediately spooked for having said it.

But that didn't compare to how spooked she felt when she turned, still holding the trunk, and looked at Winterhaven . . . only to spy a light flickering on in the tower window. She blinked, telling herself it was the setting sun reflecting on the windowpane . . . then realized that there couldn't be a windowpane in a tumbledown ruin. Could there?

That question died unanswered when a cloaked figure emerged from the lower door of the tower, moving in long strides across the narrow spit and up the beach.

Josie's mind and heart raced, but she froze when he stopped and looked up, as if directly at her. *Run*, she told herself.

She turned, but his voice, carrying beyond the sound of the surf when there was no way it could have, stopped her.

"I believe you have something that belongs to

me." His thundering voice all but vibrated through the wind-tossed air between them.

Josie slowly turned around. He was standing behind her, which was impossible given that moments ago he'd been yards down the beach.

"Gregor?" But she knew it wasn't Gregor. This man wasn't old enough to have grandbabies. And it wasn't Bagan either. This man was no dwarf. Quite the opposite.

He looked around her age, late twenties, maybe thirty, but far more intense than any man of any age she'd ever met. He was tall, ruggedly built, his dark hair pulled back from his face. Unlike most of the men she'd seen in Scotland, he actually wore a kilt, with the excess tartan tossed over his shoulder like a cloak. The fabric was worn, the colors faded, like a favorite pair of jeans. And he looked just as natural in it. Beneath the plaid was a shirt that might have been linen, but in the growing dusk it was hard to tell. The shirt wasn't new and neither were the leather boots laced up his thick calves. She couldn't manage another word. Imposing didn't begin to describe the man.

His dark eyes bore full into hers. "I'm The Mac-Neil." He nodded to the box. "And that stone yer holdin' is mine."

"I—" She forced herself to choke down the hard knot in her throat. "Here." She shoved the box toward him. "Take it. I don't want it."

He stepped forward then and she realized just how big a man he really was. She forced herself not to flinch or pull back as he reached for the box with impossibly big hands. Once he had what he wanted, he'd probably leave her alone.

She breathed a sigh of relief when he grasped the box without touching her, though she couldn't have said precisely why the thought of him touching alarmed her so much. "I . . . I was bringing it here. To you."

Then he grinned and she lost all conscious thought. His teeth were a blind of white against tanned skin and dark hair. "Were ye now?" He lifted the trunk out of the cardboard box she'd packed it in, letting the latter drop to the ground ignored. "Och, but it's seen a few bad days, hasn't it."

She was still trying to get used to the reality of his presence in front of her and didn't respond. Couldn't.

He pried open the lid and pulled out the chain. "Safe and sound," he murmured, his voice quavering with some profound emotion. "Just as I knew she would be."

Josie tried not to look at the stone, had in fact been successful at not looking at it for months now. But she couldn't help herself. In his hands, the thing fairly glowed. It must be a trick of the setting sun.

She pushed her hand through her hair and somehow scrounged up a smile. "Well, it's been nice meeting you. Glad I could help." On very shaky legs, she began backing toward the door of her car.

Then he looked up and stilled her with one look. One very intense, very compelling look. "Have ye worn it?"

Josie gulped. The phrase "just say no" took on new meaning. But his eyes lit up before she could form the words and he stepped closer. The answer must have shown on her face.

"Ye have, haven't ye?" Almost in disbelief, he whispered, "You're her."

His gaze was so direct, so focused she felt as if it reached in and touched the most intimate part of her. "I—"

"If ye bear me the chain, then ye bear me yerself as well, lass." His intensity was like a live thing.

She forced her throat to work, her tongue to move. "I don't think so. I'm really sorry." She started backing up when the gleam in his eyes grew brighter, but he merely kept pace toward her. "I—I mean, I'm flattered and all, but . . . I—I can't . . . you know . . . *bear* you anything else."

"What I know is that you bear my stone." He closed the distance and lifted the necklace toward her. "Which means yer mine now as well."

Chapter 4

*T*hree hundred years. An eternity of time, but his faith had never wavered. He'd done little but think about this moment. Yet now that it was here, Connal MacNeil scarcely knew how to act. His heart pounded and a loud roar had taken up residence inside his head. His destiny would now—finally—be fulfilled.

"Come wi' me," he commanded the young woman who'd borne him the trunk. A comely lass she was, too, he thought. Short, wind-tossed curls and expressive eyes, coupled with a figure seemingly hardy enough to bear him the beginnings of the legacy he'd bargained so dearly for. Aye, she would do. Not that he could afford to be choosy.

He'd long wondered if the gods had indeed played a role in the fate of the stone, despite knowing that once the stone was set upon its way, only Fate guided its course. Had they somehow conspired with the Fates to punish him for his brothers' transgressions? He knew not. But his faith would be rewarded. His destiny was not to die on some bloody battlefield, his clan in ruin.

And finally, Fate had proven his patience and faith worthy of that reward.

He took the arm of the woman sent to fulfill his destiny and turned to make his way back to the tower. The rising tide would soon make the trip difficult.

She surprised him by yanking her arm free. He spun about to find her staring at him in a distinctly defiant manner, arms folded. "I've waited a long time for you and I'll no' be wastin' any more of it. I've a legacy to build."

Even in the twilight, he saw those expressive eyes go dark. She had quite a prominent chin, he noticed, especially when she stuck it out so.

"I'm not going anywhere with you," she announced with barely a quaver in her tone.

"A brave lass," he said, nodding approvingly. "Our son will need one such as you to protect and defend him until he is old enough to do it for himself."

Her mouth dropped open, then snapped shut again as she quickly scuttled out of his reach.

He sighed, trying to rein in his impatience. But three hundred years of waiting tended to take a toll on a man. "Ye have no say in the matter."

Her chin came up again, shoulders squared. Healthy shoulders he noticed, wondering if she labored in the fields of her homeland. He skimmed his gaze lower and was disappointed to find that her hips weren't cut from the same sturdy cloth. Narrow they were, almost mannish. Well, she was sturdy enough, he decided. She would have to be.

"I've given you back your blasted stone," she said, this time the trembling more clear in her voice, but he wasn't sure if it forged in fear . . . or fury. "In fact I came halfway around the world, or so it seems, to deliver it personally. But you'll have to understand if I refuse to accept your kind offer of rape as a token of your gratitude. A simple thank-you would be enough."

His eyes popped wide. "Rape?"

She folded her arms, but her legs weren't braced nearly as firmly as she would have liked him to believe. "That's what they call it when you take a woman against her will, which I can heartily guarantee will be the case if you lay so much as one finger on me."

She was something. All spitfire and ribald bravado. He tipped back his head and laughed.

"You're not exactly instilling any confidence in me here," she snapped.

He sighed, thinking it might have been better if the stone had brought him a quieter, obedient lass, but he was too overjoyed at its return to judge Fate's choice. They hadn't kept him waiting three hundred years for no reason.

"I willna hurt ye," he said, then took a step forward, hand outstretched, frowning when she stepped farther away.

"You'll pardon me if I don't swoon with relief."

"Och, but there's no need for such a sharp tongue."

Now she snorted with what he supposed was a laugh, though quite an unfeminine version of it. "You announce you're going to force yourself on me and I've offended *you* with sarcasm?" She bowed. "Please accept my humblest apologies, my lord."

"I'm laird, no' a lord."

She straightened and sighed. "Whatever. Listen, I'm tired. It's been an amazingly long day. I'd really like to go inside—alone—and settle in for the night. We can take up this discussion again in the morning, okay?" She didn't wait for him to answer, she simply turned her back on him and began hiking up the rutted lane to Gregor's old place.

He was so unused to being treated in such a manner—no matter that he'd lived alone for so long—that it took him a moment to react. "See here, we have much that needs discussing."

"If you want to talk to someone, put the necklace on," she called out over her shoulder, not bothering to look back. "I'm sure the dwarf won't mind listening to you."

"Bagan?"

That stopped her, but she didn't turn around. "You know him?"

"Aye. He's the guardian of the stone."

She stood stock-still for a long moment. "Not a very good one," she said finally, no longer so strident.

"You've seen him then? You know what became of him?"

Her spine stiffened and she started moving again. "Put the stone on and ask him yourself."

She was at the door when he spoke again, this time more softly. "If ye've met Bagan, then surely you know ye canno' escape what lies in store for us."

She did turn then, a trick of the waning light illuminating her face clearly to him. "Two months ago I would have said there was no such thing as Fate or Destiny. I'm still not a real fan of either."

"I'll convince ye otherwise."

Was that a smile curving her lips? He couldn't be sure, but he heard the music in her voice for the first time. "You're not off to a real great start."

"Are ye challenging me, then?"

There was a long pause. So long he fully expected her to disappear inside without another word. When she did finally speak, what she said surprised him. "What is your name?"

"I'm The MacNeil."

"Your given name."

What was she up to now? "Connal."

That seemed to give her pause. "Family name?" Then she waved her hand. "Never mind. I really don't want to know. Night." Then she was gone.

He let her go, looking down instead to the trunk he held tightly against his chest. The stone had been returned. He could scarce believe it was true. He glanced at the closed door. And with its return, another challenge.

It made sense, he supposed. Nothing had ever come to him easily. He'd had to bargain his soul to get this far. Gods knew what else was expected of him. But he'd waited this long, he'd do whatever it took, make whatever sacrifice was necessary. She was finally here . . . and she would be his.

A yellow light glowed to life behind the windowpane. "I am up to this challenge, fair one," he said. "And any others ye care to lay in my path. See if I'm no'."

⁊⁊

Josie sat up in bed with a start, breathing heavily as the last vestiges of the dream misted away. "Oh, thank God," she whispered, pressing a hand to her racing heart. She'd been dreaming, that's all. Dwarves and magic stones and demanding men with long black hair and flashing black eyes . . . she'd made it all up. Then her vision cleared and she realized she was not in her own bed, or her own house. Hell, she wasn't even in her own country. She hadn't been dreaming after all. Dammit.

She flopped back on the feather down and frowned at the beamed ceiling. The beamed ceiling in Gregor's croft. In Scotland. "Why me?"

Thankfully no one answered that question. She wasn't up to any more supernatural discussions at the moment. Or discussions with supernaturals, for that matter.

She peered out the small loft window. But as it never got fully dark this far north in the summertime, it was hard to tell what time it was. She rolled over, looked at her travel clock, and groaned. "Why am I awake at six o'clock?"

Well, she wasn't staying in bed. That would lead to more sleep . . . and more dreams. She rubbed at the goose bumps on her skin as recollections of the exact nature of some of those dreams drifted through her mind . . . and her body. She really didn't want to think about that . . . or the fact that, in her dreams, when he had put his hands on her, she'd responded in a way that had given a whole new meaning to the term "consensual sex."

"Enough." She flung the quilts off and forced herself out of bed. Gregor's place was small and sparsely furnished. The Spartans would have been right at home, she thought with a smile. The lower level was actually one large room that comprised both living area and kitchen. The loft was all bedroom with a small bath tucked in the alcove. She stepped closer to the little window, pushing open the cantilevered panes so she could see more clearly. She stilled when she realized the view from the loft was focused directly on the castle ruins.

Part of her wanted to pull away, tug the windows shut, close the curtains, and pretend none of it had happened. She could drive to town, beg a room or sleep in her car at the dock until the next ferry arrived. She didn't care where it was heading. The stone had been returned, she'd done what she set out to do.

And yet she couldn't turn away from the window, or stop from searching out the tower windows for a glimpse of him. She scanned the beaches, but there was no sign of him there either, not even footprints left behind from an early-morning stroll. She spent a moment or two wondering if she really had dreamed the whole thing. Maybe the blasted trunk was still tucked in the boot of her car.

But she knew it wasn't. It was tucked in that tower. In the possession of The MacNeil.

She wrapped her arms around her middle. Why hadn't anyone told her the tower was still inhabited? Maybe that was the real reason Maeve had been so leery of her staying out here. Maybe he was some kind of eccentric descendant who thought he was laird of the nonexistent MacNeil clan.

"Except he knew about Bagan," she murmured beneath her breath. She didn't know what to think of that. She supposed it was possible that tales of the clan guardian had been passed down from generation to generation. Still, she'd spent two months convincing herself the dwarf had been some kind of delusion and she wasn't as relieved as she'd thought she would be to hear his existence confirmed by someone else.

She turned her gaze to the shoreline, then out to the water. Now that she was here, somehow things that seemed fanciful—okay, certifiable—back home in the States actually seemed possible, even probable. There was definitely something magical about these islands. Especially Glenmuir, where crofts and sheep dotted the hills, and the one small town was inhabited with kindly older folk who could claim to have fairies living under their stoops and seem perfectly plausible.

For all that she'd flown to Scotland on a plane, driven to this very croft in an automobile . . . she could step outside and easily believe it was centuries earlier. The fact that the croft she stood in now was likely older than most structures currently standing in the United States was not lost on her. Glenmuir was definitely a place out of time.

Her thoughts strayed again to Connal. Connal. Just thinking his name gave her the shivers, made him seem all too real. It was the same name Bagan had mentioned, the name belonging to man who'd lived three hundred years ago. It had to be a family name passed down from MacNeil to MacNeil.

Yer now mine as well, lass.

His words mixed with the dreams she'd had about him and she shifted uncomfortably, thinking once again of running. But there was nowhere to run. She was stuck here, in this land that was both dream and nightmare, for three days.

And yet . . . escape from all this confusion lay just outside her window. The beach was beautiful, the waves, though small, were breaking perfectly, and the sky was clear and sunny. She could sort this out later. The siren call was upon her. And she was going to lose herself in the rhythm of the ocean, the one place she always felt at home.

❧

Connal stood at his tower window and watched her as she made her way down the path to the beach. She was clad in a black garment that clung to her like a second layer of skin. He found himself rethinking his opinion on her hips. They didn't sway overly much, but her purposeful stride stirred him nonetheless. Och, he'd been far too long deprived of a woman's softness. But his thoughts and energies had been focused only on the return of the stone . . . and the return of prosperity to Glenmuir.

Now that the stone lay securely inside his tower walls once more, his thoughts were on her. And little else. She'd followed him into his dreams last night, whereupon his subconscious had placed a far greater emphasis on how he'd gone about siring his future heir than on the importance of the heir himself.

She crossed the beach at an angle, heading toward the water. *What is she about?* His attention was

pulled from those compact curves to the brightly
colored plank she carried tucked beneath her arm. It
was longer than she was. He once again marveled at
her strength as she carried the beam quite easily. Was
she perhaps planning to hunt him down and thrash
him with it? He smiled then, thinking that while her
refusal to accept Fate's plan was frustrating for
someone who'd waited as long as he had, her feisti-
ness appealed to him. He'd need a strong woman to
carry on once he was gone.

Gone. He could scarce believe his time here was
close to an end. He'd had a very narrow view of the
world, trapped as he was here, but it had been the only
view he'd desired. Very few ever strolled these shores.
In fact, more had left than had ever come. He'd
borne the pain of his bargain in silence, forcing himself to watch the final decline of his clan, his home, as
a reminder of why his faith must never waver.

Yet, it had. Such a long stretch of time, with nothing to do but ponder one's actions. He'd remained in
seclusion, not revealing his spectral self to anyone for
a very long time, nursing the pain of the brutal end his
fellow clansmen had come to at the hands of other,
more powerful clans. Nursing also his faith that, in the
end, Fate would deliver what she had promised. The
stone . . . and the woman who would help him return
prosperity to what was left of Glenmuir.

After a century of time, he'd finally sought out
company. It was that or go mad. Gregor's ancestors
had erected the croft and their small farm holding
by then. He'd taken to visiting late at night, when
the master of the croft was well in his cups and un-
likely to question the reality of his unearthly guest
come morning. Gregor had been a particular favorite. Quite verbose in his opinions of . . . well,
most everything.

Those visits had afforded him not only knowledge

of the world beyond this place, but of what was happening about the island itself. He'd begun to feel his faith slip as he watched his homeland near its final years. There was no new life on Glenmuir, and those who inhabited it weren't long for this world. Once they were gone, Glenmuir would fall to its final ruin. As much a ghost of her former self as he was.

Then he had come to realize Fate's reasoning. If he was being punished somehow for his brothers' refusal to accept the promise of the stone by being forced to witness the slow, torturous result of their careless choices, then his reward for keeping faith would logically be saving Glenmuir once and for all. Snatching it back from the yaw of ruin and death.

Now that time was blessedly, mercifully at hand and he was more than ready for the task that lay before him, regardless of the challenges yet to be met. But was he really ready to leave this place once and for all when he'd achieved his goal?

"Good God, yes," he breathed.

She was heading directly toward the water now. He was drawn from his musings and moved to the next opening in the tower wall. She certainly didn't plan to raft her way to the mainland, did she? She'd be heading in the wrong direction, if that were the case.

He watched in amusement. She was not a Scot, which had put him at a bit of a loss. Why had the Fates tossed a foreign-born woman into his path? Perhaps she had Scots blood somewhere in her ancestry. He shrugged off his curiosity. Destiny was often a puzzle, one not to be solved by mere men. He knew from centuries spent trying.

It wasn't until she waded out into the water, with the beam held aloft, that he began to grow concerned. "Gods, she's planning on drowning herself!"

"Nay, she's out to hunt waves."

Connal's spine stiffened at the arrival of his newest companion. "I don't recall requesting your guidance, Bagan." Their discussion last eve had done little to raise the guardian in his estimation. Connal turned to find him seated precariously in a window opening and had to forcibly resist the urge to send him toppling out of it. Not that it would do any good. Blasted guardianship protected him. Had it protected the stone as well, he might not have spent the past three centuries stuck in this bloody tower.

"Ye needn't scowl at me so," Bagan said, apparently unfazed by his chilly reception. "I've explained about the storm. Ye can hardly hold me accountable for that. Even Josie said so."

"Josie?" So that was her name. He hadn't thought to ask last night. It sounded . . . odd on his lips. Foreign. "Short for Josephine, then." Josephine. Yes, he liked that better. "Another MacLeod is she?" That would help explain the choice.

"Nay, no' a MacLeod. Griffin is her surname. And 'tis simply Josie. Something to do with being named after a family cat." Bagan waved a stubby hand. "A long story."

Connal frowned. "Yes, I can imagine. I'll hear it from her."

"Have yer way then," Bagan said dismissively.

"Had I my way, I'd have been married to the Lady Elsinor, sired a castleful of hardy bairns, and been long dead by now."

Bagan offered a cheeky smile. "Ye got half yer desire anyway." He shrank back when Connal advanced on him, grabbing hold of the window to keep from falling out.

"I'm in no mood fer yer jests, imp."

"I couldna change me fate, MacNeil, nor that of the stone. Fate has the final say, ye know that as well as I do. Twasn't as if I could raise the trunk from the depths of the ocean floor."

"Yer to have the stone's interest and well-being at heart at all times. It is the heart o' the clan, but there ye go, once again more interested in—"

"Are ye no' interested in what the lass intends to do with that board of hers?" Bagan said.

Frustrating, annoying as all hell, and quite deft at shifting the focus away from himself at the most judicious times, Connal thought. But the dwarf had a point. He turned his attention once again to the water below. She was sitting astride the plank now. "What in blazes does she think she's about?"

"I told ye. Wave hunting."

Connal didn't shift his attention from the scene below. "What would she do with one were she to somehow catch it?"

Bagan hopped down from the window ledge and waddled over to stand beside Connal. "From what I understand, one rides them."

Connal didn't respond. His gaze was fully intent on the woman astride the painted board. She'd paddled closer to the castle ruin, where the tumble of stones from the castle walls created a seawall of sorts, which in turn created a greater water surge. She was moving directly into the heaviest part of the surf and—gods!—she was attempting to steer that flimsy piece of driftwood in the direct path of— "She *is* plannin' to send herself to hell!"

Connal was out of the tower in the flash, ignoring Bagan's pleas to stop and wait and let him explain. As if he'd believe anything the imp had to say. Man couldn't even deliver one winsome bride to his side through a bit of a storm! And now his current betrothed was trying to kill herself.

Connal hit the beach running, so unnerved he

hadn't even thought to merely appear in the water next to her. He was already unwinding his kilt and preparing himself for the bitter cold of the North Sea when he came to a skidding halt as he rounded the last pile of ruinous rubble . . . aghast as he spied her standing on that painted plank amidst Mother Nature's finest fury.

But if she was intending to kill herself, she'd yet to plunge herself into the rocky depths. In fact, it looked as if she'd had a change of heart and was desperately steering the thing away from the rocks, away from certain death. Or, at the very least, severe dismemberment.

He snapped out of his daze and rushed into the surf as she neared the beach. It was only after he'd dragged her kicking and screaming from the roiling seafoam that he thought to wonder on the fact that, close up, she hadn't seemed remotely panicked. At least not until he'd come in the water after her. In fact, she'd looked joyous. And quite a lovely countenance she had when she smiled, he thought.

Well . . . she wasn't smiling now.

Chapter 5

"What the hell do you think you're doing?" Josie sputtered, pounding at his annoyingly broad chest. "Put me down! Now, dammit."

"Ye shouldna swear, lass. Isna verra becoming."

She glared at him. "Neither is dragging me off my surfboard. Not to mention dangerous."

His flash black eyes widened. "Dangerous? Ye think me savin' yer life to be the dangerous act?"

"Saving my life?" She was still sputtering, but she'd given up beating on his chest. He was completely impervious to it, as if she were but a little mouse pounding on a lion. Well, she was no mouse, as this lion was about to learn. "Did you hear me scream for help? No," she answered for him. "I was in complete control, or was until I had to flip out to avoid ramming right into you. Would have served you right, you know, but it might have damaged my board."

He was regarding her steadily now, as one might watch a crazy person they were wanting to placate. "What manner of sport is this wave hunting then?" he asked after several moments of enduring her glare.

He'd caught her off guard with the question. "It's called surfing. It's usually relaxing," she added pointedly. "You've never seen a person surf?"

He shook his head, paused a moment, then said, "So ye put yerself in front of those waves on purpose then, but not in order to expedite your passage into the afterlife."

"You thought I was trying to kill myself?" She laughed, and his face reddened.

"I'm no' in the habit of watching lassies try to harness the power of an ocean with naught but a silver of driftwood beneath their feet," he said tautly.

"Well, get used to it. These aren't the best tubes in the world by any stretch, but if I have to be stuck here for a few days, they're definitely going to get ridden." She pushed her stringy wet hair from her forehead. "So, now that you and I have an understanding, I would appreciate it if you would put me down. Pretty please," she added with a fake smile.

"I'll put ye down when I'm good and ready."

Undeterred, she tried a different tack. "You must be cold. Don't you think you should go get into something dry?" *Providing you don't take me with you while you do it*, she added silently, wishing she'd thought that one through a bit better.

"The cold doesna bother me. Nor the damp."

"Oh." Well. Of course, now that he'd gone and mentioned it, she became hyperaware of that damp chest she was clasped against, covered in a white cotton shirt that now clung transparently to his skin. His muscles were clearly defined, as was the scattering of dark hair that swirled over his pecs.

She shifted her gaze away only to find him smiling at her. Caught. How mortifying. She forced herself not to squirm, but there was no denying her body was responding quite enthusiastically to her current predicament. All the more reason to end it immediately. She blurted out the first thing that came to her mind. "I could teach you. To surf, I mean."

Bingo.

He let her feet drop to the sand, then steadied her with one hand, before taking a step back. "I dinna share yer enthusiasm for taming the waters."

She cocked her head and studied him. "You're not telling me you're afraid of the water, are you?"

"I'm no' afraid of anything." He plucked at his shirtsleeves, pulling the soggy fabric from his biceps and momentarily distracting her. "I simply dinna care to flounder about in it. I leave that to the fish."

She dragged her gaze from his arms, but his face was just as arresting. In full daylight he was even more imposing. His dark hair fell to his shoulders, his face was all hard angles, but they were relieved by what had to be the most seductively curved lips she'd ever seen on a man. And those eyes. So dark, even now in the sunlight, she swore they were fully black. But they were far from cold. In fact, it was as if they sucked up all the available heat, then focused it in one tight beam . . . a beam currently directed right at her.

She shivered, but it had nothing to do with the chilly sand.

"Yer cold," he said. "Ye should change before we move yer things to the tower."

Oddly touched by his obviously sincere concern, her guard dropped. "That's okay, really. I just— Wait a minute! Did you say move? I'm not moving anything." She popped her board off the sand with her foot and grabbed it with both hands. If he came so much as a foot closer, she was going to clobber him with it.

This made the second time in two months she'd been forced to think of her board as a weapon. Well, they didn't call them guns for nothing, she thought. But they were for shooting waves. "All I wanted to do was surf," she muttered. She lifted the board over her head and started off with very determined strides toward Gregor's place. "I'm going inside. Do not follow me." *Keep walking, act like you own the world.*

She wanted to run. All the way back to Parker's Inlet. But she was stuck here and the island wasn't big enough to hide from him. So she was going to have to find a way to deal with him and this MacNeil legend he was hung up on. He actually seemed harmless enough, unless you counted the threat to her libido. All she had to do was placate him until the ferryman came back.

Visions of how she could simultaneously placate him *and* her suddenly active libido immediately sprang to mind. She just as immediately shoved them right back out again. She was as open to an island fling with a gorgeous Scot as the next red-blooded, all-American female, but an island fling with a gorgeous-but-wacko Scot was probably not a good idea.

So she kept on walking.

"Yer runnin' again."

"I'm walking," she clarified. Confidently walking. *Away from the man that I would certainly never have wild, uncontrollable, roll-around-in-his-tower sex with.* She sighed. But she kept on walking.

"Ye canno' challenge the Fates, lass."

"Oh, yes I can," she said. Walking, walking.

"Turn around then, and let me prove to ye that there are things with no explanation, yet they exist anyway."

Don't turn around. Walking, walking. Dammit, she was turning. She propped the board on her head. "Go ahead. Knock yourself out."

"I beg yer pardon?"

"It's an expression. You really have been in that tower a long time, haven't you?"

"Three hundred years, almost to the day."

Three hundred years. Okeydokey. Definitely wacko. But she'd known that already, right? So why did hearing him say it depress her more than scare her? *Because you're still harboring illusions of hot tower sex, that's why.* Well, she was over that now. He didn't think he was a descendant of The MacNeil, he thought he *was* The MacNeil. So much for lust among the ruins.

"Yeah, okay then," she said, backing up the beach. "It's been nice." If unreal. Backing, backing.

"Ye doubt the Fates? Well, lass, I dinna have time to bring ye around to the truth of it slowly. So I'll just get right to the heart of it. Ye brought me the stone, and now 'tis time to—"

"I know, I know. I appreciate the story, really I do. I'm flattered even. But I just wanted to return it to its rightful owner. That's all I signed on for, and I've done that now. So I'd really appreciate it if we can just say good-bye, okay?"

"Why no' just toss the thing back in the ocean then?"

"How do you know I found it in the ocean?"

"Bagan regaled me with the tale last eve."

"I told you why I kept it. I wanted to make sure it got back to its owner. That's all. End of story."

"How do you explain me, then? And Bagan?"

She couldn't explain Bagan, nor did she want to. "You believe you're The MacNeil. I have no problem with that. You're out here, not harming anyone, so all's well, right?"

"I am The MacNeil. Or, more precisely, I am the ghost of The MacNeil. Either way, we're one and the same."

Well, she had to keep talking to him, didn't she? She would have been safer sticking with Bagan. A ghost. Lovely. "I'm going inside now." She would have waved, but she was holding her board, so she smiled in what she hoped was a friendly, I'm-not-terrified-that-I'm-talking-to-a-total-whack-job way.

"I offered ye proof, did I no'?"

"Yep, you did, but that's okay. I'm a total believer. Not in the baby-bearing thing," she quickly added. "But if you say you're a ghost, who am I to argue?" She was backing away more quickly now, unwilling to turn her back on him, but not willing to stand there a moment longer.

A moment later she wished she had turned her back. Because then she could have kept right on telling herself that he was the crazy one, and that she was perfectly sane.

But a perfectly sane person wouldn't see a soaking wet Scot disappear right before her eyes. A perfectly sane person would look at the sand where he'd been standing and see footprints. A perfectly sane person would desperately believe that it had all been some kind of trick of the sunlight and water.

"No, a perfectly sane person would faint," she muttered. Unfortunately, she had never been a fainter. Even more unfortunately, she was pretty sure she could no longer think of herself as perfectly sane.

Only the insane would believe in invisible little people and sexy, kilt-wearing ghosts. Her gaze drifted to the tower, drawn there by a force she couldn't explain.

Connal grinned down at her from a tower window.

No way could he have made it up there that fast. In the next instant, he vanished again. She swallowed hard, might have even whimpered a bit, trying hard not to recall how swiftly he'd moved from the beach to standing right behind her on the night they'd first met. She wondered if Gregor had any whiskey stashed in his croft as she slowly turned back toward the path leading to his house . . . only to find Connal perched on a large boulder at the top of the hill.

He looked incredibly unghostlike to her. His damp kilt clung to well-developed thighs, his shirt was unlaced midway down his chest, his hair danced a bit in the shore breezes... and his smile was knowing and not a little smug as he faced the sun. And her.

"I don't believe in ghosts," she said flatly.

He levered himself off the rock and walked down the path toward her. "Rather hard to deny what is before your very eyes."

She let her board slide to the sand and raised a shaky hand toward his chest. His shirt was cold and damp, but the skin beneath it was warm and vibrantly alive. As were the eyes she lost herself in when she lifted her gaze to his. "You don't feel like a ghost."

He grinned again, and her body was having no problem making the leap of faith. "What is a ghost supposed to feel like, lass?"

"I—I don't know. Cold. Dead."

"Och, my mortal self is dead, yes." He lifted her hand and placed it back on his chest. "But my soul still burns with life."

She yanked her hand back as if it had itself been burned. "I've lost my mind. Completely gone."

"Ye no have ghosts where yer from, then?"

"Other people have ghosts. Just like other people see UFOs. *I* am not other people."

"I'd say ye are now." His lips quirked again and she couldn't manage to look away. God, the man had a mouth made for sex.

She looked away then. But the sex part stayed in her brain. "If you're dead, then how exactly did you plan on making babies?" As soon as the words left her mouth she realized she'd blundered. Badly.

If she'd thought his previous smiles sexy, this one was downright carnal. As was the way he reached out to stroke her cheek. She should pull away. She should run. Fainting would even be welcome at this point.

She did none of those things. His fingertips were blunt and rough, but his touch was gentle. And yet it was his gaze, far too alive for someone claiming to be dead, that held her in thrall.

"Upon my death, I made a pact with the gods. They've allowed me to play ghost of the tower as I awaited the charm stone's return. Fate has tested me long, but I knew if I kept faith it would be rewarded. It was the only way to prove my clan worthy of being saved." He stepped closer. "Year upon year I waited." His voice deepened to where it resonated along her skin . . . inside her skin, until she felt as if her body had somehow come alive in a whole new way beneath his fingers. "And now you're here."

It *was* some kind of madness, she thought wildly. And yet, she didn't try to escape it. She couldn't.

He leaned down and she realized his intent immediately. A sane person would have screamed, kicked, or shoved. She stood perfectly still as his mouth descended on hers, so slowly her body ached for the contact by the time his lips brushed against hers.

Not cold, and far from dead. And neither, she soon realized, was she. She didn't lift her hands to his chest, or do anything to involve herself in the kiss in any way. She merely accepted his mouth on hers . . . and marveled at the way a single kiss brought her entire being singing to life.

When he lifted his head, she wavered slightly as her eyes blinked open again. She hadn't even been aware of closing them. "Pretty good for a dead guy," she managed. But her raw attempt at humor didn't negate what had just happened to her. Or the fact that, if she were honest with herself, she wanted it to happen again.

He smiled and pulled her fully into his arms. " 'Tis

only the beginning." And with that he bent her head back, dove his fingers into her hair, and kissed her so thoroughly and with such passion that she gave up trying to remain passive. In fact, it was almost gleeful the way she joined the melee that was the tangle of their mouths and bodies.

It was only when his hand slid down over her shoulder and closed around her neoprene-covered breast that she swam back to the surface of reality. She yanked away, or tried to, but the movement was enough to break their kiss.

He didn't force his attentions further, but neither did he let her go. Which was just as well as she was fairly certain she'd drop to a limp heap on the sand if he did.

"I—we—um . . ." She lifted a shaky hand to her mouth. "We shouldn't . . . I can't . . . really. It's not—I don't—"

"Does kissin' always leave yer tongue tied so?"

She tried to laugh, but it sounded more like a croak. "Not usually." *Just the way you do it*, she thought.

His arm was still about her waist and he tugged her a bit closer. No amount of neoprene could prevent her from feeling the extent of his arousal. "Do ye still question my ability to have ye the way a man has a woman?"

She gulped. "No." It was a rasp. She cleared her throat. "No," she said more clearly, "but I—"

He silenced her by pressing a finger to her mouth. She felt a distinct dip in the knees. What was wrong with her? It was as if she was in heat.

"I know yer no' prepared for what I'm offering you," he said. "I've waited this long, I can wait a bit longer." He slid the finger from her lips down along her jaw, then over her chin to her throat . . . and lower. "But I willna wait forever."

She opened her mouth to speak, but he just shook his head. "We're fated, Josie, you and I. It will happen."

Before she could absorb the impact that hearing her name on his lips had on her . . . he'd vanished.

She stumbled backward and almost landed in a heap on her surfboard. Deciding that might not be a bad idea, she slowly lowered herself on shaky legs until she sat firmly on the sand. Solid ground. How was it that it had felt more like quicksand a moment ago?

She couldn't begin to make sense of anything that had just happened to her, the least of which was the almost overwhelming urge she'd had to fling herself into his arms.

"I have got to get a grip," she muttered. She looked up to the tower. Mercifully, the tower windows remained empty. "But on what?"

Chapter 6

*J*osie banged over the ruts on Gregor's old bike, thinking that if there was ever a way to kill the ol' libido, this was it. She'd be walking funny for a week by the time she got to town.

And yet, though her body had moved well beyond that torrid moment she'd shared with Connal on the beach, her mind wasn't past it. Not in the least. What on earth had possessed her to allow him such liberties? She snorted. Liberties. God, she was sounding like some maiden from a Gothic romance novel. It was as if, from the moment she'd taken the ferry to Glenmuir, she'd stopped living in the real world.

Her legs felt like jelly as she climbed yet another interminable hill. *Shortcut, my ass.* The people on this island must be part sheep if they thought going this way was easier. Next time she'd stick to the road, even if it took her twice as long. But as she crested the hill, she stopped and gasped in awe.

The view was nothing less than stunning. The small village of Ruirisay lay nestled below, framed by the tumble of rocks that lined the shore. She could see the ferry dock from here and, she imagined, on a perfectly clear day maybe the mainland as well. To the north she could see the rocky hills that covered the opposite end of the island she'd yet to explore.

She made a mental note to head that way next time. In the car. To her right was the roll of hill and heather that formed the part of the island she'd driven around . . . had it just been yesterday?

She turned around then, steeling herself for the impact of what lay behind her. Black's Tower thrust from the pile of stone that once had been Winterhaven, forbidding even now that it was little more than a ruin. It wasn't picturesque, as the port town was. But it was more awe-inspiring.

As was the man who resided in it.

She resolutely turned her back. And just as resolutely ignored the chills that raced over her skin when she thought of Connal MacNeil.

She knew she had to face more—far more—than the fact that she'd tangled tongues with him this morning. She'd done plenty of soul-searching back in Gregor's cabin. Her first instinct had been to turn to her dad, tell him everything and get his take on it. But he was half a world away and grieving. No, she had to come to terms with this herself first, before discussing it with anyone. If she ever did.

She looked past the dock to the open waters, hoping beyond hope that a ferry would magically appear on the horizon. *Like Connal magically appeared in front of you on the beach?* Scowling, she pushed onward, the downhill ride not much easier on her body.

Yes, she'd seen him vanish before her very eyes. She'd listened to his explanation. And then there was the whole Bagan issue. She had to deal with all of it. She hadn't spent enough time in Scotland to absorb the more whimsical, mystical side of its history. Surfers were more interested in the wave action than recounting fairy tales. But there was no denying that being here, in a land out of step with modern times, carried with it that undeniable feeling that the magical and the mystical were possible.

What she had to accept was that not only was it possible, but highly probable. Which was why she was heading into town. She wanted to hear ghost stories.

❧

By the time she parked her bike next to the others in front of Roddy's pub, the only thing she really wanted was a drink. The constant island wind had left her cheeks ruddy, but the bright summer sun had beat down on her back, soaking her shirt until it clung to her much like Connal's shirt had clung to that amazing chest of his. *So broad and—*

She cut off that train of thought and pushed inside the store first. She slid her sunglasses off and looked about for Maeve, but didn't see her. *Might as well pick up a few things*, she thought. Gregor's bike had a wire basket on the front. She'd just have to buy things that were rutproof.

She'd put several cans on the counter and was contemplating adding a tin of cookies when Maeve pushed through a small door near the back of the store.

"Hello there," she said, her weathered face creasing into a warm smile. "Ye look a bit road-weary. Would ye care for a lemonade? I just made a batch."

"Thank you, I'd love some," Josie said with an appreciative smile. "I thought I was in pretty good shape, but I have to admit your sheep trails about wore me out."

"You biked it then?" She shook her head. "Och, dinna tell me ye took Gregor's old clattering heap?" At Josie's nod, she said, "I'm surprised you're walking upright."

Josie grinned. "So am I. My dad would say it was a

character-building trip, but I'm pretty sure the only thing I built was blisters."

"I'm in the way of agreeing with you, though I'm sure your father is a wise man. Would you like a lift home?"

"Oh no, I couldn't put you out, really. I'll manage."

Maeve poured the lemonade. "It's from a mix," she said apologetically. "We don't get much fresh fruit but what we grow ourselves."

"It's wet, right?" Josie knew better than to hope for wet *and* cold. Nothing in the United Kingdom was ever served cold, it seemed. She tried not to gulp it down, but it tasted so wonderful, she was afraid she did anyway.

Maeve was beaming at her when she finished and Josie smiled ruefully. "Blister-building makes me thirsty."

"It's the thirst of youth I enjoy." Maeve refilled her glass. "We don't observe near enough of that anymore."

She said it matter-of-factly enough, but Josie was reminded of a comment she'd made the day before about missing the sounds of children on the island. "I guess there aren't many young families on the island, then?"

"None these days, excepting for company coming to visit. Farming isn't exactly a fascinatin' career path for the youngers, and fishing even less. The last of them have gone off to the mainland to university and it's a rare few that ever come back except to visit." She topped off Josie's glass again, then began boxing up the cans on the counter. "But that's the way of things, I suppose."

"Glenmuir is lovely," Josie offered, not sure what to say. She helped Maeve finish boxing her things. "I know it's remote, but I'm surprised you don't do more of a tourist trade. The north beach is truly beautiful."

"Aye, we like to think so, but to be honest, we've never courted the travel industry much. Set in our ways here, I suppose. We prefer the peace and serenity of our day-to-day lives." She smiled as she jotted down the price of everything on a pad of paper. Technology in the way of cash registers hadn't apparently come to Glenmuir as yet. Or perhaps they simply enjoyed doing things the old way.

Josie found herself charmed by it. In fact, if it weren't for a certain Scot, she'd be interested in staying on a while. She liked the peaceful feel of the place, the way the villagers seemed to look out for one another, even outsiders like her. She'd always felt tucked away in Parker's Inlet, but it was a beach town, a tourist town, and therefore had a definite vibe to it that was entirely different from this remote place. There was a wild yet somewhat civilized feel to the island, different entirely from the Pacific islands, probably because it wasn't tropical here. It wasn't like Australia either, which had a raw, frontier feel to it.

She wondered what it would be like to work here and was surprised to realize she'd like to find out. A few ideas for new board designs had already started floating about in her mind. How wonderful it would be to sit on that lovely stretch of beach and flesh them out.

Or it would have been, if not for the damn tower and its three-hundred-year-old watchman looming over her.

"Storm's coming up tomorrow," she heard Maeve say.

"The sky is such a gorgeous blue today," Josie said. "But I know how fast that can change."

"I suppose as a surfer you live near the water back in the States."

"Atlantic Ocean. I know all about storms."

Maeve nodded. "Well, this one looks to be rather fierce. You'll not want to be out in it. I'm sure Gregor has some wood put by. It'll get cold come tomorrow night, so make sure you bank the fire before you go to sleep."

Bank the fire? Josie might have traveled extensively, but she'd always had a roof over her head and a good night breeze when central air wasn't a possibility. Heat was rarely if ever an issue. She forced a smile. "Sure will, thanks." So she'd never been a Girl Scout. How hard could it be to keep a fire going?

She paid for her supplies and broached the subject that had brought her here. "The castle ruins are amazing."

"Aye, they are that." Maeve settled her hip against the counter, apparently more than willing to chat.

Josie was more than willing to let her. "It was the MacNeil stronghold once, right?"

Maeve's brow furrowed and her mouth turned down at the corners. "Oh, ye've got the right of it. This whole island was once MacNeil land, but no more. Stubborn fool of a man left his clan to be all but decimated while he awaited his *destiny*." She said that last word as if it were a curse, then shook her head, as incensed as if it had happened three years ago instead of three hundred.

"Man?"

"The MacNeil. Connal was his name."

Josie hoped Maeve didn't notice the goose bumps on her skin, or the way the hairs on her neck lifted.

"He had a notion that possession of a charm stone was all the clan needed to ensure survival. He'd inspired loyalty in the lot of them, I'll give him that, but that loyalty ended up costing them. All while he waited in that damned tower."

"What a shame," Josie mumbled, folding her

arms to keep Maeve from seeing how they trembled. But Maeve didn't seem to notice, deep into her story now.

"In the end, it cost him his life as well. Horrible battle, that. Campbells took over, then lost it several years later to the Sutherlands, who in turn abandoned it and left it to ruin. There are still some Mac-Neils here, as there are Campbells and Sutherlands, but the strength of the island was lost when the castle was first defeated." She lifted her hands and her expression cleared. "It's a checkered and sometimes tawdry past, to be sure, but then most of our country is built on like foundations. We're survivors, we are." She smiled. "But I'm sure ye don't want to hear of it all."

"Actually, I find it fascinating," she said truthfully, despite the anxiety she was feeling. "I think it's wonderful that everyone is so in touch with the events and characters that made their country what it is today."

Maeve laughed. "For better or for worse lass. Some say we cling too tightly to the past here, but I say that it's only in understanding where ye come from that ye can know which direction to go." Then she laughed. "Of course, none of that means we don't go right back down the wrong path over and over again." She wiped her hands on her apron and straightened, signaling Josie that chat time was over.

"Does Roddy serve any food? I thought I might have some lunch while I'm in town." *And see if I can get any ghost stories out of Dougal and company.* Though she was becoming less enamored of her idea with every passing minute.

"Aye, he does. It's simple fare, but it will fill you up."

"Sounds good to me. It's really a lovely little town you have here," she said. "Stunning view across the water." She smiled at Maeve. "It feels almost magical. I appreciate your hospitality, finding me a place to stay."

Maeve's eyes twinkled. "Thank you, dear heart, and it was my pleasure. Always enjoy having another woman about, especially one so lively as you. I'm sure the boys will be glad to have you join them as well." She led the way to the door. "Just don't be surprised if they hound you to death about your surfing. You've sparked their imaginations you have, with that fancy board of yours. I imagine they've become experts on the subject since you landed here."

Josie grinned, surprised. "Have they now?"

"Oh aye. To hear them go on ye'd think they were all born with a board in their hands, though none of them had ever so much as seen one until yesterday. I expect you'll be settling more than one argument for them." She winked. "A smart lass could parlay that into an ale or two, if she were of a mind to."

Josie laughed. Again she wished her father were here, but this time so that he could enjoy this adventure with her. In a place filled with colorful characters, Big Griff would feel right at home. Ghosts notwithstanding, she thought she could, too. Or would have if not for a growing sense of uneasiness. Actually, it was more like guilt.

She hadn't expected the island history to be such a sore point with the locals so many years later. She'd assumed they'd never even heard of the charm stone, much less that it had played such an important role. How did she proceed? Did she dare tell them she'd brought the stone back? She wanted to know more first, wanted to know if anyone else had ever claimed to see a ghost in Black's Tower. But what would they think of her when they found out? Would the warmth and generosity they'd extended vanish? After only two days, what these people thought or how they felt shouldn't matter so much to her. But it did.

Maeve pushed the door to the pub and Josie was immediately enveloped in the warm, yeasty smell of the place and the boisterous argument going on among the four men inhabiting it.

"I tell you, the longboarders are destroying the sport. I'm with Tubin'Mike there. The lot should all be dragged out of the water!" Clud punctuated the statement by slamming his tankard on the counter.

"Och, yer a twit, ye old geez," Gavin shot back. "Longboards are the heart of the sport, where it all began. To banish them is to banish a part o' history. I suppose next ye'll be sayin' they should burn all the balsam boards. Did ye no' read what JaneFrom-DownUnder had to say on it? The lass is less than half yer age, yet she possesses a fair bit more wit than ye'll ever lay claim to."

Roddy shook his shaggy white head and topped off the mugs as pleasantly as if they weren't arguing at the top of their lungs.

"No has bothered to ask me," Dougal put in, "but I think perhaps there ought to be a place for both in the water. The real problem is the novices with no respect for the waves or those with more skill at riding them."

"What did I tell you?" Maeve whispered. "Ever since Roddy hooked up to that Internet, these four think they know every last thing. Last month they were debating caribou migration in the Alaskan wilderness." She sighed. "Wears a body out to listen to them. Me, I prefer the mainland papers and a good mystery novel."

"The Internet?" Josie shook her head. Apparently some technology reached everywhere. She smiled, charmed by the four men and their new-found hobby. "I think they're cute."

Maeve patted her on the arm. "Don't say I didna

warn you. And don't forget what I said about getting them to buy you an ale or two. Lord knows but you'll need them."

Josie grinned as Maeve let herself out, then turned toward the bar. "Dougal has a point," she offered.

The conversation ceased instantly as all four of them turned to face her. "Och, she's here!" Dougal exclaimed, raising his glass to her. "And obviously the one to put an end to yer idiotic claims." He grinned and pulled out a stool for her, polished it with his sleeve and gestured grandly for her to have a seat. "Here ye go, lass, and allow me to buy you a pint."

"Thank you, Dougal." She turned to Roddy. "I'd love something to eat as well."

He nodded and turned to Dougal. "Ye buying her lunch as well? From the looks of her, she's no fool. She'll let ye fill her belly, then shoot yer theories down with the last sip o' her ale." He slid her a glass and leaned on the bar with a warm smile. "Do I have the right of it, lass?"

"I can pay for my own lunch, thanks," she said, then looked to the men seated next to her. "I can't be bought." She grinned at Dougal. "But I'll thank you for that ale."

Gavin, Clud, and Roddy all roared with laughter, and after several hearty slaps on Dougal's back, he laughed as well. They all raised their glasses to her. "To Josie."

She tapped her glass to theirs and enjoyed her first sip of ale. "So, who are these surfing experts you guys are talking about?" Roddy slid her a plate filled with cheeses and crackers while he went about making her a sandwich and she happily settled in for the afternoon.

Several hours and definitely more ale than it was wise to consume at midday later, Josie had fallen in love with all four of them. Eccentric, boisterous, passionate, and, above all, dead set on being the last one standing, they'd all have made wonderful surfers. "You have that gung ho spirit it takes to face Mother Nature at her finest," she told them.

"Well now," Gavin said, "be careful, lass. We just might take ye up on that offer of yours."

"Did I make an offer?"

Gavin eyed the other three. "I believe she said we'd make fine surfers, did she no'?" They all nodded and he turned back to her, his expression smug. "Then perhaps surfers we'll become. And who better to teach us, eh?"

Josie choked on a sip of ale. Her last sip, she swore, pushing the glass away. "I, um, uh—" She thought fast, then smiled as the obvious occurred to her. "Well, I'd be glad to—" She raised her hand when they cheered, wincing at the thought of their collective old bones shattering as Mother Nature tossed them mercilessly against the beach. "Wait a minute, wait a minute. I said I would be, *but—*"

"There's always a but, wi' women, isn't there?" said Clud, the group grump, she'd come to realize and liked him even more for it.

"With good reason," she told him, then turned to face them all. "You don't have the proper equipment. The water is cold up here, you'd all need suits, gear, the works. I'm sorry, really. And you know, it's not the kind of sport to take up later in life, anyway." She immediately realized she should have stopped at "I'm sorry."

"Yer saying ye dinna think we can handle the waves, lass?" This came from Dougal and Roddy both.

"I'm just saying that your wives would likely string me up for risking your necks. But we already decided you didn't have the proper gear, so—"

"Roddy can order us some from the Internet," Dougal said. "Can't ye, Roddy?"

Roddy nodded as Josie frantically shook her head. "No, no, you don't understand. This stuff doesn't come cheap."

"You're no' kidding," Clud said. "We went to yer website. It's a crime the prices they charge for things these days. And the shipping." He rolled his eyes and took another swig of ale.

"Yer designs were quite nice, though," Gavin offered.

"My website? How did you even know I had one?"

"Maeve mentioned your last name. We did a search and up popped your name," Roddy said. "You do nice work. Much better than some of that abstract-looking stuff."

Josie sputtered between laughter and disbelief. "You guys are amazing."

They all beamed. "That we are, lass," Roddy said.

"Please, don't spend your life savings on gear, though. I'd never be able to live with myself."

"Och, dinna listen to Clud's dramatics. We've got the coin, Josie."

She eyed them all, in their worn clothing and boots, thinking of their beat-up bikes parked outside. But they each looked confident in Dougal's assessment. "We're talking hundreds, maybe thousands here," she warned them, only exaggerating a little.

Dougal waved a dismissive hand. "Last year Gavin took up day trading," he said calmly.

"Excuse me?"

"Aye, we thought he was off his rocker, too. But he did quite well for himself and the missus." Dougal leaned in. "They went on a cruise."

"So we asked him to invest for us, too," Roddy put in. "I got an upgrade for the computer. Next I'm looking into a satellite dish."

The men all sighed in joint lust at the very idea.

Josie wasn't sure whether to laugh herself sick or run screaming from the pub. Colorful characters indeed. "Okay. I give up. You win. You're grown men after all." She downed the rest of her ale in one swallow, then eyed them balefully. "But don't come crying to me if you all end up dead on the beach."

She left the pub to raucous cheers and the sound of a laptop being booted up. She thought about telling Maeve how she'd let her and all the island women down, but didn't have the heart. Instead she climbed on Gregor's bike, winced as she sat on the padded seat, and pushed off down the road.

She was halfway around the island—the long way— when she realized she never had asked them to tell her ghost stories.

Chapter 7

The bolt of lightning lit up Gregor's entire loft, jarring Josie awake. A crack of thunder had her sitting instantly upright in bed. Rain lashed the small window and thrummed the roof slanting over her head. The storm. She'd forgotten all about Maeve's warning.

She pushed off her covers, then quickly yanked them back over her again. Damn, but it was cold. And she hadn't even made a fire, much less banked one. Another rafter-rattling crack shook the house. Surely this place had weathered worse.

She should start a fire in the woodstove, she thought, flinching when the next bolt hit. She loved watching storms come in off the water back home. This felt different, though, more visceral. Probably because she was in a strange place, she told herself, ignoring the fact that she'd slept through many a storm in many a country. She reached for her bedside lamp, but nothing happened when she tugged the little chain. "Figures."

She'd feel better if she got up and did something. She could find a candle or something and lose herself in one of Gregor's books. A book and a snack. Suddenly she was ravenous. Wrapped in the blanket, she tiptoed over the ice-cold plank floor and fished around in the dark for some socks. She ended up settling for shoving her bare feet into her sneakers.

She glanced out the front window as she climbed down the stairs, but couldn't see the tower. If it weren't for the lightning, she could have barely seen the window. She wondered how many such storms the tower had weathered, just what it had taken to push down the walls of the stronghold. How had Connal felt, watching his home literally fall down around him? She shivered and decided she didn't want to think about that. Fire and food. That was all she cared about.

She maneuvered through the living room, tugging the ends of the heavy blanket behind her, waiting for the next flash of lightning to light her path. She reached out to feel for a candle she recalled seeing on the mantel, knocking something to floor before she finally found it.

"Ooops," she whispered. "Hope that wasn't anything important." The next lightning flash revealed the box of matches. A dim yellow glow flickered to life and Josie sighed in relief. Somehow light always managed to banish the demons. "Or the ghosts," she murmured, deliberately not looking toward the window.

She'd come home from the pub yesterday and gone straight inside. She'd sketched, she'd read, she'd made herself some dinner and tidied up. She'd done everything but go anywhere near the beach or the tower. But that hadn't stopped her from glancing at it every now and then. The tower had looked deserted, the windows dark even as the sun set. She didn't want to think about him now, up there in the middle of the torrent, doing whatever it was that—

"Oh no!" She'd been balancing the candle in one

hand and dragging the tail of her clutched blanket in the other, when it snagged on a tall lamp, pulling it over on her, knocking the candle from her hand, directly onto the blanket—which immediately caught fire.

Stay calm, stay calm, she told herself. She shrugged out of the growing inferno and picked up the lamp, thinking she could snag the blanket with it and drag it outside before it caught on anything else. Her hands were shaking but the plan was working, or it was until she reached the end of the cord plugging the lamp into the wall. She ripped at it, but it must have been stuck on something. "Dammit!" She dropped the lamp and leaped around the edges of the burning blanket, intending to yank open the front door and shove the thing into the rain.

But just then the door flew open, crashing against the wall, almost sending her stumbling into the fire. Before a scream could work its way past her throat, big hands roughly grabbed her, lifting her right out of her sneakers, and carried her outside into the wrath of the storm.

"Stay here," a deep voice commanded.

The blanket landed in the mud about fifteen feet from where she stood, the fire guttering out almost instantly. Then he stalked back over to her. "What in the hell were ye doing in there?" he roared, his voice somehow even more riotous than the thunder.

Anger, embarrassment, along with a goodly amount of delayed reaction, spurted forth. "Roasting marshmallows."

"What? The only thing ye were likely to roast was yer own hide. What were ye thinking, lass?" His long hair was a mass of thick, wet ropes that lashed his chiseled features, his eyes gleamed fiercely even in the black of the rain. "Do ye know what you risked? I've already lost one bride to disaster, I'll no' lose another."

She gaped at him. "I almost burned a house and myself down and all you can think about is your stupid fixation on Destiny?" Anger easily surpassed embarrassment and latent fear. She poked a finger at him. "I didn't need your help. I didn't ask for your help. I could have taken care of it myself. But most of all, what I do or don't do has nothing to do with you. If I want to jump off a cliff, you can't stop me."

His jaw clenched. "Dinna test me, lassie."

"Dinna test me either . . . whatever it is you call boys," she finished on a less-than-authoritative note.

A jagged bolt of lightning lit up the sky, illuminating his face. In that split second she swore she saw his expression falter, a brief twitch curve his lips.

"Lads," he said sternly, making her wonder if it had been a trick of the light.

She was still staring at him when the thunder literally rocked the ground at her feet. Connal's hand came up instantly to steady her. She tried to shrug it off, feeling silly for being so jumpy. Truth be told, he was making her more nervous than the storm was. But his grip only tightened as he stepped closer and tipped her face up to his.

Even as the storm raged about them, something in the air between them went strangely still as she stared at his shadowed face. All she could think about was the last time they had been this close. Part of her wanted to lean into him, into the shelter he provided. Another part of her wondered what he'd taste like in the rain. She almost pulled away then, shocked by just how much of a part of her responded to that idea. But he chose that moment to trace a blunt-tipped finger down the side of her face.

"Are ye alright then?" he asked, his tone gruff, yet oddly gentle. "Did ye burn yourself?" He reached

for one hand, then the other, and turned them over
so the rain washed over her palms.

Fine, she wanted to say. I'm fine. But his touch
caused a ripple of awareness so intense that it
drenched her senses much like the rain had
drenched her skin. What was it about him that made
her so hyperaware? She could only answer him with
a brief shake of her head.

He ran his hands up her arms, then skimmed
back the hair that was plastered to her head and face
and cupped her face again as he peered down into
her eyes. "I didna mean to roar at ye. When I saw the
fire flicker behind yer windowpane . . ." He paused,
then let out a shuddering sigh. "Ye took a lifetime
off of me, lass, that ye did." Then, surprisingly, he
grinned, the slash of white illuminated brightly, as
lightning streaked through the sky above. "If I'd had
a lifetime to give, that is."

Josie stood there, trembling, overwhelmed. By
the storm, the fire . . . by him. She was suddenly
quite aware that she wore next to nothing . . . but despite being chilled to the bone, the shivers racing
uncontrollably through her had nothing to do with
the storm. Her nipples peaked, her knees wavered,
her thighs clenched. Hyperaware, she'd thought.
Yes. Hypersensitive as well. It made no sense, especially considering the circumstances, how she could
only think of wanting his hands on her.

Staring at the rain-lashed man standing before
her, she knew the line between reality and fantasy
had permanently blurred. And she wasn't so sure she
cared any longer.

His grin faded as she continued to stand there
and stare at him. "Och, but I must have ashes for
brains." He slid off his cloak and slung it around
her, which only plastered the soaking-wet nightshirt
she wore to her already freezing-cold skin.

That shock of reality jarred her from whatever spell he'd cast, but before she could regain even a shred of control over the situation—much less herself—she found herself airborne and being held against his chest.

A small squeak of surprise was all she managed before he had her bundled tightly, like a child. Only there was nothing childlike about the sensations rocking through her.

"Come. You must get warm and dry."

She knew she was beyond help when his edict only elicited visions of him stripping the damp nightshirt off her body . . . in front of a roaring fire.

Through the haze of desire, it took a few moments before she realized he wasn't heading back to Gregor's.

"Wait. What . . . where," she spluttered. Not exactly the commanding tone she'd hoped for, but then she hadn't exactly been too worried about being in charge a moment ago when she was thigh deep in fantasyland.

It wasn't until he crossed the road and started down to the beach that she began to struggle. "Wait a minute," she shouted over the roar of the wind. "You're not taking me out there through that." She didn't need moonlight to know the surf was roiling. She could hear it.

"I thought you enjoyed daring the seas," Connal said, not breaking stride despite her squirming.

"Calculated daring, yes. Suicide, no. Can we *please* go back to Gregor's?"

He didn't so much as pause. They crossed the beach.

She should have never let him mesmerize her like that. What was wrong with her anyway? "Put me down!"

But it was as if he didn't hear her. Infuriated, she

tried to pound on his chest, but her hands were all tangled in his cloak. How had she thought him remotely sexy? He was a pigheaded, stubborn, arrogant . . . Scot.

The roar of the waves was almost deafening. The causeway over to the tower had to be at least chest deep. And surging. "*You* don't have to worry about risking your life, you know!" She wrestled an arm free and grabbed at his hair, digging her fingers in and pulling until finally, mercifully, he stopped.

Of course, he was swearing and shouting at her now, but he'd stopped and that was all she cared about.

"I'll get you to safety, now stop yer panickin'!"

Rain poured down her face and she blinked furiously against it. "What, you're going to blink us up to the tower or something?"

"Blink?"

"Whatever the hell you call it when you vanish into thin air. That trick."

"It's no' a trick. But I canna whisk you off that way, if that's what yer asking."

"Please put me down."

"I'll no let any harm come to ye. What do ye take me for?"

Thunder rocked and lightning split the sky. Shaking from cold and . . . and everything, Josie peered up at Connal and said, "A dead guy?"

His laughter filled the air between them, and just for a moment, the storm didn't exist. An instant later she was bundled tightly against him, her mouth muffled against his chest as he continued on down the beach.

So, yes, she'd reluctantly been forced to believe in ghosts. She'd also been forced to admit she was seriously sexually attracted to one ghost in particular. But lust didn't equal trust.

Josie did her best to hold her breath as she prepared herself for the impact of the cold water. Her lungs began to burn, her spine stiff to the point of aching . . . but the surf never surged up to claim them. She wriggled again, doing her best despite the fact that she had no arms to maneuver with.

"Hold still," he commanded, then swore under his breath as he banged into something. "Yer no' making this any easier for either of us. Now be still, damn ye. We're almost there."

Almost there? How could that be?

And then suddenly the roar of wind and surf ceased. She thought her ears had popped, the change was so abrupt. And the rain. She couldn't feel it pelting the cloak and her bare feet that were sticking out from beneath the hem. She was about to start struggling again when he relaxed his hold on her. He didn't put her down, but she was able to shrug her arms free and shove the cloak off her head and shoulders.

Not that it helped matters any. It was pitch-black. So much so, she couldn't see his face, which couldn't have been more than a few inches from her own.

"I have to set you on your feet. Stay where I set ye, so ye don't hurt yourself, ken?"

She was just grateful enough to feel the firm—and more importantly dry—ground beneath her toes not to argue. "Yeah, yeah, I ken."

There was a scraping sound, then a yellow glow erupted in front of her, making her squint and block the light with her hand.

The glow dimmed almost instantly and she realized he'd lit an old oil lantern. Still, she had to blink a couple times before her surroundings came into view. Not that she could really see much of them. Most of her surroundings at the moment were Connal.

"You're hovering," she said, ruthlessly tamping

down the libido that seemed to have a mind of its own. "Where are we?" She tried to lean around him and see. The walls on either side of them were made of stone, the floor beneath her feet was dirt or hard-packed sand, she couldn't tell. The ceiling wasn't much higher than she was tall, in fact Connal had to hunch over. "Is this a tunnel?"

He smiled. "Ye dinna think any Scot worth his plaid would build a place out in the water without an alternative means of access, do ye?"

She didn't answer him. Instead she turned around to look to see where they'd come from, but there was only a stone wall. She waited for the frisson of fear, the commonsense reaction that came when a woman realized she was trapped. Trapped with a man she didn't know, couldn't trust.

But the fear didn't come. She tried to peer past him, but whatever lay beyond the few feet of path she could see was quickly enveloped in darkness. "This leads to the tower, then?"

"Aye. The castle actually. Black Angus didna construct this. He hadna the means. But it was his idea. It was several generations later before the task was accomplished. It actually leads to the castle proper, but there is another corridor that leads to the tower." He turned and held the lantern out in front of him. "I havena had cause to use this in some time. But it's held up for all the years before me, so it should be passable."

Okay, so she had a jitter or two left in her. "When, exactly, was the last time you used it?"

"Not too far back. Right before the turn of the century."

"Which century would that be?" she heard herself ask.

"Eighteenth, I believe?"

Okay then. *Why do I keep asking these things?*

Better to just get on with it. She tugged the cloak around her and scooped up the part that dragged the ground. "Lead on."

He looked a bit wary of her easy acquiescence, but he nodded in approval. "I can carry ye, if ye like."

"I can manage," she said, moving in front of him and starting slowly down the passage.

"Oh, I've no doubt of that," he said, moving in behind her. "But you'll forgive me if I dinna ask ye to tend to the fire later."

The grin quirked her lips before she could stop it; she was just glad he hadn't seen it. She needed to find some control here. Connal getting all cute and charming wasn't going to help. She kept moving, not daring to look back at him, but she could feel him treading heavily behind her. *One foot in front of the other,* she schooled herself. *Don't think about what lies ahead.*

And definitely don't think about what will happen when he gets you alone in that tower.

Chapter 8

*I*t was foolish really. To be concerned about bringing her to his less than lavishly appointed chambers. Not that he had any need for mortal comforts himself... although he found solace in them anyway. Something about maintaining a sense of familiarity, he supposed.

He pushed back the heavy rug he'd hung over the open doorway. Despite the fact that he had no visitors and could remain unseen if he wished, he found he still enjoyed the illusion of privacy. He motioned her inside, holding the lantern out to guide her. "Just a moment while I light the tapers." There were several sconces on the walls and a trio of thick candles on the low stone table.

She made a small, indistinguishable noise as the rooms glowed to life and he actually hesitated before turning to her. What she thought shouldn't have mattered to him. He told himself it was only because of her obvious reluctance to accept Fate's design that he felt this unnatural need to... to woo her. Ridiculous notion really, considering he'd never had to woo anyone in his life.

And yet there was a distinct sense of apprehension coiling in him when he turned back to her. "Humble lodgings, I know. But then I have little use for lavish comforts." He said it dismissively, yet held himself still as he awaited her reaction.

She looked around, cataloging the few meager belongings he had. He followed her gaze, thinking his armchair and small side table suddenly looked unbearably worn. The rug covering the floor shabby and threadbare. He kept the place swept clean, his linens as fresh as he could manage with water taken from Gregor's pump when the auld man was sleeping it off. All that time spent waiting, yet he'd never given a thought to having to impress his future mate. It was a bit late now, but it didna make him feel any less the fool.

"Is all this real?" she asked. "Or does it all disappear when you do?"

She seemed neither impressed nor unimpressed. He wasn't sure why that stung anyway, but it did. "I assure you everything here is quite real and quite permanent, inasmuch as things can be. I can close off the corridor leading to my rooms to keep any curiosity seekers out."

"And no one mentions the light in the tower window?"

He noticed she still hadn't looked at him. "I dinna care much what anyone thinks. But I have a care when I make my presence known." He said the last with emphasis, but she still didn't turn to face him.

"So, the islanders know the castle and tower are . . . haunted?"

He was growing impatient. "I care no' what the islanders think."

She did turn to face him then. "Well, they still care about you. Or the role you played in their history, anyway."

That took him aback. So much so that he didn't know what to say.

"If Maeve's feelings are any indication of how the island as a whole feels, you're not too popular."

"You've become chums with Maeve then?"

"I wouldn't call us chums, but we're friendly, yes." She tilted her head. "Maeve's seen you then? Funny, because she didn't seem as if—"

"I've not met her or her husband. I've my own ways of knowing things. How is it that you've grown friendly with her?"

"She and her husband, Roddy, found me a place to stay. Very nice couple. All the folks I've met are friendly."

He scowled, though why it bothered him that she was making herself at home here he had no idea. It was to his advantage that she like the island and its people. Perhaps he envied her easy way of fitting in. But then, he'd no' had the chance to make a good first impression on his clansmen. "Glenmuir has always had a reputation for hospitality."

She turned from him and looked around again. "Exactly what did you do all those years ago to make these hospitable people dislike you so much?"

"Ye should get out of those wet things," he said instead, not at all interested in having a history lesson with her. Especially as it pertained to his role in it.

Her gaze swung to his, wariness filling her eyes. "I, um, thanks, but you don't have to— A fire would be fine. I'll dry out quickly."

She was stammering. He swallowed a smile. *Best to keep her off-balance*, he thought. That way she wouldn't poke about in his past overmuch. She'd be too worried about his designs on the present . . . and on her.

She had his cloak clutched tightly about her. Her curls clung to her head in damp, misshapen clumps, and her bare feet were dusty and dirty from traipsing through the tunnel. She looked like little more than a street urchin. Which did absolutely nothing to explain the surge of almost animal lust that spilled through him the instant he saw awareness bloom in her eyes.

"I really must insist," he said. "I'll see if I can find you something." He strode to the next room, fairly confident she wouldn't try to run. After all, she knew he'd just bring her back again.

He stared at his bed and the tumble of linens tangled upon it. It was large and well stuffed with down, his refuge on many, many a long night. He had a flashing image of tucking her away in here with him, tangling the lean length of her in those linens . . . and in him. He wrested his gaze away and rummaged through the trunk at the foot of his bed, pulling out a loose-fitting linen shirt and a swath of plaid. It wasn't much, but then he'd always been more concerned with comfort rather than fashion.

"Thank you," she said quietly, when he returned, the cloak falling open as she reached for the small bundle he held out to her.

He was reminded then of how she'd looked, standing in the midst of a fury, rain lashing her lithe frame, plastering the thin chemise she wore to her skin. His body tightened anew, even as he fought against it. It was all well and good that he wanted her. It made things easier, for certain. Though he'd have done his duty, fulfilled his destiny and that of his clan, no matter her earthly appearance. But this . . . this rampant need wouldn't do. He had to find some element of control. He had never forced himself on any woman and, despite knowing his destiny was right at his fingertips, he would not force her to have him.

But have her he would.

He pulled his gaze from her and reined in his

unruly impulses. "You can change in there," he said almost gruffly, then motioned to his bedroom, where he'd lit one thin taper. He watched her go, surprised she'd done so without comment. In a short time he'd already come to realize she was a fully modern woman, one who had her own ideas and spoke them freely, with the full expectation that they be received with a weight equal to his own. He thought he'd prefer her silent and easily led. It unsettled him to discover that wasn't entirely true.

He busied himself in front of the modest fireplace, wishing the stacking of wood and lighting of tinder would drown out the rustling of fabric behind him. It didn't. It was as if he felt every caress against his own skin.

"Here is your cloak," she said, coming up behind him. "It's pretty wet, but if you spread it before the fire—"

He turned then, and froze in the act of reaching for the sodden material lying over her arm.

She stilled as well, then looked down at herself before looking back at him. He was almost relieved to see the challenging light return to her eyes. Almost.

"I'm perfectly aware I look ridiculous," she said defensively. "I have no idea how to put these things on."

She did look ridiculous. Entirely so. And yet the heat pulsed through him anew. "It's a definite skill," he said, unable to tear his gaze from her.

She was lithe of body, aye, but not a small or petite woman, and still his shirt hung on her frame, enveloping her, lending her an air of fragility he well knew she didn't possess. And yet . . . Perhaps it was the clumsy way she'd wrapped the plaid about her hips, tucking the end in her waist rather than draping it over her shoulder.

Could she possibly know how artfully his shirt clung to the tips of her breasts? Or that his fingers ached to push apart the gaping neckline just an inch or two farther to expose the roundness of her breasts to his gaze?

His throat tightened, as did the rest of his body. He'd do well to move away, or, at the very least speak, defuse the sudden tension in the room.

She suddenly seemed to realize where his attentions were directed, because she frowned and crossed her arms, covering herself. "You're blocking the heat," she said, her tone returning now to the surly one he'd so quickly grown used to. Had he really missed it?

"Aye, it would appear I am," he murmured.

She folded her arms even more tightly about her. "Men," she muttered, then circled the small room the opposite direction he did and stopped before the fire, presenting him with her very stiff back.

He wondered if she realized how regally she stood, or that her frosty demeanor did little to diminish his growing fascination with her. He wondered a bit at it himself. It had been a long time since cunning or the development of strategy had been something he needed to worry about. He shouldn't have been surprised to discover that the challenge of the chase enticed him, invigorated him.

War was where he'd been trained to excel, strategically speaking. Looking at her frowning countenance, he suspected battle strategy might very well be necessary here. And yet . . . where to begin? He felt clumsy, rusty.

The first rule of battle was to reduce the enemy's defenses while increasing your own. To that end, he moved away from her, toward the small larder he'd created in a narrow antechamber next to the hallway door. "I don't have much in the way of foodstuffs, but I do enjoy cheddar and bread with my wine. Would you care for some?"

Rather than catch her off guard, she merely said, "I didn't know ghosts ate and drank."

He moved in behind her rigid frame. "There are some pleasures even we insist on retaining."

There was a long pause and the scant space between them fairly vibrated as the tension shifted, grew.

Then, quietly, she asked, "Such as?"

Had he imagined the hoarseness in her voice? The underlying note of interest?

So much for building his own defenses, he thought ruefully. He'd managed to lower hers, yet one roughened little whisper and his body was galloping on, rushing headlong to the denouement. "Food, drink, the warmth of a fire," he responded tightly, barely resisting the urge to touch her, to trace a finger along the delicate line of her neck, the curves of her broad shoulders. Her strength, he was surprised to find, called to him.

"That's . . . that's all?"

"What other creature comforts would you have me want?" he said, just beside her ear.

The slight catch in her breath undid him. He did touch her then. Just the barest whisper of his lips on the side of her neck. She shivered and he dug his fingers into his palms to keep from pulling her against him. "There is the taste of a woman," he said roughly. "Yet I have no' been allowed to sample such a delight."

She stiffened slightly, then, after a moment, whispered, "At all?"

He found himself stiffening as well, though in an entirely different way. "If I am to prove my worthiness, then I must only taste that which is my destiny."

She turned then, but backed quickly away when he

reached for her. He took hold of her anyway. "I'm no' going to attack you." He moved her bodily away from the fire. "I was only tryin' to keep you from torchin' my finest plaid. You and fire are not comfortable bedfellows."

Despite the abrupt end to their provocative interlude, he grinned. There would be more. He knew this, and despite her frown, he suspected she did, too. "Ye needn't thank me, lass. 'Tis okay."

She overcame her embarrassment swiftly and made a face at him, which had him grinning rather than scowling. Such a change from the simpering lasses that had paraded in front of his brothers and himself.

To his great dismay, she folded her arms over her chest once again. Where she stood now afforded him a delightful view of her profile as the glow from the table lantern lit her from behind.

She bent down somewhat and intercepted his gaze. "You're worse than a construction worker, you know?"

"A construction worker?"

"Men who build things and leer at women."

"I suppose I've built my share of things, but I dinna leer."

She merely stared at him.

"Och, leering is no' the same as admirin'."

"Not from where I'm standing."

"Women," he said darkly, wondering why he hadn't just tossed her on the bed first thing. His ancestors would have. Hell, his own brothers had. And it was precisely that impetuosity and lack of forethought that had landed him in the position of being forced to bargain his soul to the gods to save the remnants of his clan and any hope they had for a future.

"You . . . you said something about cheese?"

"Have a seat by the fire," he said, then with a devilish

wink as that sort of attention seemed to unnerve her the most, he added, "but no' too close, lass."

"Ha, ha." But when he took one step toward her she quickly made herself comfortable in the arm-chair that fronted the fire, arranging the folds of her plaid as a queen would her fur-lined robes.

He stifled another smile as he went about collect-ing food and mead. Aye, she'd make his son a good mother. There was a small twinge somewhere near his heart when he thought of it. He'd always thought of his clan's future being in the hands of his son. His. Not theirs. He'd never really thought of it that way, other than to pray his faith in the Fates wasn't misguided and there would someday be a wee bairn to lead on where he had failed.

But now he found himself turning, imagining the oddest things. A babe in her arms as she sat in front of the fire. Would she sit in this very room, then? Not likely. He turned back to his tasks, ignoring the chill that chased out the warmth inside him. He'd naught be here to see what she did, his bargain hav-ing been met and filled. So why imagine such a thing? He strode back to the fire and, with a clatter, placed the stoneware on the footstool she'd pushed to one side.

"I thought you'd want to sit on that."

"Nay," he interrupted her, sinking to floor beside it. "I've no need for softness," he said, not caring how she took his surly manner. He'd gone soft him-self there for a moment and would do well to guard against such lapses if he wanted to remain in control of things.

He heard the wine splash in the tankard and forced his attentions back to her, though he kept his focus on the food. He sliced the cheese and flipped it onto a hunk of bread, then repeated the motion and nudged it toward her side of the platter.

"Interesting knife," she said, quickly picking up the food when he darted a glare at her. She took several bites, then, apparently unable to remain silent for more than two minutes—had he really thought this trait intriguing?—she said, "Is it a family heirloom?"

He glanced down at the dagger, then back to his food, the fire . . . anything but her. "'Twas my father's."

"It's really interesting. The pattern on the handle is— Can I see it?"

To her credit, she barely flinched when he swung his hard gaze back to hers as he flipped the dagger over in his hand. He presented the handle to her.

"Thank you," she said, with just a whiff of sardonic amusement. She held his gaze for a moment longer and just like that the mood changed. She quickly shifted her gaze to the blade.

Oh yes, Connal thought, *the chase is definitely on.*

"The workmanship is amazing," he heard her say. "That's one thing we've lost."

He turned to find her shaking her head in dismay as she admired the scrollwork on the handle.

"This bothers you?"

"Too many things are production made." She looked at him and shrugged. "People don't want to pay for craftsmanship, for the extra attention to detail."

"You say this as if it were a personal affront."

She smiled. "Well, my business hinges on those people who do feel the personal touch is worth paying for."

He was about to sip his wine, but lowered it instead. He'd been so caught up in his own destiny, he'd given no thought to the life she'd led before coming into his. The first ripple of concern chased along his spine. He washed it away with a swig of mead. "What is this business of yours, then?"

"I'm a graphic artist."

Ah, he thought, *a painter*. He nodded, relaxing. He supposed that would be enriching for their child. "Art is no' for everyone, I suppose." He, himself, had barely paid it passing attention. War had consumed most of his life.

"True. Especially when it's on a surfboard. But I do okay."

He'd just bitten off a hunk of cheese and almost choked on it. "You paint . . . those boards you ride?"

"And quite well, she said modestly."

"You call that art?"

Her smile vanished. "Why yes, yes I do. And so do a number of the elite surfers in the world. Along with collectors. My work graces the walls of any number of fine homes."

"Ah, then you paint on canvas as well."

She was scowling now. "No. They hang the boards. My father's boards," she added pointedly.

A point he was at a loss to understand. "What good does it do to hang a slab of wood meant for wave riding on a wall?"

Heat filled her cheeks, sparks flew from her eyes. He really shouldn't feel so energized by it, he thought, but it was there, as exhilarating as tasting the fine skin of her nape.

"Oh, I don't know," she snapped. "Maybe the same reason you hang swords meant to slice people up on yours? She pointed over the fireplace.

"Hardly the same thing. I don't call that art."

"You probably wouldn't know art it if bit you on the . . . kilt."

"You may have a point," he conceded, with as much grace as he could muster. "I was never much for the fripperies or adornments."

She looked around his room and said, "I think it's safe to say that's an understatement."

"Do ye now?" He bit off another piece of cheese,

rethinking the wisdom of goading her. After a moment spent hating himself for wishing he'd feathered his nest with the finest silks, just to show her he could give her fine things—which he couldn't—he grudgingly asked, "How did ye come to paint on these boards?"

"My father. He was a world-class surfer in his day, worked part-time for some of the more well known board designers when he was younger. He was intrigued by the whole process and became a shaper."

"Shaper?"

"The one who creates the shape of the board. They're not all the same."

"A craftsman then. And a sportsman."

"He is both, yes."

"Successful, I take it?"

She nodded. "Very. His work is in high demand. They are one-of-a-kind. Anyone who buys a Griff's Gun knows they're getting quality."

"Gun? I thought you said—"

"It's slang, for surfboard. For shooting waves."

He gave her a look. "That much I deduced on my own."

She smiled and he decided it might be worth wading through the complexity of her moods after all, simply for the opportunity to make her lips curve so enticingly.

" 'Tis a family business then, this board building and painting?"

"Aye," she said, her grin a bit saucy. "I roamed all over the globe with him growing up. In fact, I had planned to help my dad with the shaping and glassing, even took a few engineering classes. Art was more a hobby of mine. My mom was an artist."

"Yer mum? What does she think of you traipsing about the world?"

"She died just before I turned two." Her expression turned a bit wistful, but she'd said it matter-of-factly.

" 'Tis a loss that's difficult at any age." He hadn't meant to share that. In fact he wasn't in the habit of sharing at all. He braced himself for the unwanted pity or, more likely, the spate of questions she was likely to ask. She surprised him by merely nodding.

"How old were you?" she asked quietly.

"I was in my twentieth year."

"You have memories of her then. I don't remember mine. I have a few photos, but mostly their photos were the ones she took of my father surfing. I do have some of her artwork." She smiled with a warmth that took more of an edge off the chill in the dank room than the fire had. "In fact, she was the inspiration for the work I did on my first board. It was a present to my dad. Then I did one for myself. It was for fun, I wasn't thinking of it as a career. He hung his in the shop, it piqued some interest, and the rest, as they say, is history."

Connal didn't claim to understand it all, but he had no trouble with her avocation as long as it didn't interfere with their destiny.

"Were you close to your father?"

Her question surprised him from his thoughts. "I'm no' so sure you'd describe it as such. He was responsible for readying me and my brothers to rule our clan when they were called upon to do so."

"Was he sick then?" She shook her head. "I can't imagine losing both of my parents."

"He was no' sick. We had to maintain a readiness to defend our land against those who would usurp it and the power it commanded. There was no time to waste on the learning or appreciation of art."

She didn't look chastised. "Even as a child?"

"Even as a child."

She nibbled on her bread, seemingly lost in thought. "I'm sorry," she said at last.

"For?"

"It doesn't sound like a very happy childhood. I know mine was odd compared to just about anyone else's, so maybe I'm no judge. But I can't imagine having that kind of pressure, from such an early age. So . . . I'm sorry."

Her understanding was unexpected, and he would have thought, unwelcome. And yet he found himself responding before he could think better of it. "It was no' so bad. I played at swords and learned my maps and strategies. I thought it was a fine upbringing. I would have brought my own son up the same way." *Had I had one.*

"You never had any children?"

He shook his head. "I became laird in my twenty-first year. I was too busy holding what was left of our land and keeping my clan fed and housed. When the time finally came and the stone sent . . ." He looked into the fire. "It was too late."

She put her tankard down and scooted forward in her chair, looking at him in disbelief. "You don't mean to tell me you believe the clan was defeated because a necklace was lost at sea."

He sent her a swift glare. "Ye know nothing of it. And I lost my bride that day as well."

Either she didn't see the warning in his eyes or she ignored it. He suspected, much to his dismay, it was the latter. "Did you love her so much you could never marry another?"

"It was no' about love. Marriages were arranged for the benefit of the many, no' the emotions of the two."

"Well, I think that's sad. If you didn't love her, why didn't you marry someone else? Surely there was another powerful liaison to be made with some other poor unsuspecting clan wench."

"No' without the stone."

She laughed in disbelief and his temper soared higher. "So you let everything go to hell?"

"We already were in hell." He rose to his feet. "Proving my faith in the stone to the gods was the only chance we had left."

She tossed down her bread and stood. "You honestly believe that, don't you?"

She turned away from him and something snapped. He grabbed her and spun her around, temper spinning beyond his grasp as well. "Aye, I believe it," he said roughly. "And here you are, living proof that I was right."

"And what good does it do you now?" she demanded, trying unsuccessfully to jerk free. "It's three hundred years too late."

"It's never too late." His dark gaze stormed into hers. "I've proven my faith and Fate rewarded me with the stone's return."

"Well, I don't care what you think you've proven. You might have sold your soul, but I didn't sell mine."

"I had nothing left," he said, his voice quavering with barely restrained fury. "I rode into battle that last day with naught to my name, to my clan's name, but my honor and the determination to do what I must to my dying breath." He leaned closer. "And that dying breath came all too soon, but not until the ground around me was soaked in the blood of women and children, and my own as well." He swallowed hard against the bitterness that for so long had threatened to consume him, destroy him. "When the light came, I offered the one thing I had left. My eternal soul. But I didna sell it. I traded it. For the soul of my son."

Chapter 9

The way he said it, so intently, almost reverently, sent a shiver through her. If this hadn't involved her so . . . intimately, Josie might have even cheered for him. But she was involved. "I didn't get you into this mess," she said, but her bravado was slipping as his gaze continued to bore into hers with such ferocity.

"Nay, but it is yer fate to see me out of it." He pulled her to him, his mouth just above hers.

She pushed against his chest, hands fisted, whether in temper or to keep from grabbing at him, she wasn't quite sure. She wasn't certain of anything at the moment. The entire situation was beyond absurd really, yet here she was, smack in the middle of it. And not truly in any hurry to leave. "I don't believe in Destiny or Fate," she said, "at least not blindly like you do."

"And yet, here you are." He tilted her chin. "Meaning ye chose to be here of your own free will. Either way, the outcome will be the same."

"Pretty damn sure of yourself," she said, but her voice was quivering, as was her body, pressed as it was against the hard length of his. And dear Lord was he hard.

His hold gentled then and a smile teased the

corners of that sinful mouth of his. She hadn't forgotten how it felt. In fact, at the moment, she could think of little else.

"I've made ye swear again."

"You make me want to do a lot of things," she muttered, but it was obvious he heard her quite clearly.

"I'd have thought I'd rather make you smile, but I find I have a strange attraction to all your moods."

"How flattering," she said dryly.

"I should think it would be. Are ye no' still unwed because most men canno' keep up with yer moods . . . and yer mouth?" His gaze dropped to her lips just then, drying her throat and stifling the biting comeback she was surely about to make. "I dinna have such a problem with ye." He grinned then and she swore her inner thighs actually twitched. "Such is Fate's way, eh?"

She was going to have to ponder that statement at a later time, because he kissed her then, and her entire world was reduced to the mind-bending feeling of his lips on hers.

"Open for me, lass," he murmured against her mouth.

This was nothing like the other kiss they'd shared. There was no tumultuous storm, nor waves pounding the beach. She quickly realized there didn't need to be any external forces of nature . . . he was an overwhelming force in and of himself. Her mouth opened of its own volition beneath his and she was lost.

Josie didn't consider herself inexperienced, but she was instantly aware that she was in far over her head with this man. Ghost. Whatever. He felt—and tasted— pretty damn real at the moment. Her body raged, ached, all but screamed for him to release her from the stingingly sweet tension that he was building inside her with every second his mouth remained on hers.

Maybe it was some kind of otherworldly spell he was casting, she thought wildly, surprised she could think at all.

His mouth shifted from hers then, and she was clutching at his hair, dragging his mouth back to hers, fiercely unwilling to leave unfinished this maelstrom of emotions he'd ignited in her, and damn the source!

She felt him chuckle and that only fueled her on. "You started this," she said against his mouth, "and you'll damn well finish it."

"As I said, yer moods are an intriguing maze, but one I'm willing to puzzle my way through." He pushed his hands through her hair, cupping her head, lifting her face to his.

"Whatever," she said, pulling his mouth back to hers. "Just don't stop kissing me."

"Gladly, lass," he said, and returned his formidable attentions to her mouth. His hands skated down her back and cupped her hips, tucking hers tightly into his.

"Yes," she sighed in heartfelt gratitude, feeling incredibly wanton and not caring. It was as if she were possessed and all that mattered was satisfying this screaming need. And he was the only one who could do that.

She clutched at his hips, almost growling in pleasure. She might have clawed off both their kilts, but he stilled her with one strong arm behind her back. She squirmed, her mouth fiercely commanding his, but he pulled back nonetheless.

"Connal—"

On hearing her say his name, his black eyes flashed as if truly lit by some inner demon. Rather than douse the inferno raging between them, it only served to fan the flames higher.

"Ye will be mine," he said hoarsely. "Ye are mine, Josie."

"Just finish me, Connal." Begging, she'd been reduced to begging. But the wild light in his eyes only grew brighter and she knew she'd do a whole lot more than beg if that's what it took. Tomorrow she'd be sane, tomorrow she'd be rational.

She tugged at his kilt, almost whimpering in frustration as his mouth did wicked things to the side of her neck. Then his hands came up and over the aching tips of her breasts and she moaned, forgetting completely what she'd been doing even a second ago. "Don't stop that."

"Never."

His thumbs were thick and perfect as they rubbed back and forth. "Dear God," she managed.

"Aye, I owe them I do," he murmured against the damp skin of her neck. Damp not because of the storm, but because her entire body was in heat.

He sat in the armchair and pulled her down on top of him, somehow managing to push his shirt off of her shoulders as he did. The plaid she'd wrapped around tugged loose and she let it slide low on her hips even as he shoved it up her thighs and shifted her so she straddled him.

He lowered his mouth to her breasts and she arched her back, fisting her hands in his long hair, wishing, praying, pleading that this night never end. Then she'd never have to face tomorrow.

That was her last thought as he slid her up snugly against him and she discovered the answer to the eternal question. No, Scotsman didn't wear anything beneath their kilts. And, an instant later, she was profoundly grateful that she hadn't either.

"Hold on to me," he commanded, as he shifted his attention from one breast to the other.

"Yes," she said, arching her back, opening herself to him, "just please—" Her plea ended on a long, very loud groan of absolute perfect pleasure as he pushed inside her. "Oh God, oh yes," she cried as she moved forward again, and came the instant he filled her completely.

She rocked against him, rode him shamelessly, until the last vestiges of quivering orgasm finally left her. It felt like an eternity . . . and she soon realized that eternity wasn't enough. "I don't know what's wrong with me," she murmured to no one in particular.

"At the moment, you're perfection," Connal said roughly.

Her face was buried in his hair, her entire body was slicked with sweat, and she felt like she could sleep for a hundred years. Three hundred. But just as the first edge of cold, harsh reality began to nudge its way into her brain, she felt his lips begin a slow, torturous journey along the side of her neck, then lower. And when he nudged her back slightly, to allow him access once again to her breasts, she told herself she was simply too spent to stop him. But he proved that untrue almost immediately. He flicked one nipple to life with the tip of his tongue, then, while she moaned softly, moved to the other one.

He was still alive and hard inside her and she was already moving on him by the time his fingers replaced his tongue . . . and his tongue began a rather insistent mating ritual with her own.

She dueled with him, sparred and parried, and felt the sweet climb begin again. She didn't have time to be amazed, she was too busy single-mindedly pursuing that same exquisite release her body had already learned could be hers. Addicted, she thought, she could easily become addicted to this. Otherworldly sex rocked.

It was hearing his uneven breathing that spurred

her beyond seeking her own pleasures. She slowly took control of the kiss, commanding the duel . . . and him. He was gripping her hips now, pushing hard into her as she gripped the back of the chair in order to remain astride him. The guttural noises he made shoved her even closer to another climax. "Yes," she panted as his rhythm increased and she did her damnedest to keep up. "Yes, yes, yes."

Her muscles clenched, gripping him tightly, and when he roared through his release, she screamed through hers.

Stone walls were a good thing, she thought mindlessly, lying limply against him.

"The gods have surely gone mad," he said raggedly.

She couldn't move, couldn't even lift her head to look at him. She was numb, and hoped to stay that way for as long as mortally possible. Mortally. She felt a hysterical giggle rise in her throat and fought to quash it. There had been nothing mortal about what she'd just done. Or, more precisely, to whom she'd done it.

"What amuses you?"

"Ghost sex," she managed, then snickered despite her best efforts not to. Oh, she was giddy with exhaustion and . . . and everything else. She really didn't want to talk. Or think. Especially think. She only wanted to feel. Feeling was safe. Feeling was good.

He nudged her head up. "Am I to be insulted?"

"God, no. It was incredible. You were incredible. I'm thinking of having you bronzed." She did laugh then, reveling in the sheer delight of such intense pleasure. "All of which is to say, damn, you're good."

"I'm beginning to see the positives in yer swearin'." He smiled then and her world felt remarkably right. So she nestled back against him and when his big hands began to slowly stroke her back, she let sleep tug her under. Sleep would be safe, too. As long as she never woke up. Yep, she'd just stay right here, in fantasyland . . . the ghost and the pussycat.

❧

It wasn't a ghost or a pussycat that woke her up. She had no idea what time it was, or even what day for that matter. There were no windows, only the glow of a fire burned low. She was in the tower. In Connal's bed. She rubbed her eyes, yawned and stretched, wincing as some of her muscles protested. She grinned through the pain. What a night. She didn't even remember moving to his bed. She shifted to her side, but had already known she was alone. Had he tucked her here after she fell asleep in his arms?

A sleepy smile curved her lips.

"I dinna wish to startle ye."

"Jesus Christ!" Josie shrieked and flew upright, clutching the bedcovers to her chest. Her bare chest. She blinked and tried to calm her thundering pulse. There was someone else in the room . . . and it wasn't Connal.

"Bagan." She groaned and flopped back on the bed, pulling the covers over her head. "I knew I didn't want morning to come."

"A fine good day to you, as well, lass," he said, if a bit dryly.

She didn't want to have a conversation with Bagan. Or anyone else. She wanted Connal. In bed. Naked. Doing things to her that kept her from thinking. And conversing.

"I didna mean to disturb yer slumber," he said.

"Well, ye didna succeed too well at that," she said grumpily. Then she remembered the rules and groped her neck. No necklace. She sat up again, clutching the covers. "How can I see you without the necklace? What's going on? What's happening to me now? I am really getting tired of—"

"Whoa, whoa, lassie. 'Tis all right." He smiled, looking well pleased. "Aye, 'tis as right as it could be."

"That would depend on whom you're asking. Why can I see you without the stone?"

"The laird of the stone can always see me."

"Connal, yes, I know that. But how does that change me being able to see you?"

He smiled again and settled into the corner chair. "You now belong to the laird. Yer hearts have joined."

Josie felt the stirrings of a headache. "You know, I really just wanted a nice peaceful morning." And maybe some more mind-bending ghost sex. She dipped her chin and heaved a sigh, then looked back at Bagan. "So, you're basically saying that because I had sex with Connal, I can now see you all the time?"

Bagan plucked at the folds in his kilt. "That is a rather coarse way of sayin' it, but aye, that is the way of things. I'm to guard ye both now, as the stone has made its match."

The tension that Connal had so deliciously rid her of last night crept back along her spine, making her doubly irritable. "Meaning?" She eyed him steadily.

Bagan gamely held her gaze. "The bairn, lass. Ye might be carryin' the little lad as we speak."

The tension ebbed, the relief sweet. Josie smiled. "I'm no' carrying any bairn."

"How can ye be so certain. The Fates—"

"Can't circumvent the Pill, as far as I know."

"Pill?"

She nodded. "Small, hormone-filled tablet that prevents women from getting pregnant. Marvelous invention."

Bagan looked quite concerned. "You've taken this pill?"

She nodded, seeing how upset he was and knowing she should feel bad. But she was hardly going to get pregnant just to make the dwarf happy. "Every day."

Bagan sighed and stroked his chin. "Well, this is an unforeseen complication." He seemed lost in thought for a moment, then a spark lit his bright blue eyes. "How many of these pills do ye have with you?"

"Enough," Josie shot back. The ferry was scheduled for tomorrow. Then she'd sail away from this madness. She idly wondered if Connal would be up for one last night. *Greedy, aren't we?* She swallowed a grin. *Sue me.*

Bagan seemed unfazed by her remark, which should have alarmed her, but she was still daydreaming about another possible encounter with Connal.

He slid from the chair and waddled to the door. "There are clean clothes by the hearth for ye. Once yer dressed, I'll escort you back to the croft."

That jerked her from her fantasies. "Where is Connal?"

Bagan turned and sent her a look. "What of it? Ye dinna need him now that ye've had yer pleasure of him, aye?"

Josie did have the grace to blush. "I wanted to thank him." She quickly added, "For helping me with the fire." Now that she thought of that, she realized she had no idea what kind of damage had been done. She had to take care of that before she left. Gregor didn't even know he had a houseguest, much less one that had tried to torch his cottage. "I'll let you know when I'm dressed," she said, sadly accepting that her fling was over. Oh well, she thought, it would provide her with many a warm recollection. She smiled as she picked up her clothes. More than warm.

Then she realized that they were, in fact, her clothes. She shot a quick glance to the door, wondering who had retrieved them from the croft. Bagan, or Connal?

She dressed quickly, gave one last lingering look at the small, Spartan rooms. Somehow none of that had mattered last night. Were Connal to stride back in the room that moment, she thought it probably wouldn't matter now either.

Trying to ignore the twitch of desire, she called for Bagan, who led her back down the tunnel.

"Is the tide in?" she asked, wondering why they were going this route.

"Oh, aye, you could say that."

The storm. Duh. She'd forgotten all about it. She'd been too busy making thunder of her own. The surf would likely be huge. She felt the adrenaline surge and she grinned. That was just what she needed. A good couple hours working the kinks out of her muscles.

They rounded a corner in the tunnel, only to arrive at the dead end Josie recalled from yesterday. "How does this work, anyway?" She started feeling along the stone for some kind of secret switch or something.

Bagan held a lantern, but there had been small sconces lit all along the passageway this time. "What do ye mean?"

"The door to the outside. Is there some kind of trick to opening it."

Bagan looked perplexed. "It's right there, behind ye."

Josie whirled around and damn if there wasn't a slender opening between the stones in the corner. "How did I miss that?" But the question went unanswered as she stepped through it only to be pelted by a cold rain. "Oh, great."

The surf was deafening, which was likely why

Bagan was tugging on her shirt. She turned, and he handed her Connal's cloak.

"Put this over yer head, lass." He went to step around her, as if to lead.

"No, that's okay," she shouted to be heard over the deafening surf. "I can handle it from here."

"Nay, lass," he shouted back. "I'm to stay with ye, unless Connal is about."

That stopped her. "What? You're kidding?" She didn't even bother to stand there and argue. All her sympathy for him being stuck out in this weather evaporated as her temper rose. "I do not need a chaperone," she sputtered as she stalked up the beach. "And I'll be damned if I'm going to have you around, underfoot, questioning my every move."

If he was answering her, or even keeping up with her, she had no idea, and refused to turn around and find out. How had such a wonderful night gone to hell so quickly? But then, when Bagan was around, that was par for the course. Well, it was only for one day, she told herself, then she'd be sailing out of here. Certainly she could manage to coexist with him for that long without killing him. If he didn't manage to kill her first.

As she neared the cottage, her concerns turned to the damage from the fire. She hoped it wasn't anything she couldn't repair or at least arrange to have taken care of after she was gone. She'd have to leave Gregor a letter explaining everything and apologizing. Busy thinking up what she was going to say, she almost tripped over Bagan as she stepped through the front door.

He smiled and waggled his fingers at her in a little wave. "Welcome home, lass."

She was going to ask him how he managed to be here first, then noticed he was bone dry and remembered he didn't have to follow the laws of mere mortals like her. "Only until tomorrow," she advised him, then turned around to get her first look at the damage. Only there wasn't any. She also realized she hadn't passed the sodden blanket out in the driveway either.

She faced Bagan once more, who was looking rather pleased with himself. "Did you do this?" she demanded.

"Och, ye think she'd be pleased with my efforts," he said with a sniff. "Worked me little fingers to the bone for you, I did."

She raised a brow, skeptical of that announcement, feeling smug when she saw the tinge of blush bloom on his cheery little cheeks. "Worked up a real sweat did you?" She surveyed the room again. "Must have been real hard, snapping your fingers like that."

There was a loud huff from his direction. " 'Twas more complicated than that, lass. But the fire did its job, so I wasna put off by a bit of cleanup."

Josie turned slowly. "What do you mean, the fire did its job? That fire started by accident. I tripped."

Bagan examined his nails, then some spot on the ceiling. "Aye, well, that ye did."

Josie thought back to the night before as best she could. She'd come down the stairs, lit the candle on the mantel, then turned and tripped over the lamp. Only when she visually retraced her path now, she saw that the standing lamp wasn't anywhere near the mantel. In fact, it was by the chair near the front window. Which, now that she recalled, was where it had always sat.

Not making a real effort at restraining her temper, she let loose on Bagan. "I could have been hurt! I could have burned this place to the ground. If Connal hadn't shown up when he had—"

"Aye, but he did," Bagan pointed out, not looking at all abashed by her outburst.

"I could have had third-degree burns by then!" She swung back around, looking for something to throw at him. She'd never been a violent sort, but this . . . this . . . miniature Scotsman could drive anyone to commit any number of violent acts. "I can't believe you'd risk something like that. What were you thinking?" She stalked to the small kitchen, but managed to keep from reaching for anything sharp.

Bagan followed her. "I only thought to bring the two of ye together, 'tis all. I've ne'er met with resistance such as yours in all my years as guardian to the stone. I never actually meant for the fire to start."

She turned on him. "What? Exactly what did you think would happen when I tripped over that lamp?"

"I didna know ye'd be carrying a lit wick, lass. I simply thought—" She apparently looked fierce enough now to penetrate even his thick little head, because he actually took a step back. "If ye were to cry out, that 'twas all."

"And you thought he'd hear me through that?" She motioned to the front window and the storm still raging on the other side of it.

"Oh aye, he'd have heard ye."

He said it so certainly, it actually made her pause. And in that moment she decided it really wasn't worth fighting about. It was over and what had happened had . . . well, she could hardly complain about the outcome, now could she?

As if he were reading her thoughts, Bagan smiled at her, that damnable twinkle back in his eyes. "It all worked out well then, didn't it?"

She growled in his general direction, then sighed and nodded. "Oh aye. That it did, I suppose."

Bagan scuffed his boot along the fringe of the

rug. "So, there'd be no need to go tellin' The MacNeil about my hand in this, would there then?"

She looked at him, surprised, but quickly realized her advantage. "Why yes," she said, her smile actually making him a bit nervous. "I think we can come to some sort of mutually satisfying agreement."

Chapter 10

S he's done what?"
  Bagan nudged at the sand with his boot. "She canno' be carryin' yer babe. She's taken a pill to keep her barren."

Connal turned away from the water and looked toward the croft. Bagan had been out of sight since yesterday and now he knew why. But that wasn't what angered him. He'd done little but think on his night spent with Josie. And not once had he thought that Destiny might have put her plans in motion.

"You wait until now to tell me this?" he demanded tightly, perfectly willing to let Bagan think his anger was directed at him.

"Ye said my job is to watch over her now."

"Ye don't have much to watch over if she's barren, do ye now?"

Bagan said nothing, leaving Connal to stalk along the shoreline. The rains had finally ended, but the storm had left the beach strewn with flotsam and jetsam. The sun was setting and there was still no sign of her. He'd expected her to be tempted by the heavy surf, but she'd remained in the croft all day. When the dwarf had finally emerged, Connal had actually been happy to see him.

That feeling had dimmed.

"I know this hasna gone as it should," Bagan began.

"An understatement if ever there was one."

Bagan paused, then cleared his throat, drawing Connal's attention. "It's simply that . . . well, in all my time as guardian to the stone, since your ancestors took on its blessing, naught like this has e'er happened. With your father, and those that came before, each embraced what the stone promised as did those betrothed to them. More importantly, they embraced the promise in each other. It was from that happiness what came joy and prosperity. I know not what to do, or what rules apply. I only wonder if perhaps—"

"It's obvious they are testing my faith still," Connal stated flatly. "I know they were angered by my brothers' refusal to believe. The fates have made me wait long, tested me well. But I have proven—"

"Dinna ye remember what the gods said to ye, in that moment ye lay there, bloodied and dyin', beggin' a second chance to secure yer clan's future?"

The last thing Connal wanted to be reminded of was that day, and those that followed directly after it. Years of days, centuries of days, spent helplessly watching the ragged remnants that were his clansmen, though there were precious few men left among them. It was mostly the aged, the women, and the children left by the time battle claimed him and took the life of their last laird. And he watched as others came to claim the few left standing. Forced to observe as what had been his to protect was taken, destroyed, ravaged. But rather than dim, his faith had been forged even stronger in that time. It was all he had to cling to. His only hope, and theirs.

"I told them I'd prove to them my faith in the stone, as my brothers had not. My soul was the only thing I had left to bargain away."

Bagan moved closer, and quietly said, "And do ye

recall what they said to ye? They said that you'd naught to prove to them. That the only one you had to prove anythin' to was yerself."

Connal swung around, fists clenched. "And haven't I done just that? Proven to the gods, to Fate, and to myself that my faith in the promise of the stone is strong enough to outlast any test? And they're no' done testin' me, I ken that, I do. It is why the stone isna working its magic as yet." His thoughts went unbidden to the previous night. Magic, aye that she'd been. "But it's begun. And I'll do whate'er it takes to see that this land doesna fall to its final ruin, that Glenmuir is given the chance once again to prosper, so that future MacNeils will know the pride of this isle."

"Maybe Destiny willna deliver it to ye. Maybe she has some other idea in mind. The gods themselves never promised anything, they only said—"

"They said they'd grant me eternity to await the promise of the stone. And it is here, is it no'?"

"And what if that promise is no' to be the bairn ye seek? They never promised anything other than time."

"What else can it be? I promised my soul in return for one to lead on in my place." He leveled his gaze at the guardian. "So they continue to test me, I accept the challenge. You yourself said no one had thwarted the stone's promise before."

"But you didna thwart—"

"My brothers did." He waved a hand, tired of this dialogue. It was one he'd already had with himself a hundred times over, a thousand even. "And I am willing to pay for their sins. Have been paying. Surely that is enough, or they wouldna have granted me the time. And Fate surely wouldna hae brought the stone home to me, in the hands of a woman, if no' to allow Destiny to fulfill her promise of hope."

The imp fell silent and Connal finally turned his back on him, more weary than he could ever remember being. He'd spent the last hours thinking like a man. It was time he thought like the laird he was. "Can ye find this medicine of hers?"

He turned just in time to catch the immediate, instinctive resistance in the dwarf's eyes.

Connal sighed in disgust. "Don't tell me she's captured yer heart in such a short time. Ye may be her guardian, but yer loyalty is still to the clan first." He held Bagan's gaze directly. "I want the medicine in my hands tomorrow."

"Perhaps she's expecting ye to visit her tonight. Ye could retrieve it yourself."

Connal shot him a glare.

Bagan sighed, clearly unhappy. "Fine, fine. I'll do wha' I must."

Connal turned for the tunnel, wanting to burn off this sudden excess of energy. He'd like nothing better than to burn it off inside that croft . . . inside of Josie. But he didn't need to cloud his mind with more thoughts of her sweet taste. Until he removed this . . . barrier between them, there was no point in it anyway.

His renewed focus did little to ease his frustration. Or his desire for her. She was a weakness that he could ill afford right now. After all this time, neither could he afford any mistakes.

"Will ye no' be seein' her tonight then," Bagan called out after him. "Is there a message I can deliver for ye?"

Connal paused, then turned and said, "No manmade barrier will keep me from fulfilling my destiny. Our destiny." He started to go, then stopped once again. "Find it, Bagan."

It was simple enough to leave the tower and Bagan behind him. However, Josie didn't leave his thoughts so easily. The sun set and the night turned into the longest one he'd spent since his death. He haunted the tower, stalked the beach, and fought against the need to go to her, until he'd finally stormed back to his rooms. But there he was confronted with the lingering essence of her presence. Her scent clung to his bedclothes, clouded his mind. And there was no solace to be found in the chair fronting the fire. In fact, he didn't think he would ever be able to fall asleep in front of the fire again.

The sun broke the horizon right about the same time as Connal's weakness broke him. However, it was Bagan who met him at the door to the cottage.

"Where is she?"

Bagan swallowed hard, but said nothing.

"You did find them, didn't you?"

He fluttered one stubby-fingered hand in a vague motion. "Actually—"

"Och, spare me. I'll do it myself." He pushed past the little guardian and entered the croft. He knew immediately that she wasn't there. She hadn't been on the beach, either. He spun back to Bagan. "Where is she?"

"In—in town."

Connal worked to reign in his temper. "Fine, that will give us time to find those blasted pills and get rid of them." He climbed the stairs to the loft.

"She's taken her things with her," Bagan called out.

"I can see that." Swearing, Connal popped out, then back in below. "Why are you here, then? Why are you not with her? It's a wonder you didn't lose the damn stone instead of drowning with it!"

Bagan ignored the slight and gave him his most winning smile. "She will be back, my laird."

Connal growled and stalked to the door. Her car was not in the drive. He hadn't even noticed, his thoughts being so single-mindedly on finding her. " 'Tis a small island, but I am no' comforted at the thought of her packing up and taking up residence a farther distance from the tower. It was your responsibility to make certain she—What?" he demanded when Bagan's gaze suddenly wavered.

"She was no' relocating to new lodgings. She was plannin' to catch the ferry."

For a split second Connal felt as if he'd been run through yet again with a mighty sword. Gone? It was simply beyond reasoning. She was destined to be his. Destined to be the one to bring hope back to Glenmuir in the form of his son. The next MacNeil.

She couldn't simply leave. He wouldn't allow it.

"There willna be a ferry after such a storm," Bagan offered quickly when Connal rounded on him again. "She'll be forced to return."

"Ye never should have let her go in the first place."

Bagan made a helpless gesture with his hands. "She's no' a woman ye tell to do a certain thing. In fact, I'd say that would be the swiftest way to ensure that she does the opposite."

"Then use her woman's logic against her." Connal waved off his reply. He hadn't factored in that she'd try to leave him. Barrier or no, he realized now he should have kept her in his bed, wedded her needs to his, if not her heart. And the woman had a voracious need . . . He shook off the memories and turned on Bagan. "Pop off to town and determine when this ferry departs."

"But—"

"If I'm to keep her from leaving, I must be able to cut off her route of escape. I'm a warrior, Bagan. I'm no' willing to allow my opponent to retreat from the battle."

"If I may be so bold as to suggest—"

Connal glared at him, but as usual, the dwarf seemed impervious.

"She is no' supposed to be yer opponent, m'laird, but yer partner. You plan to have her raise yer child, do ye no'? Perhaps it would be wiser to turn her attentions toward championing you instead of runnin' away from you."

"I do not need you of all people to be telling me how to take control of this situation."

"I've explained that I've no' encountered these difficulties before, but I've no' done anything to prevent the charm stone from workin' its magic. In fact, if it wasn't for me, ye'd have never had cause to rescue—" He stopped suddenly, coughed. "Yer right, I should pop on over to town."

Connal narrowed his gaze at Bagan, but was not in the mood to discuss whatever shenanigans he'd been up to. Right now he was concerned with one thing only: finding Josie Griffin and getting her back where she belonged.

In his bed.

*

Josie sat in her car, arms folded, focusing intently on the horizon. But no matter how hard she stared at the whitecaps, not even a shadow of a boat emerged in the distance.

"Dammit." She was tense, hungry and half expected either Bagan or Connal to pop into her car at any second. The waiting and wondering alone were close to unnerving her. Now she was faced with accepting the fact that the storm had thrown off the ferry schedule. Which meant going back to Gregor's place. And dealing with Bagan.

And facing Connal.

God knows she didn't need to spend any more

time thinking about him, but a fat lot of good that realization was doing her. She could think of little else except how his hands had felt skimming over her . . . and the things he could do with that mouth of his . . . No, she'd been strong enough not to go running back for seconds, to end the whole little fairy tale and head back to reality. Hopeful that sanity would return shortly thereafter.

She sighed, backed the car down the ramp, and turned to town. No, she wasn't ready to face Connal again. Not yet. Maybe not ever. And Bagan . . . she didn't think she could take any more of his assistance. This morning he'd thought to prepare her some breakfast and almost succeeded in burning Gregor's croft to the ground after all.

She'd told him she was going out to check the surf, when in fact she'd been strapping her board and gear onto the car. She'd come back in to find him sorting through the bag she'd left packed on Gregor's bed, waiting for the moment she could sneak it past him.

It had taken only five seconds for her to realize he'd been looking for her pills. So much for their tentative accord. When she found out Connal had set him to the task, they'd ended up in a shouting match which culminated in her storming out, daring him to try to stop her. Fortunately for both of them, she thought, still stung by the whole exchange, he'd let her go. She only hoped Connal found him before he'd had a chance to work his magic on the croft.

"Serve the little imp right to have to explain the torch marks on the kitchen walls." She pulled up in front of Maeve and Roddy's place, but made no move to leave her car. Maybe she could beg a bed from them for a night, she thought, and brightened a bit. Surely the ferry would be able to cross by tomorrow.

Dougal pulled up on his bike just then, tipping his hat to her as she climbed out of the car. "Something happen out at Gregor's place?" He nodded to the car, obviously packed with her belongings.

For a split second she worried that someone had seen the fire the other night and reported it. How would she explain the lack of damage? "Why do you ask?"

"Oh, sometimes Gregor claims he sees—" He broke off, apparently thinking better of whatever he'd been about to say. "Never mind, lass. Usually in his cups he is when he tells such stories. 'Tis nothing. Yer okay then?"

"Everything's fine," Josie said, but before she could pursue Gregor's drunken claims, Dougal's expression fell.

"So you were thinking to leave us then, with no surf lessons before you go."

Josie had the grace to blush. It wasn't that she'd intended to leave without saying her good-byes, she'd just been mad and in a hurry to leave before Bagan or Connal could stop her.

Plus, she supposed she hadn't really thought they'd go through with it, that it was just another one of their larks. But Dougal's hangdog expression told her they'd actually been counting on it. "You didn't really go and order gear, did you?"

He shrugged. "Roddy has been looking on eBay. He's a cagey sort though, won't bid on something unless he's checked out the references and such. He's been trying to work a shipping deal to the U.K. Monstrous rip-off for sure." He took his glasses off and wiped them on his sleeve, not looking at her. "Suppose I should go tell him not to bid on anythin'."

Josie felt awful. She hadn't believed they really meant to go through with it. Not really. "I wasn't planning to stay. I—I thought you all knew that."

"Dinna worry about it, lass. We're used to folks going rather than coming."

How had she gotten herself in this situation anyway? Josie sighed and tried like hell not to think about things like Fate and Destiny. She worked up a smile and said, "Well, it appears I'm not going anywhere quite yet. The ferry must have changed its schedule because of the storm."

"Aye, happens often as not."

"Must make it hard for you all to count on things like mail and supplies."

Dougal turned his attention to her, his voice warming a bit. "Island living has its ups and downs. It's all in what you want from a life, I suppose. There's nothing I can't do without for a few days."

"Unless it's surf gear and you want your first lesson before your instructor heads back to the mainland."

Dougal chuckled. "Well, there is that now, lassie, there is that." He opened the door to Roddy's and swept an arm in front of him. "After you, Madame Instructor."

What choice did she have? She was a guest of Glenmuir for at least another day. She saluted Dougal and led the way into the pub. Maybe a sandwich and an ale would help her figure out what in the hell she was going to do next. Maybe three or four ales, she amended, when the rest of the quartet hailed her entrance like a hero come home from the wars.

"Caught this one tryin' to leave the island."

All three faces fell and Josie was torn between scowling at Dougal and digging a hole to hide herself in.

"I'm sorry, really, it's just that—"

"Afraid we'd show her up on that board of hers, most like," Dougal butted in, then shot her a wink. "Now with the ferry off schedule, we've a few more days to convince her to give us a shot at it." He turned to her. "So, what do ye say, Josie lass?"

The other three men turned somewhat anxious stares her way. And what was she supposed to do? So she nodded, and they all cheered. She only felt marginally better.

A few more days? What was she supposed to do? How could she explain she didn't want to go back to Gregor's without sounding even more ungrateful than she'd already come off looking today? They'd done nothing but treat her well since she'd stepped foot on the island.

"I've found the most likely source for our gear," Roddy told her almost gleefully, turning to pour her an ale without even being asked.

"Are you sure this is what you want to do? I mean, it's an awful huge investment for—" She wasn't sure how to finish without insulting him.

" 'Tis alright." He patted her hand. "Dinna worry, Miss Josie, we know what we're about. Now, I've some roast beef today, if you'd like. Or a bowl of Maeve's stew."

"The stew sounds good," she said. She sort of liked the way they took care of her. Not that she needed taking care of. She'd done a fine job of that all her life. Whatever her dad hadn't been able to handle, she'd handled just fine all by herself.

Her dad. She accepted the ale from Roddy, then asked, "Is there a phone I could use?" She lifted a hand and smiled. "Don't worry, I'm calling collect."

Roddy's bushy brows furrowed. "Storm knocked out our switchboard, such as it is. Pain in the arse it is, too, since I canno' get on-line until Maeve gets it fixed. Don't suppose you know anythin' about electrical wiring?"

Josie shook her head. "Sorry." The call to her dad would have to wait. Not that this upset her overly much. He would be getting back from Hawaii today and would expect her to be home by now, but with everything going on, she'd forgotten to leave him a message saying she'd stayed on. Well, she hadn't exactly forgotten, more like she'd procrastinated. Mostly because she didn't know what to say. She could hardly lie and tell him she'd stayed with Finola, since she'd likely left a message of her own thanking her father for their participation in the competition.

No. She was going to have to tell him something, and that something was probably going to have to be the truth. Or at least part of it. But which part?

She tuned back into the conversation and realized they were talking about the storm.

"Haven't seen one quite like that for as long as I can remember," Clud was saying.

"That was one for the record books it was. Took down Old Ian's last tree, it did." Gavin chuckled and sipped his ale. "Sent the sheep into a panic. We'll be weeks sortin' them all out again."

"Och, go on with yersel', Gav," Clud said. "This isle has seen its share of storms, I'm telling ye. This was no' the worst it's seen, though I suppose Josie here probably believed it to be the second reckoning." He turned to her. "How was it out at Gregor's place? Rattled the roof but good, no doubt. Probably what sent ye packin' up this morning, wasn't it?"

He was handing her the perfect out. She could have kissed him. "I've seen some wild storms in my time, but that one was pretty intimidating. I guess I'm not used to being so remote and all . . ." They were all nodding and she knew that now was the time to ask if there was somewhere else she could stay. But instead, she heard herself ask, "Has anyone ever said anything about the tower being haunted?"

All three men paused, midsip, and glanced at each

other. Gavin slowly lowered his mug to the bar. "What brings ye to ask such a question? Do you think ye saw something out there?"

"I—I'm not sure." She was a terrible liar. But what was she supposed to say? *Oh, I saw something all right, in fact, I made wild, passionate love to it. For hours.* She should have kept her mouth shut.

Roddy folded his arms and leaned on the bar. "What exactly did you think ye saw?"

Good going, Josie. "A—a light. Or something. Coming from the tower windows."

Clud waved away her concern. "Och, was likely just the lightning playin' tricks on ye."

"So you're saying the tower isn't haunted?"

"Oh no, I didna say that, lass. There's been tales of those claiming to have seen things out that way for a long time."

She looked at him. "How long?"

He shrugged. "Oh, years. As children we used to tell stories late at night about the dead MacNeil who failed his clan and was forced to haunt the tower, awaiting his true love." He laughed harshly and sipped his ale. "Gregor thinks he talks to the dead, but then Gregor spends too much of his time soused in ale, he does."

"Oh, now you've gone and done it, Clud, you oaf," Gavin said. "She's gone pale as Maeve's shortbread." He leaned over and patted her hand. "Dinna ye listen to him, lass. He's right about auld Gregor. Man would claim to see a UFO if he thought we'd believe him."

Josie managed to swallow the bite of stew she'd taken. *His true love. More like his true broodmare,* she thought disgustedly. As much as she wanted to plead fear and beg for a new place to stay, she knew she couldn't do it. It was bad enough she'd hurt their feelings, she'd not hurt their pride. If it ever got out that she'd brought the charm stone back to the island, that she'd known all along about "the dead MacNeil," much less that said dead MacNeil thought *she* was his true love . . . well, she didn't want to imagine the expressions on their faces then. No, she'd just have to go back to Gregor's and wait it out. It was either that or drive to the far end of the island and sleep in her car. Actually, that idea had some merit.

"When is the next ferry?"

Clud, Dougal, and Gavin exchanged a glance, then looked to Roddy, who cleared his throat and turned to her. "Well, likely it will be here three days hence."

Three more days? Three days of Bagan's inadvertent tyranny? She gulped. Three more nights of not flinging her newly discovered multi-orgasmic self at Connal?

Roddy cleared his throat again and began wiping down the already shiny bar.

Josie forced the images of Connal and exactly how he'd go about extracting those multiple orgasms out of her mind and turned her attention back to Roddy. "What is it?"

" 'Tis nothing, it's just that—" He broke off, shot a scowl at his comrades, then let go a deep sigh. "It's just that we've got our hearts set on trying out this surfin' and even if I manage to get the order sent today, we canno' get our gear here till the second ferry next week. I dinna suppose ye can stay that long. Can ye?"

Josie looked at their wrinkled, shadow-bearded, expectant old faces . . . and knew she was lost. Fate and Destiny be damned. She swallowed a sigh, telling herself she was staying of her own free will. Not because of some charm stone, and certainly not because of a three-hundred-year-old ghost with incredibly talented fingers.

No, she was only staying so she could commit quadruple homicide by trying to teach four seniors to surf. Much better.

"I'll need to get ahold of my dad when the phones are back up and working. He's expected back home soon and I need to let him know I'll be working from here for a while."

"Phone call is on the house," pronounced a jubilant Roddy, who hurriedly filled her mug again. "And we'll pay ye." At the look on the other three's faces, he stared them down and said, "Won't we, boys?"

"Already payin' for the gear—"

Clud's grumble was cut off when Gavin elbowed him in the gut. "Ye want her to stay, or not?" he whispered fiercely. "It's no' a cruise, but it'll be fun. Most fun we've had since we put those sheep in Old Bidda Stewart's loft."

Josie wagged a finger, trying like hell to not be charmed and failing miserably. "Now, this isn't like when you were kids, you know. Surfing is—"

"Oh, they weren't talkin' about their childhood exploits, lass," Roddy piped in with a laugh. "Hell, this was just last spring."

Josie's mouth dropped open. "I've been conned by a band of senior delinquents."

Clud actually smiled. "Ye've promised us now. And I'm sorry I grumbled about the payment. I'll be glad to toss in my share."

Josie looked at them consideringly. "Well, it will cost you . . ."

Always the crafty one, Dougal leaned forward, intrigued. "What have you in mind there, lass?"

"If I'm to work from here, I'll need some art supplies. Nothing too fancy, but—"

"Aye, just make us a list. Roddy will order it up when he orders our gear."

"And you'll have to sit for me."

They all looked at her, nonplussed. "Pardon?" Gavin finally asked.

"I've been toying with an idea for a series of designs inspired by my trip here in Scotland."

"And ye want to draw our auld mugs?" Roddy laughed and Dougal and Gavin joined him. "Who'd want to buy a surfboard with our ruddy likenesses drawn all over it?"

"I think it's a fine idea," Clud said, surprising them all. He turned to Josie. "I'd sit for ye, lass."

"Thank you," she said with a grin. "You can be first. Tomorrow afternoon?"

He paled, but in the face of the other three's avid interest, he nodded stiffly. "I'd be proud."

"Great." She turned to Dougal. "You can be next," she told him, trying hard not to grin when he paled a bit himself. She leaned over and patted his hand. "Dinna worry, lad," she said with a dry imitation of his accent, "I don't paint nudes."

She thought that Roddy would burst an internal organ, he laughed so hard at that one. So she turned to him next. "Well, I might make an exception. If your wife doesn't mind, that is."

They all howled as his face turned beet red. Maeve came in just then, telling them the phone line was repaired and asking what all the uproar was about.

"Josie's gonna draw Roddy in his birthday suit, Maeve. What think you of that?"

Maeve looked to Josie and winked. "I think Josie here'll finally realize why a Scot wears nothing beneath his kilt."

Roddy roared with laughter and came around the bar to give his wife a resounding kiss. "Married the best one of the lot, I did."

She snagged his towel and snapped his backside with it as he walked back around the bar. "Aye that ye did, and don't ye be forgettin' it." She tossed the rag after him and turned to Josie. "Come now, I'll save you from the deplorable influence of the likes of these."

Josie wondered if she knew about the surfing lessons, but decided now was not the time to explain just who the bad influence was around here. "I need to use the phone, if that's okay."

"As long as the webmaster there doesna need it, yer welcome to it."

"Just let me know when yer done, lass," Roddy called out. "And give me that list of supplies ye'll be needin'."

"Supplies?" Maeve asked as she held the door for Josie.

Josie pasted on an innocent smile. "Well, since I'll be staying for a while, I thought I'd get some work done."

Maeve brightened. "You're staying on for a bit then? Well, that's wonderful news. I'm sure Gregor won't mind. I had a call from him before the storm. He'll be stayin' on with his daughter a bit on Mull. Looks like the new wee one has captured the auld codger's heart." She breezed on into the store. "I've just made some lemonade. Why don't ye come and sit with me for a bit. With no ferry today, I've got nothing to shelve." She winked over her shoulder. "And you can tell me all about those surf lessons I'm certain they've conned ye into. You know, I'm thinking maybe I might want to try—how do you Yanks say it?—hanging ten?"

Josie didn't know whether to laugh . . . or sincerely consider taking heavy medication. "Sure, why not?" she said weakly.

Chapter 11

I told ye she'd be back." Bagan swung his legs and leaned out the tower window.

Connal restrained himself from tipping him the rest of the way out. He'd spent a very tense night waiting for Josie's return. Even knowing she couldn't leave the island had done little to ease his mind. He paced the tower, then stopped by another of the tall window slits, unable to keep his attentions away from her, as if she'd disappear again if he took his eyes off her for a moment too long.

She had unloaded her car and was now inside the croft. But she had that black skin suit on, so she would likely be back out shortly to take her shot at taming the waves. They were still high from the storm.

"I dinna like her tempting the fates the way she does, balancing on that stick of wood."

Bagan smiled merrily. "You could always go down and stop her."

"I might do that very thing." Connal scowled and kept his attentions on the croft. "Where did you go last night?" he murmured, willing her to reappear.

"She was with Roddy and Maeve."

He swung about. "Ye knew of her whereabouts and didna come report them to me?"

Bagan looked at him as one might a thickheaded

child. "I am her guardian. Of course I know where she was."

"And what of your responsibility to me?"

"I told ye she'd return and she did." He slid down from his precarious perch and waddled across the room. "Were ye that concerned about her welfare?" He stopped and cocked a bushy white brow. "Or were ye more concerned with whose bed she might have been warmin'?"

Connal forced a laugh. "I never once gave that a thought." *Liar.* He'd thought of little else, which was ridiculous and he knew it. "Considering the average number of years on the men of this island, I was hardly worried."

Bagan's expression remained shrewd. "Aye, then what were ye so concerned about?"

Connal tightened his grip on his control. The dwarf could be maddening at times. Most times, he thought. "Her general welfare. Is it no' so hard to believe? After all, she is the future mother of the next MacNeil."

Bagan looked hurt. "I was with her, m'laird. No harm would have come to her."

Connal merely lowered his gaze at him until he fidgeted and drew small circles on the dusty floor.

"In the future," Connal stated evenly, "I want to be made aware of her whereabouts at all times? Do ye ken that, Sir Guardian?"

Bagan huffed. "There should be trust between a stone guardian and his—" At Connal's growl he hurriedly nodded, and said, "Aye, aye, I'll do my best." He sidestepped toward the window. "In fact, I'll begin now by tellin' ye she's heading for the water with her board. And she's no' alone."

Connal swung about. Jealousy had never once been spawned within his heart. He'd have to give said heart for that to happen, or so he'd always thought. Yet, though it was still firmly his own to command, merely the idea that Josie was going to share her surfing experience with anyone but— He stopped in midthought. Surely he hadn't been about to wish himself onto one of those death traps she rode. Nay. But he wasn't keen on her offerin' to teach anyone else either. He didn't understand her predilection for tempting the forces of nature so, but he already realized it was what she'd built her life upon, so therefore, something she held very dear. He paused again. Was it that *he* wanted to be the one with whom she shared the things dear to her heart?

Nonsense, he told himself, and stalked to the window. She was to serve one purpose, that of raising his son to manhood. It was good that the Fates had chosen someone witty, seemingly intelligent— other than her death wish on the waves—and no' too hard on the eyes. It was pointless to consider whether he would have come to care for her, since his time with her was limited in any case.

All internal debate ceased the instant he spied her guests. Two men were following her down the sandy incline toward the pounding surf. They were each old enough to be her father, perhaps even her grandfather, nonetheless he felt his gaze narrow. Just what were they about?

A blanket was spread on the sand and the two men made themselves comfortable as Josie chatted quite amiably with them. She was smiling and gesturing to her board, then to the water, then back to her board. She laid it flat upon the sand, then lay on it herself, making a paddling motion with her hands, as if she were in the water. The two men clung to her every word and motion. As she was in her wave-hunting gear he understood their close attention . . . and didn't like it overly much, no matter their age.

He folded his arms and continued to watch her lesson, as it was clear now that's what this was.

Not once did she look up at the tower. In fact, to look at her, one would never suspect there was a night she'd spent here, in his very bed. He vowed then he'd have her there again, and soon. Perhaps it was the clearest way to seeing this done. But first there was the little matter of removing a final barricade.

"Bagan, now would be the time to search her belongings and—" He turned as he spoke, only to discover the imp had left him. "Bagan!" Nothing. He should have toppled him out the window when he had the chance, for all the good his guardianship was doing him. Hell, he had half a mind to blame his entire predicament on the little meddler.

He turned his attention back to the window, only he looked to the croft instead. Perhaps Bagan was, even now, taking advantage of Josie's absence. He wished he could be more optimistic, but as he had no other recourse, he ground his teeth and hoped for the best.

His gaze drifted to the old men. Gregor's cohorts most like. He wondered if she'd spoken to them, or anyone else, regarding his continued residence in the tower. He knew Gregor had likely told stories, but just as like no one believed the auld sot. What would the reaction be if *she* told them? And how would she explain her burgeoning belly once he'd planted his seed firmly within her?

It mattered little, he supposed, for it would all come to pass, regardless of what they thought. His son would grow into a man, bring life back to the island and with it prosperity and hope for its continued future. A future that would never have dimmed had his brothers not turned their backs on the stone. He knew history had laid the blame with him, with his dependence on the stone. He didn't care.

He wasn't doing this for his own greater glory, but finally to do for his people what he'd pledged to do when he'd become their laird. He had sold his soul for them. And history be damned for what it believed.

Josie's lithe body and animated expression pulled his attentions firmly back to the present. So, she would teach these old men her passion.

Passion. She'd managed to stir his.

His body tensed as he watched her . . . and he found himself devising a campaign. A strategy designed to realign her attentions to *his* passion. Namely, fulfilling destiny.

Only it wasn't destiny he thought of when she ran into the waves wearing that second piece of skin.

His heart pounded as she cheated death several times over. It took all of his willpower to stay put and not drag her from the waves . . . and straight into his bed. The gods be damned, but there was something primal about what she did out there on that water. The thundering inside him was not all fear for her safety.

He could tell himself his reluctance was because the old men were there, that he was not prepared to reveal himself to anyone but her. Or that the Fates would certainly not have brought her to him after all these long years, only to allow her to dash herself against the rocks.

But those rationales were not what kept him riveted to the scene below. His own blood surged as she pushed to a stand amidst a swirl of white foam and churning water. She was magnificent . . . and his blood sang with the need to conquer her, to make her his own, in a far more indelible way than merely planting his seed in her. He was a warrior born and raised, and he would not be satisfied with anything less than her total acquiescence to him.

He all but willed her to look up at him then, to make some sort of contact with him in that moment, something to confirm to him that they shared a bond that went beyond the boundaries of earth. A confirmation that she was, indeed, his, by not only the will of Fate, but by his will as well.

And, beyond that, he wanted to see evidence that he was not the only one filled with this raging need.

She pulled herself from the foam and climbed the beach with her board, without so much as a glance in his direction. Her attentions were focused exclusively on her pupils.

He narrowed his gaze and pushed away from the wall. "That, Josie mine, is about to change."

ॐ

Josie was tired, but not the blissful sort of fatigue that usually accompanied a morning spent on her board. The sets were coming in close and high, just the way she liked them. And it was as exhilarating as always to be out here, just her and her board, taming the wild water. But her attention was splintered.

Not just because Clud and Dougal watched from the shore. She'd thought inviting them over for a presurfing class had been inspired. In fact, she was planning on having any of the four of them over, Maeve, too, as often as possible. Hell, she'd give the whole damn island surfing lessons if it meant keeping Connal at a distance. At least, she assumed he wouldn't pop up as long as she had guests.

But he was taking a toll on her anyway. She was having a very hard time not looking toward the tower, wondering if he was watching her even now, and what he thought of her guests. Not that it mattered, she told herself. She was in charge of what she did, when she did it, and with whom.

So naturally all she could think about was doing it

with him. She sighed and dragged her feet through the undertow, onto the beach.

"Amazing!" Dougal called out. "Yer like a fairy sprite on that thing."

They really were charming, all four of them. Of course, Old Bidda Stewart might not agree, she thought, smiling.

"Ye are a talent on the shortboard," Clud added as she approached their blanket. "And an artist to boot." He nodded to her board. "Is that one of yer own designs then?"

Josie turned it around and nodded as she gazed fondly at it, like the old, dear friend it was. "My dad designed the board. It's one he did a number of years ago. At one time this shape was used by half of the top ten surfers in the world," she said proudly.

"Aye, aye, but 'tis the artwork we're talkin' of," Dougal insisted.

She looked at the design and her smile warmed further.

"There's a story to tell," Dougal said. "I see it in yer eyes." He patted the blanket. "Tell us the tale, Josie lass."

"It's not all that exciting." But she shrugged and sat on the corner of the blanket, glad to pull off her hood and shake her hair out. "Actually, I designed it as a little joke, albeit a time-consuming one. On my dad. It was for his sixtieth birthday." She nodded at the board, which depicted her father sprawled like some *Cosmo* centerfold. "That's him, in his younger days. Although he'd be the first to tell you he's only gotten better with age." She rolled her eyes, but both Dougal and Clud nodded quite seriously, as if this was a perfectly natural conclusion for any man to reach.

"I'm sure he was well proud of ye for going to the trouble," Clud said earnestly.

Dougal nodded in agreement. "Quite an honor, immortalizin' him that way."

She laughed at that. "He certainly thought so. He paraded that thing around the beach for months. The ladies loved it, to be sure. But then Big Griff hasn't generally needed a billboard to help him in that department."

Dougal and Clud shared a quick look.

"What?"

Dougal waved a hand. "Nothing, nothing. So, how did you come to have it?"

"You know, I don't actually recall. I rode it in a competition once and did pretty well. I guess I tended to take it out more and more after that, even though the technology and designs improved a great deal." She laughed. "My dad says it's my way of walking all over him, even when I'm out on the water. Of course, even now, it's the only way that's going to happen. My dad is a natural."

"With the waves and the ladies, it would seem," Dougal said, almost reverently.

"To be sure."

Dougal and Clud nodded, waited a respectful moment or so, then Clud nudged him and Dougal cleared his throat.

"Are ye really thinking of displayin' us in a similar fashion?" Dougal finally asked.

Surprised, she looked from him to Clud, who was eyeing her board with an expression that fell somewhere between hope and horror.

She couldn't help it, she winked at him. "I think it would be a big seller, don't you? Yanks love anything Scottish. Especially Scotsmen."

Clud blushed, but puffed his beefy chest out somewhat. Dougal waved off his display with a huff of disgust. "If yer wantin' a real Scot, Josie, look no further." He puffed his own rather thin chest out for her and gave her a gander at his biceps. It wasn't too bad, actually, but she really wished she'd resisted the temptation to tease them. She should have known better.

"Impressive," she told Dougal, laughing out loud when he smiled smugly at Clud. She climbed to her feet. Best to nip this in the bud right now. "I hope you enjoyed what you learned today."

" 'Tis all a right bit more complicated than we supposed, what with ocean currents and wind direction and all. Ye've given us something to think on, for certain."

She nodded at Dougal. "Hopefully Roddy and Gavin can make it out later this afternoon." Maybe they'd all realize this was no walk in the park and put an end to their latest fascination. She picked up her board again, resisted the urge to look up at the tower again, and heard herself ask, "Would you care to come in for some tea?"

Both men hurriedly got to their feet, brushed off the sand, and folded up their blanket. "Why, don't mind if we do," Clud said.

"Here, allow me," Dougal offered, taking her board. He only dipped a little under the weight, but recovered impressively.

Probably had to be pretty strong to lift sheep into a loft, she thought, but kept the observation to herself.

Once back in the croft, she said, "I need to shower, so just make yourselves—"

"We've been to Gregor's many a time," Dougal said, waving her off. "We'll start the tea for you."

Josie nodded her thanks and headed up to the loft, only to come to a dead stop when she saw her bed. And the man presently lying on it.

Her heart leaped to her throat . . . the rest of her body pooled with heat.

A slap of a cupboard door from below shook her from her momentary hot flash. "What are you doing here?" she whispered fiercely.

Connal smiled at her, though it wasn't a casual smile if the glittering light in his dark eyes was any indication. "I figured this was the one spot they wouldn't be accompanying you to. Only after that display of machismo on the beach, I did have some doubts."

"Ha, ha, very funny. You can't stay here."

"On the contrary, lass, I can stay wherever I will myself to stay."

"Fine. I'll go."

He merely stretched and made himself more comfortable. "Were you no' going to change before makin' yer escape?"

Had she really dreamed of going to bed with him again? Actually, they hadn't gone to bed. They'd gone to chair. Whatever. He looked pretty damn fine on a bed, too, as it turned out. But it couldn't happen again. He had all these far-fetched ideas about how she fit into the grand scheme of his life. She had to swallow the hysterical urge to laugh. Far-fetched? His life? The former went without saying, after all, he was a centuries-old ghost. Which more or less negated the latter.

She rubbed her temples, her amusement fading. She only wished a similar death to her libido. "Listen, we can't do—that, again. Ever."

He cocked one dark brow. "That?"

"You know perfectly well what I'm talking about. It won't happen again."

He rolled to an entirely too graceful sitting position and swung his feet to the floor. He wore black fitted breeches today, which were nice—really nice. But she found herself thinking how much nicer he'd look just now in a kilt . . . with all that bare thigh exposed.

Stop it, Josie. Sheesh, a person would think she

was desperate or something, the way she— He stood
then and everything froze but her pulse, which went
into immediate overdrive. She lifted a suddenly
shaky hand. "I mean it, Connal. No more hanky-
panky."

He smiled and her knees wobbled a bit. "Hanky-
panky? I'm no' familiar with the term."

She narrowed her gaze. "I imagine you can figure
it out."

He stepped closer. "Oh, I have quite a vivid imagination, Josie lass. In fact, I've spent an inordinate
amount of time imagining how I'll have you again."

"I—I have guests," she stammered. "Right downstairs. This very minute. Making tea." Dear Lord,
but she wanted him again. She took a step backward,
grasping the stairwell railing for balance. Sex for the
sake of pleasure was one thing, when both people
were consenting adults who understood the rules.
Connal didn't understand anything but what he believed. She absolutely couldn't do this.

"I'm—I'm not staying on the island," she blurted
out. "I'm only here now because the storm threw the
ferry schedule off. So there's no point in wooing
me." Wooing? Where had she come up with that?
He wasn't wooing . . . he was seducing. And doing a
damn fine job of it, too.

"I'm aware of your attempt to flee yer destiny.
That you were thwarted by nothing less than such a
dramatic display of Mother Nature should tell you
something."

"Oh, so now the storm is the Fates' way of sending
me a sign?"

He shrugged. "What else could it be?"

She shook her head. "I'm going downstairs. When
I come back up here, I expect you to be gone. Understand?"

He moved unexpectedly fast. She was up against

him before she realized what was happening. Then his mouth was covering hers and nothing else registered. He invaded her mouth, took without asking, demanded without apology.

She was already swept in before she thought to deny him, if that would have been possible. He ended the kiss as abruptly as he'd begun it. Looking at him now, she didn't doubt he was the warrior he claimed to be. Her heart pounded, her throat was dry... and the bathing suit she wore beneath her neoprene was soaked... and not with seawater.

"That is what I understand, lass," he said roughly. "Now, you'd best dispatch of your guests or they'll be treated to the screams I'll elicit from you when I make you come apart for me again." He stepped closer. "And again."

Chapter 12

Connal stared in disbelief out of the loft window as Josie rode off on Gregor's dilapidated bicycle, following her two guests. The brief white shorts she now wore displayed the fine length of muscle in her thigh as she pedaled off. Apparently she'd left some clothing in her vehicle, not that it mattered if she had an entire wardrobe at her disposal. Clothing was not necessary to the plans he'd made for them, and she'd well understood that.

He had been so certain, beyond a wisp of a doubt, that she would comply. He'd had her exactly where he wanted her. Aching for the release only he could provide her. At least on Glenmuir he was the only one who could. He swore under his breath at the images that accompanied that thought, not liking the notion that she could have other lovers once he was gone.

He took the stairs to the lower level. He was doing that a lot more of late . . . expending energy as a mortal would. But he found he had a great deal more of it to expend. He'd have much rather divested himself of it in a far more pleasurable way, but—

"Things didn't go as planned, I see."

Connal glared at Bagan, who was perched on the counter next to the kitchen sink. "Why is it you only decide to spend time in my presence when you wish to annoy me?" He waved a hand. "Dinna answer that."

"I believe I explained that commanding her to do something was only likely to have her do the exact opposite."

"I dinna need yer counsel, Guardian. In fact, I had hoped your absence earlier was a sign that—"

Bagan waved a little pink wallet. "Done. Though I'll be tellin' ye, I had no liking for the task. She should be a willing part o' this."

Surprised and pleased, Connal took the packet from him and examined the white-and-green pills inside. "She knows exactly where I intend this thing between us to lead."

"Which is why she is presently pedaling for town?" Bagan slid off the counter. "Yer strategy is brilliant, I must say, m'laird."

Connal lifted his eyes to the heavens but refrained from asking the gods why they'd saddled him with a three-foot-tall conscience when his own was working perfectly well. "As ye said earlier, 'tis no' like she can leave the island. If she gains some measure of confidence in flaunting her independence, that is all fine and well with me. I can be a patient man."

A small noise, sounding suspiciously like a snort, erupted behind him, but when he turned on Bagan, the imp's face was full of angelic innocence.

Connal knew his expression was anything but at the moment. "I believe three centuries of waiting proves my point. But mark my words, Guardian, patience or no, I will have what I want. I sold my soul for it. I'll no' be letting it simply walk away from me."

❧

Josie slipped off her sneakers, then let her feet dangle over the edge of the sheer cliff. The late-afternoon sun felt good on her shoulders and she tipped her face to it as well. If only her life were as carefree as the breeze, she thought. She looked down at the shoreline. The northern tip of the island was little more than a tumble of rocks, with no beach and little vegetation. A hardy sprig of heather here and there was the only color amidst the otherwise dark stone. The waves pounding the rocks kicked up a spray that misted the air and cloaked this end of Glenmuir, making it feel remote, cut off, even more so than Gregor's little croft. Which suited her needs perfectly.

Not that she suspected Connal couldn't search her out, if he was so inclined, but at least she'd make him work for it. She sighed and lay back on the rock, framing her eyes as she looked up at the clouds scudding across the brilliant blue sky. *How did I end up in this mess?* she asked herself for at least the thousandth time since landing on the island.

She'd left Dougal and Clud at a hilly crosspath midisland and headed this way, leaving them to go on back to town while she explored. Glenmuir was truly stunning in its diversity, the change from the green, heather-dotted east end to the dramatic cliffs of the north captured her imagination and not a little of her heart. The connection she felt to this place would have been intriguing if it hadn't been all wrapped up in tales of Fate and Destiny.

She let the mist cool her sun-warmed skin, wishing she could stay in this little place out of time forever. But Gavin and Roddy were due at Gregor's later, and she figured on arriving right about the same time. That was if her butt lost some of its numbness by then. How did these people ride bikes on paths so rutted anyway? And their butts were a great deal more bony than hers, too.

She smiled, thinking of Dougal and Clud's excited chatter on their ride back. Both were even more eager now to test their prowess on the waves. If she wasn't so terrified of them shattering every bone in their bodies the first time they took a spill, she'd actually be enjoying this. Of course, she thought with a smile, if their bony backsides could handle the skeleton-rattling rides to and fro on those bicycles, maybe they were in better shape for surfing than she gave them credit for.

She continued to look up at the clouds, her thoughts drifting to her father. Had he gotten back yet? Had he gotten her message? She'd left one telling him she'd stayed on to check out this little island she'd heard about, and that a storm had stranded her a bit longer than planned. It was the truth, anyway, if a very pared-down version of it. She knew he wouldn't mind in the least, he was always encouraging her to enjoy her freedom, her youth, and her growing bank account. She smiled. She and Griff had a lot of traits in common, but wanderlust wasn't among them. She'd already had her share of adventures, just growing up with him.

When he'd decided on settling in Parker's Inlet, she'd been surprised, but happily so. She was as ready for a slower, more steady pace of life as he'd claimed to be. She'd wondered if maybe he was doing it for her, if some latent parental gene had finally kicked in and he'd suddenly felt guilty for dragging her all over the place. She grinned. Big Griff was the last man to be swayed by what others saw as the norm.

If anything, he worried constantly that his need to set himself apart from the cutthroat, competitive politics of his sport and industry had stifled her own sense of adventure. She'd argued with him on many occasions that she was perfectly happy where she was. And she was perfectly happy with her life. Or had been before that stupid trunk had tumbled its way into it.

And just like that her thoughts drifted right back to Connal. Again. There really was no escaping him. Not on this island . . . or anywhere else she feared.

"Ye have him worried, ye know."

Josie shrieked and almost slid off the edge of the cliff as she scrambled up to a sitting position. Her eyes had drifted shut somewhere along the line and she hadn't seen Bagan pop up next to her.

"You could have killed me!" She clutched both hands over her racing heart and scooted another foot or two back from the edge.

He looked honestly taken aback. "I merely thought to sit and dangle my feet with ye for a spell." He clambered to a stand. "But if my company is no' appreciated, then I suppose—"

"Oh, for heaven sakes, don't go off in a pout." Geez, what was it about the little pain-in-the-kilt that made her care about him anyway? "Next time whistle or something before you just pop next to me, okay?"

Bagan nodded, sniffed, then sat down once again beside her. "I'd thought to come and apologize to ye."

Now Josie was surprised. And wary. "Oh really."

He looked at her, all sincerity and cherub cheekiness. "Aye, really. I shouldna' hae argued with ye back at the croft. 'Tis only that I must still answer to Connal." He sighed, quite a long-suffering sound it was too. "He is no' an easy master to please, I confess."

Josie found herself stifling a smile, though she couldn't have agreed with him more. Connal was rather . . . demanding. She abruptly shifted her thoughts away from just what he'd demanded of her a few short hours ago. And even more abruptly away from just how badly she'd wanted to give in to those demands. But Bagan, for all that he spoke the truth, was so obviously working her, she was interested despite knowing better, in where he was headed with this. "What obligation has he burdened you with now?"

Bagan glanced away, but not before Josie spied what looked like real discomfort flashing across his face. So, he wasn't being a drama king. Well, not as much as usual anyway. "Bagan?"

He cleared his throat, but kept his gaze out to sea. "I, well, ye see, lass, I have an obligation to the both of ye. Now that yer his, you know I'm to guard ye until the blessed event takes place."

Blessed event. She sighed. "We talked about this, Bagan. I don't need or want a guardian. Not to mention there will be no 'blessed event.'"

"Aye, well, that remains to be seen."

"And just how does he propose to make that happen? Even if I was to—you know," she stammered, "And I'm not planning on it, but even if a miracle were to happen and I end up in—" This was impossible. "All I'm saying is, nothing can happen even if something happens, okay? As long as I'm taking—" She broke off as Bagan's face flushed a bright red. And not in embarrassment regarding the subject matter either. "Tell me you didn't."

"As I said, I have an obligation to the both of ye."

"You took them?" She climbed to her feet, hands fisted on her hips as she loomed over him. "How could you do that?" Especially considering the great pains she'd taken to hide them. Apparently she should have kept them on her person at all times. "I can't believe you'd betray me that way." She laughed. "What am I saying? Of course I can believe it. You'll do anything to save face with him, given how badly you screwed things up last time."

Now Bagan scrambled to his feet, all offended and outraged. "Oh ho, now, lass. I believe you were the one to tell me it weren't my fault. About the storm and all. And now yer the one to go and cast stones."

She glared at him. "Don't tempt me."

He didn't even have the grace to look abashed. "I'm no' doin' this thing for my own pride," he said stubbornly, "but for the good of the clan."

"I'm not *in* the clan!" she shouted. "Nor do I want to be. How can I get it through your head that I didn't want this, still don't want this, and will never want this?"

Bagan didn't even blink at her outburst. Instead he merely cocked his head to one side, as a considering light came to life in his eyes. "Yer sayin' ye dinna want Connal as yer own."

"Thank you. Now you're listening to me."

"So then, there are no worries regardin' me havin' yer medication now, is there."

"That's not the point and you know it."

"Ye've already made it clear yer going to leave the island on the next ferry, so you can replenish yer supply then, true?"

Now it was Josie's turn to look away.

"Lass?"

She scowled, then relented. "Fine, fine, okay. Yes, I was going to leave. And I will." She cast her gaze downward. "Just as soon as I give some lessons to the guys at Roddy's."

"Pardon me? I didna hear that last part." He was grinning now. "Did you mean to say . . . surfing lessons?"

She sighed. "Yes," she said, then pointed a finger at him. "Which is the only reason I'm staying. At all."

Bagan raised his chubby palms to her. "Oh, I believe ye, lass." He straightened his kilt, fiddled with his hat a bit, smoothed the sash across his chest. "In fact, I was just now tellin' Connal that you had no plans to stay."

"Oh thanks, I'm sure that went over well."

"I wasna tellin' him anything he didn't already know. He was well aware of yer aborted attempt to take the ferry, lass. In fact, I'd venture to say that, as close as he watches ye, there is naught ye can do that he willna know about. I thought ye'd at least ken that by now."

"Yeah, yeah, I ken it," she muttered. So, he was watching her closely, was he? Why that sent a shiver of awareness—and not the kind filled with dread either—down her spine, she couldn't say. She'd felt him watching her on the beach earlier, had known that was the cause of the pull she felt, to look up at the tower.

But she'd resisted the pull then, and she'd resist it again. And again. And as many times as it took until she was ready to board that ferry.

He was obviously worried about that resistance, too, she realized. Why else show up as he had, right there in her bed? It was so obvious he was trying to use the power of sex to sway her to his will.

She glanced out to the water again as she felt her skin heat. So, okay, she'd wanted to sway. The sex had been that good. But she'd had good sex before—maybe not quite as earth-shattering, but then she'd only had mortals up until now. Still, she knew what it was to feel good. But normally she didn't obsess over it, or the partner she'd shared the pleasure with.

But then, nothing had ever come close to being like this.

And, no matter how she'd talked up her willpower, to Bagan and herself, she knew she was only so strong. She'd walked away today, or pedaled as the case may be. But repeated exposure to Connal, and Connal's single-minded determination—especially where mind-blowing sex was involved—would likely wear her down at some point. She was, after all, only human.

But she'd had a backup plan. Her pills. Even if she finally broke down and admitted to herself that she was perfectly willing to wallow in meaningless, if fabulous, sex with him . . . at least she knew she wouldn't get pregnant. As if that made it all okay. Her forehead began to throb.

"I didna mean to bring ye such troubles," Bagan said. "I came here to apologize for my role in ending your attempt to thwart Destiny. Not that it would have been thwarted anyhow. But Connal . . . well, he was never one to leave things entirely to the Fates."

That snapped her from her thoughts. She faced Bagan once again. "That's not the way I heard it."

Bagan's bushy white brows drew together. "Have ye been talkin' to the townsfolk about Connal then?"

"God no. I'm already one step away from being committed. And that's voluntarily, mind you. I don't need to let everyone else in on my psychosis."

Bagan simply looked blankly at her.

She shook her head. "Never mind. I haven't told anyone about any of this. But I have asked questions about Connal's role in shaping Glenmuir's history."

Bagan trotted over to her, all concerned. "Now, now, don't be too quick to judge him, lass. History has no' been too kind to him, that is true but—"

"Gee, I wonder why?"

Now Bagan pulled his contrite look on her. She merely folded her arms and stared at him.

He held her steady gaze for a moment, then on a lingering sigh that would have brought tears to the eyes of Broadway veterans, he said, " 'Tis my role that has brought the most tarnish to the MacNeil name. I was the one trusted to bring the stone, and his intended—"

"Oh no, you're not pulling that on me. One minute it's all your fault, the next minute you're shocked and offended to be so much as whispered about in conjunction with the downfall of an entire clan."

Bagan's expression returned to being shrewd and somewhat miffed in the blink of an eye. "Well, I hardly think it's fair to judge me so harshly."

Josie laughed. "I don't know what to think of you." She waved him off from replying and finally let go of her anger. "I do know you honestly care for him, or you wouldn't be here."

"I'm here because I honestly care for you, too," he said quietly, so quietly she actually thought he meant it.

They held each other's gaze for a long moment, then Bagan gestured to the cliff edge. "Have a seat, lass, and let me tell you a bit about Connal and the real history of Glenmuir."

Josie found herself torn by the surprising offer. There was no denying she was curious, beyond curious, to know more about Connal. She also knew that learning more about him was risking feeling more for him than she already did. That stopped her cold. Surely all she felt for him was a need for screaming orgasms. What else was there between them at this point? He was demanding, stubborn, rude . . . and great in bed. Or chair. Whatever. But that was the only source of her fascination with him. It had to be.

Didn't it?

Bagan positioned himself on the rocky ledge, then patted the ground next to him.

Josie wanted to step back. Run for her bike. Pedal away from Bagan and the temptation to learn anything else about a man who already took up entirely too much of her thoughts. But she didn't. Couldn't.

She sat down next to Bagan, albeit back a few feet from the edge. "Okay, I'm ready." Which was a lie. She had the feeling that where Connal was concerned, she'd never be fully prepared.

"I'm no' so sure where to begin. 'Tis a long and complicated story."

"I don't have anywhere to be until late this afternoon." And the longer this took, perhaps the better. More than likely, if Connal knew Bagan was with her, he'd leave well enough alone. "Why don't you just start from the beginning?"

Bagan fiddled with the soft fringe on his sporran, then finally dropped it and looked out to sea with a small sigh. "Perhaps it's best if I tell you the history of the stone, as well as Connal's management of it. It was Connal's great-grandfather, Ranulf, who came into the possession of it when he married a lass by the name of Mairead. Her family was directly descended from the Druids and had some rather powerful notions about things such as gods and Fate and Destiny. Their own powers were rumored to be strong and many steered clear of them for that reason. Not Ranulf. He fell deep in love with Mairead and was made a bride gift of the charm stone from Mairead's own mother. It was then my guardianship began.

"Charm stones were no' so unique in that time, however the special gifts attributed to this particular stone were detailed to Ranulf with great care and caution. So taken was he with Mairead that he didna doubt her powers, nor those of the stone."

"I suppose having you pop up was rather a strong reason to believe, huh?"

Bagan nodded, oblivious to the gentle teasing note in her voice. "But that was only part of it. Ranulf was a man who believed in defending his own with power, might. Loss of life amongst his clansmen was not only accepted as a way of life, it was anticipated, calculated. However, his possession of the stone changed that. He quickly learned that the stone did indeed fulfill its promise. His love for his wife changed him and when they had a son—"

"Connal's grandfather?"

"Aye, Domhnall. When he came into the world soon after their union, Ranulf was a changed man, wanting do what he must to preserve life, rather than cast it so quickly into battle. He learned the powers of strategy and politics as means to gain what he wanted, resorting to war games only when necessary. The clan did prosper and all believed in the stone's promise from then on.

"His son, Domhnall, was raised with this knowledge. His wife, Rowena, was chosen with the stone. His heart was hers and together they saw the clan's prosperity continue. Domhnall and Rowena had several daughters, then a son. Connal's father, Alasdair. He married Eilidh, the stone's choice and that of his heart as well. Connal and his brothers were raised to revere the stone and its powers."

"He had brothers?"

"Aye. Two older, two younger."

"Then how was he clan chief?"

"His oldest brother, Ramsey, was somewhat the headstrong renegade. He had left the island to be educated on the mainland. He returned when Alasdair passed on, to claim his rightful place as MacNeil laird, but he was filled with notions that his family was heretical for their beliefs in ancient Druid ways. He cast the stone aside and made his own decisions, which was the beginning of the downfall of the

Glenmuir MacNeils. He abandoned the strategy and political mediation that had kept the island peaceful. Greedy to expand their wealth, he took up the sword and the shield once again and led the MacNeils back into bloody battle."

Bagan fell silent and Josie didn't know what to say. He painted a vivid picture, that sitting here, on the very land where it had taken place . . . it was as if she could feel the clash and clang of battle resonating in the misty sea air around her.

"What happened then? How did Connal become the chief?"

Bagan smiled briefly, clearly pleased by her curiosity, then his expression tightened as he resumed the story. "Ramsey fell in battle quickly. He'd never married, nor sired any children. So the next in line, Edmund, became laird. Edmund was quite close to his brother and he too shunned their mother's desperate urgings to return to the beliefs that had brought them so much happiness. Eilidh kept Connal close to her, even as her younger sons took up arms with Edmund and headed into battle."

"Connal was a mama's boy?" She shook her head. "I'm having a hard time with that picture."

Bagan stared hard at her, not at all amused by her input. "With Edmund and his youngers off warring, he was the only one with the sense to remain behind to defend Winterhaven. Connal had always held to his parents' beliefs, much to the chagrin and very public tongue-lashings of his older brothers." His expression changed from fierce to empty in the blink of an eye.

Josie found herself holding her breath. Finally, she could stand it no more. "What happened?"

He looked at her, immeasurable sadness in his eyes. "War claimed them all, with naught to show for it but the decimation of most of the clansmen along

with them. Connal was left as chief to a clan made
up of women, children, and aged men. Hardly the
legacy his father, and the fathers before him, had
dedicated their lives to building. His guilt knew no
bounds."

"But he wasn't to blame! It was his brothers'—"

"He was The MacNeil," Bagan said quietly. "All
responsibilities were laid onto his shoulders and he
took the mantle without question. With that mantle
came the responsibility for the desperate times the
clan had fallen on. He wasn't much more than a
lad then, and took his role very seriously. Stronger
clans were gathering their strength, preparing to
take Glenmuir and what was left of its prosperous
fields and farms. He had no warriors, no might, no
armor. He had only one thing, and it was the one
thing he'd been raised to believe in."

"The stone."

"Aye. He'd seen firsthand, suffered firsthand, the
consequences of no' following the ways of his ancestors. So he did what he believed best. He sent the
stone away—"

"To Elsinor."

Bagan nodded. "She was betrothed to Connal by
Ramsey when the stone's legacy had been cast aside.
The MacLeods would have been a powerful alliance.
But with the MacNeils' downfall, the MacLeods broke
the betrothal. Connal had me take it to her anyway,
praying the legacy and promise of the stone would
sway Elsinor. It was all he had to offer and his clan's
one chance for survival."

Josie tried to imagine the decisions he had to
make, the crushing obligations thrust on him. "How
impossibly difficult that must have been for him."

Bagan nodded, the gleam leaping to life in his
eyes once again. "Aye, that it was. His beliefs were
strong and deeply seated. He knew there was no

other way. He felt that after his brothers' abandonment, the gods were testing him and he had to prove his belief to them, his faith. He knew the stone would return, his faith absolute. But when the Fates punished him anyhow and time finally ran out, he offered his own soul in exchange for his clan's last and only hope."

"What if he had looked for another bride sooner—"

Bagan shook his head. "Ye still dinna understand. He had nothing but the stone to offer and it was lost to him. It wasna as if he sat and waited, leaving what was remained of his clan unaided. He did what he could, mustered what strength he could, and when they came to take from him as he knew they would, he fought valiantly and bravely. But it was for naught. And upon his death, he still would no' give. The gods granted his spirit would remain here, in a sort of purgatory, given time to wait on the stone, as only Fate could guide it back to him. It was the only hope for redemption. Perhaps no' that day, or that year, or even a hundred years hence. But the last MacNeil was no' going to simply allow his people to disappear for all eternity. His soul was all he had to offer them . . . and he gave it willingly. He couldna change how his story was told upon his death, nor did he care. If he looked the coward or the fool, so be it. He knew otherwise." He looked to Josie. "And now, so do you."

Chapter 13

She must come to him.

Connal paced his rooms. He would not go to her again. It had been difficult enough watching her charm yet another pair of old men early this eve. Bagan had only bothered to make a brief appearance, and that had merely been to tell him that Josie planned to stay on Glenmuir, but just long enough to teach the aged ones about surfing. As if he needed reminding that she wasn't fully his yet.

That was about to change.

Visions of appearing in her bed, right now as she slept, of pulling her body beneath him, bringing her to full alertness as her need grew to match his, watching her come apart again, hearing the pleasure screams ripping through the night—

"Enough!" He threw himself into the chair fronting the fire, then just as quickly stood again. His imagination needed no further stimulation. He was going mad and she was completely at fault. Never had he been so preoccupied with thoughts of a woman. Yet, she was never more than a wisp away from his fevered mind. It was almost a sorcery of some kind, the way he couldn't stop thinking about her.

He had endured three hundred years of abstinence . . . and yet he knew that had nothing to do with it. "Bloody hell and damnation, I dinna even know her," he muttered. His sole and only purpose was to see his bargain fulfilled, which could only happen if he sired an heir who would follow through on the stone's promise to see Glenmuir thrive once again. Knowing her beyond her fitness as mother to that heir mattered naught. So why this obsession with her? One that was going well beyond the siren call of passion.

And yet, passion was all that was needed. His only concern should be that the stone had brought her to him and his faith in the ancient promise was about to be fulfilled. Or he'd bargained his soul for nothing.

A cheerful voice filled the room behind him. "Perhaps ye should stop thinkin' with what dangles beneath yer kilt and begin thinkin' to seduce her with what lies up here."

Connal spun about to see Bagan tapping his forehead. If he'd had his sword, he'd have run the little bastard clean through. He turned his back on him. "Leave me if ye know what's good for ye, Little Guardian. I'm in no mood for yer guidance this eve."

"She doesna know you either, ye know. Not the man himself. 'Tis her mind ye should be targetin', my lord, no' her body. If ye wish to win her heart—"

Connal spun back around. "I've no intention of winning her heart. 'Tis only her womb I'm interested in conquering." The dwarf flinched and he felt a slight twinge for his crudeness, but hard was what he had to be to make decisions for the good of all . . . no' for the good of one. Especially when that one was himself. "If ye've no stomach for it, yer welcome to leave. But dinna paint this up to be anything pretty. It's an alliance, a promise to fulfill, nothing more."

Bagan's expression smoothed, his blue eyes unreadable. "Fortunate it was for your mother then, and your grandmother, and her mother before her, that their men didna think on them so coldly."

Connal did flinch then. He'd not thought of it like that, nor did he care to have it put to him that way. Not at all. "That was different. They had the great fortune to select their alliances and the gods blessed them with matched hearts. I'm no' so greedy as that. I realize I'm fortunate enough to find absolution for Glenmuir. I canno' hope for personal joy as well."

"What of her joy? Are ye so callous then?"

"I'm willin' to do what I can for her, but that canno' be what drives this, Bagan."

The dwarf shook his head. "Now 'tis you who dinna see. I've spent much time thinking upon this since my return. I believe it was their willingness to risk their hearts to one another, no' simply blind faith, that caused the stone to lend its prosperous charm to their causes. Perhaps 'tis why the stone failed with Elsinor—"

"She never wore it."

"True. But you insist on thinking of this as an alliance only, and it might fail again. Until you realize that your heart must be as committed as your mind, you willna succeed in yer mission, Connal."

He was gone before Connal could respond.

"Daft is what he is," he grumbled, pacing once again. The room was suddenly too close, too stifling, too filled with visions he'd be better off forgetting. "As if there were a hope of that."

He stalked out from the tower, crossed the causeway to the beach, and began what had become a nightly trek along the shore. Midsummer nights rarely darkened beyond twilight, but the clouds had

come in, which was fine with him as black skies
matched his mood. As he walked, his thoughts
skipped to that rare occasion when, as a child, his father would walk with him along this very strand. In
the winter he would point out the stars, naming
them for Connal so that he felt a certain kinship
with them, always above him, a celestial chaperone
of sorts. In the summer they'd look for the solstice
lights that flashed and streaked across the skies, the
sight so wondrous it was as if some fairy magic were
at work.

Tonight there was nothing above, no celestial
chaperone, no fairy magic. Only endless dark . . .
and the doubts that naturally came to be when faced
with such an endless abyss.

He smiled dryly and shook his head. "Morose
MacNeil," he murmured, thinking the name was far
too apt of late. He turned and headed back to the
tower that, even in the dark, loomed ominously on
the horizon. Yet his gaze was pulled to the croft,
though he couldn't quite see it. Had Josie ever spent
a night naming stars? His lips quirked again, as he
thought it likely that she'd spent a great number of
nights exploring some folly or other. It was her nature. An adventuress she was. One he had to tame if
he were to prove himself worthy of the bargain he'd
made.

With that thought in mind, he shifted his destina-
tion to that of the croft, and her bed. The one way
proven to him so far. No matter Bagan's claim of
hearts and such. If he began where he'd met with suc-
cess, surely the rest would follow. Still, he strode the
beach rather than leap directly there. Patience. Best
he harnessed that particular trait of his, one she'd
sorely tried of late, before dealing with her again.

As he neared, he spied a light in the tower. His
tower. Bagan? His instincts told him otherwise. This

time he did take advantage of his spectral powers, disappearing from the beach and reappearing a blink later in the shadowy corners of the tower. It was dark now, and empty.

He crossed to the stairwell that led directly to the causeway, but no light flickered in the depths below. He turned and faced the only other exit from the tower. At least the only obvious one. He silently descended the short, curved stairwell, rewarded almost instantly with a pale flicker of light just before it winked out as the lightbearer turned a corner.

And he knew who that lightbearer was . . . and where she was heading.

He grinned. So, she'd come to him after all. Aye, just as he'd known she would! It was only Bagan, filling his head with needless worries, who had caused him to doubt himself. He popped on ahead, lighting enough torches that she'd find her way, then paced his bedroom waiting for her.

Should he await her in bed? Och, too eager. Perhaps he should pretend slumber. Aye, being awakened by her could be a pleasurable thing. Or, perhaps he should pretend to catch her as one would a thief, demand to know why she'd intruded on his privacy, as if he'd given her nary a thought since their last conversation. Not that he wanted to do battle with her, quite the opposite. But there was no denying that when riled, Josie Griffin was a sight to behold . . . and harnessing all that independent energy of hers could be advantageous to his pleasure as well . . . and hers.

There was a rustling in his antechamber. She had arrived. His body leaped at the mere thought of her here once again, alone with him in the privacy of his own chambers.

"Dammit," came her furious whisper from the next room.

Connal frowned. What was she about? He returned to his spectral self, invisible to her as she cautiously entered his bedchamber.

She heaved a brief sigh of relief upon finding the room empty. Or so she thought. "Okay, where would they be?"

His temper flamed now, dousing his passion. She hadn't come here to beg him to take her to his bed. Nay, she was the thief in the night he'd been willing to pretend her to be. And he knew precisely that which she sought.

His first instinct was to make himself visible to her, preferably in such a way as to give her a good start, then presume her intentions to be amorous in nature. Let her explain her real reasons. But then he had another thought.

Why would she be looking for that pink packet unless she was concerned about needing it? The only reason she could be concerned with keeping her womb barren . . . was if she feared there were to be an assault on it in the first place.

"Come out, come out, wherever you are," she sang softly.

Connal's skin prickled with a quite visceral sense of awareness, though he knew it was not him she called for. He wanted it to be. And be damned the reasons why.

She doesna know you. Bagan's words came to him, despite his unwillingness to hear them. *Nor do I know her,* he thought. Though, looking at her now, as she gingerly poked about his room, he thought perhaps he knew her better than he suspected. Aye, there was much he'd learned of his close observations of her. She was tenacious, both in his arms and upon that board of hers. She was generous, at least with others. All who met her seemed taken with her in some way. He'd told himself his interest was decidedly carnal, but why bother to continue observing her laughing with her guests? If his only purpose was to get between her legs once again, then why watch her assault the waves for hours on end? Why wonder what she was about when she was out of his direct sight?

And why are you standing here pondering questions that have no answers when she is directly within your grasp?

He reappeared that instant, leaning casually in the doorway to his bedchamber. "Perhaps you are snooping about for these?"

She let out a short scream and spun about just as he pulled the small pink wallet from the folds of his kilt.

"Surely you dinna think I'd leave something of such import lying about."

"Surely I didna think you'd stoop so low as to steal it in the first place," she shot back, her temper quickly usurping her surprise. "And I wasn't snooping. I came here to demand my property back face-to-face. You weren't here, so I took it upon myself to retrieve it."

"You must be concerned about needing them if you're worried about recovering them."

"It doesn't matter *what* you took," she insisted. "It's the point of it. You had no right."

He straightened away from the doorframe and strode to her. To her credit, she didn't back away from him. "So," he said quietly, "you had no concerns regarding the possibility that we'd end up here . . . again."

He held her gaze directly, challenging her to respond to him honestly, already knowing her well enough to understand that a direct challenge would be next to impossible for her to ignore. He saw this clearly, perhaps because it so closely mirrored his own temperament.

"I think we both know that last time was a—an aberration."

"You consider my attentions to you aberrant behavior? I thought what we shared was quite natural, if somewhat intense."

"You know what I mean. It really can't happen again."

He stepped closer still, until the air stirring between them seemed to thicken, edged with a sense of anticipation. "Can't it?"

"You—you want what you want. To you this is fulfilling some sort of pledge to your mother. To me—"

His body went stone cold. "What do you know of my mother?"

"Bagan thought I would be more sympathetic to your campaign if I knew the real story."

He tamped down his fury at the imp's interference. "And what is it you think you know now?"

"I know you're an honorable man, a man with deep faith in your convictions. A man who was wronged by his own siblings yet took his responsibility to his people so seriously that giving his life for them wasn't enough. He gave them his soul as well."

Connal was shaken by the quiet tenacity in her words. He'd never heard himself defended in such a manner. "I assure you," he said equally quietly, "that I hold myself in no special esteem. It was something anyone in my position would have done."

"Your brothers didn't."

He looked down. "Dinna canonize me, Josie. My brothers didna have the faith in the stone I did. It would be a waste of time to wish things different. I worked with what the Fates gave me. I'd no' change that if I had to do it again."

When the silence expanded, Connal stepped closer to her. "Yet with all this newfound knowledge, ye still seek to thwart our destiny." He thought of Bagan's insistence that he should somehow woo her. Perhaps there was merit in it. She was a romantic, it seemed, touched as she was by his role in history. He lifted his hand, ran a fingertip along the length of her jaw, just skimming the bottom edge of her lower lip. "Is it courtin' ye seek then, lass?"

"My future isn't here, Connal," she said, if somewhat shakily, as he shifted his touch to the tips of her curls.

He heard the words, her denial . . . but the truth was she hadn't stepped away, had made not one single move to end his contact with her. Her words told one story . . . her eyes told another. Did it truly matter if he simply seduced her into giving him what he wanted?

Right now his body was shouting at him to push forward, take what he knew he could have. It was hard to hear any other logic. "You are here now, are ye no'?"

"But—"

He placed his finger across her lips, his body tightening to the hardness of forged steel when her trembling sigh caressed his roughened skin. "But that is all I ask for, lass. This moment. Now." He wound his fingers into her hair and pulled her close, tipping her head back as he did, maintaining his direct gaze into her rapidly darkening eyes. "Give me this night, Josie, and I'll allow you to decide where to spend the next."

She'd bristled slightly at his use of the word *allow*. He dismantled her attempt to pull back by taking her mouth with his. He'd intended a decisive victory, an instantaneous capitulation from her the moment he claimed her. But her fingertips skated hesitantly across his shoulders even as he pushed her lips apart to allow his invasion, she moaned softly as her body began to yield . . . and yet those fingertips curled inward, still indecisive.

It shouldn't matter. Her body would lead her and he could convince her to follow its urgings, he was certain of it. And yet, now, a victory won this way seemed wrong to him. Unworthy.

He broke off with a vicious, self-directed epithet and stumbled away from her, leaving her reeling unsteadily in the middle of the room. *Damn Bagan for all his emotional mumbo jumbo!* This was his handiwork, this worm of doubt that he'd so insidiously planted within him. He should have her half-naked right now, panting for him, begging for the release he himself was all but begging for as well. What possible care could the gods have as to how he managed to conceive an heir, as long as the consummation took place?

He whirled around, intending to stalk directly back over to her and begin again where he'd left off. But one look at her stopped him dead.

Her body swayed, the very slightest of movements, but he was keen to it anyhow. She could be his, still. But it was her eyes, a bit wild, still unfocused, and mostly confused, that had halted his action.

"What is it ye want from me?" he demanded hoarsely.

That brought the clarity back to her expression, the temper back to her cheeks. "Sex," she said, holding his gaze directly now. "What else?"

Damn if she didn't make him want to grin and shout with frustration all at once. "I believe I was willing to provide that for you."

She'd folded her arms over her chest, a shield of

sorts and the only outward indication that she was still uncertain of taking what she so boldly claimed she wanted. "I didn't stop you."

"Ah, but you did."

Her eyes widened in denial, then narrowed as temper moved dangerously close to routing desire. "What exactly do you want from *me*?" She lifted her hands in a helpless gesture, then dropped them to her side. "To hear me say I want you? That the sex we had was the best, the most mind-blowing thing I've ever experienced? Do your gods require more from me? After all, it isn't like you want me for anything more than a vacant uterus to fill."

Her words, so bold and crude, shocked him. Yet, hadn't he just said the very same thing to Bagan? Wasn't this precisely what he wanted to hear? Absolution for any and all guilt he might have for her unaccepted role in this?

And yet it only made him feel a hundred times worse.

This was idiocy! If Bagan didn't succeed in driving him to madness, Josie would. He wanted to tip his face to the heavens and ask if the gods were enjoying their little melodrama. Instead he took in a deep breath, then released it all at once. Somehow through all this he had to be the one to think clearly, to understand the path he was to take.

He raked his fingers through his hair, loosening the leather thong he'd tied it back with, not caring when it fell to the floor. "Had I no' stopped," he said finally, quietly, "ye would have given yerself to me. Is that true?" He looked to her then, unsure of what he wanted to hear.

She waited, then sighed and nodded. "I think that was a safe bet."

"Why?" He waved off a response. "I mean to say, despite whatever sympathy Bagan managed to inspire in you, ye obviously have no real desire for this fate that has been thrust upon you. You say you would give in for the pleasure I can give you." Even he shivered slightly at that, the air between them still that dense with unfulfilled need. "I agree that what we shared the other night was an experience unequaled for me. If we're swapping truths, then I'll confess I've thought of little else since. And yet . . . the compromise ye were willing to make simply to experience that again doesna ring true for me, from what I know of ye."

She looked at him, squarely and without rancor, and very simply asked, "Since when does that matter to you?"

Since the moment I felt the doubt in your touch, he wanted to say. Yet her question was far more the point. Was it not?

"It shouldn't. But I find it does."

"So you shouldn't care about whether there should be happiness or joy or any other kind of fulfillment between us, as long as the basic tenet of reproduction is met?"

"This is no' about happiness, mine or yours, but about giving Glenmuir a chance for a future. I can only do that by leaving behind someone who will carry on for me. That is all that matters. All that can matter."

"Then your parents, your grandparents, even your great-grandparents, were simply extraordinarily lucky with their charm stone matches? Only you are to be denied?"

Bagan had already hit him with this, and yet hearing it from her didn't affect him any less significantly. In fact, if anything, it affected him more. "I'm no' in the same position as they were."

"You expect nothing for yourself, then."

"Ye forget, lass. My life is already over. There is nothing else left for me."

She fell silent for a moment, then said, "What of your clansmen's obligation to fulfilling their own happiness?"

"I was their laird," he said simply. "It was my responsibility to do for them whatever I could."

"Connal," she said quietly, "there is no clan left to be responsible for."

"Do ye think I dinna ken that?" he said just as quietly. "Do ye think it's been easy sittin' here in this tower, watching those that remained upon my death, few as they were, fall to the control of others? Watching everything I've been raised to revere pillaged and torn asunder?"

"That was centuries ago. They're all free now. Those that are here now anyway. I think they're pretty happy. Sure, they know they could have gone commercial, gone for the tourist buck, but they chose to stay to themselves and live their lives quietly."

"They know not what could be theirs, know not the happiness of this isle when it rings with the laughter of children, the promise of that laughter ringing for centuries to come." Connal held her gaze. "Glenmuir is dying, Josie. I've watched its death throes quite closely for three hundred years. Ye've been here all of one week. Ye see them making peace with the inevitable. They know the children are gone, yet make no gestures to change things. When they themselves are gone . . . there will be nothing left. Maybe they can accept that, but I know what Glenmuir can be because I've seen it, lived it. This Glenmuir is no' the legacy my mother and father raised me to accept . . . much less leave behind."

"And you think one child will change all that?"

He stepped closer then. "He will be The MacNeil. Blessed by the gods, with the will of the charm stone behind him. Aye, I believe he will change everything. I have to."

Chapter 14

J osie was moved to silence by Connal's intensity. She found herself wishing the right woman had found the stone, the woman who could give him what he so desperately wanted. "I'm sorry," she said softly, and meant it.

He cocked an eyebrow in question and she was unsure what to say. "You know I want you, I can't deny that," she began, then faltered when his eyes flashed to life and she felt it clear down to her toes. Her voice wobbled a bit. "But I don't want to have a baby. I'm not saying I never do, but when I do, it will be with a man I plan to build a life with." She looked at him earnestly. "Connal, what kind of life do you think this child will have? It's hard enough with two mortal parents." She shook her head and laughed humorlessly. "This entire thing is insane."

Connal moved close to her again, cupped her face, and stroked her lips with the pads of his thumbs. That focused intensity of his all but beamed from his eyes. "Ye'll make a fine mother, Josie. Yer strong of mind, of body, and of will." He drew his thumb across her bottom lip again, pressing slightly at the center, allowing the smallest of sighs to escape.

She shuddered with pleasure, knowing she should back away, from his touch, his look, his words. But she couldn't. Or wouldn't. She'd told him she only wanted him for sex, partly in anger and frustration, but mostly because it should have been the truth. And yet, when she'd said it, it had felt like a lie. She no longer understood all the reasons why she was drawn to this man, but the fact remained she was. Indelibly so.

"Come to bed with me, Josie," he murmured as he lowered his mouth to hers, letting his hands drift to her shoulders, then pulling her tightly against his body.

"It won't change anything," she whispered.

He flashed a smile at her then, and her body flashed hard in response. "Everything has changed, Josie Griffin. Nothing will ever be the same again. Ye must know that."

She didn't know anything, she thought, her mind and body in turmoil. Then he kissed her, boldly, confidently, with the assurance of a man who knew exactly what he wanted and exactly how to get it. Normally she would be put off by that. At that moment, however, she found herself swept away by it. As if giving in to him absolved her of all responsibility. It didn't, and wouldn't. She knew that and realized she didn't care. She was in his arms, feeling the most amazing things, and nothing else seemed to matter.

His seduction wasn't smooth, or practiced. It was a wild thing, barely restrained. His lips and tongue didn't taste her, they consumed her. He plundered her mouth as a pirate would, taking what he wanted, certain it would be his. She felt weak and unbelievably strong at the same time. Never had she felt so desired, so wanted. Never had she desired or wanted so strongly in return..

"Connal," she said, a hoarse whisper against the side of his throat.

"Aye, 'tis me." He lifted his head, his fingers stilling from the devastatingly carnal path they'd been intent on following. Whatever he found in her eyes made him grin. "And glad I am to know you ken it." His own eyes darkened, and he added, "For as the stone has cast you as mine . . . so has it cast me as yours." He rolled onto his bed with her, pulling her on top of him. "Make me yours, Josie Griffin."

Dear Lord. She was trembling, her heart pounding, as she looked at the man proclaiming himself hers. She badly wished she could make this merely another romp in the hay, a night of debauched revelry or whatever they'd have called it three hundred years ago . . . but there was far more in his eyes than the desire to get himself laid. And, being brutally honest with herself . . . she admitted this had already gone well beyond some kind of sexual fantasy fulfillment for her.

"Ye think too much," he said, surprisingly gently for all the ferocity of need that had arced between them only moments before. "Can ye no' just—how do you say it? Go with the flow?"

She smiled then, surprised and charmed by his attempt to lighten things up. Mostly because he'd pulled it off, and with such frightening ease. "You're supposed to be all rough and demanding," she said, "ravishing me against my will until I no longer care what's right and what is wrong."

He smiled, obviously willing to play this game. "I believe I can still manage a good ravish, if yer heart is set upon it." He skimmed his hands up her sides, letting his thumbs skate across her breasts, brushing ever so deliciously across the tips of her nipples. His smile broadened to a bold grin when she trembled and her thighs clenched involuntarily against his waist. "But I do no' care to force a woman." He kept his gaze focused tightly on hers as he continued to brush his thumbs against her nipples.

She gasped and tried to keep from arching her back. It took amazing willpower.

"Nay," he went on, his own voice a bit rougher, "I find I much prefer it when yer as demandin' of what I can give ye as I am willing to give it."

Her eyes drifted shut and she let the pleasure he was wreaking within her take over. She moved on him, his own stifled groan of pleasure only urging her on.

"That's it, Josie, take what ye want." He pushed her top off even as she was already clawing at his own.

Her will to end this slipped from her fingers along with his shirt. She smoothed her hands across his warm chest, toying with him in the same manner he toyed with her, never so gratified as when he gasped in return.

"Ye think to ravish me?" he managed, rather hoarsely.

She'd have never guessed how much fun he could be to play with. Adrenaline pumped into her, along with ever-increasing need. "Aye. Aye, that I do," she responded saucily, and bent down to circle his own nipple with her tongue. He bucked beneath her and gasped in surprise. Josie felt instantly drunk with sexual power. "Don't stop touching me," she demanded.

He moved beneath her now, as she went back to tracing rings around him with her tongue. His fingers moved swiftly and amazingly deftly to her inner thighs. He slid his palms up and let his fingers move beneath the edge of her shorts. She cried impatiently against his rapidly heating skin when he stopped, just shy of his goal. His hands were so big, her shorts too tight.

"Connal, please."

Then her world tumbled and she found herself

on her back, with Connal looming large and dangerously aroused above her. She could have come right then and there. Her shorts disappeared down her legs, panties with them, until she lay naked beneath him. And reveled in it. Her hips moved, knowing what they sought was oh so close.

She reached for him, only to have him take her hands and pin them down to the bed beside her head. He straddled her then, bare himself but for his kilt. She moaned as the velvety hard length of him brushed her belly, made somehow more erotic as the rough wool of his kilt skimmed across her wildly sensitized skin.

"Look at me," he commanded.

She hadn't even been aware of closing her eyes. She opened them to find Connal's face mere inches from her own. "What do ye want, Josie? I'll hear it from your own lips."

She tried to buck her hips, to show him exactly what she wanted. As if he didn't know! But his thighs were rock hard, clamped on her own, making her incapable of moving. Being trapped like this should make her angry, make her want to resist giving in. Yet all she wanted was to feel him slide down her body, then back up again, with that glorious part of him snugged deeply between— She moaned at the mere thought of it.

"I'm no ravishin' ye," he said, his lips quirking just the tiniest bit. Just enough to provoke her.

"Ye could," she shot back.

"Make yer demands of me, Josie. Tell me what ye want."

"You know damn well what I want," she managed.

He shifted slightly so he brushed against her, nudging himself into the soft skin of her stomach.

She ground her teeth against moaning for him again. "I want you to let go of my hands."

His eyebrows lifted. "And why should I do that?"

She looked him straight in the eye. "So I can run my fingers down the length of you. Feel you pulse in my hand."

His pupils shot wide and his thighs tightened, even as she felt him twitch against her. Josie swallowed hard, wondering at the wisdom of pushing him like that . . . but the wetness between her legs only urged her on.

"Would you like that?" she said, wanting to scream from the sweet edge of tension riding along every nerve. "To feel my hands like that?"

"Aye," he managed, jaw tight.

"Then let go of me."

He grinned at her then and sat up, still gripping her wrists. He balanced his weight on his legs as he easily held both her wrists in one grip. He used his free hand to remove his kilt, tossing it aside, eyes shining in delight as her gaze moved unwaveringly to see the full glory of what she'd been feeling rubbing at her.

He took one hand and guided her to him. Somehow the power had shifted again and her gaze shifted to his. His eyes were glittering as he wrapped her palm around the throbbing length, curling her fingers around him. This was unbearably erotic, watching him use her hand to stroke himself. Her hips jumped despite being trapped beneath him. Her other hand flexed in his grip, eager to touch him, to feel . . . anything. Dear God, but she might come if he didn't let her—

He groaned then, deep and long, almost more of a growl. Their gazes met as his hand dropped away, leaving hers on him . . . to do as she pleased. He released her other hand as well. But as she moved to touch him . . . so did he move to touch her as well.

She fought to keep her eyes open as his fingers did amazing things to her nipples. But their gazes were locked on each other's, as if by some greater force, each of them bearing witness to the havoc of pleasure they were wreaking on the other.

She fought beneath him to move her hips.

"I feel the same need," he rasped.

"Then take me, dammit!"

The grimace of restraint that had locked his jaw broke then, into a grin so wickedly erotic she felt herself reach the first edge of climax right then and there.

"As you command, my lady," he told her, then slid down her body . . . and surged back up and into it in one bold stroke.

Josie cried out and lifted herself onto him, opening herself to this sweet invasion, locking her legs tightly around him to ensure he stayed right where she wanted him. Where she'd always want him, she found herself thinking as delirious waves of pleasure built inside her.

She grabbed at his hips, urging him on. "Faster, harder. God, Connal."

"I couldna be any harder," he managed, and they both gasped and laughed simultaneously.

And just then, for one brief moment, their gazes met, held . . . then broke apart again, the air filled only with the sounds of two people slaking their lust for each other.

He did push harder, she did move faster, almost furiously so, reaching for that brilliantly mind-blowing release he'd driven her to once before . . . and trying to pretend that was all this was about.

"Come apart for me," Connal growled just then. "I want to see ye find the stars."

Josie's eyes blinked open even as he drove into her

again, to find his gaze locked on her, his eyes so dark they were almost black, glittering with intent, the focus so tightly wound that she spiked instantly into a climax so strong it robbed her of breath, the glimmers that had come before it paling in significance to this overwhelming rush of sensation. It was all she could do to hang on to him and ride it out.

"That's it," he said, moving faster, grabbing her hips and shifting her higher so he could plunge deeper. "Hold on to me, Josie . . . and reach for the stars again. There are hundreds, thousands. I would give them all to you."

She was gripping his shoulders, then his head, pulling his mouth to hers, almost blind with need at that point, looking for something, something . . . needing— His mouth came down on hers, his lips pushing hers open, so he could invade her mouth as he was invading her body. She felt completely possessed by him, her entire body his to take, his to command. His.

This time the groan of release came from deep within her. She felt as if her body would shatter with the soul-piercing pleasure that ripped through her. She reached for more stars . . . and found a galaxy of them.

But even as their twinkling lights faded and her body still jerked with release, she knew she hadn't found what she sought . . . not all of it. She opened her eyes once again as he stroked her hair, damp now, from her face. He was still deep inside her, raging hard with need, but he held himself still, and from the tic pulsing in his jaw, not without enormous self-control.

"Why did you stop?"

He continued to push the hair from her brow, his gaze penetrating hers, as if he too were looking for something. "I've never met a woman who takes so much joy in the pleasuring a man and woman can give each other."

She supposed she should be embarrassed, only he'd said it with a touch of awe and wonder, and made her flush with pleasure instead. "I've never met a man who could give me such joy," she said, before she thought better of it. It was true, but the instantaneous surge of . . . she couldn't even describe it, something primal almost, she'd seen in his expression, told her she might have wanted to keep that bit of information to herself.

Except at the moment she couldn't seem to care overly much. Because he did bring her joy. Blissful amounts of it. At least when they were like this he did.

But along with admitting that her feelings had gone beyond the physical came the curiosity to know more of him. Surely if he could be this generous, capable even of laughing, a man who enjoyed blissful amounts of pleasure himself . . . surely there was more to him than the tortured, almost-angry clan chief she'd dealt with the rest of the time. The thought was tantalizing. The desire to find that man was dangerous.

"Ye've gone from me," he said, kissing her neck and making her body arch into his. How was it he knew just where to touch her, just how to elicit a continued response from her no matter how wrung out she felt? "Your body is here, mine to take, but your thoughts have traveled far."

Her body, his to take. Yes, she thought, there was no denying that any longer. But the rest? "My thoughts haven't traveled far at all," she said softly, then nudged his mouth up to hers, sank her fingers into his hair, and kissed him. Not the dueling tongues, piston-imitating kind of carnal kiss he'd given her moments ago.

No, she was seeking something else this time, too curious to find if he would be receptive to it to listen to the warnings clanging in her head . . . and more distantly in her heart.

She kissed him softly, slowly. She made love to his mouth, but gently, wooing his response rather than demanding it. If he was surprised or confused by this sudden change of pace, he didn't show it. In fact, he seemed to enjoy it . . . and he was a quick study, she found out a moment later. His own hands sank into her hair, his body pinning hers to the bed. He returned her kisses with devastating gentleness. His hips moved just as slowly, pushing himself within her gently, even as he felt fiercely hard.

The combination undid her and she came again. This time it was swift and somehow soft. She cried out and he took the cry into his mouth even as he moaned. Ripple after ripple washed over her with excruciating gentleness and yet he kept on, gently pushing into her, kissing her softly, on the neck, the cheek, the eyelids, the lips.

"Again, Josie mine," he whispered against the shell of her ear. "Again and again."

"I want . . ." She trailed off on a light moan as he moved her up . . . and over again. Could a person simply drown in her own pleasure? She thought she might find out. "I want you to . . . You . . . Your turn." It was the best she could do, she was both breathless and so deeply sated she felt drugged with it.

"It has been my turn since I entered you," he said. "Wrap your legs around me, Josie," he urged her, already pulling her thighs up tight. "Let me sink deeply into you, so deeply that you will feel joined to me even when we are no longer like this."

She did as he asked, knowing at that moment

she'd have done anything he asked. And when he lifted her up, higher, then higher still, and moved deeply, so deeply into her . . . they both groaned as he pulsed into her, his climax one long, low growl of release.

She managed to open her eyes to see his squeezed tightly shut, his expression . . . she wasn't sure. Blissful yes, but there was something else—

Then his eyes blinked open and he looked down at her, into her, and said, "We have done it, Josie mine. We have well and truly done it."

Of course we have, she wanted to say, preferably with a dry, oh-so-witty little laugh. About as well and truly as any two people could, she would add. But there was something else in his tone. Something . . . fateful. "What have we done?" she whispered, even though she wasn't sure she really wanted to know.

Somehow she'd stepped into the rabbit hole and fallen deeply into a wonderland of her very own . . . only she was no longer certain she could find her way back out. There was no ferry ride out of this place, no plane ticket, no wave of a magic wand.

He smiled then, a grin of such pure happiness and joy . . . neither of which had anything to do with sexual fulfillment.

Suddenly she felt a chill deep inside her, and not a little fear. "Answer me," she demanded softly.

He ignored her sudden urgency, apparently too distracted to note her withdrawal. He slid from her body and rolled to his side, carrying her with him even when she put up a little struggle. She should be clearing her head, exiting this sensual fog he'd gotten her lost in. Something had just happened, something far more involved than two people making love.

That stopped her. Not having sex. Making love.

No. She didn't love him. She didn't even know him. But she'd wanted to, wanted to show him there could be more, and she found she still did. And there could be more. Dangerously more, she thought as she looked up into the chiseled perfection of his face.

"Connal," she said, but he quietly hushed her, tucking her easily against his chest, as if they'd spent hours, nights, in this very spot. His hands were toying with strands of her hair, and he felt so immensely relaxed she found it hard not to follow him and let the delicious lethargy claiming her body take her mind along with it. Sleep beckoned, and she was in his arms . . . probably he hadn't meant anything by what he'd said. He'd just been feeling as exultant as she had. And yet, she heard herself asking, "Explain what you meant. What have we well and truly done?"

He slid his hand down to her belly. "This."

She stilled, even as she acknowledged she'd suspected this was exactly what he'd meant. Had he thought that by making her miss a single pill, she'd be fertile again? She had to tell him, to explain . . . to shatter his momentary peace. But he'd said it so surely, with such obvious awe, that she couldn't find it within her to do it. Not now.

So she said nothing. She let him tuck her head back against his chest, not sure how she felt about leaving him to imagine that he'd finally completed what he'd waited three hundred years for. She should probably feel used, except she didn't. What they'd just shared . . . well, it had been fully shared. If there had been using, then they were both guilty of it.

Her thoughts were a jumble, not made any clearer by the slow stroking of his fingertips now along her spine. No, she didn't feel remotely used at the moment, she thought as sleep reached into her and claimed her. She felt . . . cherished.

"I dinna think I could feel such joy," she heard him whisper.

"Neither did I," she murmured, safe in the knowledge that it was all a dream.

Chapter 15

A re ye sayin' ye love her, then?" Bagan wanted to know.

Och, why he had gone and shared the news with the imp was beyond him at the moment. "Couldna ye just be happy for me, for yersel' as well, and not ask a thousand questions?"

Bagan hopped down from the window. "I explained this to ye. This is no' about the bairn, lad, 'tis about giving yer heart. And I canno' see where ye've done that." He waved his hands in the air. "I'm no' so certain ye've even located the thing within ye as yet, much less given it to another."

"Very amusing," Connal said, then scowled. He'd awoken this morning feeling . . . well, he couldn't even describe it. Fulfilled, perhaps. So much so that his empty bed had only mildly upset him. He'd set out to find Josie, make certain all was well with her . . . and also make certain she knew there would be no more surfing now that she carried his heir within her. Only he'd encountered Bagan the Worrier instead.

"I dinna mean to amuse, m'laird. I mean to warn ye no' to get yer hopes up. The stone's promise has yet to be fulfilled."

Connal turned to face him. "I know what happened between us, Guardian. 'Twas . . . celestial."

When Bagan merely raised his white eyebrows, he said, "Dinna give me that look. I know I sound foolish, but there is no other way I can describe it. Only the gods would have enabled two people to join themselves as we did. Surely that union was blessed."

Bagan tapped his chin and paced. "Hmmm," was all he said.

"What is that supposed to mean?"

Bagan paced on, silent for a moment, then turned to face him. "Ye say ye felt as if the gods had blessed ye. That it was no ordinary rutting about."

"It was no' rutting!" he all but shouted. "It was—"

"What?" Bagan asked, suddenly very interested in his answer.

Connal folded his arms and stared once again from the tower portal. "It was no simple slaking of pleasure is all I meant to say."

"Hmmm," Bagan responded again.

Connal whirled about, this time he'd wring the dwarf's neck for certain, only he found himself alone in the tower. "Just as well, imp," he warned.

But as he looked once again out across the water, he couldn't help think on the guardian's words. This wasn't about surrendering his heart. He'd already surrendered his soul, surely that was enough. And it wasn't as if he found Josie abhorrent, in form or in intelligence. Nay, the Fates had seen to that. She'd do well in parenting their child.

Somewhere deep in his heart there was a small clutch as he imagined it, truly pictured her with a bairn in her arms. Their child. He knew he wouldn't be part of that picture, and felt that small clutch grab at him once again. He swung away from the portal. It didn't matter. His own needs and desires didn't matter in this. Josie would do what Fate had sent her here to do and that was all that mattered.

His part in this was done. He'd have to trust her as he'd trusted in the promise of the stone.

Trust her. That was asking much, but it was little enough when the alternative had been to allow Glenmuir, and the hopes of all who came before, to die. His fists tightened and his heart began to pick up speed. Now there *was* hope. There would be another MacNeil to rebuild Glenmuir!

He moved to the stairs, a maelstrom of emotions swirling inside him. He must find Josie. Merely to ascertain that she was well, and to put a few rules into place, he told himself. It wasn't because he'd missed seeing her awaken this morning, nor was it due to his own need to have her once again, taste her.

That stopped him cold. His bargain met now, there'd be no need to have Josie again. Nor to hold her, taste her. This time the clutch was lower and his heart felt as if it paused in midbeat. With all his strategizing, he'd not stopped to think that part through.

He'd only moments ago told himself his own needs and desires couldn't interfere, shouldn't. And yet . . . the idea of never touching her again . . . he couldn't even think on it without feeling that odd ache in his chest.

He tried to shake off the malaise. He should be celebrating, joyous in the rebirth of hope for Glenmuir. He'd been through much this past night, that was all. The fulfillment of a three-hundred-year-old bargain was enough to toss anyone's emotions about and he'd had a tempest full of them. He resumed his descent. But just because he'd have no need for her in his bed did not mean he was about to leave her alone completely. Nay, he would be involved in this venture, at least in as much as the gods would allow.

That thought had him slowing again as another realization sprung forth. He was still here today. He had not gone on to his greater glory . . . or to whatever plane the gods would see fit to send him. As Bagan had reminded him, they'd merely granted him the time to see the stone returned, his mate with it. But surely they knew as he did, as they'd not taken him the moment he held the stone, that it was only in creating a new life, the next MacNeil, that his destiny would be completely fulfilled.

Now that time had come. Finally, blessedly, amazingly. His knees folded and he sat hard on the stone step as the totality of this fulfillment washed through him. He'd truly done it.

The emotions that swept through him were close to overwhelming, but he recognized and could not ignore that not all of them were joyous. Josie would go on alone. At some point, the gods would call him back. Whether it be at the child's birth . . . or in the next instant, he did not know. And shouldn't care. He'd done what he set out to do.

Why then was there this piercing emptiness inside him?

He rubbed at his chest, then pulled his hand away and tightened his fingers into a fist. He'd managed this long with his focus intact, he'd not lose it now with the end so close. But see her he would, as mother of his unborn child and nothing more.

He stood then and finished his descent. He was across the sandspit and halfway up the beach, heading for the croft, when he saw the footprints. Narrow and long, but perfectly formed . . . just like their owner.

He turned and looked down the shoreline and spotted her, trailing just along the water's edge, head bent as if deep in thought.

"And Lord knows where those thoughts are this

morning," he murmured. Best he had as much influence over them as possible, he told himself as he took off behind her, struggling to keep his newfound determination from wavering. He'd think only of the bairn, no' of the feel of her, the taste of her, or the way they'd laughed even as they'd gasped in anticipation of their roaring completion.

Swearing silently as he struggled to block those images from his mind, he strode purposefully along the shoreline toward her.

She stopped and looked over her shoulder before he caught up. She remained where she stood, waiting for him, but with her hand shading her face against the rising sun, he couldn't see her eyes to be certain of her thoughts.

"Hello," she said finally, as if at a loss on what else to say.

Now that he stood here before her, he realized his own tongue was not under his command either. She was . . . stunning. Her hair was a short tangle, tossed lightly about by the wind. Her legs were sheathed in some sort of soft gray fabric that clung to her hips and thighs, the bottom band tight and shoved up to just below her knees. Her top was also soft, white, and she wore nothing beneath. His body stirred and he willed his attentions elsewhere. His thoughts as well. But visions of last night assaulted him anyway. She'd been magnificent then, and despite thinking it impossible, she was even more magnificent to him now. And try as he might, his thoughts had very little to do with wee bairns.

He turned and looked out to sea. He'd have to get past this if he were to play any role in her life now. Any moment could be his last, and he wanted to spend whatever number of them he had left with her. And his unborn son.

"Would you care for company on your morning

stroll?" he asked, quite proud of his polite demeanor, which had cost him much since what he really wanted to do was take her in his arms and feast on those lips, taste her once again, have her beneath him so he— Dear Lord he needed to find control.

He shifted his attention to her when she didn't answer, only to encounter an unreadable expression on her face. "Is it so odd that I'd wish to accompany you?"

She folded her arms. "What's odd is you being so polite about it."

He smiled then, even though her words stung a bit. "Have I been such an ogre then?"

She didn't smile in return. "At times, yes. And don't get me wrong, I'd rather the polite act than—"

"Act?" He heard the bluster in his voice and worked to tone it down. " 'Tis no act. I spied you walking the beach and wished to spend time with you. But if that is no' to your liking then—"

She reached out for him when he swung about, stopping him, then dropping her hand quickly when he turned back to face her. "I'm sorry," she said. "It's just—" She lifted her hands, then dropped them again. Now it was her turn to look out to sea. "I'm confused this morning and I guess I was hoping to get my thoughts together before facing you."

The first wisp of concern prickled the back of his neck. He didn't stop to consider the consequences and acted on instinct. He reached for her, took her arms in his hands and pulled her around to face him, so close that their knees almost brushed. "What thoughts are those?" he asked, searching her eyes. "Is it the bairn then? Are ye worried about being alone here to raise him, away from yer family?"

He knew he'd hit on the problem right off. Her gaze shuttered, then she looked away. He tipped her chin up. "Josie, listen to me. I know this must be overwhelming to you, but I have faith that you were chosen wisely."

She pulled from his grasp, or tried to. "There won't be a baby, Connal." He let her go then and she stumbled back a few paces. She found her balance, then stood her ground firmly. Pushing the hair from her face, she sighed, and said, "I'm sorry, that's not how I wanted to say that. I know you have a great deal riding on this."

It's not all about that, he'd been about to say, then stopped when he realized it. What in the blazes was wrong with him this morning? "What do you mean, about the baby?" He moved closer, but she backed away, hand raised against him. The prickle of alarm became a full-fledged taste of fear. "Nothing happened to ye, did it? Josie, you must tell me. Is that why ye left my bed? Did something happen this morning?" Could something go wrong so quickly? He didn't think so, but his knowledge in this area was sorely limited. Maybe there was some way to—

"I wanted to tell you last night," she said, mercifully interrupting his careening thoughts, "but you looked so happy, so . . . well, blissful is the only word I can think of to describe it. I—I didn't want to ruin that." She looked down at the sand, pushing her toes into it. "And maybe I didn't want to ruin the rest of the night for myself either." She nudged the sand again. "So there."

If he wasn't so concerned and confused, he might have smiled at that last part. That she'd enjoyed herself and hadn't wanted the evening to end pleased him greatly. Too greatly perhaps, but that was for examination at another time. "What was there to tell me?" He stepped forward then, but again she shielded herself from his touch. That stung him almost as much as her previous declaration had pleased him. "Tell me now, Josie," he demanded, perhaps a bit more stridently than was prudent.

"I started my period this morning."

He flinched despite himself. He didn't have to ask her to explain what she meant, that much he understood. "I see."

"I'm sorry," she said again, every bit as sincere. "But it wouldn't have happened anyway. Just missing one pill wouldn't have made me fertile; besides, it was the wrong time anyway. That's what I was going to tell you last night. I was already at the end of my cycle—"

"Please, enough."

The silence spun out between them as he allowed the full import of her news to sink in. He didn't doubt she spoke the truth and wasn't about to ask for proof even if he did. His heart banged slowly, settling a bit lower in his chest now.

No wee one. No bargain met. He should have been crushed, devastated at having his greatest hope rudely snatched away before he could even fully comprehend all of it. But what filled his mind, and perhaps even some small part of his heart, was a sort of joy. There was no other word for it. Because he realized what else this news meant. He lifted his gaze to hers. He would have to claim her again.

As if she saw the intent in his eyes, she stumbled back, splashing a bit in the seafoam. "Connal, this doesn't mean I'm willing to— We can't—" She kicked at the water, splashing him, but he didn't flinch and continued toward her. She squealed then, turned, and ran off down the beach.

"A chase is it ye want?" he called out.

She spared a glance over her shoulder, but it wasn't fear he saw on her face. Or anger. It was . . . anticipation.

And that was all it took. That wee spark in her eyes. He had the fleeting thought that it would always be so between them, but refused to ponder it. He was too busy racing down the beach after her, his heart suddenly as fleet as his feet.

As if she could feel him near her, she darted up the beach, then back down toward the water, sending him on a merry chase. She squealed again when he lunged for her and barely missed, but she was grinning now. She kicked more water up at him, then again took off running.

He gave chase, surprised to realize the sound of laughter on the wind was his. "Yer mine, Josie," he yelled out. "I'll have ye no matter how fast ye run."

"Oh yeah?" she tossed over her shoulder, then darted straight out into the water.

He thought his heart simply stopped inside his chest when she dived cleanly into the waves. Without a second thought, he was in the water after her. He dived through the first wave, surfaced . . . and didn't see her.

He turned about, looked at the shore to see if she'd ridden in with the surf. Nothing. He spun back around. "Josie, where are you?" Real alarm filled him when she didn't surface and there was no bairn to conveniently place the blame on this time. "Josie!"

He felt a tapping at his back and whirled about. "Thank God. Dinna ever give me a fright such as that ag—"

"Tag. You're it." She was smiling up at him one moment, then gone beneath the foam the next.

"Josie!" he thundered, no longer in the mood to play games. "Come back here."

Her head bobbed up a surprising distance away. "Make me," she said, then disappeared again.

Damn the woman. Did she think him part seal?

Chasing her down the beach was one thing, but he was not going to flounder about in freezing-cold water after her. He'd had enough of this. He climbed toward the beach.

He was almost out of the water when he heard the strangest sound behind him. Like a chicken cluck-ing. He turned and found Josie, who was several yards down the beach and waist deep in the water, flapping her arms and making that ridiculous noise.

"Whatever are you doing?"

She merely continued, backing away from him as he walked toward her.

"I demand that you leave the water this minute."

Her eyebrows lifted at that and he swore under his breath, remembering the consequences for giving her orders. But he'd be damned before he'd beg. And he was *not* going back into the water.

She stopped clucking and skated her hand across the top of the water, sending a sheet of it directly at him. "Come on, you were so close. Don't give up now."

"When you are cold enough, you will come out."

She smiled and shook her head, as if he were a par-ticularly dull-witted lad. "Oh, I don't mean close to catching me. I could have you chasing me for hours."

She lowered her arms then and he got his first glimpse of just how perfectly transparent the water had left her white shirt. And how pebbly hard the water had rendered her nipples. Hours, he thought. Nay, he'd catch her instantly, then spend those hours delighting in making her pay for her little es-capade. He imagined they'd both enjoy that a great deal more than this ridiculous game.

"What I meant was that you were almost close to having fun." She folded her arms across her, at-tempting to hide the fact that she was shivering.

"Ye'll catch your death. Come out of the water."

"Why did you stop? Didn't you ever play in the waves as a boy?"

"Josie."

"Answer me and I'll come out."

He sighed. "There was no time. I was in training."

She gaped, then said, "What could a small boy possibly need training for? It's not like you were next in line for the clan throne or anything."

She almost got a flicker of a smile with that. Never once had he thought any of those years something to smile about. "There was no throne, that's for royalty. I was being trained to fight. Second sons and any who came after were to be soldiers."

"I got that from what you told me before. But surely they didn't expect some little five-year-old to—"

"I've answered your question, now come out of there," he interrupted, not at all liking the fact that she was championing the boy he had once been. When she stood her ground, he swore. " 'Tis the way things were done, like it or no'." She didn't budge. "Och, ye drive a man mad, Josie."

She grinned at that. But didn't move.

He surrendered. "Aye then, I suppose there might have been a time or two that I wasted an afternoon away playing at swords. Is that what ye so badly needed to hear?"

"Playing at swords, huh?" She shook her head, but began to wade toward the beach. "That's not exactly what I meant, but I suppose it'll do."

He moved toward her, to do what exactly he wasn't aware. He was simply drawn to her. But she moved beyond his reach, plucking her shirt from her skin and wringing out the excess water.

"Ye should get out of those wet things."

She snorted. "You wish." She bent to wring out the legs of her pants, which were pushed up beyond her knees once more. "It's a bright, sunny day. I'll dry out quick enough." Done with her chore, she set off again down the beach, without even so much as a look in his direction.

Once he got over the shock of being so roundly dismissed, he frowned. He'd not chase after her a moment more today, nor would he beg for her company. He would return to his tower. She'd come to him at some point, as she had before. All he had to do was wait. He bit back an oath.

Lord, but he was tired of waiting.

She bent down then and retrieved something from the sand. "Connal, come here. Look at this."

Thinking she'd found something of import—and refusing to acknowledge the deep sigh of relief her summons had wrung from him—he went to her. Grudgingly, or so he hoped to appear. "What is it?"

She turned, smiling bright as the sun, and showed him her treasure. "Look, I've never seen one like this. What do you call it?"

He frowned. "A seashell. Certainly you have them where you're from."

She rolled her eyes, a habit she was far too fond of around him. "I know it's a seashell. I meant what kind is it, what's its name?"

It was bad enough she made him race about this morning, but he drew the line at being made sport of. "I've never made a study of them," he said dismissively, when in truth he'd never been aware they had specific names.

She didn't seem to care, her attention was already back on the shell. "I'll have to ask Maeve then."

"What is so important about it?"

She looked at him again in that way of hers. "I collect them."

"Shells," he said, certain she must have meant something else.

"Aye," she said with a saucy grin. "It's a hobby. Not that you'd know anything about that," she added dryly.

He shouldn't be offended as he'd never once thought himself in need of adopting some mind-numbing task such as the collecting of shells. "Whatever do you do with them once you've harvested them?" he heard himself ask.

"I put them around. Some are on shelves, some in glass bowls." She shrugged. "They're pretty. I like looking at them."

He took the shell from her fingers and examined it. It was a dull gray on one side and pure white on the other. "Aye, I can see where this would add to the beauty of your surroundings."

She snatched it back. "You wouldn't understand."

He had no earthly idea what made him do it, but he took her arm when she went to turn away, and said, "So help me understand then."

She eyed him warily. "Really?"

"Dinna test my patience. Ye've already made me play the seal today."

"Och, well, we wouldn't want you to have too much fun all in one day, would we?"

"Fun? You call floundering about in ice-cold water fun?"

She poked his chest. "I heard you laugh."

He gripped her finger and held it tightly. "What of it?"

"Didn't it feel good?"

"All I remember is the cold." Which was a lie. Looking down into her shining eyes, all he could remember was how badly he'd wanted her last night. And how he wanted her even more right now.

"Do you have any pockets?"

"I beg your pardon?"

"In that kilt. Pockets?"

He had his sporran strapped about his hips, soggy though it was now. "What are ye in need of holding?"

She slid her hand from his, then took hold of it and turned it palm up. She placed her prized shell in the middle of it, then folded his fingers over it. "This. Don't let it break. It's really a perfect specimen."

As are you, he found himself thinking.

Then she was grabbing his hand and tugging him down the beach. "Josie, really, I—"

She didn't stop. "What, you have business meetings this morning? Something more important to do than brooding in that tower of yours?"

"I dinna brood."

"Ye could hae fooled me," she said in her rapidly improving brogue. "Come on, we're going shell hunting."

"Shell hunting."

"Aye. Give me an hour and I'll show you all the finer points of finding the perfect seashell. We can start a collection for you, dress up those dreary rooms of yours."

"Dreary are they," he said, knowing perfectly well they were that and worse.

"Dreadful," she said, then shot him a teasing look. "Though I rather like that chair."

His entire attitude underwent an abrupt change.

"Oh no you don't," she warned. "Shell hunting." She gripped his hand with determination. "I should never have said that."

He found his own smile then as he let her tug him on down the shore. "Ye were the one spoutin' off about the wonders of playing. I could show you—"

"Oooh! Look." She let go and bent to retrieve yet another shell. It was different in shape, but otherwise looked pretty much the same to him. "Connal, lo—"

He cut off her exclamation with a kiss. He didn't even think about it, he simply had to. She allowed the kiss, but only after a moment did she sigh and lean into it. He broke it off almost immediately, or they'd both be getting sand in places he'd rather they not.

"What was that for?"

Because you're so beautiful, sometimes it makes my heart hurt. She was positively shiny, so full of life, he began to see just how dull and dreary he must seem to her. "Ye want me to enjoy this adventure, then I'll have a kiss every so often, so I remember why I let you drag me about."

"Ah. So it's all about sex, then. Men." She shook her head, but didn't seem overly upset.

"I am that, aye."

"Oh aye, that you are." She simply pushed his chest when he went to take her in his arms again.

He found he liked this kind of playing. The intensity was still there, the aching need, stalking right around them. But between them, her teasing would dissolve any and all frustrations. With nothing more than a quick smile and a wry word she'd push him beyond simple physical awareness until his entire being was engaged, her every breath awaited with barely restrained anticipation. He'd never experienced such a thing, had never known it was possible to feel such a connection to another person.

"I'm not saying I would have traded sex for an hour of shell hunting anyway," she went on, "but you do recall that I told you earlier that I'm having my—"

"Aye, aye, ye dinna have to tell me again." Please God, he added, hoping like hell the sun didn't highlight the color rushing to his face. She laughed then and he scowled, which somehow comforted him as it was the role he was most familiar playing with her.

"So, are you going to stalk off now that you can't have what you want?" It was a dare pure and simple.

And she had no idea what he wanted. Hell, at the moment he was beyond reasoning it out himself. But there was no ignoring that glint in her eye. Swearing silently, he took her hand in his and set off down the beach at what could only be termed a march. "Shell hunting we go."

"Oh please, your enthusiasm is simply too much."

He shot her a look. "Ye'll do well to take yer victory without gloating."

She made a face and sketched a bow, awkward as it was with him all but dragging her down the beach. "Aye, my lord. Anything you say, my lord."

He said nothing as she fell into step beside him. After a while, she wove her fingers through his. When he looked down at her, she simply smiled up at him, then turned her attention back to the sand. No, he'd certainly never experienced anything like her.

Perhaps there was something to this "having fun" after all, though the joy in collecting flotsam still eluded him. But he left his hand joined to hers as they continued their hunt.

Chapter 16

T he suits'll be here on the next ferry. They guaranteed it." Dougal's eyes gleamed with excitement as he told Josie the news.

The ferry. Her one means of escape. Funny how she'd forgotten all about that. "When will that be?" she asked, leaning her bike against the wall outside Maeve's store. She'd promised to stay and teach them to surf and she would keep her promise. That was all it was. *Liar.*

"Two days from now."

"And the next one after that?"

Dougal's smile faded a bit, but he squared his shoulders and tried to maintain the enthusiasm he'd shown only moments before. "That's the thing, Josie. They're predictin' another storm by week's end and so . . ."

"And so?" she prompted when his gaze drifted down to his feet.

"Like as not it'll be delayed again." He looked back up at her, hurrying on. "But that will give us a chance to test out some bigger waves, aye? With our instructor still here to guide us."

"I still can't believe you guys are going to all this trouble and expense on a lark. What if you hate surfing?"

He shrugged, that charming glint in his eye. "I suppose we go back to sheep hoisting."

They both laughed, then Josie said, "Still, Dougal, I—"

"Och, dinna worry so about the whims of old men, lass. We know what we're about." He took her hand in his bony, but surprisingly strong ones. "We're all so very grateful to ye for staying on. I know 'tis a lot to ask of ye, but you're making the bunch of us verra happy, Josie." He grinned again and pumped his fist. "We're stoked."

That made her laugh again. "Stoked, huh. You've been on the Internet again, haven't you?"

"Aye," he nodded proudly. "We're hopin' to rip the back end wide open we are."

She stifled a sigh, then shook her head. Charming indeed. There was no way she could change her mind, and truth be told, she didn't want to. She'd never seen such enthusiastic and willing pupils, and despite their age and fragile bones, she thought their determination alone would see them go the distance. So she'd be stuck on the island another week or so. Somehow she wasn't as upset by the notion as she would have been a day earlier.

She smiled to herself. Connal never had quite gotten the hang or even general principle of shell collecting, but he'd tried . . . or put up with her making him try, and that had meant a lot to her. Enough that she'd woken up this morning sort of hoping to see him. Instead she'd woken to smoke filling the kitchen and had a nice burned breakfast compliments of Chef Bagan.

Connal had disappeared after their shell hunt, he'd been strangely subdued on their walk back and hadn't popped up again all day. She'd found herself looking often toward the tower during her surf lessons that afternoon, but there'd been no sign of him. She hadn't felt him watching her either. It had been oddly disappointing. She'd intended to question Bagan when she got back to the croft after her lessons were finished, but he'd been scarce as well, until this morning's breakfast fiasco.

When Connal hadn't shown up during this morning's beachcombing walk, she'd decided he'd figured she wasn't worth the trouble of being around, seeing as he couldn't seduce her into bed. It was insulting and more than a bit hurtful to have to face the fact that that was still all she was to him. After their beach walk, she'd sort of thought, maybe, it was more than that. That maybe they could actually be friends as well as lovers.

She'd decided to get out of there for a while and take the bike into town. It was a gorgeous day, bright sunshine and the wind was balmy. She'd marveled again at the stark beauty of Glenmuir, thinking she'd never tire of seeing its green hills and heather carpets. She also marveled that her backside had apparently become seasoned, because it was barely numb after the jarring ride.

"I'll go tell the boys yer here," Dougal said. "Are ye coming in for an ale?"

"I've got to see Maeve first, then I'll be over. I need to work out a deal with Roddy."

Dougal's expression clouded. "Deal?"

"Don't worry, it's not about the surfing. But if I'm going to be here that much longer, I'm going to need to use his scanner and Internet connection on occasion to send my work back home."

"You've been designing?" His face split wide. "Is it our board then? The one ye were talkin' about?"

She couldn't hide her grin. He really was simply too adorable. "Well, not exactly." Although she had done some preliminary sketches. But she wasn't ready to show them yet. "I've actually got several ideas started, but I need to get some input from my father, see what he thinks."

Dougal nodded. "Aye then, I'm certain Roddy can be accommodatin' of that for ye." He leaned in and winked, "We're all a bit anxious. Ye'll have to forgive us. This is the most fun we've had since—"

"Old Bidda Stewart's sheep?"

"Aye, I believe this ranks right up there. Possibly surpasses it." Nodding happily as he reflected on it, he tipped his hat and disappeared into the pub.

Josie shook her head, no longer bothering to wonder how she'd gotten caught up in this. She had a definite soft spot in her heart for all of them. It would be hard to leave them after all this, she thought, then shook her head and laughed. She'd probably find them posting on some surfing bulletin board online. Who knows, they might even start a cult following and get other surfers out here to their beach. Nothing would surprise her with that crew.

She pushed into the store and waited for Maeve to come out from the back.

"So nice to see you, Josie," she said with a bright smile. "What can I do for ye?"

"I guess you heard about the gear coming in." She expected Maeve to roll her eyes and snort, so she was surprised when she nodded avidly, a conspiratorial gleam entering her eyes as she leaned over the counter.

"Oh aye, that I have. What the men don't know is that I went on Roddy's computer and sort of added to their order a bit."

Josie raised her eyebrows. "Oh?"

"Oh, indeed." She pulled a piece of folded computer paper from her apron. "I've been wantin' to show ye this." She unfolded it and laid it on the counter. "What do you think? Too flash?"

Josie looked at the bright blue-and-yellow neoprene suit Maeve had picked out for herself and swallowed hard. "Um, no, no, not at all." She looked up and smiled. "The blue will bring out your eyes."

Maeve flushed with pleasure. "I've been hopin' to catch you. I was going to drive out later today and ask about getting a private lesson or two." She hurried on as she folded the paper once again and carefully put it back in her apron. "I know you're busy here, what with your work and the boys comin' by, but . . ." She finally trailed off and gave Josie a lift of her shoulders and a hopeful look.

"You're serious?"

She nodded. "The boys shouldn't have all the fun, now, should they?"

Josie simply gave up and nodded. "I'd be glad to work with you." She grinned. "After all, we women surfers have to stick together in this sport."

Maeve's face broke into a wide grin. "Aye," she said with a relieved laugh. "Aye, that we do." She darted a gaze to her hands, which were fiddling with the hem of her apron, then glanced nervously back to Josie. "I don't suppose ye'd be willin' to take on maybe another student or . . . or two. Posey Sutherland and Bidda Stewart were thinkin' they'd like to see what the fuss is all about." Her eyes twinkled even as her cheeks flushed. "Yer lessons have become quite the talk of the island."

Josie swallowed hard. "Really?"

"Oh aye. Yer almost a celebrity, especially staying out on the coast road, all reclusive." She leaned forward, "Lends an air of mystery to ye, ye know." She laughed. "Shame it never did the same for old Gregor."

Josie laughed lightly, a bit stunned by this news. She couldn't help but wonder what would have happened if anyone had happened to drive down to see her when she and Connal had been frolicking in the waves. She frowned then, wondering if anyone but she could see him. They'd have thought her more a loony than a celebrity if they'd seen her splashing about and talking to no one.

Maeve's smile faded. "Yer no' angry with me, are ye?"

Josie smiled immediately, even if her thoughts were still a bit confused on the whole matter. "No, no, not at all. Like I said, we women have to stick together. By all means bring them by if they want to come." Then she realized and said, "Did you say Bidda Stewart? Is she—"

"Aye, that's the one." Maeve's face was flushed with pleasure. "Just imagining the looks on the boys' faces is all she talks about." She spun about. "Oh, this is the best news!" Josie thought she might do a little jig right then and there. She flashed her a twinkling smile. "Ye've brought spark to this place, Josie, that ye have."

Now it was Josie's turn to flush. "I really don't want to disappoint anyone, I'm just—"

"Just be yourself, lass. I'm no' trying to embarrass ye. I only wanted ye to know we've come to enjoy yer sunny smile. Perhaps it's the spirit of youth transforming us all." Before Josie could respond to that, she winked and said, "So, what can I get you?"

Maeve's heartfelt enthusiasm was a bit overwhelming, but there was no denying it made her feel good. "Since I'll be staying on a bit longer, I need to get some more supplies for my pantry." She didn't mention that Bagan had gone through most of what she'd already bought. How a man could ruin not one can of soup, but six of them, and so badly, she didn't know, but the dwarf had managed it. And that had been after losing all the eggs. She'd kindly, but firmly, barred him from the kitchen from then on.

"Not a problem," Maeve was saying, "you just load up what you need and I'll drive it around when I come later."

"Great. Thanks." Josie took the basket Maeve handed her, then paused. "Um, there is one other thing. I need to have a prescription filled. How do you go about doing that here?"

Concern filled Maeve's face. "Are ye feeling poorly? Have ye been ill?"

"Oh no, no. Nothing like that. I, um, it's not—" She gave up and just spit it out. "It's for birth control pills."

Maeve looked momentarily nonplussed, then smiled, apparently relieved it was nothing serious. "We have an apothecary on the island. Old Drummond, though he's usually out fishing this time of day. But he doesna have that sort of thing in stock, I'm certain." She smiled ruefully. "I dinna think there are any ladies left on Glenmuir who have to worry about such a thing any longer." She paused and sort of sighed, then shook it off and smiled again. "I'm certain we can fax the information over to Dunegan's on the mainland and get him to include it in our next parcel post. I'll have Clive make certain it gets to the ferry. He's a good one, Clive."

Josie sighed in relief and said a silent prayer of thanks to Clive. "Thanks."

Maeve winked. "We women surfers have to stick together. I'll see that it gets done while ye do your shopping."

Josie finished up and went to Roddy's next, where she made a call to the car rental place to extend her rental—which the boys overheard and promptly demanded to help her pay for, despite her assurances that it wasn't necessary—then had a talk with Roddy about using his computer to e-mail her father. A glass of lemonade and a hearty bowl of stew later and she was back on her bike, smiling and actually looking forward to Maeve and her friends coming for their first lesson later on.

It was amazing how quickly she'd become a part of island life, and how fond she'd grown of the place. She found herself wishing Connal had simply been some sort of reclusive Scot she'd met while on holiday and decided to have a wild fling with. In that case, this would have been the perfect vacation. And she wouldn't find herself brooding over him, she thought, then shook off the thought and laughed at the idea of fitting Bagan into her simple vacation scenario.

"The odd, but endearing sidekick," she murmured, then smiled and shook her head at her fantasies as she bumped over the last part of the path leading to the croft. Apparently her butt had only toughened up enough for a one-way journey as she began envisioning in great detail the warm bath she'd be taking this evening.

The tower loomed ahead as she rounded the last bend. She tried not to look at it as she pedaled toward the driveway, but couldn't prevent one little glimpse to see if there was any movement in the tower. She scolded herself for being disappointed to find the portals dark. There was no dark-cloaked figure striding up the beach either.

"Of course, why should he bother since he knows he can't get laid," she muttered harshly as she turned to let herself into the cottage. Mad at herself for still harboring hurt feelings when she shouldn't care one whit about him, she almost tripped over the basket someone had set on the porch stairs. "Bagan," she muttered under her breath as she managed to hop past it without falling and breaking a leg or an arm, "one of these days, buddy, one of these days. Pow, straight to the moon."

She half expected the imp to show up and gently worm his way back into her good graces and was only partially relieved when he didn't. She turned to look at the basket, wondering why in the hell he'd put it there, then stilled completely.

Her throat tightened a bit. "Shells," she whispered, then knelt by the basket, only wincing slightly at the ache of protest in her backside. She picked up first one, then another. There was a jumble of them, all shapes and sizes, some whole, some only in parts. She felt the pressure build behind her eyes as she looked again toward the tower. It was still dark and there was no sign of him.

She looked back to the basket of shells and let out a long, slow breath. Had he really gone shell hunting for her? She sorted through the pile again, immensely touched even though she tried to tell herself she shouldn't be. Hadn't she just gotten done telling herself he was a sexist pig jerk out for only one thing? So what if it was a three-hundred-year-old bargain made with the gods and not just about getting his rocks off? And so what if physical gratification was all she'd hoped to get out of the deal? Didn't that make her a sexist pig jerk, too?

"That's different," she mumbled, knowing it was nothing of the sort. She sighed again. She'd already admitted it had turned into something more for her. But what? Friendship? It wasn't as if she could have a future with him. Looking at his peace offering, had she really believed she could befriend him and leave the physical part of their relationship behind? Had she really believed he'd accept that? That she could?

She scooped up the basket and headed inside. Only

to be shocked again. The croft smelled of jasmine, and candlelight flickered from the second floor.

This time her eyes narrowed and she didn't feel that short wash of pleasure over her skin. "So this isn't a token of friendship," she said out loud. "It's a seduction." She sighed and set the basket down, trying not to be disappointed. Would she ever learn? "Well, you should have saved yourself the trouble," she called up the stairs. "I already told you I'm off the seduction list for a few days. And after that I'm simply not interested." It was a total lie. Even though she was miffed that he thought he could just come in here, set the scene, and get her to fall gratefully into bed with him again, there was a part of her that wanted to do exactly that.

"Yeah, the part that's gotten addicted to screaming orgasms," she muttered. "Well, you're just going to have to get over it," she told herself. To him, she called out, "I'm not coming up there, so you might as well put the candles and yourself out."

Nothing. Not a sound, not a word.

"Fine." She was hungry, starved even, so she went to the kitchen to see if there was anything left to eat since she'd left all her groceries with Maeve. She had some crackers and a bite of cheese, pretending she didn't remotely care that there was probably a naked man waiting for her upstairs. He was going to grow old waiting, she decided, then shook her head. One thing Connal could never do was grow old.

Which, when she thought about it, had its upside. Imagine a lover who never aged, she found herself thinking, her body reacting favorably to the suggestion. "Oh for heaven's sake." She slammed the cheese down, as disgusted with herself as she was with him, and marched up the stairs, determined to put an end to this whole thing right now.

Only he wasn't up there. And looking at her bed, it appeared he'd never been up there. It was still the same tangle of sheets and mushed-up pillows she'd left this morning. She spun around, looking for the source of the flickering candlelight, only to discover it was coming from the tiny bathroom.

"A ha! The old 'take her in the shower' trick. And apparently it's a really old trick if they were trying that even in your day. Why am I not surprised?" She stalked into the bathroom . . . only to find it empty as well. "Humph." She didn't know what to think. Several candles were grouped on the edge of the sink, another one or two occupied the narrow shelf that hung on the wall just above the tub. The tub was an old claw foot, deep and narrow, and presently filled with water. She tested it. Warm. Perfectly so.

She dried her hand on her shorts, totally stumped now. Had Bagan done this? She snorted. No way. The croft would have burned to cinders by now. Or flooded.

She sat down on the toilet seat lid and simply stared at the whole display. "What does this mean?"

Then she saw the note. It was a sheet of what looked like heavy vellum. She picked it up and realized it had been torn from her sketchbook. He'd looked through her sketchbook? Warmth that had nothing to do with the steamy air flushed her cheeks. She'd done more than sketch Dougal and gang in her book. She might have done, oh, one or two little sketches of Bagan. And maybe a few more than that of Connal. What had he thought of them?

Hell, she didn't even know how she felt about them.

She unfolded the paper to find several lines of dark, slashing script. Some of the letters were oddly formed, so it took her several tries to decipher it.

The water is to soak in. How ye survive riding that contraption of Gregor's I'll never know.

Then there were several words that had been scratched out, followed by:

I hope the shells are up to your standards. I still dinna see the need to keep them lying about. Maybe now ye can leave the rest alone.

And then it was signed, *Yours, Connal.*

Yours.

Is that what he truly felt? Or did he only think so because his gods told him so? And why should she care? She went to fold the note, but stopped and read his words again. She smiled. *Not exactly a love note, Josie.* And yet her heart dipped a little anyway.

This thing between them—whatever the hell it was—should feel wrong. Or at the very least dangerous. She'd fantasized about this being a highland fling. Only he wasn't anything so simple as that. She was messing with things, elements of nature, or whatever, that she didn't really understand. She should end it, completely. In fact, if she were smart, she'd leave the island on the next ferry, surf lessons or no surf lessons.

Did she honestly think she could keep pretending this was simply a slightly unusual vacation? Pretend that because she'd fallen in love with the people here, that the rest would somehow magically turn out okay? Because whatever she did or didn't believe about Connal's gods and his bargain with them, much less her role in all of it, the fact remained he wasn't mortal. And really, who in the hell knew what would happen to her if she kept fooling around?

She put the note on the sink by the candles, then pulled the lever for the plug so the water would drain.

She needed to think . . . and figure out what she was going to do. And the best place to do that was out on the water, or walking next to it. Since she was going to surf later when Maeve got here, she opted for walking. Besides, she was just distracted enough that she'd probably end up on the rocks if she took her board out now.

She grabbed her sketch pad and stuck a few pencils in her pocket, thinking if walking didn't do the trick, maybe she'd find a quiet spot and let her mind drift while her hand moved across the paper.

And yet, even as she left the house and started off down the shore, she had the feeling that her tried-and-true methods of dealing with her problems weren't going to help her today. But then, she'd never quite faced problems like the ones she was dealing with now.

۶

Connal stood in the tower and watched her retreating figure. Something was wrong. Hadn't she liked his gestures? Dammit, he wasn't good at this sort of thing, but he'd made the effort, hadn't he? And what exactly was he trying to do?

Go to her.

He shouldn't have left her alone, but he'd been confused by the things she'd made him feel yesterday. He'd needed the time to think. And then today she'd been gone and he hadn't been able to get her out of his mind. He'd found himself wanting to do something for her, show her . . . what?

He swore and spun away from the window. This was all getting far too complicated for him.

Go to her. But it was clear she wanted to be alone. She'd taken the drawing pad with her.

His body heated as he recalled the sketches she'd made of him . . . and how it had made him feel. She was quite talented, but it wasn't pride in her skills he'd felt. No, it had been something far more primal.

What had she been thinking as the ink spilled from her pen, taking the form of his face, his body? She'd drawn the tower, too, only as it had been during the storm. Raging waters, windswept beaches, lightning splitting the dark skies. Aye, she drew with passion. Just as she did everything else.

His body tightened further and he swore as he spun away from the window. This shouldn't be so damn hard. He should know what to do.

Go to her.

Chapter 17

*A*s always, she felt him before she saw him. She flipped her sketch pad shut, not that there was anything to hide. Her pencil hadn't made one move across the paper. Her thoughts were just as stuck.

"Hello," she said, keeping her gaze out to sea.

He didn't say anything for several long, tension-filled moments. She was just about to look up at him, when he said, "Can I sit wi' ye?"

Surprised that he'd asked, she still managed a shrug. "It's a public beach. At least, I think it is. You can do whatever you like." Feigning indifference was difficult enough when she'd spent the past hour thinking of nothing else but him. But when he sat down next to her, his body radiating that energy it always seemed to give off, well, it took all her remaining willpower to keep her gaze calm and unaffected when her own body was anything but.

He didn't say anything for several minutes, just studied the water. Until finally he heaved an impatient sigh, and blurted out, "So, what exactly did I do wrong? I thought ye'd be pleased with the bath I drew for ye. I was only trying to show you—" He broke off and swore under his breath. "Never mind, I dinna ken what I was trying to do."

"You didn't do anything wrong," she said quietly.

"Then why did ye leave?" He motioned to her pad. "Yer not even drawing."

She turned to look at him finally, and as always, looking at him made her insides jump. Only this time her heart was doing a little leap of its own, as well. He looked too damn good. Strong, sexy . . . and endearingly confused. But rather than get angry and stomp off, he was here, trying to figure things out. And isn't that what she wanted, too?

"You looked at my sketches. They weren't public property."

"Ah, so that's it then. I suppose I should apologize for intruding. But I won't."

She raised her eyebrows. "Won't you?"

He shook his head, the wind whipping his long hair back from his face. "Nay. I was only looking for paper to leave a note, but once I saw what you'd drawn, I couldn't put it back down." He paused, looking more intently at her in that way he had, the way that made her feel like she was the only one in his universe. "It was a part of you, and I find myself drawn to learning all I can about you. This was a part I didn't know."

"And now you think you know me?" She was gripping her pencil so hard she thought it would snap. "Because you looked at a few drawings."

"I didna say that. Perhaps it was but a tiny peek inside yer mind, to how ye see the world. And me."

She couldn't contain the little shiver that raced over her. "And how do you think I see you?"

"Like a man. A lover." There was a touch of awe in the words, and he looked at her again. "Your lover."

The shudder of pleasure was stronger this time and she told herself it was a good damn thing it was the wrong time of the month. "You are both of those things," she said, if a bit shakily.

"Aye, but if asked to describe myself, those are the last two things I'd have applied. I am laird first, last, and always. Never something as simple as a man, never something as selfish as a lover."

"Why is it selfish to love?" She waved a hand when his eyes darkened, ignoring that sudden rush it gave her to imagine, even for a blink of time, that she would ever hear words of love from him. When he looked at her like that, it was all too easy to— "Surely your people didn't expect all your devotion to belong to them alone or that you didn't deserve any personal pleasure. Your father did, your grandfather, and his father loved."

Now Connal looked away, that dark look of passion that had filled his eyes at the mention of the word love going flat and empty. "I was no' as fortunate as them, to have the luxury of a life that could include both commitment to my people, and to a family."

She thought about that, tried to imagine what it would feel like to carry such an immense burden, and couldn't. "Maybe you should have anyway," she ventured carefully. "Maybe it would have symbolized hope to your people, that you'd found happiness."

He sighed then, the deep, almost-anguished sigh of a man who'd spent too many years analyzing his every action. "That's what I was doing by sending the stone out." He looked down at his hands, then back up at her. " 'Twas no' only my people I had to please, Josie, but the gods as well."

Josie shook her head. "I'm sorry. I know you believe that with your whole heart. I guess I just don't believe in that higher purpose or plan. Not like you do anyway. I think we're supposed to make our own destiny, that we have some hand in our fate."

"My brothers thought that and almost destroyed us all." He picked up a broken piece of shell and skipped it across the water. "Beliefs might be different now. But I can only act on what I believe in, what I know to be true as I see it."

"And maybe," she said, very softly, "what was meant to be was that your clan didn't survive. What if that was supposed to be their fate, their destiny? And yet, you didn't accept that. You fought it just like you think I'm fighting it now." She sighed. "I guess I'm just confused."

He picked up another shell, then tossed it back down and shifted so he faced her fully. "So am I."

"About which thing?"

"The bargain I made. The destiny I tried to thwart. Maybe it wasna meant to be. Maybe you are right and this is all some sort of grand entertainment, a celestial play for the gods, with me cast as the fool."

"You don't really believe that."

He took her hand in his, looking at it as he ran his wide fingers over her slender ones. "No, I don't." He tipped his gaze up to hers. "Because I look at you and I know that I did the right thing in bargaining, that my belief in the stone was right. Perhaps things do happen as they do for a reason, Josie. Perhaps the stone was lost at sea because you were the only one intended for me . . . and it had to wait for ye, as did I."

Her heart began to thunder like the pounding of heavy surf. "Connal, I—"

He turned her hand over and lifted it to his lips, placing a heartbreakingly gentle kiss in the center of her palm, then curling her fingers inward as if to hold on to the promise of it. "I know ye dinna feel as I do," he said, "and I canna force you. Nor can I blame ye." He let go of her hand and she felt such a sense of loss, of abandonment, that she had to fight the urge to clutch at him again.

"But I do feel . . . something," she said. "I just can't

make the giant leap from what I feel, whatever that is, to bearing a child. It's too—" She waved a hand helplessly.

"I know that. Which is why I came to ye."

Stunned by the admission, she could only look at him.

"I have been focused only on the outcome, as you pointed out, forcing the destiny I've bargained for, waited for, on us both, with little thought to anything else. But, lately, I . . . I find myself thinking about my own wants and needs. And I find myself wondering about your wants and needs, too." He paused and looked away, then blew out a shaky breath before looking her directly in the eye. "So I've decided that the only way to deal with this is to have faith in the Fates' grand design. The stone brought ye here. If I'm to trust its choice, I have to trust it all the way and stop pushing. Ye'd think one thing I'd have learned after three hundred years is patience, but this is no' easy for me." He sighed heavily. "In fact, 'tis the most difficult thing I've ever done. But if the rest is meant to be, it will come to pass. Pushing harder willna make it so."

"Meaning what?"

He lifted a shoulder, but his eyes betrayed the tension he felt. "Meaning I will leave ye alone to take those pills as ye wish. Or the ferry, if that is yer plan. I willna stop you from leaving."

"Even if it means that you waited all this time for nothing?"

His expression filled with some emotion she couldn't describe. The corners of his mouth curved just a bit. "I already know I didna wait for nothing," he said quietly.

Josie didn't know what to say. Much less what to feel.

"I'll leave ye to yer drawings," he said then, and started to get to his feet.

She grabbed at his arm. "Wait, wait."

He slid her hand from his arm and stood anyway, looking down at her with the late-afternoon sun at his back. "Ye know where to find me if ye want me." And in the next blink, she was staring at the sun and nothing more.

Josie squinted and looked away. "Damn. Damn, damn, damn." She slid the sketch pad to the sand beside her and dropped her head to her hands, raking her fingers through her hair as she tried to make sense of everything that had just happened.

He'd come to set her free. Let her off the hook. "Say good-bye," she whispered. Her heart clutched at the mere thought of never seeing him again, and yet she knew he wouldn't appear to her now unless she purposely sought him out.

Did she want to?

Hell yes, she wanted to, she thought. And that wasn't only her body talking. She felt like she'd finally begun to know him, dammit, and she wasn't ready to walk away yet.

Which meant what? Pursuing him now, unless she was intending to fulfill his desire to have an heir, was unfair to him. And possibly her as well, since she'd likely only come to want him more . . . but not necessarily the rest of the package deal. So he'd done the right thing, cut them both loose of this bargain. He was letting Fate guide its own course. If he lost everything, so be it.

Which really pissed her off. Dammit, she wanted him to fight for what he wanted. *Her?* No, she thought immediately. The baby was what he was fighting for. Wasn't it? But that was what he thought he was *supposed* to be fighting for. What she meant was that he should be fighting for what *he* truly wanted, for his own heart, his own needs, the hell with the clan and his supposed obligations to them.

Which brought her back to what it was she thought he truly wanted. *Her?*

"No," she muttered, "that's just what *you* want him to want." She groaned and flopped back on the sand. She was a hopeless head case.

"And so what if he does, Josie," she said out loud, her words whipped away by the breeze. "What if he does decide he wants you, the rest be damned? He's a freaking three-hundred-year-old ghost. Not the best prospect for a long, enduring relationship." Not to mention difficult to explain to friends and family.

She laughed. Yeah, she'd become that crazy old woman who lived alone in the croft, ranting on about her secret ghost lover. Which brought up the whole complication of her aging while he stayed forever young.

"Argh!" *Enough of this torture*, she told herself. She rolled to her feet, brushed herself off, and grabbed her sketch pad. She had surf lessons to give shortly. That was about all she could handle at the moment. "At least I'll be dealing with mortals."

❧

Josie ended up being very thankful for her mortal friends. They were the only reason she made it through the following couple of days without losing what was left of her already admittedly shaky mind.

Maeve had been an avid pupil, as had her friend, Posey, the one with the shaky marriage. Josie wasn't sure learning to surf was going to help in that department much, but that wasn't any of her business.

Her star student, however, had been the surprising old Mrs. Stewart. And old was the mildest of adjectives one could use to describe this woman. Her wrinkles had wrinkles. Josie's initial reaction on seeing her climb out of Maeve's car had been to call off the whole thing. This woman wouldn't last one second out there and no way was Josie going to be responsible for putting her into an early grave. Early being a somewhat subjective term. But still, she wasn't going to be a party to it.

Then Mrs. Stewart—or Bidda, as she'd commanded Josie to call her—had plucked Josie's board from its resting place against the side of the croft, propped it up, and toted it on down to the beach as if she was balancing nothing more than a basket on her head. It was only when she'd barked at Maeve and Posey to stop standing about, wasting her class time, that Josie had snapped her mouth shut and moved.

Maeve had given her a helpless shrug, to which Josie could only nod in understanding. Apparently no one stopped Bidda from getting what she wanted. She'd had to hide a small smile as she'd followed the ladies down to the shoreline, thinking that next time the boys decided to hoist some of Bidda's sheep, she might actually be willing to help them out.

She did smile now as she stood on the ferry dock and watched the boat draw closer. The boys, as she'd come to think of them, were all crowded at the edge, as if their anxiousness could will the boat to go faster. She couldn't deny that there was still some small part of her that wanted to get on that ferry and get as far away from here as possible, escape the endless thoughts of Connal and what he wanted and what she wanted . . . and what fate could possibly have in store for them.

But the larger part of her couldn't imagine leaving

here. For the first time she felt like a vital part of the community, rather than the reclusive artist-slash-surfer.

She'd never really meant to become reclusive, being a social enough person. She supposed after all the traveling and hopping about the globe she'd done, she'd just enjoyed the solitude, the peace and quiet that allowed her to create. She had friends, other surfers mostly. She hung out with them on occasion, though she guessed she'd term the friendships fairly casual. Of course, she had her dad and his crew. They were family to her, and Parker's Inlet as normal a home as she'd ever had. She was happy, fulfilled. She'd never really given any thought to being more involved, community-wise, or felt that she was missing out on something by staying tucked away in her bungalow.

Until this moment, standing here on this dock, surrounded by a bunch of anxious Scots and feeling just as excited about the shipment of gear as they did.

The boat chugged closer. No, she realized, she was in no hurry to leave this place, these people. Her people. She laughed at that. Her people. God, now she sounded like Connal. But she hadn't meant it that way, she just felt like she belonged here. *Yeah*, she thought, *among the other eccentrics. I fit right in.*

Dougal turned to her, grinning like a little kid on Christmas morning. "I don't suppose we could bribe ye to give us a real lesson this evening could we?"

"I'll help you go over your gear tonight. You all have to try it on and make sure it fits. Tomorrow morning will come soon enough."

He pouted as she patted him on the arm, then shouts from the boat drew their eyes to the water.

Someone was waving from the deck of the boat and the men were all waving and hollering back. Josie, however, stood rooted to the spot, frozen, certain her eyes were playing tricks on her.

"Wha—?" was all she managed to get past her suddenly tight throat.

Roddy turned to her and gave her a wink. "Now ye see why we brought ye down here. 'Twas no just the gear we had shipped in, but a wee surprise for ye as well, Josie lass."

She'd half suspected something of the sort was going on, but she'd thought it was just the art supplies she'd ordered. She thought maybe they'd gone and done something foolish, like order her a drafting table or something. But this . . . she'd never suspected this. "We?" she squeaked, as her heart bumped, then began pounding furiously.

"I hope yer no' mad at us," Clud said. "He made us keep it a secret."

She looked at them all. Gaped, actually. "You *all* knew?" She looked back to the ferry . . . and the man shouting hello from the deck. Big Griff. Her father. Was here. On Glenmuir. "But how? Why?"

Roddy threw his arm around her shoulders. "I'd only order from the best, and figured who else could I trust but the man who taught our teacher? We got to e-mailing each other and we sort of told him about the lessons ye were going to give us and well, he decided to bring the stuff out personally." He laughed and hugged her. "Dinna be angry wi' us for not tellin' ye."

"I'm—I'm not." And she wasn't. She was too shocked to feel anything. Her father. Here. A grin finally split her face and she waved madly back at Griff as the reality finally sunk in.

It seemed to take forever for the ferry to dock.

She was on the ramp even before it was fully secured. "Dad!"

"Josiecat," he said, his big voice booming even over the groan and squeal of the boat being moored.

She was swallowed in his embrace seconds later. "What are you doing here?"

"Well, I thought I'd come meet the merry band of fairies and pixies that had stolen my daughter away from me."

Josie laughed past the brief blink of panic his comment caused. Connal. The charm stone. Bagan. Talk about your fairy magic. But she refused to think about that right now.

"Surfing lessons is it?" He nodded to the group of men clustered at the bottom of the ramp. "To these fine young gents?"

"Now, Dad, you of all people should—"

He laughed. "I'm just teasing you. But I was sort of hoping there'd be at least one under the age of fifty in the group. You know, one you'd be giving more personal lessons to?" He looked down at her, his eyes twinkling.

"Since when have you wanted to play matchmaker with me?"

He hugged her. "Oh, I've always wanted to see you happy, little cat."

She pulled back and looked up at him, honestly surprised. "I am happy."

"You're stuck with a bunch of old people. First me and my crew and now these guys."

"I'm not stuck with anyone. I happen to love you, and I like these guys, too." She grinned. "A tad eccentric, the lot of them," she said with a brogue, then smacked him on the arm before grabbing his hand. "You'll fit right in."

Griff laughed and let her tug him down the ramp,

where introductions took place with a hearty host of slapped backs and shaking of hands. It was like a reunion of old friends and Josie wondered just how long they'd all been e-mailing each other. She shook her head in bemusement and followed as Griff was swallowed up and all but carried off to Roddy's pub, where ales were had and stories shared before finally someone remembered the boxes of gear.

"Dear Lord, we left it all sitting on the dock," Gavin said. "After all this, we went and forgot it."

"No ye didn't."

They all turned to find Maeve standing in the doorway. "It's over in the store. I signed for the lot of it."

Roddy came out from behind the bar and kissed her. "Thanks, love."

She swatted him, but let him kiss her again. "Ye might want to hold off on those kisses until ye see what's in the boxes."

He frowned and the room all but stilled. "What d'ye mean? Is there something wrong with the gear?" He looked to Griff, who just shrugged.

"Shouldn't be," he said. "It's all there as far as I know."

Roddy looked back to his wife. "Maeve?"

She looked to Griff and winked. He winked back. Then she smiled up at her husband. "Yer no' the only one with surprises up your sleeve."

Roddy looked from Griff to Maeve and frowned. "I'm no' thinking I like surprises."

Griff roared with laughter and Maeve flushed furiously and swatted him again with her towel. "Roddy!"

Roddy flushed a bit, too, but laughed as well. "I wasna really worried," he said, pulling her to him. "I know yer a happily married woman."

She let him buss her loudly on the cheek, then said, "Just see as ye keep it that way, laddie."

Roddy's eyebrows lifted as everyone hooted and hollered, then he grinned devilishly, and said, "We'll see to the unpackin', then we'll see to the rest."

Maeve pulled out of his arms then, cheeks dark pink. "Enough of this foolishness," she said, though any fool could tell if she'd been anywhere else she'd have had Roddy right where she wanted him, Josie thought, blushing a bit, too.

She caught her dad grinning at the display in obvious affection and spent a moment wondering why he'd never remarried. She'd asked him more than once, though it had been years since the last time, back when she was a young teen experiencing her first crush. He'd told her then that he'd been blessed with finding his soul mate and although their time together hadn't been for as long as he'd have liked, he was content just knowing such a love could exist.

Funny, she hadn't thought of that in years. She grinned to herself and took another sip of ale. Of course, for all his talk of soul mates, he'd certainly not lived the life of a monk since her mother's death. Far from it. And yet, she thought, as she sipped some more, he had never been remotely serious about any of them.

She supposed that was why she'd been so surprised by his matchmaking comments. Griff had never struck her as the type to worry about that kind of thing. He was much more the type to live for the moment. And he did, with gusto.

She studied him as he got up and followed Roddy and Gavin next door to retrieve the gear boxes. Tall, strong, and still quite handsome if she did say so herself. She'd never once felt sorry for him or thought him to be lonely or unhappy. Had he honestly worried that she might be either of those things?

She was distracted from that train of thought when they came back with the boxes, followed by Maeve and Posey. Josie wished she'd had a camera to capture the expression on the boys' faces when Bidda stepped in behind them.

"Can I help ye, ladies?" Roddy asked, obviously as surprised as the rest and just as obviously hopeful they were here because they'd developed a sudden thirst for an ale.

"No, no," Posey said. "We're here to look at our order."

There was a moment of dead silence, followed by the sound of Dougal clearing his throat. "*Our* order?"

Posey beamed. "Aye."

Roddy looked to his wife, who smiled back at him and said, "That surprise I started to tell ye about before you got all hot to trot."

Josie almost choked on her ale, laughing.

Somehow that sound drew the attention of all four men to her.

"What?" she managed, trying to look completely innocent.

"What have ye to say about this?" Clud demanded.

She sat her tankard down and stood. "I have to say that the ladies have every bit as much right to learn to surf as you all do. I'm an equal opportunity instructor." She winked at Maeve, then turned back to them. "Now why don't we stop all this and have a look at what you bought? I've been waiting all day for this fashion show."

"Fashion show?" Dougal asked, swallowing hard.

"Oh, aye. Only way to see if the gear is proper. Consider it part of your training." She waved at them all. "Dad and I will sit right here while you all go and try your suits on."

"All of us?" Roddy looked from Maeve to Bidda, then back again when she gave him a swift elbow to the ribs.

"All of you."

Chapter 18

O f course, if she kills the lot of them, you won't have a legacy left to worry about," Bagan offered, looking down from the tower at the surf lessons commencing in the swirling waters below.

Connal merely grunted, not up to sparring with the little guardian today. A week had passed since their talk on the beach and she'd yet to come to him. He'd been relieved when the ferry had come and gone and she'd remained, yet there would be another ferry, then another.

He looked to the skies. Though blue and cloudless today, he knew another storm brewed out over the waters and was heading this way. Were the Fates proving he'd done the right thing, that his faith in the stone's promise was being rewarded by stranding her here longer, giving them more time together? He'd struggled long and hard with the decision to leave her be, to trust in that faith that had delivered the stone back to him, along with Glenmuir's future.

But this sitting about and doing nothing was driving him mad. It was one thing to await the stone and his promised one, even for what had felt like eternity, but to stare down upon her, day after day, and trust that it would all work out as he believed . . . as he had to believe—

"Three hundred years to ponder the meaning of it all and ye still are too stubborn to see it." Bagan made a tsking sound and shook his head.

"Too stubborn to see what, Guardian? Am I no' supposed to trust the stone? The gods and Fates have conspired to fulfill the destiny I so dearly bargained for. Surely they wouldna allow her to leave without seeing the rest of the bargain met. The storm on the horizon is proof of their commitment, is it no'?"

Bagan rolled his eyes. "They had no deal wi' ye, Connal, other than to allow yer miserable carcass to haunt this tower waiting on the stone."

"A stone which has been delivered . . . and yet here I remain. If no' for the promise of an heir, then what for?"

"The stone has already delivered on its promise. 'Tis only waiting on you to fulfill it. And yet, here ye sit, doin' nothing to secure it. Yer father and his father before him were smart enough to seize the opportunity provided and make it theirs." He hopped down from the portal ledge and waddled closer. "Your opportunity is finally at hand. And if ye fail in this, ye have no one but yerself to blame."

"But I canno' force myself on her, Bagan. I will no'."

Bagan merely smiled and took Connal's hand. "How many times must I say it? 'Tis not about the babe, laddie. It's about yer heart. And hers. Where the heart goes, the rest will follow."

Connal looked to the tower window, and when he looked back, the imp was gone. He sighed heavily and, thoughts swirling like the black clouds that would soon cross the horizon, his attention was drawn inexorably to the scene below once again. He watched Josie smiling, her father's booming laughter filled the air as well, as they guided the islanders through the vagaries of wave hunting. They were starting in the shallows, which, he thought, was wise. If she could keep them there, perhaps they'd survive this insanity they'd undertaken.

Her father looked to be a hale sort and it was clear there was a deep well of love and respect between them. It caused him a momentary twinge near his own heart. Not for the lack of such a relationship of his own. His father had loved him well and he knew it. The pang came from imagining having such a relationship with his own child . . . and realizing that would never come to be.

But watching her, he knew he could trust her to do it for him. She had the heart and the love for it. And yet she'd told him once that she'd only bear the child of the man she loved.

"So, how do I make you love me enough to bear me a son?" he murmured.

'Tis not about the babe, laddie. 'Tis about yer heart.

Bagan's words floated through his mind. What possible good could come from him gaining her heart? Or losing his own to her? Unlike his father, and his father before him, he was not destined to share a life with her. Wouldn't losing their hearts only bring pain to them both when the inevitable happened and his time here came to an end?

But if she would only commit to bearing the child of one she loved, what other path did he have to travel?

He looked down at her as she helped guide one of the ladies toward a small swell, showing her how to steer the board to the left, then the right. And as he stood there alone, apart from her and the zest and excitement for life that seem to radiate from her every movement . . . he admitted something to himself in the quiet of the tower room. His heart was already compromised.

It was what had made the waiting unbearable, he realized. And worse, despite what he'd said to Bagan and even to himself these past long days, his wanting of her had precious little to do with getting a bairn in her belly. He wished it were so, had tried to will it to be so. But, if he were to be brutal in his honesty, he was actually fearful of that moment ever happening, as it would mean never seeing her, touching her, hearing her, tasting her . . . ever again. There should be guilt to accompany those selfish thoughts and guilt he indeed had. It was the only thing that had kept him in this tower. Yet he could not take his eyes off of her, nor stop thinking about her.

That and the hurt. The hurt he felt because his heart was the only one involved. Care for him she might, enjoy his attentions she did, but she didn't feel for him the depths of emotion he'd come to admit he felt for her.

It shouldn't matter. He was laird first, man last, if at all.

And yet it was the man who stood there and wanted. Wanted like he'd never wanted before. It had nothing to do with his people, or the prosperity he'd bargained his soul to reclaim for them.

It simply had to do with him. Wanting her. And more than that, wanting her to want him back. Not for the pleasure he could give her body . . . but for the pleasure she would have in just being with him. A pleasure he well knew existed, because he felt it every time he looked at her.

Because he knew he was done waiting. Only this time when he left the tower, he didn't leave it as a laird. He left it as a man. A man determined to have his woman's heart. The rest would have to sort itself out.

‰

Josie waved at her father as he and Dougal climbed into Griff's rental car. She'd offered to have her father stay in the croft back when he'd first arrived, even though she could only offer him a couch. Typically, he'd already found himself a place to stay before the fashion show had ended that first night in Roddy's pub. And hadn't that been an evening! She smiled in remembrance of Clud in his neon green-and-black body suit. But the capper of the evening had been Bidda in her bright pink-and-black neoprene. Where she'd found the bright yellow plastic flower she'd somehow adhered to the side of the hood, Josie didn't know. And wasn't sure she wanted to.

But her dad had told her he was taking Dougal's spare bedroom. "We young bachelors prefer to hang together," he'd told her with a grin.

She'd teased Dougal about not initially offering her a place to stay, to which he'd blushed furiously and babbled something about it being unseemly for a young woman to stay with a man alone. If he only knew, she'd thought at the time, about Connal.

But Dougal was obviously thrilled to host their newest guest, so she'd happily waved the two of them off when they'd left the pub that night, just as she did now.

But as she closed the door behind her and turned to look at the croft, she wished she'd been more selfish and had begged her father for some company.

She didn't think she was up to facing another night alone, thinking about Connal. Wanting him. Bewildered at what to do about it.

She'd gotten so desperate she'd even hoped for Bagan to show up, but apparently with all the islanders coming and going at all hours, he'd decided to remain out of sight.

She sighed and climbed the stairs to the loft.

She'd take a shower, then find something to eat, maybe dive into that romance novel she'd been surprised to discover on Gregor's shelves. The clouds had begun to roll in as their lessons had ended for the day. Apparently the storm that had been predicted was going to happen after all.

Her father hadn't said anything about them leaving on the next ferry. In fact, he'd said nothing about leaving at all. He looked to be having quite the time here, so much so that she hadn't had a moment alone with him to ask him about the funeral, or what he was doing a half a world away while his business was left sitting. Well, with the storm coming, they'd have the time now since lessons would likely be called off for at least a day or two and the ferry grounded.

She wanted to tell him about Connal. Ask him for advice. She laughed as she peeled out of her wet suit. Asking her father for relationship advice was like asking Jerry Springer for family counseling. Her laugh softened to a wistful sigh. He had loved her mother, though, so he did know something about it.

She sank down on the edge of the bed. Surely she didn't think she actually loved Connal. She hadn't been with him long enough to have developed that depth of emotion for him. Had she? She'd always thought love was something that came about slowly, evolving over months and years of time spent together.

And yet . . . when she thought about him, her heart raced. And her heart raced often these days. She found herself looking at the tower all the time, hoping for a glimpse of him. A crush, lust, that was what it was. After all, he was gorgeous, virile, great in bed . . .

She sighed wistfully. He also had integrity and

honor, he respected her and her wants and desires, despite the conflict with his own. He was loyal and determined.

And he'd looked at her with those dark eyes of his and told her that waiting three hundred years for her hadn't been in vain.

Her heart swooned anew. She flopped back on the bed and sighed. So maybe she wasn't *in* love with him. Maybe. But she was falling in that direction. Hard and fast.

"So what do I do?" If she went to him, they'd end up in bed at some point. And her pills, despite Maeve's fax, hadn't arrived on the ferry. She certainly couldn't pop into the store and pick up some condoms. Josie snorted as she tried to imagine explaining them to Connal, much less showing him how to use them.

There was a crack of thunder just then and she sprang off the bed. She peeled the rest of her gear off and hopped into the shower while she still had light. Scrubbing her hair and skin, her thoughts strayed right back to Connal. Hearing the rain pounding on the roof made her think of that night in his tower, when they'd made love during the storm.

Made love. She paused under the hot spray, soap running down her body. There was that word again. She'd always been careful to think of it as merely having sex. Really hot sex. Highland fling sex. Never lovemaking. That was something that couples did, people with relationships.

"How in the hell am I supposed to have a relationship with a three-hundred-year-old ghost?"

But the fact of the matter was, she was caring less and less about the immortal aspects of the man in her life. And she knew then that she wasn't spending another night alone in bed, thinking about him. Wanting him. They needed to talk.

She finished rinsing and got out, only then realizing that the part of the pounding she'd been hearing was coming from below, not above. Someone was pounding on her door. Her first thought as she hurriedly pulled on sweats and a T-shirt was that her dad had come back, worried about her. She could tell him—he'd have to know at some point if she was going to continue carrying on with Connal, right?— and get his reaction.

"Dad? Hi, I wanted to talk to you," she practiced saying on the way to the door. "I met this guy and I think I'm falling in love with him. What does he do? Well, see, he haunts this tower, has for three hundred years, and he wants me to have his love child." Yeah, right. She groaned, feeling a headache coming on as she opened the door.

Only, when she flung it open, it wasn't Griff standing there.

"Connal." It was all she could manage.

The storm tossed behind him, the dark castle ruins highlighted as lightning streaked the sky. The pelting rain plastered his dark cape to his shoulders. Rivulets of water ran over a face made more taut by the way his hair had been pulled tightly back from his face.

Her heart pounded harder than the rain, her body leaping with joy even as her mind raced ahead of it.

"Will ye let me in, Josie?"

She backed away, almost stumbling, and motioned him inside.

He took his cloak off and shook it outside before coming in and closing the door behind him. The croft suddenly seemed smaller, more confining. He was all-consuming. He'd certainly taken her breath away.

She grabbed his cloak, clutching it and the few precious moments hanging it up afforded her. But when she turned back to him, she was still at a loss about what to say, what to do. Which was a partial lie. She knew what she wanted to do.

She wanted to tell him she'd been on her way to see him, that she'd given in, that she wanted him and damn the consequences. But he'd come first, and she had to know why before she laid her heart out. "Why—why are you here?"

He stood there, white linen shirt damp and clinging to his chest, black fitted pants somehow making his legs look even longer and stronger, leather boots completing the picture. "For you," he said, his voice barely reaching her above the sounds of the storm.

She backed away from him even as she fought the urge to fling herself at him. "I'm not . . ." She trailed off, swallowing hard as he took steps toward her. "I'm not ready, Connal." And that, she realized, was the truth. She wasn't ready to damn the consequences, no matter that she wished she was. "I do want you, but I can't give you everything you want."

"I'm no' here as The MacNeil, Josie. I'm here simply as Connal. And all I want is you."

Dear God. She didn't think she was strong enough for this. He looked at her like he could consume her. And damned if she didn't want to be inhaled at the moment.

"It's supposed to be different," she said quickly, trying like hell to hang on to her integrity and respect his needs like he'd respected hers. How did he make it look so easy when he'd done it? "Relationships, I mean. First you have dating." She continued backing up. "You know, going out to dinner, talking into the wee hours, discovering all the things you both like, the things you don't." He kept coming, his expression unreadable. She backed around the couch. "Then, of course, comes the sex." His eyes flared at that and she raised a hand, backtracking even faster. "Then more talking, lots more. And, eventually, if you're lucky, really lucky, you get commitment." She skated by the loft stairs, circling her way back to the front door. "I never was really lucky. Not that I worked all that hard at it. I—I never really gave it much thought, actually." She was babbling now, but didn't care. He was still coming for her. "I always thought it would happen when it happened, you know? Love, commitment, marriage, babies. In that order."

"Stop running," he said.

"I'm not." But she was breathless by the time she got back to the front door. She stopped, her hand on the knob, uncertain whether she should just ask him to leave . . . or run into the storm herself. "I'm not running," she said again, as much to herself as to him. "I'm explaining." She gripped the doorknob more tightly as he stopped just in front of her. "I'm explaining why I can't do this, Connal." She took a breath and looked up into his eyes. "I can't do this. I can't give you what you want. I need more."

"You want this commitment then? The offer of marriage?"

It shocked her hearing him say it. So much so that she spluttered, laughing out loud, even as some small part of her heart yearned to believe the offer was real. "I was not angling for a proposal." So what *did* she want?

With a far gentler touch than she could have imagined, he tipped her chin up so she looked directly at him. "I wish to give ye what ye want, Josie. Only I dinna know how to go about givin' it."

She swallowed, which was difficult over the sudden lump in her throat. "I-I—"

The smallest of smiles flirted at the sides of his mouth. "I've finally done the impossible. I've rendered ye speechless."

She tried to give him a look, but suddenly it was all too much for her. He was offering her . . . what? *Just what you want*, she thought. *Whatever you want him to offer*. She pulled from his grasp and left the doorway, moving so she put the couch between them. Even with the distance, thinking was almost impossible. "Why?"

"Why?"

"Yes," she said, shoving her hair from her face, suddenly impatient. "Why do you want to give me whatever I want? Are we bargaining?" She'd seen in his eyes that he hadn't offered himself as some sort of calculated strategy. But maybe she needed to hear that from him.

"'Tis no bargain I seek." He didn't come closer this time. "'Tis only the path to yer heart I wish to travel."

"What about the rest?" she choked out, forcing the rest out onto the table. "The baby?"

Now it was his turn to wipe the rain from his face as he searched for the words. He looked back to her and she saw the sincerity, the raw emotion on his face. "I can only think of you. I dinna want ye to leave, Josie."

"Why?"

He frowned now. "Because I want you here. With me."

"And this doesn't have anything to do with the baby you've waited three hundred years to make. The one you're convinced will single-handedly restore wealth and happiness to this island." She shook her head, even as her heart knocked hard a few times inside her chest.

He came to her then, but she folded her arms across her chest. He sighed heavily, maybe even swore beneath his breath.

Finally, she gestured to the couch. "Why don't you sit and I'll make some tea." He looked like he was going to argue, then scowled and sat anyway. For some reason this made her smile. This was the Connal she knew. "Maybe we'll at least get to the talking to the wee hours of the night part," she murmured before heading to the small kitchen.

Her hands trembled as she boiled the water and steeped the tea. Where could this possibly lead but them back in bed again? And where did she want it to lead if not back to bed?

"Why couldn't I fall in love with a regular mortal guy?" she muttered, then squealed when Connal spoke from directly behind her.

"Do ye want help carryin' that?"

It was only then that she realized what she'd said. Out loud. Her breath caught as she looked at him, but he apparently hadn't heard her. It whooshed back out in a relieved sigh as she handed him the tray. "Thanks."

He carried it to the small table fronting the couch, then sat, looking up at her expectantly. Which is when the ridiculousness of this whole thing hit her. They couldn't simply sit here, sipping tea, and calmly figure out what in the hell it was they were both doing tangled up in one another.

"It can't work," she blurted out.

He paused in the act of pouring tea for them both—somehow looking really sexy while doing it—and looked back at her. "What won't work?"

She flopped down beside him. "This. Us." She hiked a knee onto the cushion as she turned to face him.

"It's fair to say we want each other, right?" She took the look in his eyes to be a yes. A big, pulse-racing yes. "So where can that lead us? I mean, even if we can forget, for the moment, that you need an heir, which, frankly, is really hard for me to get past—"

The teapot clattered back to the tray just before he gripped her flailing hands. "Josie, I am no' here about the bairn!"

She actually believed him, which only made what she had to say next more frustrating. "Even so, I can't go to bed with you again. My pills have run out."

He sat and stared at her. And her heart sank.

"So," she said quietly. "If you're not here to make a baby, you certainly came here expecting to get some practice in. Am I right?" Of course, she had no right to judge him considering she'd done little but think about "practicing" herself of late.

"I willna lie and say I have no' thought of you . . . of me. Of us. Together in such a way again. I've never experienced anything like you."

Her heart could barely take the things he said. It was harder and harder to cling to the cynical when she so badly wanted to revel in the romantic.

He cupped her face and she simply couldn't make herself pull away. "But 'tis no' why I came here tonight. I spoke the truth about it being yer heart that I want."

There it was. The pathetic thing she'd wanted to hear. What all women want to hear, she tried to tell herself, but the cynic inside her was receding quickly. She made one last stab at it. "But you'd take my body if it was all I had to offer."

He merely looked at her then, his gaze steady on

hers until she wanted to squirm at the directness of it, the intimate penetration of it. "Days ago, I'd have said yes. Perhaps even hours ago."

"And now?" She was trembling again.

"I've had your body, Josie. 'Tis wonderful, and I'll no' deny I want it again. I dinna think I'll ever tire of it, in fact." He reached out and stroked one blunt finger along the side of her face. "But 'tis no' enough."

"What more can I give you?" she asked shakily. His touch was undoing what little control she had left.

He looked her straight in the eye. "Yer heart." He took her hands, and for the first time she could feel the fine tremors in his own fingers. It was only then that she realized he was nervous, too. And it changed everything.

"I told you I came here as a man. A man who is afraid of no' doing the right things to keep his woman here," he said roughly, as if the words were being torn out of him. And maybe they were.

"Connal—"

He pressed his lips to her fingers, halting whatever she'd been about to say. His eyes searched hers. "A man who doesna want to see his woman sail away from him."

She was shaking now. His woman. Just hearing him say that sent a thrill of awareness through her she couldn't deny. A thrill she liked, dammit. And wanted to experience again. And again.

"I dinna wish to lose your smile, the sound of yer laughter." He stroked her face, her lips. "And I admit, I dinna want to wake up knowing I'll never taste ye again."

She swallowed against the sudden tightness in her throat. "What can come of it?" she whispered, completely undone by his words. "What can come of us?"

He pulled her into his arms then, and lowered his face to hers. "That is why I am here. To give us the chance to find out."

Chapter 19

Och, but her taste inflamed him. Once he settled his mouth on hers, he was fairly certain even the gods couldn't have dragged him away. He'd done right in coming to her—for she accepted his kiss with one of her own.

She took as hungrily as he did and he lost himself in the knowledge that her needs met his. It was a sweet promise that somehow, this would all work out.

He pulled her on top of him and slid down into the cushions, never wanting to let her go. Aye, how she fitted herself over him. Nothing could be as right as this. Surely this was meant to be.

He wove his fingers into her hair, holding her mouth to his, plundering her. More, he wanted more. He slid his hands beneath the soft shift she wore. Her skin was warm, smooth and his to caress. It left him reeling, this drunken immersion into sensations that flooded him simply by touching her.

Her hands skated over his skin as well, as she peeled back his shirt, tugging it from his breeches, sliding her hands—gods yes—over his chest. His hips pushed into hers, blindly seeking, and the sweet pressure she returned almost undid him right then and there.

He skimmed his hands up her sides, brushing the

pads of his thumbs over her nipples as she arched
back above him. A moan tore from her lips, lips
reddened from his kisses and all but begging for
more. He could give her more. He would give her all
he had.

And that was what stopped him.

For, beyond pleasure, he had nothing to give.

"What's wrong?" She whispered the words against
his cheek. His hands had stilled completely, and now
so had hers.

"I canno' take ye, Josie," he said hoarsely, his
body still trembling with need.

She smiled at him then, her eyes shining with
trust. Trust in him. He'd never do anything to shatter that.

Then the smile shifted to one of promise. "I believe there are other things we can do, that won't be
risky. Or have things really changed that much in a
few centuries?"

He looked into her teasing eyes and understood
more clearly than ever before that his heart was well
and truly lost. "How was it that you came to me?"

She leaned down and kissed him. "Destiny."

He cupped her face. "I've nothing to offer ye. No
future."

Her gaze didn't so much as flicker. "I'm not asking for promises."

"But—"

"Are you going anywhere right now?"

"Nay."

"Then that's all I need to know." She kissed away
his response to that, and, in the end, he realized he
didn't need promises either. Other than the promise that neither of them was going to run away this
time.

He kissed her deeply, pouring everything he felt,
his confusion, his needs, his wants, into it, until

they were both panting, bodies writhing for what they could not have.

"About these other ways," he managed hoarsely.

She laughed a bit breathlessly and slipped off him, standing shakily beside him. "You once drew me a bath I foolishly wasted. Would you care to share one with me now?"

Connal's entire body leaped. But even as he stood, somewhat shakily, he wondered at the wisdom of stripping off what little barrier their clothes provided. "I'm no' so sure 'tis wise."

She took his hand. "I think I can change your mind."

He smiled then. "I think yer probably right."

He followed her up the stairs and watched from the door as she filled the deep, claw-footed tub and set about lighting candles. "In case the power goes out, of course," she said with a teasing grin.

"Aye, of course." He folded his arms as he studied her. She had a graceful way about her, not delicate, but certain in her actions, sure of her body and its abilities. He thought of her on her wave board, her confidence even under the pressure of the thundering wall of water chasing just behind her. She thrilled him, even when he worried for her. He'd not deny her any pleasure if it was in his power to give it to her.

"Well, are you just going to stand there?"

He let thoughts of all the things he couldn't give her drift away as the steam rose from the scented water. For now, he'd focus on what he could give her.

He stepped to her and drew her shirt over her head in one simple movement. She didn't move away from him or try to hide herself. Instead she reached for the laces at the front of his own shirt, loosened them the rest of the way and removed his shirt much as he had hers. He slipped his fingers along the inside of her waistband, enjoying her sudden inhalation at his touch. He unfastened the catch and let the fabric rustle to the floor. She stood naked and perfect before him.

"Do all women in this day wear no undergarments?" he asked.

"Does it matter?"

His lips quirked. "As it happens, no."

She laughed, and reached for the front of his breeches. He stepped back and she merely raised her eyebrows. "Perhaps 'tis best for me to do this. I fear your fingers brushing me at this moment might ruin an otherwise interesting bath."

Her pupils widened and it was all he could do not to simply take her where she stood. With incredible restraint, he peeled the damp fabric down his legs until he, too, stood naked before her.

She looked at him openly. It was nothing she hadn't already seen, but he found he enjoyed her frank perusal. An enjoyment made obvious by his state of arousal. "Well, are you just going to stand there?" he tossed back at her.

She glanced back up to his face. "I'm quite enjoying standing here, as it happens."

He took her hand then and pulled her into the tub with him. She gasped as his body brushed against hers at the same time the warm water lapped at their skin. He moved so he sat leaning against the high end of the basin, arranging her facing away from him, between his legs.

"I dinna think this is such a good idea," he murmured against the damp skin of her neck.

"Oh?" She moaned softly as he drew his tongue along her nape. "I think this is the best idea I've had in ages."

He nudged against the delectable curve of her backside. "I want you, Josie. This is torture."

She wiggled back against him. "Yes, it is." She picked up the bar of soap. "Here. You first."

He took the cake from her and dipped it in the water. "How am I to wash myself when—"

She took his hand and drew the soap across her breasts, a small moan escaping her as she did so.

"Ah. I am beginning to see the pleasures of no' bathing alone." He drew the soap across her breasts again, then decided it was unfair for the cake to have all the fun. So he lathered his hands and used them instead. "Stop yer squirming or I'll no' be able to control myself."

"You have no idea how good this feels," she said, through what sounded like gritted teeth.

He scooped up the soap and pressed it into her hand. "Show me."

She swiveled then, so she was facing him, on her knees between his. "Where to begin," she said, a devilish glint in her eyes.

"Anywhere you desire," he said, meaning it. His entire body was so responsive right now she could wash his toes and he'd likely burst.

She soaped his chest, reminding him again just how sensitive a man's own nipples could be. She moved along his arms, carefully lathering him down to each finger until he found himself quite short of breath. She then found something else to lather, at which point he lost his breath altogether.

"Josie—" It was all he was able to manage.

She released him an instant before he disgraced himself, then stood, water sluicing down her body. She carefully stepped out of the bath and grabbed a towel.

"Allow me," he said, his voice unsteady. His legs were shaky as he climbed from the bath and took the towel from her. He patted at the water droplets that clung to her skin.

"I'm not fragile, you can rub harder," she said, lifting her arms for him.

He stepped closer and pulled her arms back down, so they rested on her shoulders. "Nay, but yer skin is delicate and I'd no' abrade it."

She traced a finger along his chin and the fine shadow of whiskers that lined it. "You didn't seem to mind doing just that the last time we were together."

He hadn't thought it possible for a man to blush. "Aye," he said, finding his own smile as hers grew. "That was different."

"Aye, it was." She flung the towel away. "Come on, let's do some more abrading." She tugged him in the direction of her bed, then let go and dropped to the bed on her back.

He'd never seen a more welcome sight than Josie Griffin in all her glory, splayed across white linen sheets. And he'd never experienced a deeper sense of frustration at not being able to take what was so willingly being offered. Something he wanted more badly than he wanted his next breath.

"It will be okay. Trust me."

He found he did have trust in her. It was a riveting moment, giving that part of himself over to another, and not nearly as difficult as he'd imagined it would be. Not with her. She smiled and crooked her finger then. He didn't need further urging. He lowered himself on the bed, next to her rather than on top of her as he wished, gritting his teeth as she ran her hands over him. "Yer pushing the boundaries of risk, lass."

She pushed him over onto his back and started kissing his chest. "Trust me."

"It's the trust I have in myself that's in question."

She ignored him, moving her attentions lower, dipping her tongue most startlingly into his navel. His hips jerked and he moved to sit up, but before he could speak she slipped her hand around the pulsing length of him. He dropped back to the bed, groaning as she stroked him. His groans turned to growls when she lowered her mouth to him.

"Gods in heaven have mercy," he said, not wishing anything of the sort. He wanted no mercy. In fact, she was welcome to continue for all eternity.

His hips jerked well beyond his control as she continued and he felt himself surging forth. He gripped her shoulders, her head, sinking his fingers into her hair, intent on moving her away at the last moment, but she merely looked up at him, while she took him inside her . . . and pushed him over the edge.

He shouted through his release, then all but dragged her on top of him. When he found the breath to speak, he said, "Josie, ye didna need—"

She kissed him quiet. "I did. For me, as much for you." When he looked skeptical, she said, "I want all of you." Then she smiled. "I'm greedy that way."

He smiled then, too. And rolled her to her back.

He kissed her hard, then dipped his tongue to her breasts, eliciting a squeal of delight from her. He then discovered that she, too, gasped when her navel was invaded with a warm tongue. He slid that tongue lower. When she stilled his movement with her hand, he looked up. "I find I'm greedy, too."

"Just because I—"

"Hush and allow me my pleasure." To punctuate his desire, he dropped a kiss quite intimately between her legs.

He felt rather than saw her head drop back to the bed. "Far be it from me to come between a man and his pleasure."

"Smart lass." And he went back to enjoying her. She moved so exquisitely beneath his tongue, her moans of delight making him hard once again. He found his own exquisite pleasure in driving her farther, higher, until bliss overtook her.

Her skin was heated and damp when he crawled back up beside her. The strength of his desire for her amazed him, even now that they'd both been sated. He was of the mind that there would never be such a thing as being sated with her.

He stroked her hair from her forehead and dropped a kiss there. She turned to him, murmuring softly and curling into him. She pressed a soft kiss just above his heart. And while he was trying to come to terms with the disconcertingly tender feelings her action invoked, he felt her drift to sleep.

So he held her. And thought he could forever.

&

The rains continued unabated the following morning. Josie awoke first and watched Connal sleep. He looked so damn . . . mortal, she thought, then forcefully shoved all doubts and fears of their future aside. With the weather as it was, she would be left alone today. All day. Alone. With Connal.

She would have killed for a box of Trojans.

But there were other things they could do. She sighed blissfully, remembering them all. Connal had awakened her somewhere in the middle of the night, touching her, tasting her, until he drove her yet again over the edge. She quite eagerly returned the favor, then stroked his hair as he slumbered deeply. She wanted him then, she wanted him now. She couldn't ever imagine a time she wouldn't. She wanted him in her bed every morning. She wanted him in her life every day. "Don't push it," she warned herself. "Enjoy what you do have."

Connal roused then and pulled her to him even

before he'd opened his eyes. She rolled in to him as naturally as if she did so every morning. She kissed him awake, then smiled when he looked at her with something very close to awe.

"What?"

"I enjoy finding ye here, next to me, when I first open my eyes. 'Tis a lovely sight."

She blushed. It was that or cry. Then her stomach rumbled and the moment passed.

"I think I've finally depleted yer vast stores of energy."

She would have denied it, told him she was perfectly content right where she was, but her stomach intruded once again and they both laughed.

"Come on," she said. "I'll teach you the joys of cooking."

As it happened, Connal attended his lesson as fiercely as he attended her pleasure. She enjoyed his pride at finally mastering turning an egg over and keeping the yolk intact. So what if it was on his tenth try? He was a determined man, but then she knew that about him already.

He ate with gusto, then noticed her staring at him and stopped midbite. "What?"

"Nothing. I just enjoy watching you."

"I'm no' doing anything all that exciting."

She could have told him that watching him breathe excited her. "I guess I never thought about this before, but do you need to eat?" Once the question was out, she could have kicked herself. Reality had intruded its ugly head and she was the one who'd invited it in. "Never mind."

"No, 'tis all right." He put his fork down. "I dinna mind answering anything ye care to know."

"But—"

"I want to know ye, as well as a man can. And I

want ye to know me the same. So ask. And dinna worry about the next minute, or hour. Agreed?"

She nodded and did her best to push her fears away once again. "So, do you? Need to eat?"

He shook his head. "I exist as I am no matter what. But I can still enjoy all the mortal pleasures, if I wish to."

She swallowed hard, thinking of the mortal pleasures he'd enjoyed giving her. "And do you? Wish to, I mean?"

He grinned then, the teasing light back in his eyes. "Are ye askin' me if I've pleasured other women? Mortal women?" Then his eyes darkened and he reached across the table to take her hand. "Since I've waited for you, I've had no other."

She put her own fork down. He'd said that once before. This time, it was different, even more meaningful.

"What else do you want to know?"

She could only shake her head.

"Then 'tis my go." He settled back in his chair. His hair was sleep-tousled, his chest invitingly bare. "Tell me about your father. I can see that you are close to him."

She nodded, then finally found her voice. "He—" She smiled then and shook her head. "He's hard to describe. A gypsy, I guess, is a good start. Sounds better than oddball or eccentric, right?"

"He does no' seem so odd to me. He is full of life, his laugh hearty. And when he looks at you, you can see pride and love in his eyes. The look of a man who knows he's left the best part of himself behind to carry on when he is gone."

Josie could only stare at him, tears gathering at the corners of her eyes. "Thank you. I wish I knew I could live up to that."

"I only speak the truth." He studied her, in that disconcertingly intimate way of his. "And ye will. It's in yer heart."

He got up then, and cleared both their plates from the table. She watched him as he put the dishes in the sink. He appeared at ease, but she wondered. Wondered if his talk of leaving the best of himself behind hadn't triggered thoughts of his own three-centuries-long quest to do the same. Only his reasons for wanting to wouldn't be the same as her father's.

Yet, when he turned around and she caught his contemplative gaze, she wondered if even he understood what his real desires were anymore.

She stood then and pasted a smile on her face. "I told you once that I thought you needed to have more fun."

She thought he might have winced, but she pushed on, undeterred. "Cards? Do you play?" Then she remembered the beautiful hand-carved pieces set up by the fire. "How about chess?"

His eyes lit up for only a second, but it was long enough.

"So, you do play."

"Gregor and I have had a few midnight matches, aye."

"Drunken chess, huh?"

Connal grinned then. "Made it easier to beat the auld sot."

"What, having three hundred years of practice wasn't enough of an edge?"

"Practice never makes perfect." Gazing at her quite directly, he added, "Unless it's perfect practice."

And just like that she wanted him. Again. Always. "We *are* talking about chess." She said it as much to remind herself as him.

"Aye. What else would I have meant?" His eyes gleamed as he crossed the room toward her. He took her hand and for a split second, she thought he might drag her upstairs to bed. Or right to the floor. She was fairly certain she wouldn't have objected to either. But he pulled her instead to the chess table. "You'll be white."

She sat down and tried hard to remember why she'd thought this was the best way to spend the day. "Why do I have to be white?"

He looked at her then. "Because I am always the black."

"Ah. So, perfect practice or no, you just maybe take this game a little seriously, do you?" She flexed her hands and cracked her knuckles. "Well, I'll have you know that as I spent the larger part of my formative years traveling all over with my gypsy father, we had little in the way of things to entertain ourselves in most of the places we stayed. It was pretty much either cards, books . . ." She looked up at him. "Or chess."

He blew the dust from the board, realigned the figures to suit himself, then smiled up at her, supreme confidence in his gaze. "Your move."

੨ፇ

Three hours and much consternation later, Connal shouted, "Your king is mine!"

Josie barely managed to refrain from sweeping her arm across the board. Or flinging her king at his oh-so-smug face. "Fine then. You were lucky. This time."

His eyes lit up. "You care to go again?"

She groaned, certain he would gladly sit another three hours. And not too sure he wouldn't trounce her again. "There is a downside to your immortality." She glared across the board at him. "You'll always outlast me."

"You need a respite then?" He was already around the table and pulling her from her seat. "Another bath perhaps? Or maybe you could show me how that other contraption works."

"The shower?"

"Shower. 'Tis like bathing in the rain, then?"

She'd never thought of it that way. "I suppose it is."

He took her hand. "Come then." He looked at her meaningfully. "It will be fun."

"I've created a monster," she muttered, but she quickly forgot how much she hated to lose when he pulled her up the stairs and began stripping off what little clothes he wore.

As it turned out, there was something incredibly sexy about having a man wash her hair. His fingers were so strong, she moaned in appreciation as he massaged her scalp. "You could make a fortune doing that."

He didn't respond. Instead he turned her around and tipped her head back into the spray. When she lifted her hands to rinse her hair, he used his own to spread the foamy white suds all over her body. Her knees went decidedly weak as he knelt and made sure all the soap was gone.

When he leaned in closer, she braced her hands on his shoulders, then massaged his scalp, mostly to make sure his head didn't move from the exact spot it was in.

She'd never come in the shower before. But she did now. Twice. And if she had her way, she would again. In fact, she thought this could easily be worked into her daily routine.

Limp and wishing there was a wall she could lean on, she leaned on him instead. "I—you—should be . . . your turn."

But he turned off the water instead and pulled the

curtain back. Then, without a word, he lifted her from the tub, wrapped her in a towel, and carried her to bed.

He moved to lie beside her, but she needed to feel him on top of her, she wanted his weight pressing her down, to feel him move between her legs. He resisted her tugging. "Connal, please," she whispered.

"But—"

"I want to feel you inside me."

His jaw clenched and she saw the same need warring in his eyes.

"You can . . . you can stop, just before. I know it's not fair, but—"

He didn't need further urging. He pulled her hungrily beneath him and drove into her with a loud growl of pleasure. She came again instantly, shockingly. She locked her legs around his hips and let the pleasure rush through her. Nothing had ever felt so complete to her. "I don't want you ever to leave," she whispered. She'd meant leave her body . . . but when she said the words, she knew she meant something else entirely.

He pushed more deeply, then held himself rigidly still, as if his entire body was clenched against the need to roar into her. She wanted badly to urge him to do just that.

He thrust again, then pressed his lips to the side of her neck and held himself there, fully inside her. "I never want ye to go," he said, then thrust again before pulling out.

She held him between her legs, if not inside her and they both moved, hips thrusting, until the air was filled again with the groans of release. This time his as well as hers.

He collapsed onto her and she held him there. *I love you.* The words were there, so clear she thought she'd spoken them.

She shifted him aside, gently, then silently went to the bathroom to clean up and hopefully gather her wits. But it didn't help. She walked back into the bedroom and looked at him, sprawled in her white sheets, his chest rising and falling evenly as he dozed, and the words still shouted in her mind, over and over. She loved him.

She slipped back into bed and he moved toward her, tucking her body into his, even as he slept. Her eyes filled and she pressed her lips to his warm skin and gave in to the need. "I do love you, Connal." She closed her eyes. "The gods help us both."

Chapter 20

*J*osie stretched languorously before finally forcing her eyes open. She knew instantly that Connal was no longer beside her, but didn't worry. Instead she stretched again, smiling even as her muscles protested a bit. She listened for sounds of the bath or shower, but there were none. In fact, there was no sounds of water at all, inside or out. Despite the pale gloom of light coming in the window, the rain seemed to have stopped.

"Well, pooh," she said, thinking that with the end of the rain, her classes would resume. Would Connal stay? Would he finally consent to appear before others? And how in the hell would she explain his presence on an island where everyone knew everyone else?

She decided she didn't want to think about that at the moment. It was late afternoon, judging by the light, so she had the rest of today and all of tonight before she had to worry about what came next.

She sat up and pushed her hair back, then smiled as she got out of bed. Knowing Connal, he was downstairs trying his hand at cooking again. She didn't smell anything burning, so that was a good start, she thought, pulling on his white shirt. It dropped just past her hips, so she pulled on a pair of panties, then went downstairs.

The kitchen was empty. As was the rest of the croft.

She frowned, but refused to get worried. After what they'd shared, she knew, *knew,* he would not leave her. Maybe he'd simply gone back to the tower for something. Her lips curved. If he had, he'd done so naked, as the rest of his clothes were still on the floor upstairs. "Must be nice to be able to pop in and out of places."

So, with her confidence firmly in check, she fixed them both an early dinner. She was famished and figured he would be, too.

But the shadows grew longer, and longer still, and he didn't return. Anger finally crept in as she ate her dinner and a good portion of his, then rinsed the dishes and put the leftover food away. Did he expect her to come to the tower then? And what if he did? Would she go? She really didn't think he would play this sort of game with her, not now. But maybe what happened between them hadn't invoked the same powerful feelings for him as it had her. Yet, even as she thought that, she knew it wasn't true.

He hadn't said he loved her, and maybe he didn't, not fully, not yet. But his feelings for her were most definitely powerful. The most powerful she'd ever felt.

"So, dammit, where did you go?"

She pulled on sweats and shoes and went outside. The air was warm and humid, the sky dusky, and the ground a vast sea of muck. Still, she made it across the road and looked through the gloom to the beach. The tide was roaring and it was in. There would be no going to the tower. Despite her exit with Bagan, she had no idea where the exact location of the opening was in the rocks. There was no light in the tower portals either.

She turned back to the croft, fear finally beginning to crawl past the anger. "Where did you go?" she whispered, but the only response she got was the howl of the wind.

&

By four in the morning, she was calling for Bagan to appear. No luck there either. By morning she was torn between self-pity and wanting to commit homicide. She'd known, hadn't she, that this was going to have a bad end? But she'd never imagined he would simply abandon her this way.

She climbed the tower the instant the tide was low enough, searched his rooms, all vacant. No Connal. No Bagan. She even looked for the damn stone, but all she found was the trunk. Open and empty.

She was hiking back up the beach to the croft, feeling hollow and emotionally ravaged, when Roddy pulled up in his tiny little car, packed with Dougal and her father. He got out and waved, grinning broadly before shouting, "I hope we're still on for this morning. The lassies will be along a bit later."

Josie wanted to yell at them to get the hell away from her, that she was too busy feeling bewildered, lost, hurt, abandoned . . . and scared. She was never going to see him again. She felt it. Knew it. She thought she might throw up, her stomach was twisted in so many knots.

Then her dad climbed out of the car and looked down at her and she wanted more than anything to race to him, fling herself into his arms, and sob her heart out.

In the end, she neither screamed nor sobbed. No point in bewildering her father and Dougal as well. Besides, she had no idea where to begin . . . much less explain how it had ended. It took every last ounce of energy she had to paste a smile on her face and wave back. "We're still on," she called out above the roar of the surf. It was probably for the best, she thought. It would keep her busy, so she wouldn't feel compelled to fling herself out of the tower window. Which, the way she felt at the moment, she'd have only done after flinging every last thing he owned out the window first.

ॐ

Classes lasted well into the afternoon. The men had finished with learning about currents and wave formation several lessons ago, so she'd showed them the pop-up stance and they practiced it in the "soup," the shallow waves that broke near shore. It was obviously they'd been practicing their stances at home as well. If she hadn't been so miserable, she'd have smiled for real.

Gavin was doing very well, and even Clud had surprised her by being more agile than she'd given him credit for. Dougal, on the other hand, was getting extremely frustrated, so her father had stepped in and taught him an alternative way that seemed to be working. Roddy was struggling, too, but was bull-headed enough to wave her and Griff off as he tried again and again to pull his feet under him and remain crouched on the board without falling over sideways.

Maeve and the girls had arrived while the men were still practicing and Bidda had complained bitterly about not being allowed to learn this part herself. Josie explained they had to learn more about how the ocean was going to move beneath them, how to read the water, the waves and the currents, before actually learning the mechanics. Privately, she had no idea how a woman of Bidda's age and bulk was going to perfect the pop-up technique. She could only pray her father had an answer for that one when the time came.

She was emotionally and physically wrung out when they finally piled back into Bidda's car, Griff along with them as he'd stayed behind to help her out. He'd looked at her questioningly a few times, as if he realized something was off. The one time he'd managed to get a private word with her, she shrugged off his concern and muttered something about the storm keeping her from sleeping well. She wasn't sure he bought it, since she'd never had that trouble before, but he'd accepted it and left her alone. Probably relieved to be off the hook, she thought, but without any rancor. At the moment she just wanted to crawl into a hole and sleep for a very long time. Three hundred years ought to do it.

But once everyone was gone and she was faced with the prospect of going back into the empty croft, she thought about chasing after them and begging to go along. Instead she forced herself inside, though she carefully didn't look at the bed, or his clothes that still lay scattered about. She wasn't up to dealing with that yet. As it was she'd spent the previous night on the couch. "Well, that's going to have to end at some point, just like this pity party," she told herself firmly, and marched to the bathroom. "And it might as well be now."

She yanked on the shower knob, stripped out of her wet suit, and climbed in, determined to just wash and get out. No lingering under the spray, no thinking about how it had been when they'd showered together.

She did fine until she reached for the bar of soap. She swore she could feel his hands on her, even though she was quite well aware she was alone. So alone. One tear sprang from her eye, then another.

Then she was sobbing, openly, wrenchingly. Standing beneath the pounding spray, naked in body and spirit, pouring her heart and soul down the drain.

By the time she got out, she was totally spent. But after kicking Connal's clothes beneath the bed, she tossed and turned trying to sleep, until she thought she'd go mad. So she dragged on sweats and a T-shirt, grabbed her new, extrawide sketch pad and forced herself down to the beach. Maybe she could lose herself in her work.

The sunset was gorgeous and she forced herself to accept its beauty, if not its promise of a brighter tomorrow, as she traipsed along the water's edge. But it was too windy to draw and frankly, her heart wasn't in it anyway.

Her heart. It was deeply dented, if not completely broken. She finally stopped and forced herself to sit down and take stock. After a deep breath, she stared out to sea. "Okay, enough. You've got to think this through. Figure it out." So she did. Or at least tried to.

Why would he have gone? Where would he have gone?

He was here because of a bargain he'd made with the gods to allow him to create an heir. But he hadn't done that, as evidenced by her period. They'd been careful after that. Except for that one last time, but even then . . .

She clamped a hand over her mouth, whispering "No!" through her fingers. Her other hand crept along her flat belly, even as she fought against the truth she suspected.

She looked down at her hand. At her belly. It hadn't happened. Couldn't have. It had only been once. And he'd stopped in time. Besides, it had barely been twenty-four hours since they'd been together.

And every argument she'd just made was what every pregnant woman told herself, right?

Pregnant. It couldn't be. She dropped her head to her knees. She couldn't be. She didn't feel any different. She laughed then, though there was no humor in the sound. "Yeah, just what they all say."

She lifted her head and, stunned as the possibility began to sink in, looked back toward the tower amidst the tumble of castle ruins. "Is that what we did, Connal? Did we make a life between us?"

It was such a huge thing to contemplate, she couldn't manage it. So she sat there, staring at the setting sun, and tried to simply allow it to filter into her brain. And her body. And her heart.

But even when she finally got up to walk back to the croft, she simply couldn't wrap her mind around it.

"Well, you're going to have to eventually," she murmured as she let herself back into the croft. She forced herself to eat something, then dragged herself back to bed.

After an hour of staring at the ceiling she got up, fished Connal's shirt out from under the bed, put it on, then crawled back under the covers. There she hugged the soft linen to her body and discovered she still had tears to shed. Wracking torrents of them. And when she was completely empty, sleep finally claimed her.

❧

A week passed. Josie spent as much time as she could with her students. The rest was spent working or down at Roddy's pub. Anything to keep from being alone with her thoughts.

Gavin had been the first one to tackle the real surf. She'd purposely waited until the poststorm surge had died down, but it was still a challenge. For the boys and for her. It was hard, being so close to the castle and not feeling the weight of Connal's gaze staring down at her. She'd caught herself glancing up there too often, but the disappointment at finding the tower empty every time was too keen and, after three days, she forced herself to stop looking at all.

Gavin had handled himself fairly well in the smaller swells. Enough that Clud was encouraged to try it out as well. Roddy was next, but it wasn't until the second day that he actually got to his feet. Dougal came last, but surprised them all by having the best run of that day.

Josie was just thankful that they didn't break their necks.

The ferry came several days later and she accompanied her father down to the docks. She'd grown used to having him around in the short time he'd been there, but she knew he had to get back to the business. She drove them there in her rental, which he was going to take back for her and turn in. Dougal had talked Bidda into letting her borrow the old Renault she'd had stored in her barn since she'd given up driving years before.

"I'm going to miss you," she told her dad, never meaning it as much as she did right then. She never had told him. It seemed best to just let it go, seeing as it was over and done with. But no matter how she tried, she suspected there was an undeniable melancholy air about her that her father hadn't missed, despite her ability to fool the boys and Maeve.

"Are you sure you want to stay?" he asked.

She found a smile then and laughed. "Bidda would kill me if I left now. And no way am I letting the boys be the ones to take her out for her first ride."

Griff laughed, too. "True, true." Then his smile

faded and he brushed a strand of her hair from her cheek. "Are you okay, Josiecat?"

She paused, her lips trembling the tiniest bit at the gesture. She found a breath and a smile to go with it and said, "I'm fine. You've got my sketches, right? I put them on the backseat—"

"I'm not worried about your work. I'm worried about you. You seem . . . different."

"I guess I am," she said, knowing he couldn't know just how much different she was. She turned and looked over her shoulder at the town of Ruirisay, at the small huddle of buildings that bravely fronted the sea. "This place has changed me." She looked back to her father. "I like it here." And she realized as she said it, that she meant it. In a way that had nothing to do with Connal or her original reasons for being here.

Her father nodded in agreement. "I know what you mean. A week or two ago I might have questioned it. No young people here, surf not all that challenging."

"South Carolina isn't exactly the pipeline either, you know," she teased.

"I know," he said, quite seriously. "I worried that I stuck you in that place."

She pressed her hand to his arm. "I love it there, too. You know that." Though, honestly, at the moment she couldn't imagine going back to her tiny bungalow and living alone among strangers and tourists. It unsettled her enough that she leaned in and kissed him on the cheek. "And I love you."

He blushed a little, then chuckled and bussed her back. "I love you best, Josiecat." Then he looked down the road to town as well. "You're right though. There is something about this place that pulls you in."

Josie followed his gaze, but in her mind's eye, she saw the castle ruin and Black's Tower. "Yeah. Yeah,

there is." She shook off the image and all the emotions that came with it and turned back with a determined smile on her face. "But we're a team." When
he opened his mouth, she talked over him. "Dad,
I'm twenty-six years old, a grown woman. It's not
like I couldn't have left Parker's Inlet if I'd wanted
to. I'll be back on the next ferry. Or the one after,"
she said when he just looked at her. "I just have to
finish up with the lessons. I don't want to go until
I'm sure they're not going to kill themselves out
there. I'll fax you whatever work I get done in the
meantime. Besides," she added with a grin, "I have
to come back to work on the boards the boys ordered
from you."

"And the ladies?" he added, a teasing grin of his
own curving his lips.

She rolled her eyes. "We're still discussing ideas.
Bidda says if the boys can have their own likenesses
on their boards, then she wants Mel Gibson on
hers." She sighed. "I'm working on alternatives."

"Good luck," her father said with a chuckle.

"Thanks, I'll need it."

The truck driver came back from his delivery to
Maeve's then and told them it was time to board
the car.

"Be right there," Griff told him, then surprised
Josie by pulling her into his arms for a tight hug.
"You take care of yourself, okay?"

She hugged him back, perhaps a bit more tightly
than he was expecting himself. "Yeah," she whispered. *I have to, I'm pregnant.* It was there, on the
tip of her tongue, but in the end, he broke the hug
and tousled her hair the way he'd done a million
other times and the moment passed.

Besides, she'd already figured it would be better
to tell him when she got home and the time came

where she couldn't hide the obvious. Maybe by then she'd have figured out just what to say. "Take care of yourself, Dad. Now that I'm not there to keep an eye on you and all. Maybe I should send word back, warn the female population."

He laughed, his gaze shifting again past her to town. She thought there was something there, something a bit wistful? Then he was waving and climbing into the car and she let it go. "I'll see you soon," she said.

And with another smile and a wave, he was gone.

Josie watched until the ferry was a small dot on the horizon, then rode Gregor's bike back down the road to town, somewhat surprised no one else had come to see Griff off. She said as much to Maeve when she arrived at the store, who smiled gently. "Och, we gave him a proper sending off at Roddy's. We thought ye might like the time. For all he's been here, the two of ye haven't had much time together."

Because I planned it that way, she thought, but only nodded, and said, "Thanks. I love my father dearly, but he's more in his element surrounded by people." She grinned. "Preferably with a mug in his hand."

Maeve laughed, then said, "Oh! Almost forgot." She fished a small parcel from the box of goods the deliveryman had brought and handed it to her. "Better late than never," she said. "I'm sorry for the delay. It's island life and we're used to it, but I know you're no'. I hope it doesn't cause too much trouble for ye."

Her pills. Josie didn't know whether to laugh or cry. Cause her trouble? If Maeve only knew. She managed to smile and nod. "No, it will be fine. Thanks." She took care of the bill, turned down an offer of lunch, saying she had to work before their afternoon lessons, and headed for the door. "Besides, I'm still coming up with alternate art for Bidda's board."

Maeve's eyes twinkled. "I believe she has some ideas as well, though she didna give me the details. But forewarned is forearmed. And Josie," Maeve added, causing her to pause in the doorway, "we're so glad ye stayed on. And no' simply for the lessons. We've all come to think of ye as our own. I'm no' sure how we'll handle it when ye leave us." She sniffled a bit, then laughed and wiped at her eyes. "Go on now before I embarrass us both."

Josie could only nod, surprised and touched. She left, smiling, her own eyes a bit teary. "I'm no' so sure how I'll handle it either," she told herself.

※

Another ten days passed. She stopped going to Roddy's as often, as she'd run out of reasons to explain why she wasn't joining them in an ale. Instead she worked like a demon possessed, taught lessons, surfed alone as often as she felt she safely could, and rode Gregor's bike all over the island. Trying to escape her thoughts, she knew. And it worked, most of the time, but she didn't feel any better for it. In fact, she didn't feel much at all.

The high point of her days was the time spent on the beach with the gang. After much practice, the day finally came when the ladies felt confident enough to take Josie's board out past the shore breakers.

Bidda had tackled the waves first, but—thankfully for Josie's heart—opted to ride the board in on her stomach. Griff had given her pointers, but she still hadn't mastered her stance and until she did, Josie counseled her to stay flat. Maeve acquitted herself nicely, finding a few short, but well-executed rides.

But, to all their amazement, it was quiet little Posey who bested them all. In fact, Josie thought she was a natural on the water.

"See, you don't need me at all, you can just watch Posey here," she joked. Everyone was quick to protest, but she figured they had to know she'd probably be leaving soon now that their lessons were essentially over. Josie wasn't sure what she wanted to do. She had to go home at some point, and it was probably well past time to leave this place. But at the same time, she wasn't ready to. She had grown as fond of everyone here as they had of her. And, though she knew it was foolish, she couldn't deny the feeling she had that by being here she was still somehow close to Connal.

And then there was the possibility that she was carrying his child. A child he'd wanted raised here. She'd managed to shove all that from her mind, but it was growing harder to do each day. She'd have to see a doctor, get vitamins or whatever. Deal with it, face it.

She helped everyone pack up and made arrangements to meet Bidda at her place to go over the final draft of the art for her board. They'd compromised and Josie had done her own takeoff of the hero from one of the more passionate-looking romance novel covers in Gregor's collection. Thank God Bidda had finally agreed to let her clothe the guy.

She waved them good-bye then turned back to the croft. But instead of going inside, she picked up her board and headed back to the beach. She needed some one-on-one time in the water. The swells were hardly worth riding, so there was little danger of her hurting herself.

Or the baby.

She blocked the thought and paddled out.

But the waves weren't doing their job. The tower

loomed too large and dark over her shoulder today. The distraction finally drove her out of the water altogether and she headed back inside.

She showered, tried to eat, but her stomach was a bit off. Part of her wondered if this was the beginning of morning sickness—despite the fact that it was late afternoon—but she was pretty sure it was leftover nerves from watching Bidda paddle out to sea.

She opted for a bath instead and grabbed the book she'd been reading from the table by the couch. A mystery novel this time. Gregor's romance collection was simply too painful to contemplate. The last thing she felt like doing was reading about someone else's happily ever after.

When she stripped down to get in the tub, however, whatever happily ever after she might have still had left in her was stripped off right along with her clothes.

Her stomach wasn't off because of morning sickness. Or Bidda risking life and formidable limbs. It had been cramps. She was having her period.

Josie simply stared at the incontrovertible proof, her emotions in turmoil, the rest of her in shock. Undeniably, there was a part of her that was relieved that she wasn't pregnant. So why was she crying?

And she was. Little gulps that turned into silent sobs, which grew stronger, and louder as she climbed in the shower and stood numbly beneath the spray. She could barely see and her chest was heaving as she dressed and stumbled back to the bedroom. She found Connal's shirt and buried her face in it, sinking to the floor beside her bed. "I'm sorry," she whispered hoarsely. "I'm so sorry."

She couldn't get beyond it, couldn't form a single thought. She merely hugged the shirt to her, rocked herself, and let the grief wash through her until she was completely wrung out.

When the tears finally stopped, she rested her head on her bent knees and tried to get her shuddering breaths under control so she could put her thoughts in order.

She hadn't wanted a baby. Wasn't remotely ready for one, much less the explanations that would have had to come with it. And yet . . . it had been her last chance at carrying a part of him with her forever. For that, she grieved.

She lifted her head and stared, unseeing, as another realization came to her. "Then why did you leave me?"

As that thought sank in, her entire body went cold. If she hadn't been pregnant, then why had Connal disappeared?

"I think I can help ye with that."

Josie choked on a scream and scrambled to her feet, clutching Connal's shirt to her chest as she whirled to face the owner of that voice. A voice she hadn't heard since before Connal's disappearance. A voice she'd been reduced to begging for in the darkest hours of the night.

"Bagan."

He sat in the chair by the bed, his own expression easily as ravaged as her own.

"Aye, lass. 'Tis me." He slid from the chair. "I've come to explain."

And just like that Josie's emotions veered from deep, freezing grief to blazing, volcanic temper. She tossed Connal's shirt on the bed and stalked over to him. "Well, it's about damn time!"

Chapter 21

Not in here," Josie decided abruptly, when he started to talk. If her emotions had been in tatters moments before, they were completely beyond piecing together now. "Downstairs."

She waved an arm and he scuttled ahead of her, apparently thinking better of popping out of her sight.

Once downstairs, Bagan walked to the window. Josie sat on the edge of the couch, but staying still proved impossible. She stalked to the kitchen and began making tea. Anything to keep her hands from going where they longed to. Which was around Bagan's neck. Though he'd yet to tell her a thing, it was obvious just looking at him that he'd been at least partly responsible for the agony she'd put herself through these past weeks.

He cleared his throat, then did so again when she slammed the mugs on the counter.

"Go on," she ordered him, still unable to make herself even look at him. "Start at the beginning."

"I'd counseled him," Bagan said. "Repeatedly. Told him it was no' about the bairn, but what was in his heart."

Josie's hands stilled with the tea egg only half filled. When he said nothing more, she said, less tersely this time, "Go on."

"He thought it was part of the bargain he'd made, but I'd given it much thought and knew the gods had granted him only the promise of the stone."

She turned then, forgetting all about the tea. "Which was what?"

Bagan stared at her, then simply said, "Love."

Love. But she had come to love him. And she thought he'd come to love her. "I think we were figuring that out."

Pain filled Bagan's cherub face and his lips twisted downward. He looked down to his hands, which were tightly fisted. "I know that now."

"What did you do, Bagan?" she demanded quietly.

He looked up at her, tears swimming in his great blue eyes. "He kept insistin' the stone's promise of hope could only be a bairn, that he'd proven his faith to the gods and they'd allowed him to stay on to reap that final reward."

"But you'd come to believe differently."

He nodded, sniffling. "I thought back to what the stone had brought to those who had possessed it, followed its guidance. And that was love."

"You're the guardian of the thing and yet you didn't already know this?"

His small hands flailed, then covered his face as he dipped his chin. "It's always worked before," he said hoarsely. "I've never had to question its exact powers, only oversee its unions. Which have all borne fruit, but only because—"

"So what did you do with it?" she asked, remembering with a chill that the trunk had been open and empty when she'd found it.

"I simply thought that if it wasna there between you, if he knew its promise had been fulfilled merely by bringing ye to him, he'd move past the nonsense of the bairn and see what was plainly before his own eyes."

Josie was trembling now. "What did you do with it?" she repeated.

Bagan's voice shook, his expression beseeching her understanding. "I tossed the stone in the sea."

Josie's eyes popped wide. "You did what?" she shouted.

Bagan blanched. "I know, I should hae thought my actions through more clearly. I knew I would no longer be here to guard over ye, that I was flinging my own self to sea along with the stone. But I thought it was a worthy sacrifice to what I knew you and Connal would have."

"What? What would we have?" She tunneled her fingers into her hair, tempted to go ahead and rip it out, then let her hands drop to her sides. "What are you trying to say?"

"I thought he would see that the stone had done its duty, that his destiny and the hope he had for Glenmuir was fulfilled in you. He had only to give you his heart to prove himself." Tears slipped down his face now. "Ye were so close. So close." He crossed the room, taking her cold, fisted hands in his own stubbier ones. "Josie, lass, I didna know. I swear it. I wouldna hae done it if I'd known."

Josie tugged her hands free and tried to make sense of it all. "I understand why you disappeared with the stone. But why Connal, too? He didn't do it."

"Och, that's the worst of it. I've angered the gods so. They'd agreed to allow him to remain here until the stone was delivered, until he'd proven himself, naught to them, but to himself. When I threw it back to sea, they felt their bargain had been tossed back with it. He'd failed in their eyes. And they—" His voice broke on a sob. "They called Connal home."

Josie stared at him, but said nothing. Then she

turned abruptly and headed for the front door. She had no idea where she was going, but she knew she had to get out of there, had to move, to breathe, to think. The only thing she didn't want to do was feel. And that was impossible when she looked at Bagan.

"Wait!" he called after her. "I canno' come but only once. Please hear me out."

She whirled on him then. "What else is there to say? You screwed up. Again. Only this time everybody paid." She didn't care that she was hurting him. She wanted to inflict the same pain he'd given her, no matter that his motives had been pure. She ignored his flinch and faced him down. "I don't ever want to see you again. Why are you even here? It's not you I wanted to see. Why did they send you?" Even she heard the pained edge of hysteria in her voice and knew she had to get out now, or she'd only say more things she'd regret.

"It was my mistake," Bagan said. "They weren't going to let me come and explain, but I made them see that you shouldn't be hurt for what I'd done."

She laughed harshly at that. "A little too late for that now, isn't it?"

"Josie, lass—"

"And what about Connal? Wasn't he hurt?" The instant she asked she wished she hadn't.

Bagan's remaining composure crumpled. "Aye," he said roughly, tears now filling his throat. "He cast me off for good. I dinna blame him. I failed him in the worst way possible. I am no' fit to be guardian of anything." Tears coursed down his cheeks. "I had only thought to protect his heart. I didna want him to toss it aside. It was the one valuable thing he had to offer. No' the stone." He buried his face in his hands, his shoulders shaking. "I didna mean to ruin it all. I didna mean to." Whatever else he might have said was lost in his tears.

Even with the anger and pain filling her, she couldn't harden her heart enough not to respond to his anguish. She understood it all too well herself. Slowly, she made herself cross the room toward him, finally reaching out a shaky hand and touching his shoulder.

He jerked his head up, his eyes more red than blue now. "I know ye can never forgive me. But please dinna hate Connal for what I did. That is why I came back most of all. He was as innocent in this as you were."

"I don't hate him," she said, then sighed heavily, suddenly too tired to fight any longer. "And I don't hate you."

Bagan shocked her by throwing his arms about her thighs and burying his face in her hip. "I dinna deserve yer forgiveness."

She patted him awkwardly, then gently pried him loose. "It wouldn't have made any difference, would it?" she asked, realizing the truth of it as she said it. "I mean, even if you hadn't interfered, what good would it have done for us to fall in love?"

He just blinked up at her as if she'd gone daft. "Why, it would have changed everything."

She shook her head. "It would have just been more painful when the time came for him to go. Bagan, I did—do—love him. I'm not saying what you did was right, but maybe it was better to end things sooner rather than later." She shook her head. "I don't know where it would have led, but it could only have been worse in the long run." She looked at him. "What could we have truly ever had together?"

"Ye could have had everything," Bagan whispered.

Josie knelt in front of him, all her anger, all her grief, gone. Or maybe she was simply too numb to feel anything anymore. "I'm sorry for all of the pain we've been put through. But please make sure he knows I'll never regret one moment of the time I spent with him. If you can do that for me, I'll be indebted to you forever."

Tears welled up again and he could only nod.

"And tell him—" She broke off as her own throat closed over. "Tell him I'm sorry. About the baby. He waited so long . . . I didn't want him to fail, it was just—" She couldn't finish.

"It was never about the bairn. Only I didna know he'd come to realize that himself." Now it was Bagan's turn to offer solace. "If it's any comfort to ye, he wasna angry about the bargain being lost. He was only angry at being taken from ye."

Josie's heart did a ridiculous and painful flip inside her chest. "Thank you," she said, standing up again. "Thank you for that."

Bagan nodded miserably. "I only wish it were more." Then he shook his head, and murmured, "If only he'd told ye."

"What?" Josie asked.

But Bagan was no longer standing in front of her. She whirled around. "Told me what?" she shouted. But she knew there would be no answer. "Dammit!" She curled her fingers against the urge to throw something. "Damn him for always doing that to me." She raked her fingers through her hair and tried to get herself under control. "Can't even apologize without raking up something else to torture me with." The kettle she'd put on whistled just then, making her jump. She swore as loudly and creatively as she could as she stormed back to the kitchen. "Should have never picked up that stupid trunk," she muttered.

But as she dumped the water down the drain and tossed the tea, silver egg and all, into the trash, she knew she didn't mean it. Emotional roller coaster and murderous feelings aside, she'd meant what she said.

She didn't regret one minute of the time she'd spent with Connal.

≈

Three days later she was packed up and sitting at Maeve's, waiting for the truck driver to finish his delivery and saying her final good-byes.

"Ye'll come back, now, won't ye?" Gavin asked.

"Ye wrote down our e-mail addresses, right?" Dougal added.

Clud shuffled his feet. "We're goin' to miss ye something fierce, Josie. Breath of fresh air in these parts, ye've been."

"That she has," Roddy agreed mistily.

Maeve bustled up just then. "I've packed ye a lunch to take with you on the ferry." Her eyes looked overly bright and Josie prayed with everything left in her that she wouldn't cry. She never wanted to cry again.

So she hurriedly took the bag and leaned in to give her a hug. "Thank you, Maeve." She sniffed as she straightened, pasted on as bright a smile as she could and turned to face the collected group. They'd already done this last night in the pub. In fact, her head was still aching from the send-off they'd given her. "And don't worry boys, you won't get rid of me that easily. I want reports on how you're doing once the boards get here. In the meantime, remember what I taught you and keep practicing."

They saluted her with only a few suspicious sniffles between them, then the deliveryman was mercifully clearing his throat behind her. "Beggin' yer pardon, but we have to get going."

"Right," she said, "Sorry." She turned back to them and the words just came out. "I'll come back."

Their eyes lit up and Roddy sent up a cheer that made her ears ring and her stomach pitch. She amended her list to include no more ale.

"I can't promise when, but . . . but I will be back." *Someday.* When she could face looking at that tower and think back fondly on the time she'd spent with Connal. Instead of now, when looking at it made it feel like her heart was being squeezed out of her chest in a giant fist.

"Bring Griff with ye," Dougal said.

They all agreed. "He's a right fine bloke, for a Yank," Clud put in.

"Stories the likes of which Roddy's place has never heard," Gavin agreed.

"And never will again," Roddy said, nodding somewhat sadly.

"Okay now, yer getting' maudlin on us all," Maeve cut in. She put her arm around Josie and walked her to the door. "I'd offer them all to see ye off, but like as not they'd all be blubbering like babes. Best ye say good-bye now, while they can still smile." She winked at Josie. "Then they can go get good and drunk over some ales while trying to outdo each other with paeans to yer youthful effervescence."

"Youthful effervescence," Roddy repeated. "I rather fancy that." He laughed then and the tension broke. They all gave her one last cheer and then she was outside and following the deliveryman to his truck for the ride to the dock. Her surfboard and bags had been stowed in the back.

She waved one last time, throwing a kiss and wink just to make them all blush, which they did. And so she was smiling as she turned back to face the road ahead.

The road ahead.

She swallowed a sigh and the smile faded. She should be happy, or at least relieved, to be leaving.

She missed her father. And it had been so long since she'd seen her bungalow she'd forgotten what it looked like. It would be good to be back in her own bed, under her own roof.

Yeah, she thought morosely. She couldn't wait.

Thoughts of Bagan and the things he'd told her popped into her head, as they had off and on since he'd popped back out of her life. For good this time, she was certain. The pain was still fresh, but the anger had faded. She'd meant what she said, too, about them both probably being better off ending it sooner rather than later. Then there was the guilt. She hadn't quite managed to work her way past that yet. Because, no matter what Bagan's cryptic remarks had meant, she did feel as if she'd failed Connal.

She sighed and climbed out of the truck when it stopped at the ferry landing, then turned and looked back at Ruirisay. The misty spray of the ocean cast the small row of buildings in an almost dream-like glow. She did love this place and the people in it. They'd become like family to her and she couldn't imagine not seeing them every day, listening to their stories, offering their advice, asked for or not. She realized then that part of her sadness in leaving was the knowledge that Connal had been right. They were all happy enough here, but the truth was, the island would die when they did. And after that, who was going to be left to see to the future of Glenmuir?

She stood stock-still as the answer flooded her brain. *No.* But her heart was already picking up speed, then it began to pound in earnest as the answer refused to be ignored. "No. You're insane even to think it," she told herself.

"Miss?"

She jerked around to find the driver looking at her. "The ferryman says it's okay to board."

"Okay, yes, right. Just a minute." She turned back toward town, forgetting all about him as her mind raced on with her solution.

Her insane, foolish, reckless, and quite terrifying solution.

"Maybe it *was* Destiny that brought me here," she whispered, hardly daring to give voice to the idea. She stared hard past Ruirisay, to the castle she knew lay beyond it on the western shore. "Maybe Bagan was right and the stone's promise wasn't the bairn," she said, picturing Connal as he'd been that first time, striding up the beach to claim his stone, and her. "Maybe the promise was just me."

"Miss?"

"A second, just a second," she said, waving him off. She felt a bit dizzy, but the feeling welling up inside her, along with the fear and adrenaline . . . was joy.

She spun back around, jumping on that feeling, latching on to it with both hands—and her whole heart—and refusing to let go, even in the face of the terror that came screaming in behind it. The stone had promised love, and she did love Connal. Just as she loved the legacy he was to leave behind. Glenmuir.

"I won't be taking the ferry today," she blurted out, before she lost her nerve. *Or any other day.* She hoped.

The truck driver looked nonplussed, but the ferryman just waved him on. "I've got a schedule to keep," he said. "Are you coming or no'?"

"No," she said, letting the grin split her face. *Dear God, what was she doing?* "Wait," she called out, racing after the truck.

"Well, which is it going to be, lassie?" the ferryman said, a touch of exasperation in his voice.

"I just need to get my stuff. Off the truck."

The driver and the ferryman exchanged looks, then with a shrug the driver got her stuff off and even helped her carry it back to the dock.

"Thanks!"

"Dinna thank me," the driver said with a smile. "Yer the one who has to get this stuff back to town."

"I'll be fine," she said, knowing that at the moment, her gear was the least of her problems. The enormity of her decision was still sinking in. But she clung to the joy she felt . . . and ignored the fact that she hadn't a single clue how she was going to pull it off.

She waved at the driver as the ferry cast off, then turned and faced the island. Her island.

"I'm here to save you," she said, then hugged herself before laughing out loud. She felt lighter in her heart than she'd ever expected to feel again. It was the right thing to do, no matter how paralyzing the decision felt at the moment.

She shaded her eyes and glanced heavenward. "I'm fulfilling the promise of the stone, Connal. And your promise to your people. Because they're my people, too."

She looked down at the stuff piled by the dock and decided it wouldn't hurt anything to let it sit until she could borrow Bidda's car and come retrieve it. *Wish me luck,* she thought, then said, "Ready or not, Glenmuir, here I come."

She was halfway to town when she was forced to admit that she wasn't going to be able to save the island single-handedly. By the time she reached Maeve's, the beginning of a plan had formed in her mind. She needed help. And she knew just whom to call. After all, they were a team, and had been all her life.

She pushed into the store, surprising Maeve with a wave and a cheery hello.

"Is something wrong with the ferry?"

"Not that I'm aware of. Can I use your phone? I'll cover the charges."

"Wha—? Why, certainly." She bustled in the back and came out with her portable. "Here ye are. What is happenin', Josie? Ye look like the proverbial cat with a fat canary tucked in its belly."

"I'll tell you after I make this call. Go round everyone up for me, okay?"

Maeve looked at her curiously, then nodded and waved her off to make her call. "They're all right next door." She bustled off as Josie connected with the overseas operator.

Then the phone was ringing and a voice was on the other end.

"Dad?" she said breathlessly. After taking in and expelling a deep breath, she took her first step. "I have a proposition for you."

Chapter 22

*A*re you guys coming?" Josie was all but bouncing on the balls of her feet. It had been two weeks since she'd placed the call to her father. It amazed even her just how much had been accomplished in such a short period of time. But then, she should have known never to underestimate Griff when he was set to do something.

And he'd taken her suggestion to think about moving his business here and run with it at a shocking speed.

"Come on, the ferry will be here any minute."

Maeve looked to Roddy. "We don't want to intrude."

"He'll be up here soon enough," Roddy agreed, then smiled. "And after that you'll be lucky to have a minute alone with him for the next six months."

Josie grinned. "You're probably right. Okay, then, I'm off." She dashed to the door. That's all it seemed she did these days, dash, dash, dash. When she wasn't on the phone getting information on obtaining proper permits and business licenses, she was scouring the island for possible places for her dad to set up shop. They'd need a place for the designing and shaping, and probably a separate building or location for the glassing. She had a short list of places all ready for him to inspect. Of course, on Glenmuir, the list wasn't going to be that long anyway.

She also wanted to look for a place for herself. Gregor was making noises about staying on in Mull indefinitely, but she didn't know for sure yet. There'd be time for that later.

She spun around at the door and ran back to hug Maeve and kiss Roddy on the cheek. They both blushed, but the pleasure sparkling from their eyes told the real story.

"Thank you both for all you've done to help me. I couldn't have done it without your support."

Maeve patted her arm. "We think what you're doing is wonderful." She looked at Roddy. "I know the boys were skeptical at first, but once they knew Griff was behind the idea one hundred percent—"

"Hey now, I was behind the idea," Roddy cut in. "We were in a rut here, Josie, thinking our way of life was the only way, but ye brought a spark of life back to the island and we know now what we were missing. I just didn't see how it was all going to work." He winked at Josie. "Didn't account for that Yankee ingenuity."

"You mean hardheadedness," Josie shot back. "You know, everyone told my dad when he left Hawaii for the East Coast that he'd be out of business inside six months. I guess they don't understand that he's not in it for the profit. He loves what he does. He just needed the space to do it without all the industry pressure."

"Well, he'll have plenty of that here," Dougal said, strolling in from the pub next door.

"Exactly." Josie beamed.

"And ye say he's already got some lads lined up to come take a look-see with him?"

"Freddie Granger and Tuck Sopponi. They won't be coming till the next ferry over, though. Trust me, they'll fit right in here." She'd known Freddie since she was twelve and Tuck had been her dad's glassman since the move to Parker's Inlet. Freddie was about the same age as Griff, but Tuck was younger, with a wife and two little boys. She was nervous about him picking up and moving over here because of her wild idea to relocate Griff's Guns, but bringing new blood—young blood—to the island was the whole point.

"He won't be able to run the whole shop with only those two, will he?" Dougal asked.

Josie turned a considering eye toward him. "You thinking about coming out of retirement? Because I imagine you and my dad might be able to come to some sort of agreement." She knew she'd said the right thing when a shrewd look entered his eyes. "In fact, he'll need someone to help him set up ads on the mainland, maybe the Internet too, for other help."

"Doesn't Margaery have a cousin or something that does employment work?" Roddy asked Maeve.

"I think you're right." She looked to Josie. "I'll ring her up and ask. Now, you'd better hurry off or you'll miss the boat."

"Right!" Josie did dash this time. She took Bidda's car rather than the bike, in case Griff hadn't rented one of his own.

She parked at the dock and watched the ferry heading in. It was still a good ten minutes out. Which gave her ten minutes of nothing to do but think. She'd tried not to do much of that, other than as it pertained to putting her plan into action. But now that it looked like it was going to happen, she couldn't help but think about Connal.

Did he know what she was doing? Did he approve? She realized it might not be exactly what he had in mind, and that moving one business here was not going to single-handedly change the prosperity of the island. But she'd had long talks with her father and even longer ones with the residents of Glenmuir.

They had all agreed they wanted change, that while they didn't want the peacefulness to change overly much, they were saddened by the fact that there were no young families here any longer and accepted the reality that if they didn't do something about that, the island life they and their ancestors had built over hundreds of years would die out. Josie saw Griff's Guns as exactly the kind of jump start Glenmuir needed. A small increase in capital, a slow growth of new islanders, and perhaps, down the line, other small businesses, and the families needed to grow them.

"It's a start, Connal," she whispered. "Some will be Yanks, some Scots, and some are even MacNeils." She sighed, feeling the familiar tug of loss in her heart. All of this still hadn't come close to replacing her need for him and would likely never fill that hole completely. But she felt closer to him somehow. "I hope you're at peace," she whispered, "wherever you are." She gripped the handle as the ferry neared, then added, "I miss you. I wish you were here to do this with me."

Then, before fresh tears could spring to life, something she'd managed to avoid this far, she jumped out of the car and walked closer to the water's edge.

She saw three men standing on the prow of the ship, above the unloading area. One stood apart from the others. Had Tuck and Freddie made it after all? she wondered.

But as the boat neared, she could see that one man was Griff, and if she was not mistaken, that was in fact Freddie standing next to him. But the other man . . .

The ferry drew closer and her heart slowly came to a stop. She was hallucinating. Her talk with Connal in the car had produced some kind of momentary psychotic wish fulfillment. Because she could swear that was Connal, standing on the prow of the ferry.

She blinked, squinted, shaded her eyes. It was still him. His hair was pulled back, and he wore what looked like khakis and a polo shirt instead of a kilt and laced-up linen shirt. But it was definitely Connal MacNeil.

"Or someone who looks just like him," she murmured, standing there in a form of suspended animation. She was simply unable to believe what she was seeing, unwilling to allow even one glimmer of hope to spring to life inside her chest. For she knew she'd never withstand having it snuffed out again.

Then they disappeared from the prow as the boat docked and moments later there was her father, swallowing her up in a huge bear hug. "Look who I brought with me," Griff was saying, stepping back to allow Freddie in to hug her.

"We've missed you," he said, giving her a peck on the cheek.

"Me—me, too," she answered, trying to give her father and Freddie her full attention, but unable to keep from darting looks past their shoulders.

Griff noticed and looked behind him, shifting slightly . . . and suddenly there he stood. Right there. Not ten feet away.

Josie couldn't breathe, much less speak.

"Have you met?" Griff asked, looking confused. "We met this chap on the boat, with his friend. Says he's come to claim some land left to him by his ancestors." He stuck his hand out and said, "What was your name again, son, I'm sorry."

But the man only had eyes for Josie. Eyes she'd seen every night in her dreams.

"Connal," he murmured, almost distractedly, his gaze focused so intently on her. "Connal MacNeil." His voice almost brought her to her knees.

"Everyone calls me Griff," her father said, shaking Connal's hand, before turning to Josie. "This is my daughter, Josie Griffin."

She opened her mouth, but no words would come out. The whole scene was so surreal she was certain she was dreaming the entire episode. And she didn't want to do anything that might jar her out of it. Because right now it felt very damn real and that was all that mattered.

Griff looked at Josie, then back at Connal. Josie had no idea what he thought of the two of them standing there, looking thunderstruck, but couldn't seem to make herself care at the moment.

Griff finally winked and nudged Freddie. "Well, I think we should just make ourselves scarce here, huh?"

"What?" Freddie asked, also staring with great interest at the two of them. "Oh, yeah." He winked back at Griff. "Right, right. Come on, I'll help you with the car."

The two of them disappeared back onto the ferry, leaving her here with . . .

"You look just like him," she finally choked out. Because in the span of the last five seconds, she'd finally figured it out. The gods were giving her a gift, for what she was doing for Glenmuir. They were giving her Connal's great-great-great . . . whatever. Well, no matter how simply looking at him made her body ache, he wasn't *her* Connal. "I'm sorry to keep staring, it's just that—"

Then he took a step forward. "Josie."

She stilled again, her breath caught in her throat. No man said her name that way, except for one. "Connal?" she whispered. "Is this really you?"

"You were, perhaps, expecting someone else?" His eyes were searching hers, his expression almost fierce despite the forced humor in his tone.

"I thought . . . my father said you were here to see land belonging to your ancestors."

"Aye, that is true. It has been in the possession of the MacNeils for centuries longer than I've been alive." He stepped closer still. "Or dead."

"But—" Her heart began thundering then, until she thought it would simply burst from her chest. Yet, despite the overwhelming urge to fling herself at him, cling to him until forcibly removed from his arms . . . she stepped back, though putting even an inch more space between them took every scrap of control she had. "How? And . . . why?"

"It was you who did it," he said, dead earnest now. "Your commitment to me. To our future."

"Our—" Her voice was shaking badly now. "*Our* future?"

He nodded. "The gods told me that I had naught to prove to them, only to myself. I didna understand, thinking that by proof they meant to prove my faith in the stone. Once I had, I could only think that the stone's promise was an heir."

"Bagan said—"

"He was right. What I had to prove was that I could give my heart, that the faith I needed to find was faith in myself, faith in valuing that which only I could give."

Finally, as if he couldn't stand apart from her for a moment longer, he reached out to touch her. She shuddered hard, her legs shaking with need.

"My love." He pulled her into his arms and it was the place she so badly wanted to be, the place she'd never dreamed she'd be again, that she went willingly, shattered heart be damned.

She touched his face, ran trembling fingertips

over his lips. "It really is you, isn't it? You're really here." Tears sprang to her eyes. "I do love you, Connal. I didn't get a chance to tell you before, but I did. I do."

His eyes blazed with passion, with life, with promises not yet made. "That was where I failed ye truly," he said, touching her face now, tracing her own lips. "I had come to realize that my heart was yours, but I thought I needed to secure yours first before declaring myself. I thought I'd have more time to figure it all out—"

"Time." Her heart skipped one beat, then two. "Are you—? How long—?"

He pulled her arms around him and tilted her head back. "As long as ye'll have me."

"But the bargain—"

He kissed her, as if he couldn't wait another moment, another breath. And took what little breath she had away. There was all the passion she remembered, and something more she'd never felt before.

"The gods were very angry to have the promise of the stone tossed back to sea. But you showed them the promise had been fulfilled." He stroked her face. "What you've done, your love for me, for Glenmuir . . . fulfilled the stone's promise. And the gods realized I'd fulfilled my own."

"The gods—"

"Allowed me to ask for one thing." He looked into her eyes, life as she'd never seen it sparking in his own. "I asked for life, with you."

"I don't understand, do you mean . . ." Her eyes widened as he nodded. "Mortal?" she whispered, not daring to believe it.

"As mortal as you. I hope ye dinna mind, I'll no' be popping in and out. Ye'll have to put up with having only a mortal man to love you." He took her mouth then, kissing her deeply, until she well and truly believed what he'd said. And when he lifted his mouth from hers, he looked into her eyes and said, "I do love you, Josie Griffin. My heart is yours."

She hugged him tightly, tears welling in her eyes, unable to stop them, but not caring, for these were tears of joy. Indescribable, impossible joy.

A slight clearing of a throat intruded on their moment.

"Oh no." Griff. And Freddie. What must they think of the scene she and Connal were creating? She looked up at him, but her joy was too immense, too huge, to worry about anything at the moment. "I guess I can always tell them it was love at first sight, right?"

"Them?"

"My father. He has no idea. About us. Nobody does." She went to gesture behind him, scrambling madly for what she was going to say to Griff, but there was no one there.

Connal took her face between his hands and kissed her again. "There is one small thing I have yet to tell ye." He frowned slightly. "Very small."

Certain she could handle anything so long as he didn't move from her sight, she said, "What?"

"The gods saw fit to render mortality on someone else, as well, though I'm no' certain if it was as a blessing or as punishment." He shifted around and pulled her to his side as he did.

Standing just behind him, wearing a simply awful mustard yellow polo shirt, with plaid trousers and a matching tam, was Bagan. He wiggled his fingers at her. "Hello, Josie."

Josie's mouth dropped open, then she looked from Bagan to Connal, then back to Bagan. "Really? Mortal?"

Both Bagan and Connal nodded. Only one of them was smiling.

She started to laugh, then laughed even harder, until she clung to Connal, who was beginning to look seriously alarmed. "Are ye okay?"

"Oh aye," she said, still grinning. "I'm as okay as I've ever been in my entire life." She looked to Connal. "Wait, he does get his own place to stay, right?"

Connal nodded. "Of course."

She leaned in, and whispered, "He needs serious wardrobe help."

Before Connal could reply, her father and Freddie reappeared. "Well," Griff said jovially, "looks like you've all made acquaintance rather quickly." He eyed the arm Connal had placed possessively around Josie's back.

"We've, uh, we've met," Josie stammered.

"So I see." Griff looked Connal over, then looked at Josie. He had to see the joy beaming from her, she thought, because he nodded, smiled at Connal, and said, "Care for a lift to town, laddie?"

"That's okay, Dad," she said quickly. "I'll drive him in." Then she smiled. "But Bagan here needs a lift."

Bagan started to complain, but one look from Connal had him nodding and smiling, thanking Griff for his kindness.

"See you at Roddy's?" Griff asked her. "We have a great deal to go over."

"I'll be there as soon as I can."

"Fine then." He gave Connal one more considering look, then climbed in the rental car with Freddie. Bagan waved from the back window as they headed toward town.

Josie waved back, then turned to Connal and pulled him right back into her arms. "Please tell me this isn't a dream. I don't ever want to wake up."

He tipped her head back and leaned in to kiss her.

"Aye, 'tis a dream. A grand dream. For there are none better than those that come true." He kissed her then, hungrily, like a man staking his claim.

When he lifted his head, they simply stood there and stared at each other, as if each of them was still afraid to believe in what was right in front of them. "I'm sorry for the pain," he said, brushing at a stray strand of hair.

"You're here, that's all that matters." She rested her head on his chest, reveling in the steady beat of his heart beneath her cheek. His arms felt perfect and strong around her. She thought she would be content never to move from this very spot. "I'm sorry... about the baby. I thought, for a time, but—" She shook her head, unable to put what she felt into words.

Then she felt his finger beneath her chin, lifting her gaze up to his. "It wasn't the destiny due us. No' at the time." He kissed her so gently it brought fresh tears to her eyes. "We'll have our bairns, Josie. When the time is right for us." He pulled her to his side and they both turned to look at the island. "But first, we have another destiny to fulfill."

In that moment, she had never been more certain that Fate and Destiny did indeed exist. And it had nothing to do with a cold stone set in hard metal. She looked up at the man she was destined to spend the rest of her life loving. No, Destiny was a living thing, ever-changing, ever-forming... its strength founded on the hearts of those who loved enough to give it the wings to fly.

She glanced up to find him gazing at her. A teasing grin came from somewhere to curve her lips. "So," she said, taking his hand and tugging him toward Bidda's car, "when do you want to start your surf lessons?"

"My what?"

"It'll be fun."

"Fun."

"Yeah, you remember. Fun?"

He grinned then, that devilishly wicked grin she'd almost forgotten he possessed. She took one step backward, but he tugged her hand and she came flying back up against his chest. "Ask me again in about an hour," he said, the words almost a growl against the side of her neck. "When I have you naked and beneath me in bed."

She was already panting. "I—good idea." She groped behind her for the door handle. "I'll drive."

"Good idea."

"Oh no. My father—"

"Can wait." He was already peeling her shirt open.

"Yes," she decided, somewhat breathlessly. "Why yes, he can." She gasped when his fingers brushed over her. "I think this is going to be the shortest courtship in Glenmuir history," she said, leaning her head back to allow him full access to . . . anything he damn well pleased.

"Aye," he said, lowering his mouth to her. "Aye, that 'tis." He caught her gaze just before his lips brushed her skin. "The MacNeil is back."

"Aye," she said, then her eyes drifted shut on a sigh of pleasure. "Aye, is he ever."

Epilogue

The sun at his back felt wonderful.

He looked toward the shore and his heart filled with such happiness he could have burst with it. He thought, once again, how undeserving he was of it. But he'd accepted it all the same, thanks.

There were two of them, frolicking in the waves. Josie and her daughter, wee Isabella. If he squinted, he could just make out the other two strolling away down the shoreline and into the afternoon mists. Shell collecting, most like, he thought. Young Griff was quite enamored of his collection and his father, when not busy representing his people in Parliament, took his job as guide and collection curator quite seriously.

Aye, it was a rich life they all led. No' because of money, though Glenmuir was prospering in all ways a man could measure it. Josie had continued her work with her father, as well as teaching the island children—and many of their parents—to surf. Clud helped her out on occasion. Dougal and Gavin both worked for Griff part-time. Bidda and Posey had gone and opened what they called a bed-and-breakfast, catering to the slow, but steady trickle of surfers that came to examine Griff's wares. Roddy handled most of the shipments on the Internet.

Another fine invention, he found himself thinking, making a mental note to check his e-mail later.

Right now there was a perfect swell building behind him. He stuck his stubby hands in the water and paddled his custom-made shortboard—very short board—over so he could catch it.

Then Bagan popped up in a perfect front-footed stance, caught the shoulder . . . and ripped the back end wide open.

Note from the Author

The idea for this book began when I read a story about the current MacNeil clan chief signing a one-thousand-year lease with Historic Scotland, to ensure continuing renovations of the clan seat, Kisimul, on the Isle of Barra. The terms of the lease are a pound note a year, and a bottle of Scottish whisky. Sounded reasonable to me! Legend has it that Kisimul has been the MacNeil stronghold since the eleventh century. The fact that the property had stayed for so long in MacNeil possession intrigued me and I started digging around a bit. I found the Isle of Barra to be charming and its history and that of the MacNeils quite interesting.

The needs of my story, however, meant altering that history a great deal, which I didn't want to do. So, although I use the MacNeil name, my characters, their heritage, and their actions, are completely fictional. And while the Isle of Glenmuir is certainly inspired by Barra, it is my own creation, as are Winterhaven Castle and Black's Tower.

Charm stones are real, however, and have a long and colorful heritage in both Scottish and Celtic history. The MacNeil Stone is my own invention. If the MacNeils had a clan charm stone, my research didn't uncover it.

And in case you're wondering, yes, you really can surf in Scotland. Barra, Tiree, the North Coast, and Pease Bay are a few of the places favored by the small, but hardy band of Scots surfers.

About the Author

Born and raised in Maryland, Donna now lives in Virginia with her husband, sons, and growing menagerie of dogs and birds. She can be reached online at www.donnakauffman.com or by mail at PO Box 541, Ashburn, VA 20146.

Turn the page for a sneak peak at the new exciting
romance from Donna Kauffman

The Last Bridesmaid

Coming soon from Bantam

*K*iller column today, Tanz."

Tanzy adjusted her phone headset and hit save. "Thanks, Martin. Let's just say I was inspired."

"I'll say. The reader response to your last bridesmaid angle has been amazing. Who knew there were so many of them out there?"

She snarled silently. "Yeah, who knew. I'm thinking of forming a club." It had been two weeks since Rina's wedding and fodder for her twice-weekly column was still spewing forth. Apparently she wasn't, in fact, the last bridesmaid on the planet. She'd heard from a whole slew of them in the past ten days. "Listen, I'm getting Saturday's column in early. I've got that Single Santa radio thing this afternoon, then this month's stint on the *Barbara Bradley Show* is taping tomorrow morning. They're doing a Single at Christmas show for airing during the holidays." Hoo boy. She could hardly wait.

"Well, chat up this whole wolf/sheep thing you zeroed in on in today's column. I have a hunch it's going to play big with the serial solos out there."

She grinned. "I'll talk to you after I'm done taping Friday, let you know how it went." She clicked off and stared at her laptop screen, scanning back over what she'd already written, then began to type.

So, why is it we L.B.'s aren't willing to settle for Sheep like the rest of our social circle? What's wrong with a man who puts family first, who maintains a steady job, has college funds set up for his kids, and builds that nest egg for his retirement? Member of the workaday herd, never straying.

Solid, dependable Sheep Guy.

Why can't I love this guy? I've decided that, for me, it's the Wolves. They distract me from the Sheep. Men on the prowl. Totally alpha. Not interested in being domesticated. What is it about these men that makes my heart speed up in ways no Sheep ever have? I don't want to tame them. I certainly don't want to take them home to Mama. No. I, the original self-sufficient, independent, and proud of it dammit, woman wants Wolf Guy to drag me back to his lair and have his way with me. Repeatedly. But that's all I want from him. That wild rush, that feeling of being taken over by something stronger and more powerful than I am.

Maybe that's it. I'm responsible for everything else in my life: my home, my career, my social circle. I don't have to ask permission to do anything, don't have to make any compromises unless I want to. I do what I want, when I want. And I like it that way, intend to keep it that way. I just need Wolf Guy to rip the reins from my hands from time to time and allow me to give up my grip for a little while. Let's face it, Sheep Guy will never do that. And until I don't need to have my reins ripped anymore, I can't imagine joining the herd on a permanent basis.

So where does that leave me? A serial solo, straying from the herd every time that Wolf comes sniffing around, that's where. And I'm sorry to all you permanent herders out there, but at the moment, I'm thinking that's fine by me.

"Take that, Sheep lovers," she muttered and saved. She tapped on her ISP and zapped the column to Marty before she could reconsider what she'd written. After all, it wasn't called "Tanzy Tells Some of the

Things." Whatever she felt was what she wrote. No holding back, no worries about offending anyone. She was the universal bared soul of the single woman, put on display for all the world to read. What you read was what you got. Take it or leave it. Fortunately for her, a whole lot of people, both men and women, took her words. They accepted them, rejected them, debated them, heatedly at times . . . and propelled the writer of them to a certain level of fame and fortune.

She scanned her email, a dry smile curving her lips as she skimmed down the potpourri already queuing up for today's entertainment. The fame part, even at her insignificant level, had its pros and cons. She got date offers, marriage offers, offers to be saved by various members of the clergy, offers to be fixed up with sons by various mothers, fixed up with brothers by an assortment of sisters, and all around good guys by well-meaning married matrons. And that was usually before ten A.M.

The flip side was that, on occasion, she also got threats: some aimed at messing with her person in a violent manner, some litigiously eyeing her bank account. Of course, the combination of being seen on television, heard on the radio, and accessible via the Internet, was bound to bring out the less stable segment of society. She figured it went with the job. Fortunately, none of them had ever followed through, successfully or otherwise.

She spied a note from her most recent "extreme fan" as she called them and debated whether reading it would entertain or disconcert. This guy was particularly insistent if not particularly original. He was her self-proclaimed savior, the one who would love her for all time, thereby relieving her of all her single girl angst. She smiled faintly as she skimmed past his most recent proclamation of eternal devotion.

He didn't seem to understand single girl angst paid her rent. Besides she wasn't really angsty. More reflective. In an openly global kind of way.

Forgetting about SoulM8, as he so cleverly called himself, she clicked instead on an email titled "Howling 4 U." Her latest column, in which she'd only briefly debuted her "men can be put into two categories, Wolves and Sheep" theory, had been published for less than an hour. "And they're already crawling out of the woodwork." She picked up her now cool mug of hot chocolate and sipped. "It's going to be an interesting day," she murmured as she read with great amusement the letter from a guy who professed he was an actual wolf. Of the werewolf variety. He was certain her column spoke directly to him and wanted to mate with her during the next full moon. Which—lucky her!—was the very next night. She hit delete—her most effective tool when dealing with whackos—and had just opened "Baaaahed Boy" when her phone rang.

"Tanzy dear, we need to talk," the caller said without preamble.

Tanzy almost choked on her chocolate. "Aunt Millicent!" She quickly put her mug down and pulled off her headset in favor of the old-fashioned phone. She found it was generally better to be gripping something substantial, and better yet, unbreakable, whenever her great aunt deigned to call. Since there were no titanium bars within easy reach, the hard plastic receiver would have to do. "What a nice surprise."

"How nice of you to say that even if you don't mean it. At least Penelope managed to breed some manners into her only offspring before flitting off to God knows where. Now stop gripping the phone like a drowning woman clinging to a lifeline. I've only got a few moments before the car arrives and we've got much to discuss."

"We do?" Tanzy found it best to merely nod and go along with Millicent, as there was really no point in believing she'd ever have control of a conversation with her mother's somewhat eccentric aunt. Okay, "somewhat" was her being nice again. And she hadn't gotten that trait from her mother. The only thing she'd gotten from Penelope was blue eyes and a distinct mistrust of long-term commitment.

"Yes, dear, we do. It seems my dear friend from Philadelphia, Frances Dalrymple, has suffered a decline in her health. She's asked me to come visit for what might be a rather extended stay. We went to Vassar together as you might recall."

"Mmm," Tanzy replied, one she'd learned to use rather judiciously when conversing with Millicent.

"My those were wonderful years. Still feels like yesterday. Young women in pursuit of higher learning were so rare in our time, you see. We were vital, so alive." She sighed wistfully.

"Real visionaries," Tanzy said, hoping Millicent didn't think she was being patronizing. She really did admire her great aunt, and what she didn't admire she was in awe of. But she really didn't need a replay of "Millicent Harrington: The Vassar Years." She knew them by heart. "I'm sure she'll enjoy having your company. Do you want me to go by and water your plants or collect your mail?" This was an empty offer as Millicent was loaded and had a houseful of people to look after every last detail of her Presidio Heights monstrosity of a mansion, but she also knew Millicent enjoyed it when Tanzy played the doting niece.

Other than her absent mother, Millicent was the only family left and although she wasn't exactly anyone's version of a cuddly, maternal figure, she also didn't pretend to be anything other than what she was. A woman who oversaw her inherited holdings, business interests and God knew what other investments with a steely eye and a firm grip. At eighty-two she was a more intimidating figure than ever.

"Actually, in a manner of speaking, yes, I do."

"I—I beg your pardon?" Tanzy had let her gaze wander back to her list of incoming mail. "What did you say?"

"The holidays are approaching and much of my household staff has been given leave to be with their families. As I am going to likely be out of town through the beginning of the year, I didn't see any reason not to extend their leave. My holiday gift to them for all their hard work."

Millicent ran her home like a colonel ran his troops, but though exacting, she was also generous to a fault with those she valued and those loyal to her.

"That's really lovely of you, Aunt Millicent." No one called her Millie. Or they only did once. "But won't you need at least a skeleton staff to oversee business matters?" She asked this somewhat tremulously. As Millicent's only remaining heir—Penelope long since having been written off—Tanzy knew she should probably be somewhat more aware of exactly what might be passed her way when Millicent cashed it in. Considering she'd never so much as dipped her pinky finger into her great aunt's business and had less than no idea what sort of empire Millicent had truly amassed during her tenure, this would be no small undertaking.

But Millicent had never broached the subject with her, and, cowardly or not, Tanzy had been happy enough to leave her to it. She hoped she would luck out and her great aunt's lengthy list of philanthropic and charitable endeavors would be the benefactors when the time came.

Tanzy had always believed it was up to her to take care of herself, and she did so, quite well thank you.

Her Russian Hill condo didn't begin to compare, thank God, to Harrington House. And that was intentional. She lived well enough, she worked hard and enjoyed the nice things her income afforded her, but she also lived within the scope of what she was willing to maintain. She didn't like people traipsing through her dwelling, so she kept it small enough so that even she could keep it marginally clean. Vacuuming and dusting not being high on her list of fun things to do with her free time.

Millicent chuckled. It was a rather rusty, somewhat scary sound. "Actually, I do have someone staying on to handle certain matters. I've given my regrets to the round of social events. Otherwise, there isn't much to do during the holiday season. My annual endowments have already been taken care of. I'd appreciate you cleaning up after yourself when you choose to cook and, I'm sorry, but you'll have to manage on your own with laundry and other such things. I'm certain you're well used to taking care of those matters on your own."

"Laundry? Cooking?" Tanzy was nonplussed. "If I'm just dropping by to check the house and water plants and such, I won't be needing to cook or wash, but I—"

"I'm sorry, I should have made myself clearer. With everyone gone but Riley, I would feel better if I knew someone was staying under the roof. Someone I could trust."

"But you travel all the time."

"For a week to ten days, yes. But this will probably be most of December and a good part, if not all of January. And what with the winter weather on the East Coast, one never can entirely depend on airline travel."

Tanzy opened her mouth, but she had no idea what to say.

"I know this is asking a great deal of you. And I don't mean for you to spend every waking minute there. I realize you're a busy woman with quite the hectic schedule yourself. But you can bring whatever you need with you. I'll have your rooms and private office all spruced up for the holidays, so writing your column here won't be a problem. Riley is fairly unobtrusive, but I've directed him to do whatever is necessary to make your stay comfortable."

"Riley is a he?" Tanzy didn't know why this surprised her. "What happened to Margaret?" Who was her aunt's long-time personal secretary and trusted confidante.

"You've not met him, but I trust him implicitly. As can you. I'll feel so much better knowing you're both here. Margaret's about to become a great-grandmother, so I've given her extended leave as well, to stay with her son and his family through the holidays."

"That's wonderful, really. So who is this—"

"Clifford is here with the car, darling. I've left a list of things, nothing major mind you, for you to go over every night before going to bed. A brief routine, I assure you."

"Aunt Millicent, I—"

"I can't tell you how much this means to me, Tanzy dear. I'll contact you once I arrive in Philadelphia and see to my lodgings. I've no idea if Frances intends to put me up, but like as not I'll be staying at the Belleview as usual. If anything comes up, you can simply contact me there and leave a message. In the meantime, Riley can handle any other questions you might have. He's expecting you by dinnertime tonight. If that's not convenient, please let him know as soon as you can. Ta ta, darling."

Tanzy was left staring at the dead receiver. "Ta ta my ass," she muttered as she hung up. She'd been hornswoggled by a master. "Nothing about this is convenient. Which you knew when you called me. Oh so cleverly on your way out the door." Tanzy had half a mind to call this Riley person and tell him he was on his own, and not just for dinner tonight.

And who was he anyway? Millicent had never really said. Tanzy didn't remember her talking about him before. But to be honest, when her aunt started off on a tangent involving business matters, Tanzy's eyes tended to glaze over and her mind wandered. For all she knew Riley had been in Millicent's employ for twenty years.

She sighed and stared unseeing at her computer screen. Her aunt rarely asked anything of her. Actually, other than coming for Thanksgiving dinner, she never did. Which made this whole thing even weirder. She certainly didn't seem to be losing any of her faculties, mental or otherwise. But the fact was, she had asked. And despite her annoyance at being so expertly maneuvered, Tanzy owed her too much not to do this for her.

So she picked up the phone again and called Riley.

* * *

"Helloo? Anybody home?" Tanzy's voice echoed down the central hallway and up the massive winding staircase as she let herself into the Harrington estate, a High Victorian Queen Anne with all the appropriate turrets, towers, and excessive ornamentation that was popular in the late 1800s, when the house was built.

A school pal who had visited once had told their friends about the "big hairy house" that Tanzy's aunt lived in. She'd called it Big Hairy ever since. Just not in front of Millicent.

She quickly punched in the security code so the alarm wouldn't go off. Millicent treasured her heritage, but was also quite the techno-geek, enjoying all the latest gadgets. Tanzy sighed as she searched for the new pressure-sensitive light pad Millicent had raved about in her most recent email. "Hello?"

Her own voice echoed back. So where was this Riley person anyway? No one had answered her call earlier, so she'd simply planned on arriving around six and hope for the best where dinner was concerned. Of course, it was closer to seven now, but her *Morning with Santa* radio show had turned into a *Late Afternooner with Santa*. Single at Christmas she might be, but that didn't mean she had to jingle her own bells.

She sniffed the air, but no heavenly scents were wafting down the hall. Apparently she'd missed dinner. She tugged her cell phone out of her purse as she nudged her overnight bag with a toe, scooting it to the base of the stairs. She stroked her hand over the highly polished newel post. How many times had she slid down that banister, she wondered, still tempted every time she stepped foot in the place. It would be a little rough at the moment, what with the fresh pine garland woven with berries and other assorted stuff Tanzy had never learned the names of. It was only the first week in December, but Millicent always had a crew in decorating the entire place the day after Thanksgiving, which had been the last time Tanzy had been here, bailing out early that morning as the trucks had pulled up.

They'd done a masterful job as always, she noted, as she finally found the pressure pad. Faux gas lamps sprang to life, softly illuminating the front parlor. She'd take her bags up later, first she wanted to see this year's pageant of excess. Humming "Jingle Bells" under her breath, she wandered the length of the room. Every year she assumed Millicent couldn't outdo herself. Why, she had no idea, as her aunt always accomplished what she set out to do.

Tanzy punched the speed dial code on her phone for Hunan Palace, then leaned down to inspect the intricate white iris ikebana arrangement on the sideboard. Every room, including the powder rooms, would have its own holiday theme complete with coordinated color scheme and tastefully accessorized tree. Martha Stewart had nothing on great aunt Millicent.

Apparently the front parlor had been tagged Doves by the Dozen or something, given the countless delicate little birds flitting amongst the bows of the slender, but amazingly tall Douglas fir. The color scheme for the room was a blinding, yet ever-so-tasteful Winter White. Even the rug and furniture had been replaced or recovered. Well, Millicent was nothing if not a slave to detail.

"Hunan Palace—May I take your order?"

Tanzy fingered one softly feathered dove—real feathers, natch—and spoke without even having to think. "Kung Pao chicken, as hot as you can make it, two spring rolls, extra rice. Delivered please." She gave directions, then tucked the phone away as she continued to wander the length of the front room, stopping and staring straight up when she realized the chandelier had been transformed with hundreds of cut crystal snowflakes replacing the regular crystal drops. "You da man, Aunt Milly," she murmured, shaking her head.

"I thought no one dared call her anything but Millicent," came a startlingly deep voice from the doorway. "That is when they aren't addressing her as Ms. Harrington."